D0388824

Grudge Match

BOOKS BY JAY BRANDON

Deadbolt

Tripwire

Predator's Waltz

Fade the Heat

Rules of Evidence

Loose Among the Lambs

Local Rules

Defiance County

**Angel of Death*

**AfterImage*

**Executive Privilege*

**Sliver Moon*

**Grudge Match*

*A FORGE BOOK

JAY BRANDON

Grudge Match

A Chris Sinclair Thriller

A TOM DOHERTY ASSOCIATES BOOK

NEW YORK

This is a work of fiction. All the characters and events portrayed in this novel are either fictitious or are used fictitiously.

GRUDGE MATCH: A CHRIS SINCLAIR THRILLER

Copyright © 2004 by Jay Brandon

All rights reserved, including the right to reproduce this book, or portions thereof, in any form.

This book is printed on acid-free paper.

Edited by James Frenkel

A Forge Book
Published by Tom Doherty Associates, LLC
175 Fifth Avenue
New York, NY 10010

www.tor.com

Forge® is a registered trademark of Tom Doherty Associates, LLC.

Library of Congress Cataloging-in-Publication Data

Brandon, Jay.
Grudge match : a Chris Sinclair thriller / Jay Brandon.—1st ed.
p. cm.
"A Tom Doherty Associates book."
ISBN 0-765-30892-4 (acid-free paper)
EAN 978-0765-30892-4
1. Sinclair, Chris (Fictitious character)—Fiction. 2. Public prosecutors—Fiction. 3. San Antonio (Tex.)—Fiction. 4. Judicial error—Fiction. 5. Police murders—Fiction. I. Title.

PS3552.R315G78 2004
813'.54—dc22

2003071101

First Edition: May 2004

Printed in the United States of America

0 9 8 7 6 5 4 3 2 1

★

This is dedicated,

with great love,

to my family:

Yolanda, Elizabeth, Sam, and Elena.

acknowledgments

I want to thank the following people for their help, support, and encouragement:
James Frenkel, a thoughtful, thorough, but unobtrusive editor;
his assistant, Derek Tiefenthaler;
my longtime hardworking agent, Jimmy Vines;
and all the great people at Tor/Forge and St. Martin's who carefully and creatively shepherded this and my other books into existence, including art director Irene Gallo, production manager Eric Raab, publicity maven Jodi Rosoff, and editorial assistant Liz Gorinsky.
Thank you all.

Grudge Match

CHAPTER one

★ Trials end with a verdict. The victim's family sobs. Jurors look stoic, or hug each other, or at last talk to reporters. The judge nods in agreement. He thanks the jurors for their hard work. Closure is achieved. The lawyers move on to the next case.

"The defendant showed no emotion."

This is the phrase always used to describe the lunk sitting alone, or still standing to receive the verdict. He lifts his chin, or drops his head. But his eyes don't fill with tears. He has nothing to say. The person on trial has just been stripped not only of his freedom but of his singularity, as he will soon be stripped of his clothes and draped in a jail coverall. One moment he is one of us, his fate uncertain, as are all our fates, his destiny unknown. In the next second he has become part of a subhuman herd: the convicted. The guilty. Now everyone knows. What you did, what you are.

The newly convicted defendant grows an instant shell. He knows he is no longer quite present in the courtroom. He is on his way to a new life, the main feature of which is invisibility. He will no longer be among us. Even if the defendant emerges someday, he won't quite rejoin the race. Cut out from the herd, he remains one of the others. "Ex-con."

It seemed a horrible, terrifying fate. *Then why do they never show emotion,* Chris Sinclair wondered. He assumed it was because they knew they were guilty. They had it coming. The jurors had found them out. Suddenly the trial just past was revealed for the academic exercise it had been. "Okay. You got me."

Yes. We get you. And no longer have to think about you. Chris seldom did. It was rare for him to revisit a past trial, except as an anecdote.

But one defendant had shown emotion. A man of average height but broad shoulders, he had sat with the required stoicism throughout his trial, but at the word "guilty," he had gone berserker. He had slammed his fists down on counsel table, and roared as if he'd been stabbed. His pain sounded physical.

The defendant had picked up his chair, raised it over his head, and actually pulled one of its arms free. He had been advancing across the front of the courtroom—toward the judge or the jury, accounts differed afterwards—until he'd been stopped by the bailiffs, one of them rough and contemptuous, the other surprisingly gentle.

The arms of the defendant's blue suit had ripped at the seams, as if he'd been revealed. His transformation had begun. The next time he had appeared in the courtroom, for the punishment phase, he'd behaved appropriately. The defendant showed no emotion.

He was the one Chris remembered.

Years passed, and Chris Sinclair went on to other trials and other jobs. By now, Chris had been an attorney for twelve years: seven as an assistant district attorney, three as a defense lawyer, two so far as the district attorney of Bexar County, in San Antonio. Though his job now was administrative, he still thought of himself as a trial lawyer. A week spent in meetings left him peevish and restless. Many days, without knowing why, he drifted downstairs to the trial courts. There his fingers stopped tapping, his shoulders expanded, and he stood taller, with a faint smile of which he remained unaware. His physiological reactions were similar to an athlete's returning to his high school stadium. But Chris was lucky. At thirty-six, he could still compete.

So when on a Thursday morning in October, he strolled into the 186th District Court on the third floor of the Justice Center and saw an empty chair at the prosecution table, he reacted without thought, walking quickly up the aisle and through the gate in the wooden railing.

"What's happened?" he asked, standing behind the chair.

The remaining prosecutor, Bonnie Janaway, barely glanced up. To her credit, she didn't do a double-take at the sight of her boss standing over her. "Kenny's out. Spent half the night throwing up, according to his wife." Bonnie was thin and intense, with tightly compressed lips and sharp brown eyes. She continued going through her file, occasionally making a note. Across the aisle, the defense lawyer leaned back in his chair and put his hands behind his head. He and Chris nodded to each other.

"You didn't have a backup?" Chris asked his assistant.

Bonnie shook her head. "Don't need one. It's a simple case. Agg robbery. Four eyewitnesses." She snapped her fingers, still not looking up at him.

Chris could have told her from experience that one eyewitness is often preferable to more. Multiple tongues tell multiple tales, and Bill Gibs, sitting there at the defense table, was a veteran lawyer who could exploit differences in testimony.

The empty chair called Chris's name. "Mind if I sit in?" he said, taking the seat beside Bonnie.

She shot him a suspicious glance, then a totally artificial smile that looked as if it hurt her lips. "Really not necessary, Chris. We're halfway done anyway."

Chris smiled, well aware of the mixed feelings she must have. Bonnie was a second-chair; the first-chair prosecutor from this court had taken sick. This presented an opportunity to Bonnie to win a first-degree felony conviction on her own. If the district attorney sat in, he would undoubtedly take any credit for a win. Bonnie didn't know Chris well, but she knew how things worked.

"It's your case, Bonnie. I won't question anybody unless you want me to. I'll just fetch things for you."

He smiled ingratiatingly. She shrugged and went back to her note-making. Within minutes Judge Ernest Ormond took his place. After a formal exchange of remarks allowed Chris to join the prosecution team, the judge said, "Bring the defendant."

A uniformed bailiff opened a side door of the courtroom and brought out a man in handcuffs. The man wore black pants and a white shirt and looked young until he lifted his head. His dark eyes were watchful with long, bad experience. They fixed on Chris Sinclair for a long stare, then he slunk down in his chair and stared at the table as the bailiff removed his handcuffs and his lawyer talked to him. Just before the jurors entered, the young defendant took thick, black-rimmed glasses from his pocket and put them on. The glasses seemed to change his age and expression. Now he appeared thoughtful, a scholar. His magnified eyes looked watery with worry.

Chris had a tingle of apprehension. Bonnie Janaway sat studying a report. Her thick black hair, cut short, didn't get in her way. Neither did Chris. But as Bonnie called her next witness, a firearms examiner who had tested bullets found at the scene, Chris read the prosecution's file. The police offense report told him there had been a robbery at a small family-run grocery store on the city's west side. Three men had entered, faces obscured by caps and scarves, pulled out guns, and ordered everyone to the floor. Three members of the Rivera family had been in the store at the time, the owner in the office, his mother running a cash register, and a teenage daughter stocking shelves. One of the robbers had put a gun in the grandmother's face, another had approached the girl. The report blandly sketched what must have been a terrifying few minutes before the robbers had run out.

Chris looked over at the defendant and wondered which of the three he had been. The guy looked up at the ceiling as if bored. His lawyer didn't appear much more interested as the firearms examiner gave his opinion that a certain bullet had been fired from a certain gun.

Chris found that Kenny, the missing prosecutor, had taken very careful notes of the previous day's testimony. Much of it had been dry, the collection of evidence, but the first witness had been the store owner. His testimony could have been dramatic—a bullet had been fired just past his face into the wall beside him, while an armed thug stood over his daughter—but the quality of the testimony was impossible to tell from the notes.

Beside Chris, Bonnie sat looking as tight as if the case were slipping away from her. She nudged Chris's arm and he saw that she had written him a note on her legal pad: "See who else I've got out there."

He knew she meant what witnesses waited in the hall. This was a second-chair prosecutor's job, being the stage manager for the first-chair's director. That was the job for which Chris had volunteered. He hurried up the aisle of the courtroom and out.

The hallway of the Justice Center had a purified, clinical aspect. Its surfaces were varying shades of bland. Humans intruded. At once, Chris spotted the family group across the hall. They huddled together on and around a stone bench. A very young woman held a baby. A young man in a ribbed undershirt paced and glared. Older adults talked in murmurs. On the bench sat an elderly woman who must have been the grandmother mentioned in the police report. She wore a shapeless, thin gray dress, from which her hands emerged like talons, gnarled by work or arthritis. Her skin was very dark brown, her hair long and gray. She looked up at Chris and caught his attention. The plumpness of her cheeks held wrinkles at bay, but they clustered at the corners of her eyes. Her gaze, looking startled, held on him.

She looked familiar. Of course she looked familiar. In his decade-plus as a trial lawyer Chris had seen thousands of faces. Victims and their families, defendants and theirs, cops, witnesses, jurors. By this time, everyone looked familiar to him.

But the old lady seemed to recognize him, too. Her mouth opened expectantly, waiting for him to come up and give her an order.

"Olga Rivera?" Chris said, and she nodded.

He consulted his witness list and asked for two other names. The girl holding the baby turned out to be the teenager who'd been working in the store at the time of the robbery. He checked off the names and said they'd be called soon. Then he looked around the hall for any other waiting witnesses.

Just before he pulled open the heavy glass door to return to the courtroom, Chris looked back and saw the old lady still watching him. He forgot, until he saw a face like hers, how frightening the judicial system could be, even to someone not being prosecuted. That's why the victims had brought their whole family, as if they themselves were on trial. Chris gave the woman a reassuring smile that didn't help. She still watched him fearfully.

Her face stayed with him as Chris sat through the rest of the morning's evidence. He read the summary of yesterday's testimony from Kenny's notes. After the robbery, the case had languished unsolved for more than a month until a snitch had come forward. Recently released from prison, he had been asked to participate in the crime but had refused, then after it happened had reported to his parole officer that he knew who had been involved. A detective had shown photos to the victims, then arranged a live lineup, during which two witnesses had picked out this defendant.

"Jessica Rivera." Bonnie announced her next witness in a clear, loud voice. A moment later the teenager who'd been holding the baby in the hallway appeared in the courtroom. Chris smiled at her encouragingly, but the girl looked wary, as if this whole stage set had been built to catch *her* at something.

Bonnie Janaway took no pains to calm her down. She liked having a frightened witness, especially when she asked the young woman if she saw in the courtroom the man who had held a gun near her face during the robbery. Ms. Rivera looked long at the defendant, then said, "Him. The one in the white shirt."

"May the record reflect that the witness has identified the defendant?" Bonnie asked, and Judge Ormond agreed that it would be so. But everyone in the courtroom including the jurors had seen how long the young woman had hesitated. When the defense lawyer's turn came, he jumped right into that hesitation. Smiling graciously, Bill Gibs said, "Ms. Rivera, you seemed kind of slow to identify my client, may I say. Do you have some doubt?"

"No."

"Well, it's obvious who the defendant is here, isn't it? The jurors are in the jury box, the judge is wearing a black robe, and here at these tables except for Mr. Dominguez there's a nicely dressed young lady, a blond man in a suit, and me, who's probably twenty years older than the man you described. So it's not like it was a tough call, was it?"

"No," the witness said slowly, obviously not clear how she should respond.

"So you said it was the defendant. Let me ask you this, what was memorable about the robber who appeared in your store that day?"

Ms. Rivera paused again, and said, "The gun he was holding. I thought he was going to hit me with it."

Gibs nodded. The defense lawyer liked her answer. Chris waited tensely, watching the witness, wondering if Bonnie realized how badly her case was being hurt. The prosecutor sat making notes, apparently oblivious to the exchange.

"Did you know this young man before the day of the robbery?" Bill Gibs continued.

"No. I don't think so." Ms. Rivera shifted nervously in her seat.

"You're not sure? Maybe he had been a customer in the store?"

"Maybe," the witness agreed. Bill Gibs was an agreeable, friendly man. His voice made people want to go along with him.

He also had the good sense to quit once he'd gotten what he wanted. When the witness was passed back to Bonnie, the prosecutor said, "Ms. Rivera, what did you do when the robber pointed the gun at your face?"

"I looked him in the eyes. I said, 'Please don't. I have a baby.'"

Bonnie nodded. "Thank you, ma'am. No more questions."

Pretty good recovery. Chris decided this prosecution was in good hands after all. Still, Bonnie surprised him thirty minutes later when she stood and said, "The State rests, your honor." He thought she'd had more proof to bring forward. Judge Ormond dismissed the jurors for lunch, and Chris leaned over to his assistant.

"Why didn't you call the old lady as a witness? The girl's grandmother. She was in the store during the robbery, too, wasn't she?" He thought she would have made a very sympathetic witness, cowering in the witness stand as she must have done that day in the grocery store.

But Bonnie said offhandedly, "She couldn't identify anyone. Besides, she doesn't speak English."

For no good reason, that answer, along with his vague recollection of the woman in the hall earlier that morning, bothered Chris. He went out to speak to the woman and found her gone. Most of the family remained in the hallway, but the centerpiece of the portrait, the grandmother of the family, had fled. To Chris's eyes there seemed to be a blank spot on the bench where she had sat.

Chris took a drive at lunch. From the police report he had written down the address of the Rivera family grocery store. It was on Zarzamora, a long street only a couple of miles from the courthouse, and a world away. Across the Commerce Street bridge, on the west side of San Antonio, the cityscape changed from generic to specific. There were few brand name stores. Smaller businesses crowded the street instead, many of them looking on the verge of failure even if they had been in business for years. Small houses in poor repair took up some of the spaces between auto shops and secondhand stores. Pale faces grew rare, too, except around certain landmarks such as Karam's Mexican restaurant.

Rivera's, the grocery store, sat farther out that street. As Chris neared it the car began to steer itself. Chris knew when to slow down, and looked expectantly toward the left side of the street. Sure enough, that was where the store appeared. Chris felt again a tingle of recognition. The store occupied a corner. Unlike chain grocery stores, it didn't have large display windows. The two windows in the wooden front were covered by hand-lettered signs advertising lettuce and avocados.

Chris didn't get out of his car. He sat there across the street looking at the storefront as it placed itself in his memory. He had been a young prosecutor, more eager than Bonnie Janaway, so eager that on big cases he always visited the scene of the crime personally. That thoroughness had brought him to this store eight years ago. It seemed to have grown even smaller, but Chris remembered it. This was where another armed encounter had occurred, which had turned into Chris's first big trial. He pictured the interior of the store and its checkout counter, with a bloodstain on it.

And behind the counter the old lady, the same one he'd seen in the Justice Center this morning.

She didn't speak English, Bonnie had said. But Chris knew better. She had spoken English well enough, eight years ago when she had testified for him.

He drove slowly back to the Justice Center, through a bright October day when the air held a certain crystalline quality that presaged cool winds, but the sun had lost little of its potency. Chris looked more closely at everything he passed. Passersby felt his stare and turned sharply or hunched their shoulders.

In the Justice Center he climbed four flights of stairs and went to his office without speaking to anyone. The office occupied a corner of the top floor of the building, giving him views south and westward. Chris ignored the views. He went to the lone wooden filing cabinet that held cases in which he'd had a personal interest over the years. It took only a minute to find the file he wanted. He opened it on his desk. The topmost layer of papers was letters, the most recent three unopened. Chris had stopped opening the man's letters, imagining they contained only rants or threats.

The top envelope was thin. Its return address included a number and a prison unit, a stamped phrase on the envelope identifying it further as mail from an inmate. Chris tore it open and unfolded the two thin sheets of lined paper inside. There was no greeting. The letter began, "I have a sixteen-year-old son. I haven't seen him since he was twelve years old."

Chris felt a chill. He kept reading.

Bonnie Janaway remained on her own for the rest of her trial that day. Chris spent the day making a few phone calls, looking up information on his computer, and walking distractedly through the halls. People asked him questions, he even answered some, but couldn't have repeated afterward what he had said.

Anne Greenwald heard his preoccupation when she called about four in the afternoon. After thirty seconds of conversation she said, "What's up?" In a tone that meant she wanted a real answer.

"Nothing. I don't know. Thinking about some old cases."

"At least yours end," Anne said. She was a psychiatrist, mainly dealing with children, so many of her cases represented lifetime commitments. Her patients would outlive her, if all went well. Many of them would carry their childhoods with them forever, though.

Anne stood in her office, which boasted one small window. If she went to stand right next to it she could look down five stories to a parking lot. But staying back here by the corner of the desk meant the window showed her a square of daylight, blue clear sky untouched by humankind, like an abstraction of day. Framed by the white walls of her office, the square of outside looked like a hole punched in her schedule. Anne stood staring, holding the phone loosely by her ear.

She felt distracted too, but unlike Chris had no specific reason on which to blame her mood. Just one of those October things. Change of season, winds stirring, something life-altering just over the horizon.

"My next appointment canceled," she said into the phone. After Chris's short answer she laughed. "Yeah, but it was a group session. The whole group canceled. How can that be? They all got better all at once, or sicker? Maybe they're meeting somewhere without me. Would that be a good thing? You think I cured them all at once?"

"Or they all realized how sick of you they were, all at the same time," Chris suggested.

"Certainly a possibility. Maybe they're somewhere forming a gang. I've given them back their self-esteem and they're going to use it to terrorize other people. Dr. Greenwald's Crime Incubator. Can you be Professor Moriarty without realizing it?"

"I don't think anything can happen that you haven't thought about," Chris said. He made it sound like a compliment. Anne laughed again.

"So what are you going to do?"

"I don't know," he said. "I need to think. How are you going to use your free hour?"

"I've got about fifty reports I need to write. And a paper for a seminar that was due last week. I'll find something."

The top of Anne's desk looked pristine, like a well-ordered mind. But she knew that its drawers, like the subconscious, were bursting with ill-digested files.

That square of blue was having a strange effect on her. The window was closed, but Anne felt a breeze. She took a clip from her hair, letting the soft brown hair fall down her neck, its ends just brushing the juncture between neck and shoulders.

"I'll see you later," Chris said.

"Yeah," she muttered toward the phone as she set it down. "If you're lucky."

She unbuttoned her white clinical coat, sat at her desk, admiring its neatness, and with a sigh reached toward the bottom drawer.

Chris left the building before five o'clock, not an unprecedented event, but a rare one. Often when he left he had no one to tell good-bye except the cleaning crew. On this October Thursday afternoon he told no one, not even himself, as his round of pacing just took him out the doors, a not-quite-planned exit from the Justice Center. He didn't feel the air. His thoughts remained so solidly on the file he'd studied and the memories he'd revisited that he was a little surprised to find himself in his car headed north on the expressway, apparently homeward bound. He didn't remember which floor of the parking garage he'd been parked on.

Anne would have known what he'd meant when he said he couldn't think inside the Justice Center. His body had known, too. He would go home, change, and run. At least walk, maybe shoot some baskets. He would get out of the box, move freely, let his thoughts roam.

But his mood detracted from the attention he paid to normal matters. Chris couldn't have said whether anyone had seen him leave the Justice Center, whether anyone had been watching him. He had acted strangely ever since noon. Someone could have noticed. Cars hummed around and behind him on the expressway. Some followed him off at his exit. It was a busy street. Chris drove past the Quarry Market shopping center, busy with teenagers and others at four thirty in the afternoon. Traffic required some attention. The Quarry, which had started life as a huge hole in the ground out of which rocks had been dug for decades to make concrete, had turned into one of the busiest shopping areas in town after Alamo Cement relocated. The shopping center had opened since Chris had moved into the neighborhood a few years earlier. Population and traffic had grown. Generally Chris kept different hours from most of humanity and didn't notice how crowded his neighborhood had grown. Today, coming home at roughly the same time as most people, he decided he needed to move.

Besides, he had a child now: Clarissa, seventeen, who had lived with him for the better part of a year. She should be in a house, with a yard and a dog. Clarissa would have laughed if she could have seen the watercolor scene her father's mind was painting for her. Her laughter would be lighthearted but caustic and remind Chris of her late mother.

Clarissa was fine in a condominium. So was Chris. He'd been a suburban kid who had grown into a downtown kind of guy, which made a condo the perfect living space. But some days he felt it was time to grow up. Buy a house. Commit.

He felt something as he parked under a rippled tin roof in his assigned slot. A certain weight to the air as if it carried something like a stare. He turned his head and saw many windows, but no one standing behind any of them. Then he began thinking again about his long-ago first big-time prosecution, and forgot the feeling of being watched as he went up the stairs to his front door.

Inside, he flicked on lights. The condo sat dark during the day. It blinked in the light. The condo's walls used to be white. Recently Clarissa, with his and Anne's help, had painted them a bold lavender that Chris had hated at first but that had begun to grow on him. "Looks less like a clinical experiment now," Clarissa had said with satisfaction when the job was finished.

The air in here didn't feel as dead as usual, as if October had crept inside even before Chris arrived. Not noticing, Chris draped his suit coat over one of the chrome barstools at the counter that defined the opening between the kitchen and dining area. He left his briefcase there, too, pulling off his tie as he walked to his bedroom, the one on the right. He left his tie and black shoes in the closet and went into the bathroom, failing to hear the sound of light footfalls.

Chris emerged from the bathroom back into the walk-in closet. He took off his suit pants and hung them up. Barefoot, unbuttoning his shirt, he walked back out into the living room. The glass patio door caught his attention. He crossed to it and found the heavy door unlocked. Clarissa must have gone out there in the morning, and as usual forgotten to lock the sliding door when she'd come back in. The balcony held a fascination for her. Maybe she did need a backyard. Chris stepped outside, feeling a prickling along his shoulders. The patio looked down into another patio and beyond that to a parking lot. Someone could have clambered up here with difficulty, but he saw no sign that anyone had. A breeze stirred the crinkled hairs on his legs.

Stepping back inside, he felt more than heard movement. Chris stopped just inside the door, standing perfectly still. Air moved on his skin, even though the air conditioner wasn't blowing.

Chris wasn't normally paranoid, but life had been event-filled in the last year. He could name people who actively hated him. Some of those people were not the type merely to brood about their supposed injustices. This summer for a brief period he'd actually carried a gun for the first time in his life.

But he'd given that up. For a moment he regretted that decision.

Then he shook his head, closed the patio door, and walked toward Clarissa's bedroom, his feeling of alarm passing. Reason said no one lurked here. Who would even expect him home at this time of day? Something in the condo had probably moved when he'd opened the patio door and let the outside air slither inside.

He glanced into Clarissa's bedroom. It looked neat as a room in a model home, the bed made tightly. Opening the closet door, he saw her shoes lined up neatly. Just since this school year had begun, her senior year, Clarissa's room had begun to look like that of a cadet in military school. He had no idea what was up with that. But it did make it easy to see no intruder had pawed through her clothes or dresser. Chris glanced into her bathroom, but began to feel silly, so that he didn't check behind the shower curtain or even the bathroom door.

He walked back across the living room, humming, talking to himself in a disconnected murmur. His own sounds covered up the soft sound of feet crossing the living room seconds after his.

The light in the bedroom came only from the walk-in closet, white angling into the gray of the room. Chris went into the light again, dropped his white shirt into the laundry hamper, and came back out into the bedroom in his underwear, the room grown even dimmer after his trip into the lighted closet.

Thinking about things coming back, he bent over his own dresser and opened a drawer, looking for running shorts.

The sounds from the living room were even softer, too soft to carry to Chris, the slither of fabric on skin as the intruder moved. Bare feet crossed his carpeted bedroom floor behind Chris's back as he found shorts and bent to pull them on.

Arms encircled him from behind. At first the contact was so slight he thought he imagined it, then the arms drew tight across his chest, pulling him back.

Chris gasped, trying to keep his balance. He felt flesh and then hair against his bare back. He turned, trying to see, and the soft brown hair moved across his shoulder. He recognized something then, her hair or her smell or the low chuckle that she couldn't hold in any longer.

She turned with him, staying behind him, so they twirled for a moment in a strange dance. Anne began to feel embarrassed, she didn't want him to turn and see her. It had seemed like a great joking adventure, slipping in here before Chris got home, lying in wait. But joking adventures aren't for grown-ups. Even as she laughed and held him tight, she had lost her adventuress's resolve.

Chris moved in her grasp, feeling her bare skin against his. She had dropped her skirt and blouse in the living room just before making her last daring rush across the bedroom floor to attack him. He turned in her grasp. Even after he had realized it was Anne he would see, he was astonished to find her nearly naked. She smiled like a predator, brazenness her only defense against embarrassment.

"The mayor and chief of police are here with me," Chris said. "They're coming up the stairs now."

"Then this will be fun," Anne said. She stepped close, running her hands down his sides and up to his chest. More whisper of fabric. The bedroom was dim but not dark, and not even dim in a normal way. That slash of white light cut through the room from the closet, a stripe of illumination in the darkness. Anne stepped through it, her skin turning very white. She pulled Chris with her, he also flickering white as in an old film.

They stood by the foot of the bed, each with a knee up on it. Anne drew his head down for a first kiss. It did feel like a first kiss, tentative and slow, then growing more passionate. Her fingertips tickled his abdomen. His hands fell to the tops of her thighs.

They found themselves on the unmade bed without a push or a fall. Anne was behind him again, moving. Her leg went over his. She kept moving, encircling him, like a very intimate evasion, not letting him get a good grip. He was the object, she the explorer. Chris knew this mood, and let her have her way, until she sat behind him with her legs wrapped around him, as if she'd captured him. He reached back and very slowly pulled her up and over. Their mouths met again. She lay full length against him as he fell forward and sideways.

Time passed. Now there could have been other intruders in the condo; indeed, the mayor and police chief could have sat in the other room, tapping their fingers impatiently. No one in the bedroom would have noticed.

Anne murmured, "I knew you'd come here. And Clarissa has volleyball practice after school today."

This might have been an especially erotic endearment, from Chris's reaction. His last inhibition dropped. It was true that for the last six months he'd been as much a parent as a lover. His times with Anne seemed quick and secretive. But in every long-term relationship there are highs and lows, and must be an occasional renaissance of desire. Anne seemed to have felt such a rebirth lately. She'd become restless and sly, flirtatious at times in crowds. This didn't remind Chris of when they'd first begun dating. It was better.

She pushed now, reaching, feet elongating. He held her waist tightly.

The room seemed brighter, a few minutes later. Darkness no longer hid them. They lay huddled together, enwrapped, the sheets pushed down over the foot of the bed. Anne sighed, not ready to talk. Chris's thoughts had been pushed away, except the ones of her.

"You know what we should do?" he said after a while, and Anne chuckled as if he'd made a great, dirty joke.

Before he could elaborate, they heard the front door crashing back against the wall, a rush of air and movement, and a full, hearty teenage voice call, "Coach canceled practice and Suzie gave me a ride home! Anybody here?"

Anne didn't leap up. She lay on the naked bed, put her hands over her face, and laughed like a teenager.

Jack Fine walked the narrow halls inside the district attorney's offices. He had laid down a lot of scuff marks on institutional floors over the last thirty years. Jails, police headquarters, medical examiner's offices, now the DA's office. Jack no longer even saw his surroundings, though if you put him into an unfamiliar scene his eye would catch out-of-place details in a heartbeat. Twenty years as a police detective had more than trained him; investigation instincts had twined along his spine and through his nerves. He had the best eyes in the business.

People might have thought his life's work had shaped his cynical attitude, too, but people react in different ways. Jack had been completely content with a cop's life until in the course of his work he'd noticed some numbers that didn't add up in other police officers' collection and distribution of a charity fund. Jack being Jack, he had pulled on that thread and couldn't stop even when he began to see where it led. A few veteran cops had lost their jobs, including Jack. After what a lot of people inside the department saw as his betrayal, the cop shop had no longer been the clubhouse it used to be for him. He'd gotten out. An offer from a brand-new, overly eager district attorney to be his chief investigator had given Jack Fine the perfect escape at a time when he badly needed it, though he would never have let Chris Sinclair know such a thing. Jack's job inside this office included usually being the oldest guy in the room, the most hard-bitten, the one who had seen it all.

As now. Jack stepped into one of the small offices to see a lanky young man in a white shirt slumped behind a metal desk. An even younger guy in a pink shirt sat across the desk, looking heavier and more lively.

"What's the problem, Bert?" Jack asked the inert one.

"I don't think there's a problem. Just this defendant in my court who says he wants to talk to The Man. I thought I should tell somebody."

"How does he know *you're* not the man?"

The other young prosecutor laughed. "See, I told you. You the man, Bert."

At twenty-eight, the thin young man behind the desk was indeed a veteran prosecutor, even though to Jack he still looked like a high school student. Bert must have encountered an unusual defendant, one old enough to remember *The Brady Bunch* on its first run. One who wouldn't consider a kid prosecutor—even a first-chair kid prosecutor—"the man."

"Where is he?" Jack asked.

"In the holding cell next to the 290th." As Jack began to withdraw, Bert came alive enough to crane his neck. "Undoubtedly bullshit," he called. "I just thought I should tell somebody."

Jack trudged down through the building. He could feel its unpopulated quality, on a Friday afternoon. No more jurors, no witnesses waiting, all trials finished, the week's business essentially done, and the skeleton staff remaining on duty resentful at having to be there. The hallway door into the 290th District Court was locked. Jack walked around through the back corridor and into the courtroom next to the judge's unoccupied bench. The large, friendly bailiff gave Jack a nodding smile. "Hear you've got a dangerous criminal mastermind here I should talk to," Jack said.

"Really? Let me look at him again. I haven't seen a mastermind before. Closest thing we've had is that guy that spray-painted the security cameras blind. Then dropped the can of spray paint with his prints on it in the trash can on his way out."

Ray laughed, jangled the keys on his belt, and went to a side door. Beyond it sat a confined space holding an elevator that went down to the mini-jail two floors down. Inside this space next to the courtroom there were also two very small cells, for holding inmates just before they were brought into the courtroom to testify or be put on trial. After a minute Ray the bailiff brought out from this space a guy with a stubbled head, quick eyes, and a prominent lip that curled when he saw Jack.

"You ain't the man," he said.

"Hell I'm not. Compared to you I'm the damn' Secretary-General of the UN."

"I am only going to talk to Mr. Sinclair, the district attorney himself," the idiot in the orange jumpsuit said, enunciating distinctly in order to be insulting. "I have something to tell him that's a lot bigger than this bullshit they got me charged with. He'll want to deal, trust me. They'll have feds in here, too. *Hard Copy,* before it's over."

This defendant looked to be in his thirties, probably toward the tail end, though with drug users it was hard to tell. He seemed as at ease in the courtroom as he would have been in a crack house, sitting on a corner of one of the counsel tables. His feet remained shackled but Ray the bailiff had freed his hands. He folded his bony arms as Jack stood close to him, hands in pockets, looking unenticed. It required no effort on Jack's part to appear less than intrigued. "If every jerk-off with a line of crap got to deal directly with the DA, he'd spend his whole day on nobodies like you." Jack realized he didn't even know this guy's name, and didn't mind keeping it that way. "So you don't get to talk to the man unless you convince me you've got something real."

No man cometh unto the Father but by me. The quote had not played a role in Jack's upbringing, but he knew it. Among his other functions was that of gatekeeper. That's why the young assistant DA had come to him about this. And Jack prided himself on being a more reliable bullshit-detector than his boss. He looked this defendant in the eye, not ready to be entertained.

The guy shook his head. "I'm not bringing it to you."

"Why not?"

"Because you're one of them."

"One of who?"

"Cops," the defendant said with a sneer.

Jack sighed. The conversation had just ended, as far as he was concerned. The defendant sensed him about to turn away. He grew angrier.

"You've all spent years covering it up." His eyes flicked past Jack to the uniformed bailiff, taking in all uniforms.

"Covering up what?" Jack said, bored. Some of these guys at least made entertaining stories out of what they had to say, spun elaborate fantasies or conspiracies reaching all the way to the top. This guy's tale was the most recycled in the system: *Cops framed me*.

"You know it's true," the defendant said. He read Jack's reaction on his face, and their conversation became condensed. "They've been doing it for years. Cops getting away with murder. And when somebody gets close they frame him for something else. Like Mr. Sinclair's old friend Steve Greerdon. Tell him. It's true. I've got the goods."

Jack turned away, jerked his head back toward the defendant, and the bailiff nodded at the signal to put him away again.

"It's true!" the defendant called, his voice going shaky as he realized he'd blown his chance. "Tell the district attorney! You don't think he'd care that he put an innocent cop in prison?"

Jack walked out, shaking his head.

He found Chris Sinclair in his office, and Jack was glad to see that Chris was no longer in the cheerful mood in which Jack had found him earlier in the day. This morning Chris had been chipper and jovial, laughing at nothing or at his own stupid jokes, half of which didn't make any sense. Jack had been forced to leave, looking for people more beset by troubles and therefore easier to take.

Now, though, Chris paced his office looking deeply thoughtful. His face wasn't out-and-out gloomy, but it was nevertheless an improvement from this morning.

"Trouble?" Jack asked hopefully.

Chris didn't answer, showing how preoccupied he was. Jack strolled around the office, waiting. He glanced at the open file folder on his boss's desktop, turned a couple of pages, then started reading more closely, noticing for the first time the name on the folder's tab. "Now isn't this a coincidence?" he said.

Chris stopped pacing. He'd heard that. "What is?" he said slowly.

"You looking at the file on Steve Greerdon. I've just come from talking to a guy who knows the whole scoop on that story, and about the other people various cops have framed over the years."

"'Other'? So he says Greerdon was framed?"

"Sure. This guy's a repeat offender looking at life. He's got to say something." Jack saw Chris going more alert but didn't think anything of it. Chris did that regularly.

"But he happened to choose this case."

"Yeah. So why were you lookin' at it again after all these years?"

"Something brought it to mind, so I found it. I read the letters Greerdon's sent me in the past year. They're different. They've changed from what they used to be. He doesn't claim to know anything, just asks questions."

"Such as?"

"Here's a good one," Chris said. He walked toward Jack, closer to the desk, with the flimsy sheet of paper he held in his hand. "'Why was John Steger buried with full police honors, even though he left explicit instructions that he shouldn't be?'"

Chris looked at his investigator, waiting for the answer. Instead Jack asked a question. "How'd you know John left a note?"

Chris held up the letter. "How did Steve Greerdon know? Is there a cover-up, Jack?"

"No. They let me know what happened specifically so there wouldn't be a cover-up. Official notice was given where it needed to be. Everyone just chose not to go public with it. And not to tell his family."

"John Steger killed himself?"

Jack nodded. "Technically against the law, I know, but what're you gonna do to him? So we just tried not to embarrass his family. The only thing we could do for them."

Chris concurred. "But what did his note say? Anything about a reason?"

Jack shook his head. "Only what you just heard. He said not to give him a cop's funeral. He didn't deserve it."

"But you people in your wisdom decided to give him one anyway."

Jack said quietly, "That's for the family too, Chris. John was a police officer. If you don't do the whole shmeer people'd ask why. Besides, John was wrong. He did deserve it. When you kill yourself you're not in your right mind. Should we honor every request a crazy person makes? He deserved the funeral for his whole career. The way his life ended, well, that could happen to anybody."

"But who knows what else you might've been covering up inadvertently, Jack? Look how far the story gets. Greerdon's in prison, but he knows about it."

Jack looked thoughtful but not yet worried. "Steve Greerdon was a cop. Even though he's in prison, I'm sure he's still got friends, no matter what. So what're you gonna do now, Chris, open up an old closed case because the defendant sends you a couple of letters and a lying snitch mentions his name? Word of this better not get out, you'll be deluged by letters from prison."

"It's more than that," Chris said. "Something that happened yesterday."

"What?"

Chris didn't answer. He suddenly strode across his office and opened the door. In the outer office he found his tall, thoughtful first assistant, Paul Benavides, just emerging from his own office even though it was late on a Friday afternoon. The clerical staff had left.

"What's wrong?" Paul said as soon as he caught sight of Chris.

"Nothing, I hope. But I want—Where would old evidence be stored?"

"From a closed case? I'm not sure it would be kept at all. What are you looking for?"

"Blood," Chris said.

The day had grown too late to get more work done. Chris had other responsibilities. Half an hour later he picked up Clarissa from her private school. Instead of her school uniform she wore her volleyball outfit, blue shorts and a white T-shirt, with the sleeves fashionably rolled up and tied in place on her shoulders so that the shirt looked sleeveless. Clarissa immediately filled the car with noise and the smell of healthy girl sweat. Chris even thought she smelled sweet this way, and wondered fleetingly if she'd find a boy who thought so too.

She said hi but barely glanced at him. She held a volleyball between her legs and kept popping it with the heel of her hand, not hard but accompanied by sound effects: "Pow! Whap!" Her blond ponytail twirled. Clarissa didn't smile, but stared at an imaginary spot on the ball.

They had gone several blocks before Clarissa noticed Chris wasn't talking either. She looked at him and sighed loudly, which drew his attention. When he looked over at her, she said, "What is it? What are you obsessing about?"

"Nothing. Nothing."

"Yes you are, Dad. You're supposed to be interrogating me about my day. And look at you."

Even given the short amount of time she'd known him, Clarissa could spot his phases. She'd seen this one before. He'd dropped into trial mode, which gave him great concentration but also tunnel vision.

"It's nothing," he repeated, deliberately making his voice cheerful, and looking around, seeing the remains of the day. A trace of orange in the western sky, cars filling the streets, kids walking home with backpacks slung over their shoulders.

"Hey!" Chris said, like a kid with a bright idea, as if he'd just thought of this. "How about if we do something a little different tonight?"

Clarissa watched him, not fooled for a moment. She laughed.

An hour later they drove down Zarzamora Street. Anne had joined them. In fact, Anne drove her green Volvo, Chris beside her, Clarissa in back, leaning forward to peer out, like a tourist entering a foreign city. Anne, on the other hand, drove easily, at home on the west side, where she'd made many home and school visits. "Don't you think it'll be closed by now?" she said.

Chris, staring out at the streets, shook his head. "They'll be doing a brisk trade in beer, and starting to cook *barbacoa* out back, for the weekend."

They arrived at the Rivera grocery store and Chris's prediction proved true. Its heavy wooden doors stood open, flimsy screen doors leaving the store open to the street. A man with a twelve-pack emerged, taking a cigarette from behind his ear and sticking it in his mouth.

While Anne slowed, looking for a parking space, Chris said, "Wait for me," and jumped out. Anne turned to Clarissa. "What is it this time?" Clarissa shrugged. They waited indulgently, watching Chris entering the old grocery store, their expressions like parents watching a child go off to school.

Inside, Chris found himself lucky. The grandmother stood on duty behind the cash register. Of course, why not? Her teenage granddaughter would be getting ready to go out, her son busy in the office adding up the week's receipts. She had nowhere to go. As in most cultures, in this one it was older women who kept things going.

She had her back to him. Chris approached. He had changed out of his suit, into khakis and a sport shirt with the sleeves rolled up. But he still looked on-duty, compared to the store's other customers. "*Señora,*" he said. "Why did you tell my assistant you don't speak English? I remember you speaking very well."

That was an exaggeration. Chris didn't really remember her testimony for him, except the impact it had made on the jury. The old lady turned quickly and stared at him. After a long pause, during which she clearly debated how to answer, she said, "What do you want?"

"An answer to my question."

She rubbed her lips over each other, but they still looked dry. "I didn't want to testify again," she finally said. "It goes badly for me."

"How did it go badly?" he asked with genuine curiosity. A short line of people had formed at the counter, but they waited respectfully for him to finish questioning the cashier. "You told the truth, didn't you?"

"Of course! I said it just the way you told me."

"*I* told you?" Chris thought she had him mistaken for someone else.

"*Sí,*" the woman said, her voice growing more urgent, as if he had contradicted her. "You said I had to say I was sure. You said I had to sound positive about the man I saw in here."

Chris shook his head slowly. "I said you had to *be* sure. If I was going to prosecute a police officer—I was asking you were you sure he was the one."

That was the way he'd phrased it, wasn't it, when he'd prepared this witness for trial eight years earlier? He hadn't been too eager, he hadn't put words in her mouth.

But he hadn't been the only one to question her, either. Not by a long shot. Half a dozen cops had talked to her before Chris had ever seen her.

The old lady watched him nervously. Seeing his reaction, she thought she'd made a mistake. But that wasn't what Chris was thinking. He was thinking that he had.

★

A minute later Anne and Clarissa followed him into the store. Clarissa looked around curiously, noting the three aisles, the sparsely stocked shelves, brands that seemed exotic to her. A couple of customers looked back at her with the same expressions. Tall, authentically blond teenage girls didn't appear here every week.

Anne found Chris staring. She took his arm and gently led him away from the counter. "What is it?" she asked, having no idea why he was here.

"There *was* a conspiracy," he said hollowly. "I was part of it. Anne—" His eyes had grown haunted. He was no longer fully present. But his emotions were certainly engaged. His face, pale when she'd entered, suddenly went red. "My God, I think I've put an innocent man in prison."

The following week, tests on old blood confirmed his fear.

CHAPTER two

★ A decade earlier, a gang of cops had been on a quiet rampage. As far as anyone outside the conspiracy could reconstruct later, it had begun as two patrol officers cruised slowly down Cherry Street, a neighborhood from which people moved away if they could. The younger cop on the passenger side had shaken his head in disgust and said, "Look at that guy. Sitting outside the barbershop like he owns the town."

"He does own this part," the driver cop had said. "We know the scumbag's the biggest drug dealer on the east side and we can't touch him."

Silence had wrapped the two police officers for a moment, until the driver looked in the rearview mirror and saw the subject of their conversation stroll slowly away in the opposite direction.

"Maybe we can," he had said.

The arrest of Montre Williams for possession of a large amount of heroin had been only the beginning of the conspiracy. It started out fueled by honest outrage on the part of cops who knew a lot more than they could prove, who knew that they might make arrests but once the cases got into the courthouse they would swirl down the tubes as the laughing defendants walked free.

"At least we can cost them money they spend on lawyers," one cop had remarked. Perhaps that was when money entered the picture. Once someone had raised the idea that the cops couldn't hurt the bad guys any way except financially, inevitably someone had thought, Why should that money go to scummy defense lawyers?

A very young Christian Sinclair, only three years out of law school, had called this "the evil alliance."

"They got greedy," he'd declared loudly, stalking across the courtroom toward the jury. "From offering protection to drug dealers for money, they progressed to stealing money themselves. That's when this unholy conspiracy was finally dragged out into the light. When men like Steve Greerdon, entrusted with protecting the people of this city, instead began to prey on the innocent."

The defendant, Detective Steve Greerdon, had sat at the counsel table, head lowered and shoulders bunched, as if he were pushing a great weight. From underneath his heavy brows, his eyes had glared at the young prosecutor, following his every move.

Chris, looking impossibly young and full of self-righteousness that hadn't been chipped away by experience, had stood in front of the jurors and pointed. "You will never see anything worse than what sits before you today. A rogue cop. Someone we called one of our city's finest, when instead he had gone over to the dark side. While swearing to protect your lives and property, and taking your money in his paycheck every month, he was out there hurting you instead. He betrayed you, he betrayed his colleagues, he betrayed a sacred trust. How much guiltier is he than any of the thugs he ever arrested?"

Eight years later, District Attorney Chris Sinclair could remember some fragments of that closing argument. It now sounded clichéd and ridiculously idealistic to him. But he also remembered the way it had felt to deliver it, the surge of blood pumping through his body, the rush of holding the rapt attention of everyone in the courtroom. Most of all, he remembered two jurors watching him closely and nodding along as he spoke. There is no greater satisfaction for a trial lawyer.

Trite as his speech might have been, it had also been damned effective. Now, eight years later, Chris worked to undo that early triumph. Freeing Steve Greerdon proved much more difficult than sending him to prison had been. A briar patch of bureaucracy stood in his path. Chris was as solidly entrenched a member of that bureaucracy as anyone, but that didn't mean he could move it. He wrote a letter to the governor and made a phone call to the lieutenant governor. Chris expected the latter to be more effective, because he had once helped Lieutenant Governor Veronica Sorenson with a problem that could have ruined her. Sure enough, Sorenson took his call in a matter of seconds.

"What can I do for you?" Her voice sounded like one of those computer-generated messages, bright and distinct but lifeless.

"I'm sorry to bother you with this," Chris said, and quickly explained his problem. "I just wanted to ask you who I should talk to to get the pardon ball rolling."

"Cathy Jennings, the governor's general counsel. I'll call her."

"You don't have to do that. I just—"

"I'll get through to her sooner than you would, Chris. In fact, I might just walk down the hall and see her."

"Thank you," Chris concluded lamely. "Thanks for your help."

He didn't like the way the conversation made him feel, as if he'd called in a favor. But that seemed to be what Veronica Sorenson expected. This was how things worked. Justice didn't propel the criminal justice system; personal connections did.

As he waited, wondering what to do next, he imagined Steve Greerdon. How would an innocent man endure eight years in prison? Chris had been inside prison cells. The experience had shaken him. He'd moved quickly to prevent the guard from closing the door. But no one could hear those bars clang for eight years and remain as sensitive to the sound, or to the fact of incarceration. At least he hoped so.

As a prosecutor and even during his brief stint as a defense lawyer, Chris had never given much thought to the defendants who went off to prison after a trial. To Chris it just meant the end of a case: time to move on to the next one. He realized, yes, that to a defendant his own case was vitally important, but that didn't make the event intrinsically significant in the real world. People who got arrested seemed a lower order of life, prison their natural destiny. If they weren't so stupid they wouldn't end up incarcerated, but that dimness itself seemed their protection against prison life. He imagined, if he thought about them at all, that they could take it, passing through their years of punishment in a mental fog.

But now he knew he'd committed someone innocent—someone like himself—to the hell of prison. And a cop. It would be ten times worse for a cop.

"I could get him out now. Get him bench warranted back to San Antonio, get some judge to give him a bond. Who was the trial judge? Doesn't matter. I could get him out."

"Don't do anything," Jack Fine said patiently. The investigator and the district attorney walked in the vicinity of the courthouse. Jack knew Chris hadn't confided in anyone except Paul Benavides and Jack about his attempt to free Steve Greerdon. So for privacy Chris and Jack went for a walk. Chris walked faster, got ahead, then came back, too impatient just to wait for Jack to catch up. Chris would keep pace for a couple of steps, then be ahead again, moving almost as fast as his thoughts. It made Jack feel like an old man walking a puppy. Jack was busy too, noticing every important detail of the streets, listening to the sounds of car engines; his mind working as quickly as his boss's. Jack's activity was invisible, Chris's apparent, that was all. A difference in style.

"Why not?" Chris asked. "I could at least get him back here, out of prison. That hellhole. He must—"

"He'll have gotten used to it by now," Jack said calmly. "He's made his adjustments. Bring him back to Bexar County Jail and he'd have a whole new set of people to worry about. You don't want to get his hopes up. That would be worse, to bring him here and tell him what you were trying to do, then have to send him back."

"Oh, I'm going to get it done," Chris said. He put his hands in his pockets but spoke as if counting items off a list. "I got an affidavit from the old lady, my witness, who said she wasn't sure she'd identified the right person. I've had the blood tested and it wasn't his. We didn't even send it out for DNA testing back then. I've told the lieutenant governor personally that I'm convinced of his innocence . . ."

"Then he'll be out soon enough," Jack said. "Besides . . ."

"Besides what?"

They crossed Alamo Street and went into HemisFair Park, the site of the World's Fair that had been held when Chris was two or three years old. Jack remembered the fair very well. He'd had his first real kiss there, in a nook of the Canadian Pavilion. The sight of Canada on a map still looked like virgin territory to him, crisp and inviting.

"You don't want somebody working against you before you get it done," Jack explained carefully. "You don't want someone else whispering in the governor's ear. The people who set him up to begin with."

"That's why we're here," Chris said, sounding weary for the first time. "If Greerdon didn't commit that robbery, someone else did. Someone who framed him to take the fall for it. I tried to think it could've just been a series of mistakes. It could, couldn't it? A witness guesses wrong, the evidence gets mishandled . . ." He looked hopefully at his investigator. Jack squashed the idea quickly.

"A cop becomes a suspect in a crime, and the cops investigating it don't dig as hard as they can, give him every break they can?" Jack shook his head. "If he was innocent back then, he should've been found innocent. Case never should've reached a grand jury. No. As badly as you want him out now, somebody else wanted him put away. And whoever it is, they want him to *stay* away."

Jack hadn't told Chris anything he didn't know. Chris had just resisted the knowledge. But he knew: Someone had framed Steve Greerdon. They had made Chris their unwitting instrument. "Then we have to move fast, Jack. Before the governor does. You understand? I've reinterviewed the witnesses. Somebody may already be alerted because of that. I've got the blood and fingerprint evidence from the medical examiner's office. We won't send it back. What else can we seize?"

"The good stuff would have been buried years ago," Jack said.

"But not everything. Not people's memories. Who else do we need to talk to, Jack? What else can we get? What about the gun that fired the shot at the robbery?"

"Greerdon's gun."

"Was it? How do we know that?"

"His fingerprints on it. Plus testimony."

"Whose? I'll get the court records."

Jack's eyes moved slowly across the panorama of downtown, as if methodically seeking a target. "We need to know who did the investigating.

If we request old offense reports from the PD, that'll alert somebody . . ."

"We should have copies in our own files," Chris said. "I remember seeing them. I'll get them. We have to get to the officers who wrote those reports, but not first. First we have to reinterview all the civilians. Not just about who they saw but who talked to them, who slanted their stories."

"We're going to need some help."

"I have an idea about that. But the police reports, Jack—"

"If somebody planted evidence to implicate Steve Greerdon, that person wouldn't have written a report about it."

"So the officers who wrote offense reports were clean? We can trust them?"

"Not necessarily. Somebody had to write the reports. Somebody might've wanted to write them to make sure they got spun right. List the right witnesses, leave a troublesome one off, maybe."

Jack's thoughts obviously ran on different tracks simultaneously, thinking like an investigator and like a bad cop. He seemed to have no trouble with either.

"Thanks, Jack," Chris said wryly. "I knew I could count on you for answers."

But he also knew that Jack Fine would work his ass off. Nobody in town would get less sleep in the next few days. Jack hadn't known Steve Greerdon, but he understood his situation. Jack had been accused, too, during his police career. He'd been lucky enough to be exonerated.

On their way back to the Justice Center, Chris had to hurry to keep up with him.

At first Clarissa avoided the new boy. She didn't even look at him in class. This wasn't a conscious decision, she was just too busy. She had her small circle of good friends, volleyball, and tons of schoolwork every day. Clarissa attended a private school, perhaps the best in the city. Students came there because their parents wanted the best for them. Berkshire was a prep school; ninety-eight percent of its graduates went on to college, many to famous colleges. Academically, Clarissa's school was intense.

But Berkshire also served as a new environment for some kids who'd had "difficulties" at their old schools: a new start, removed from bad influences. (As if such a thing were possible, Clarissa thought wryly. Berkshire had as active a drug culture as any school. She just hadn't drifted into it, mainly because she no longer drifted. Her schedule didn't have space for it.) And, of course, Berkshire was expensive. Parents who could afford the high tuition could get their child placed here.

So Clarissa's high school was full of smart kids, rich kids, troubled kids. For a while she'd managed to forget which she was. Then Peter arrived.

When a new student transferred into Berkshire, not from out of town but from another school in San Antonio, the other kids smelled a story. Of the three reasons students came to this school, two of them seldom came to a head gradually: Parents didn't suddenly get rich, nor did they suddenly notice how smart their kid was, at the beginning of his senior year of high school. No, the third possibility always remained the most reasonable: trouble at his old school. The first rumor usually involved drugs or a gun or both. If the new kid appeared to nod off in class, other heads nodded as well, knowingly: yep, speed freak.

Someone always claimed to know the new student, through a school or family or neighborhood connection. Fanciful stories got embellished if they weren't fanciful enough. Not many of these students, bright as they were, ever read a newspaper. They didn't care what was happening across town, let alone around the world. Their gossip remained very localized, but by the same token very intense. By the end of the first week, the new kid might be a mafioso or a Kennedy, or both.

Clarissa paid no attention, but she inevitably heard some of the talk. It made her lips tighten, not because of what the students said, but because it brought back her own first days in Berkshire. Clarissa realized they must have talked this way about her a year ago. Maybe still did. In her case, they hadn't known how right they were.

Then one day she glanced back at the new boy. He sat hunched in the classic defensive posture, backpack close at hand like a security blanket. His hand moved steadily across his notebook page, but he might have been writing scribbles, or hate notes, just to appear to be paying attention to the teacher (which Clarissa considered unlikely). Clarissa got her first good look at his face and thought of the stories she'd heard: crime boss, autistic genius, placement from the witness relocation program. Her lips pursed wryly.

When class ended and the new kid gathered up his things quickly, eyes downcast, Clarissa waited until the rush of students had passed her by, then walked back, stood next to the new boy until he had to acknowledge her, and said, "Hi, Pete. What'd they get you for?"

A week before the end of October, Chris got a call from Cathy Jennings. If he hadn't remembered the name he might not have taken her call, since she didn't announce herself any other way to his secretary. When he picked up, she said, "Mr. Sinclair, this is Cathy Jennings from the governor's office. I have one question to ask: Are you sure?"

The woman obviously didn't believe in chitchat. "Yes," Chris said, trying to sound as flat and decisive as she.

"Steve Greerdon is innocent?"

"I couldn't prove him guilty. If the case came to me again, I'd dismiss the indictment. I wouldn't even try it."

"Do you have another suspect in the robbery?"

"I'm working on it," Chris answered. "It's a cold case, hard to develop new leads."

"I'd think your police department would be anxious to solve it," Cathy Jennings said, with the first hint of something like humor, or human feeling. She quickly stepped on that, her voice going flat again. "When we announce that someone is innocent, we generally like to point out the guilty at the same time. Maintain balance, like the scales of justice."

Chris didn't reply. He found himself gripping the phone tightly, as if his own future depended on this call. Cathy Jennings asked a second question. "There was only one eyewitness, and she's now changed her story? Will she stick with the new version this time?"

"Absolutely. I've done three different photo spreads with her, and she couldn't pick Steve Greerdon out."

Ms. Jennings paused, as if calculating. "All right. The governor is going to grant your pardon. And once the decision is made, we move fast. We don't leave an innocent police officer in prison one extra hour. Can you be in Huntsville this afternoon for the photo?"

She seemed far ahead of him. Before she vanished over the horizon, Chris said, "The photo?"

"With the governor and Officer Greerdon. Handshakes all around. The man who prosecuted him has now worked to set him free. The governor apologizing on behalf of the state, you personally."

Chris could picture it. What he couldn't imagine was the grip of Steve Greerdon's hand. He could imagine instead the man spitting on him, or punching him. "I don't think you want me in that picture," he said. "Let the governor take the credit alone."

Cathy Jennings departed from her prepared script to ask a final question. "Don't you plan to run for re-election?"

"Not this year. And Ms. Jennings, when you write the governor's speech, don't call him Officer Greerdon. It was Detective Greerdon."

He felt proud of having supplied information she lacked, but the governor's lawyer topped him. "He will be again," she said decisively, and hung up.

A week later Chris stood under a bridge watching tourists go by and thinking of one phrase the governor's lawyer had used. "The governor is going to grant *your* pardon . . ." He understood what she had meant. Chris Sinclair had requested this pardon, not the defendant, and the governor was granting it as a favor to Chris Sinclair. Chris owed him.

It also meant that Chris was responsible for any potential political consequences as a result of the pardon. He'd better be right this time. And Steve Greerdon had better remain a model citizen from now on.

Chris doubted Greerdon felt any responsibility to anyone. He might, however, still be carrying a grudge. Getting him out of prison didn't make up for the eight years he'd spent there, all because of Chris. That was only one reason Chris hadn't wanted to be part of the emerging-from-prison greeting committee.

As he waited to meet the man he'd wrongly convicted, Chris felt apprehensive, of course, consumed with guilt, but also curious. What would an innocent man look like after eight years in prison? What would he have become?

Had he given up hope of being released early? Maybe Steve Greerdon would be dazzled by freedom. Maybe he was so happy to be released that he'd already begun to put the experience of prison behind him.

Chris hoped so.

Steve Greerdon didn't feel either the sunshine or the breeze. He walked on San Antonio's famous Riverwalk as if walking across a prison exercise yard. His eyes didn't turn toward the shops or restaurants. He didn't notice the happy strolling tourists. And Greerdon didn't amble himself. He walked purposefully, striding along the path.

He saw the man he was supposed to meet, standing in the shade under a bridge. Chris in his blue suit stood out on the Riverwalk, but Greerdon would have known him anyway. He remembered Chris Sinclair.

Finally the pace of the place seemed to reach Steve Greerdon. He slowed down, began to glance around. His hands went into his pockets, his head went back, and he breathed deeply. He almost bumped into Chris.

They didn't even make an awkward pass at shaking hands. Chris was a little startled by Steve Greerdon's sudden appearance, close in his face. The man had a broad, swarthy face, the beginning of a brown moustache, staring blue eyes. A European peasant look about him, that extended to his broad shoulders and thick hands.

"Hello," Chris said, and Greerdon nodded. Chris turned and walked, and they stopped at the next restaurant and sat down in wrought iron chairs a few steps off the Riverwalk. Greerdon pushed his chair back into the shade of the awning, blending into the shadows. A smiling blond waitress appeared quickly and asked for drink orders.

"Coke," Greerdon said.

"We have Pepsi, is that all right?"

He gave her a look that said it was so not all right that he might strangle her, leave her body as a warning to other waitpersons, and move on to the next restaurant. Then he nodded, indifferent.

When the drinks came, Chris nodded to Greerdon's and said, "In your place I think I might have a beer."

Greerdon shrugged. "I spent the first two days about half drunk. Wasn't as much fun as I remembered. I got too much sun, too." He pushed up his shirtsleeves to show his reddened forearms. "I forgot you can get sunburned in October."

Chris moved into the shade too. He cleared his throat. "Listen—"

"Please don't tell me you're going to say you're sorry. Is there anything you'd do different now? You were just doing your job. No reason to treat me any different than anyone else you thought was guilty."

They'd both been waiting to get that out of the way, and Greerdon had beaten Chris to it. Chris nodded and sipped at his iced tea. Then he reviewed what the man had said and replied thoughtfully, "I might do things differently now. Then I was an employee, I did what I was told."

"And now you're the boss," Greerdon said easily, staring into the fizzing cola in front of him. "So you're saying if police brought you a perfectly wrapped-up case against one of their own you'd look at it suspiciously now?"

He gave Chris a big smile and toasted him.

"Police are my partners."

"Exactly."

Chris continued carefully, "I started to say, 'But sometimes we have different objectives.'"

Greerdon shrugged, appearing bored. He sat back in the shade and watched the life of the Riverwalk pass by. The stone walkways along a few miles of the shallow San Antonio River provided one of the most popular tourist destinations in Texas. One arm led almost to the Alamo, through the lobby of a hotel. Usually shady and several degrees cooler than the street above, the walk remained crowded at most times of the year. Even with Halloween just past and Thanksgiving approaching, most of the strolling vacationers and convention-goers wore shorts and T-shirts. Greerdon watched them peacefully.

"Speaking of what you just brought up . . ." Chris began.

Greerdon raised his eyebrows. "I brought up?"

"The men who set you up," Chris said. "Your former colleagues. I've reopened the case, and it's an entirely different kind of case now. Not just a robbery. Tampering with evidence, criminal conspiracy . . ."

Steve Greerdon didn't appear to be paying attention. Chris looked at him more carefully. Noticing the pause in the conversation, Greerdon glanced at him and asked a question, sounding merely polite rather than curious. "Any of the investigating officers still on the force?"

"Two of them," Chris said, "including the lead investigator, a man named Mike Green. A sergeant now."

"I doubt it was him," Greerdon said casually. "That's the last guy I'd suspect. He probably believed what he was doing, the leads he was getting. The eyewitnesses he talked to. He wouldn't have asked who else had talked to them before him." He shook his head. "Nah, the lead guy'd be clean. They'd want at least one layer of protection between them and the DA's office. At least. Whoever was behind it was so deep in the background you would never have seen their names on an offense report." Greerdon noticed Chris listening to him intently, and he shrugged. "Or maybe that's just me. Who knows?"

Chris sat and watched him, sipped his iced tea and waved off the waitress. Greerdon slumped in his chair, apparently at ease, his big arms resting on the hard wrought iron arms of his chair. His gaze had drifted away from Chris again.

"You think you could find out?" Chris finally said.

Greerdon didn't appear to have heard. He looked sleepy, his eyelids lowering. He watched someone in the crowd, then he blinked as if he'd just heard the question. "Me? I'd be the worst person to try to investigate it all. Who'd say anything to me? Nah, I'm out of it. I'm as out of it as you can get."

"I had this feeling you'd want to know."

Greerdon looked at Chris's staring eyes and sighed. He leaned forward wearily, realizing an obligation to explain. "When I first went in, yes. It was all I thought about. Getting back at somebody. Getting somebody by the throat. Just like you'd expect."

"But now?"

"It's funny," Steve Greerdon said. "When you step outside those walls for the first time in a lot of years it's scary. It's like you've just been born, but you're a grown man. Imagine a baby crawling out of the hospital and standing up and saying, 'Now what?' "

He stopped talking, but Chris didn't see him groping for words. Chris said, "I don't get you."

Greerdon spoke slowly. "It's like, I'm here but I'm not all the way here. I'm not back in the day-to-dayness of everything. I have time to ask myself what's important." He grew a wondering expression. "And I discover that that's not. Who set me up, why it happened. What difference does it make? What's gonna change if I find out?" He shook his head again. "I'm out now, that's what counts. I have my life back. That's such a blessing. Thank you for that. If I come here and jump right back into all that, they'll still be taking part of my life away from me."

"Are you saying you don't care?"

Greerdon gave him a straight look. "I really don't."

They sat in silence, Chris disbelieving, Greerdon realizing it. After three long minutes Chris said, "Have you seen your son?"

Greerdon lost his look of serenity. He nodded. He rubbed his hands together. When he realized Chris's attention remained fixed on him, Greerdon said, "You have children?"

Chris didn't want to tell him. But he nodded. "One. Teenager."

Greerdon smiled slightly. "Tough, isn't it? Even if I'd been here all this time, it'd be a tough connection to maintain. I remember."

Chris knew what he meant. He remembered from the other side. Being a teenager, feeling misunderstood and not wanting to be understood. The worst thing imaginable would be to be friends with your parents.

He and the released cop sat there on the Riverwalk for a while, watching the tourists go by and sipping their drinks. Their conversation grew minimal. Clearly they were embarked on different courses, perhaps parallel, perhaps even opposing. At any rate, discussing mutual plans would be a waste of time. They were headed in different directions.

After Chris had thought several times of saying he had to be going, Steve Greerdon suddenly spoke up more seriously. "There is something I've wondered if you wonder about." Chris watched him and Greerdon continued. "The guys who set me up were running a racket. They had a good money-making scheme going. They asked me in on it, I said no. That's why they took me out.

"But if I were you I'd wonder—did they stop after they sent me to prison? Why would they have? Seems to me they would've just been encouraged."

They sat in a different kind of silence after that, as Chris thought about this possibility and Greerdon apparently enjoyed the breezes of the Riverwalk.

Clarissa found that Peter, the new boy, didn't want to talk. It wasn't just that he didn't want to talk to her, either. She saw him pass his days in silence. Nevertheless, she made an effort. She remembered Peter from her old high school, where he'd been a hanger-on to her crowd, the fast crowd, Clarissa's gang. Seeing him recalled those days, when she'd been the coolest thing in school, self-declared. Not jocks or cheerleaders, way too cool for that. They had actually been gangsters.

Clarissa had never slipped a pencil in her pocket and walked out of a store with it, but her boyfriend Ryan had been involved in rather large-scale thefts, and Clarissa had known about it. The outlaw aura had encircled her, too. It had all seemed fun and so sophisticated, until Ryan had ended up cooling for good on the floor of an ice cream store.

Clarissa hadn't thought about those days in a long time. The sight of Peter brought them back, but not in a personal way. She remembered glimpses of her old life like a TV show she had watched without much attention.

"Did you keep running with that crowd?" she asked Peter. He shrugged, which she took to mean yes. He was a big, shambling boy who nevertheless managed to seem unobtrusive. Brown hair, not too shaggy or short, brown eyes, jeans, tennis shoes, all appearing chosen to blend in and fade away.

"Did they catch you with something?" Clarissa persisted.

"Not really," the boy said, looking away.

Not really? Getting busted was a pretty all-or-nothing event, either it happened or it didn't. She sat beside Peter and dug in, smiling. Clarissa could not have explained why she wanted to reach him. She knew people watched her talking to him, wondering about the connection between them, reviving rumors of Clarissa's own past. But the gossipers seemed unimportant. She remembered being in Peter's place. She wanted to offer him a way out of himself.

"Who's your counselor?" she asked.

He gave her a puzzled look. The first sign of life she'd seen in his fleshy face. "A therapist?" she explained. "Doctor—?"

"I don't have anybody like that," he mumbled.

Clarissa felt a small failure of understanding. Moving a kid to Berkshire was only one step. The parents also got him a counselor. Maybe Petey wasn't in trouble after all. Maybe he'd just done great on his SAT. But she didn't think so. Clarissa thought she recognized his silence, one that extended inside, an attempt to stop thinking. He needed to talk.

"Want to meet mine?" she asked brightly.

But Clarissa remained true to herself. The new boy was a small curiosity, not by any means a preoccupation. She still spent hours studying, talking on the phone or the computer with her friends, and at volleyball. There were moments on the court when nothing else existed, life was confined to that rectangle, when the ball seemed huge, and Clarissa owned it. Her coach had recognized in Clarissa a capacity for concentration none of the other girls possessed to the same extent. Even with the ball zooming toward them, most girls remained aware of who was in the stands, how their uniforms fit, an itch under the kneepad. Nothing bad, just completely human distraction.

Only Clarissa had moments of rising completely out of that, moments when she might have been the last living human playing against a team of robots or aliens. During a late afternoon game later that week she saw two players on the other team going for the ball at the same time, and knew they would get it over the net, but barely. One wasn't setting up the ball for the other, they both just concentrated on getting it over. One reached the ball first, and her fist had barely punched the ball upward when Clarissa leaped, rising higher than she ever had, head and shoulders and arms above the net, her right hand back then coming down, hard, fast, but completely in control. The ball seemed to hover for her. Then she had hit it and it went rocketing earthward like a lost satellite plunging home.

Instinct overcame training on the part of the girl just across the net, who put up a hand but only in self-protection as she ducked away. The ball glanced off her arm and hit the gym floor with a smack that could be heard outside.

The crowd of parents and friends made a collective *whoosh* sound, sat stunned for a moment, then half of them began to applaud. On the second row of the hard bleacher seats, Chris Sinclair looked at his daughter, at her fleeting expression of abstracted ferocity, and clapped slowly. To Anne, sitting beside him, he said, "I used to say she was going to break a lot of hearts. Now I'm worried about noses."

He studied her for a moment, this long-limbed, ponytailed girl, knees and elbows bent, watching the ball carefully, and was amazed again at his good luck in having her. Chris knew other parents of teenagers, heard the stories of small but continuing rudeness. Clarissa offered him no such problems, not anymore. She seemed glad to be with him. She talked. When she had a problem she told him about it. (At least, he thought so.)

But Clarissa had only been his daughter for a year. She had grown up in a lawless world, she had nothing to prove in that regard. For her, niceness *was* rebellion.

By the time she came up to them after the game, sweaty and smiling, she had returned to herself, and shrugged off their congratulations as if to say, *It's only volleyball*. They walked out of the gym and across the small campus. Anne walked a few steps away, as she always did, leaving Chris and Clarissa together, but Clarissa closed the gap between them, put her arm through Anne's in a very adult way, and said, "See that boy over there?"

Peter sat on a decorative boulder, a book open in his lap but only as coloration. He might have been waiting for a ride or he could have been planted there, waiting for the night to pass and the sun to come up so he could climb to his feet and go inside to class. "Come here," Clarissa said to Anne.

Clarissa led her over to the boy, Anne puzzled but unresisting. "Peter," Clarissa said formally, "this is Dr. Greenwald."

The boy looked up, startled. He seemed to wear invisible headphones. "Hi." He didn't rise from his seated place, and kept his hands on his book, but neither of those appeared a calculated insult, just lack of social grace.

"Hello, Peter," Anne said warmly, but having no idea what to say next. Was Clarissa introducing him because he was a prospective boyfriend? Then why to Anne and not to her father? Maybe it had something to do with Anne's profession. At any rate, she decided not to ask a question.

Adults feel awkward too.

"Peter's just started here, but we knew each other at my old school."

"Ah," Anne said. "Old school ties. They keep popping up for the rest of your life. Wait until you've been to college and graduate school, you can't get away from them. Old schoolmates, I mean."

Clarissa and Peter looked at her politely. Neither of them expected to live that long.

The gathering had reached that point where it could end too abruptly or go on minutes longer, becoming more and more pointless. "Well—" Anne began, and Clarissa quickly said, "Peter's going to come too, the next time I come to see you."

Anne saw from Peter's expression that this announcement came as news to him. "Fine," she said abstractly, not committing anyone to anything. "I hope Clarissa didn't tell you it's fun and exciting, though. We're pretty boring in my office. Nice to meet you, Peter."

She turned and walked away, taking Clarissa's arm and saying quietly, "Maybe you should let him decide for himself he needs professional help."

Clarissa laughed, and in that one startled burst of derision Anne felt a feminine kinship with her. *Yeah, right: Wait for a man to make up his mind to do something. Good one, doc.*

Anne saw Chris waiting patiently for them, determinedly not looking curious. Anne felt great affection for him, but really, Clarissa had a point.

Anne laughed too.

Dusk invaded the campus soon after. The shade under the trees grew, twisted, and stretched to absorb the last of the light. The sun went down early, now that November had come and Daylight Savings Time gone. Peter Greerdon put his book away in his backpack and walked down to the street. A few minutes later a big gray car rolled to a stop beside him. This was, in fact, your daddy's Oldsmobile. Somebody's daddy's. The back door opened, releasing a strong scent, acrid but sweet. Peter climbed in and dropped his backpack between him and the other boy in the back seat, a skinny kid who wore a stocking cap. He remained staring straight ahead, like a lookout.

The driver grinned at Peter in the rearview mirror, and the front seat passenger turned around to clasp hands high with Peter, then knock knuckles. The car vibrated slightly from the hip-hop blasting out of the radio. Four white kids pretending to be otherwise. Peter settled back, accepted the joint passed to him, and said indifferently, "Thought you guys weren't coming."

The two in the front seat gave each other wolfish smiles. "We got distracted."

Peter shook his head disgustedly. "Man, if you ever leave me stuck in this place . . ."

The others listened as Petey told tales of Berkshire School that made it sound like a minimum security prison on acid. "Freakazoids," he said wonderingly. "All their daddies got too much money and they got too many brains. You should see them all the day before report cards come out. Like Harvard gets the grades e-mailed to them. I want to hack into the computer and send 'em all failing notices. There'd be, like, mass suicide."

The other guys laughed disdainfully. They were all literally laid back, sinking into the upholstery. The kid in back drawled, "I know Petey's problem. Smart girls don't put out, right?"

They laughed again. Peter said, "Even the stupid ones won't for you, Zooster." Zooster smiled sleepily. "Ah, stupid girls," he murmured.

Tim, the driver, who preferred to be called Tyrone but couldn't get anyone to do it consistently, offered Peter a cell phone. In the rearview mirror Peter could see Tim's pale blue eyes, red-rimmed. He had a pert, freckled nose and good teeth and could have played a teenager on a TV show. "Need to check in?" he asked.

Peter shook his head. "Nah, man, I told her I'd be somewhere."

"Where? Don't tell me your old lady thinks you got friends. Or extracurricular activities."

"I forget," Peter said lazily. "I need to start writing down these excuses so I can keep 'em straight."

Skink, the guy in the front seat, opened the glove compartment. He rummaged around, then held up a Baggie containing only a minimal amount of content. "Low," he said poignantly.

Zooster in the back started singing, "How *low* can you go?" in a bass voice.

Tim glanced at the Baggie and said, "Let's do something about that."

He began to drive more purposefully. Peter felt a little shiver up his backbone. They'd never taken him along on a run before. He hoped he could just wait in the car.

He couldn't. They wouldn't let him. Tim sounded bold and tough, but wanted all the backup he could muster. "Come on, everybody out," he said loudly.

Surprisingly, they hadn't driven all that far from Peter's posh school. Berkshire was built in one of the oldest neighborhoods in San Antonio, one that had never gone out of style and in fact always seemed to be in the middle of renovation and revival. The board of directors resolutely refused to move the campus to more spacious facilities somewhere out in Loopland. So the school stayed in Monte Vista, a good neighborhood but painfully and sometimes frighteningly close to less-good ones. Tim had driven through one of those less-good neighborhoods into an even worse one, a couple of blocks that had once been good middle-class homes but that had fallen into vacancy and disrepair.

The four boys climbed out of the car, elbowing each other and snickering but failing to disguise their genuine unease. Tim rapped lightly on a shaky screen door that shivered in its frame. Nothing happened. He pulled open the screen door and knocked more loudly on the wooden front door.

Nothing happened. Peter began to edge away from his compatriots. He felt the victim of a hoax. In a moment a light would come on overhead or a trap door open beneath their feet. Skink stared at him sullenly, focusing on the one person more obviously frightened than himself. Peter suddenly felt like living down to his expectations, turning and walking quickly away, past the car, on foot all the way to the nearest phone, or even back to school.

The door opened a few inches, as if it had fallen open from the force of Tim's knock. But Tim saw something within, said a few words, and pushed the door open wider. A man in his twenties stood there, Hispanic, swarthy as the shadows within the house. He admitted Tim, then Skink, but barred the door with a long bare arm and looked Peter and Zooster over carefully. Peter felt himself turning paler and less threatening-looking.

As the scrutiny continued he said angrily, "Fine, I'll just wait out here."

"Nobody stays on the porch," the dark man said, and stepped suddenly aside. The last two boys brushed past him.

The house was dim and musty, the front room furnished in cast-off furniture, a saggy brocaded couch and two wooden kitchen chairs. Incongruously, an elaborate golden chandelier hung from the ceiling.

"He in?" Tim said. Peter heard the effort to sound gruff in his voice.

"Show me cash," the sentry said.

Tim reached into his pants and pulled out a legal-sized envelope. He opened it and fanned twenty-dollar bills. The sentry shrugged and pointed his chin toward a hallway. Apparently everyone was supposed to go down it. Peter would have thought the man inside would want to be viewed by as few people as possible, but apparently rules he didn't understand governed the situation. He followed the others, putting his hands in his pockets and trying to look inoffensive, forgetting they were all supposed to be Tim's muscle.

No one followed them down the hall.

They passed two closed doors and came to an open one at the end of the hall. They followed Tim into the room at the back of the house. It was big and open, as if a wall had been knocked down between two smaller bedrooms. Against the wall to the right a long worktable stood cluttered with equipment that could have been musically related, except for a burner with a cold blue flame at work under a small metal screen.

Two low-hanging suspended work lights burned over that table, their glare spilling out into the rest of the room. In the far back corner of the room a closet door stood open. Windows on two walls had been painted black.

Two guys and a girl occupied the room, the girl the youngest of the group. She kept her back turned to the newcomers, busy with something. The two men stared at them as if they were intruders. One sat on a swivel stool at the worktable and had turned to face them. He sat shirtless, showing a muscular torso and thick arms. He turned a smoldering stare on them, practiced with menace.

The other guy sat in an overstuffed armchair and smiled. He had bushy dark hair, blond-tipped. A broad nose, small glittering eyes, and crooked teeth. His ethnicity was hard to pin down. A pierced eyebrow gave him a sardonic look.

"Hey, man," he said, a greeting so generic it wasn't clear whether he knew Tim at all.

"Hey." Tim returned cool at him, but wasn't nearly as good at it. Then he seemed to run out of chitchat. "We were wondering if we could buy some grass off you."

The girl finished her work and turned around to face them. She reached for the worktable but missed, dropping something to the floor with a clatter. Peter felt disgusted to see a hypodermic needle. His eyes were good and the room well lighted. A drop of blood gleamed on the needle's point.

The girl's eyes were huge. She stared at them and her lips parted in a slow, slobbery smile.

She looked fifteen years old.

If the white suburban teenagers had been outside the scene they might have thought the whole production overdone, but under the circumstances they didn't feel critical. In fact, of course, their hosts did strive for an air of danger, and succeeded.

Peter wanted no part of this. He backed toward the doorway.

The man in the armchair said, "Give me the cash." He knew they had it or they wouldn't have gotten this far. "Tim produced the envelope again, opened it, and said, "How much?" Even he sounded unsure now.

Across the room, the bare-chested guy snorted with disgust. The host smiled more charitably. "All of it. Plus whatever you've got in your pockets."

Tim's fingers began to shake on the envelope, but he tried to keep his voice light. "Price gone up?"

The guy in the armchair rose from it and took the money. "Unfortunately for you, we're a little low on product just at the moment."

The muscle across the room also stood up, and smiled. "But we could use financing."

The host agreed. "We were just sitting here discussing poverty, and here you guys appear like an answer to a prayer."

Peter turned away from it, ready to run, and almost bumped into the sentry. He stood there blocking the doorway, holding an enormous black semiautomatic pistol. Peter jumped three feet to the side. He looked around the room in a new light and saw it had no other exit.

Unlike the other two guys in the room, the sentry looked angry. He was on entirely different chemicals, perhaps self-produced. He aimed the gun at Tim, looking excited to use it.

Tim pulled money out of his pants pocket and dropped it on the floor. The other guys began to do the same. The sentry didn't glance at the rain of bills. His hand shook a little as it held the gun more tightly.

"Easy, man," the host said. His tongue flickered out to his lips.

The boys moved into a bunch, except for Peter, who stood off to the side and shuffled even farther away from his friends. The sentry's eyes turned toward him. He crooked one finger on his left hand and said, "Come here." With his other hand he lowered the gun, but it still pointed toward Peter, toward his crotch.

Peter didn't move. He couldn't. His legs had turned useless. He realized he wasn't and never would be one of those guys who was good in a crisis, who could move with sudden decision. He realized the gunman didn't see how scared he was, and thought Peter was just being defiant. He realized the host had no control over this man. In the gunman's eyes he saw an inhuman urge to destroy someone.

He realized all these realizations were useless. They were the last he would ever have. The details of the room seemed to leap toward him: the individual metal items on the workbench, the girl losing her smile and looking puzzled, the host's hands beginning to move in a placating gesture. Peter should never have seen any of this. He should never have come near this place. What a stupid place to die. His throat closed up, a sob almost choking him.

The gunman smiled. The gun sank even lower. He took a slow step toward Peter, obviously relishing his fright. He grinned hugely.

The muscular guy across the room watched indifferently. His eyes were the first to move off the sentry. They widened.

The sentry was only a step or two inside the doorway of the room. A long arm reached from that doorway and grabbed the back of his shirt collar. A big hand gave the collar a twist, so it immediately tightened around the sentry's throat. He gagged and reached for his throat, including with the hand holding the gun.

Steve Greerdon reached around with his right hand, which held a gun of his own, and smashed the gunman's hand. The gun fell to the floor. With his left hand Greerdon twisted the collar tighter, choking his captive.

The muscle man took a step toward the workbench. Greerdon lifted his gun, pointed straight at his chest, and the muscle froze. Looking very alert and intelligent, he raised his hands chest high and stood still.

Greerdon bent the sentry backward, with his knee in the man's back. Then he threw him to the side. The sentry stumbled and fell and lay moaning.

Steve Greerdon glared around the room. With his left hand he reached into his shirt pocket and displayed a badge. The host's eyes changed. Greerdon saw the effect. He nodded. "That's right. But I don't give a damn about your little cheapshit operation. I might come back and burn it down just for the hell of it, though. Get out of here, boys."

Tim started to reach to the floor for his money, thought better of it, and scurried for the exit along with his cronies. Peter moved more slowly. Steve Greerdon grabbed his shoulder. He held him so Peter faced the occupants of the room. "See this one?" Greerdon said. "He's my son. Whenever you see him, you'll know I'm not more than about ten feet away. He's radioactive. Right?"

"Yes sir," the host said without hesitation. Across the room, the muscle nodded slowly, staring at Peter's face as if memorizing it.

Steve Greerdon started to back out of the room, still holding his son's shoulder. But Peter stopped. "What about her?" he said.

They all looked at the girl. She had lost her stupid smile but still seemed unable to interpret the drama before her.

"What about her?" Greerdon said, though he understood exactly what Peter was saying. Nobody moved.

Except for Peter, who walked to the girl and took her hand. "You'd better come with us," he said kindly.

The girl looked alarmed. She studied her small hand in his, then looked up at his face. His face either reassured or commanded her. She stood up slowly and came with him. She was wearing a halter top that left her back almost completely bare. Her ribs could have been counted.

"Hey," the muscle man said. He reached.

He was probably reaching for the girl, but his fingers brushed Peter's shoulder. Steve Greerdon moved. He had crossed ten feet before anyone else had time to react. His hand holding the gun went into the muscle man's solar plexus, that tender spot located just above the stomach, below the breastbone, near the heart. The muscle gasped, to no effect. He stood as if under a spell, hands hanging at his sides. It doesn't matter how much you can bench press if you can't draw a breath. The kid's face darkened, his eyes grew panicked. His shoulders heaved.

The enraged glare faded from Greerdon's eyes, replaced by a more clinical expression. "Bend over," he said. "Put your hands on your knees. It'll stop in a minute."

"Dad," Peter said quietly.

Greerdon turned and saw that the host had moved toward his chair. Greerdon's face hardened again. He advanced on the drug dealer, who put up his hands and walked backward.

Peter was watching his father closely, looking from him to the host, seeing the fear in the drug dealer's eyes. "Dad, let's get out of here," Peter said.

Greerdon took a deep breath himself, appearing to come to his senses. He gestured with his head, and Peter and the girl went to the door and out.

Greerdon looked at the prostrate sentry, clearly thinking his punishment had been inadequate. The guy saved himself by lying completely unmoving. Greerdon said, "You boys better clean up your act. In prison you'd be somebody's breakfast. Don't forget what I said."

The host nodded. Neither of the other two could move. Greerdon backed slowly out of the room.

The three hurried out of the house, following Tim and company who had hustled out too. Tim, to his credit, waited by his car. Greerdon walked up to him, shook his head disgustedly, and didn't say anything else. Tim shrugged. He would retain the memory of having a gun pointed at him much more strongly than he would anything an adult might say to him.

Greerdon pushed the girl gently toward him. "Ask her where she lives and take her home. And you better be real careful in her neighborhood."

"Yes, sir." Tim helped the girl into the front seat of the car. She huddled against the door. She didn't appear afraid, just confused.

Tim and the other two boys jumped into their car and Tim started the engine. He drove off slowly and deliberately. None of them had been stupid enough to ask anything about Peter, who remained behind with his father.

"Come on," Greerdon said.

He walked quickly down the sidewalk and his son followed.

After the visitors left, a bulky figure stepped out of the shadows beside the porch. He made sure the Greerdons had departed, then studied the door of the old house, thinking about going in and wreaking some havoc. Steve Greerdon hadn't been wearing gloves, he might well have left fingerprints inside.

The man on the porch cleared his throat harshly and spat tobacco juice onto the porch, right in front of the door. The low level dealers inside might notice it, if they were smarter than he thought.

The figure gazed out toward the street. "Not yet, Stevie," he said quietly.

CHAPTER

three

★ The first meeting with Peter had been even worse. Steve Greerdon's first sight of his son since being released from prison had happened four days earlier. He hadn't rushed to see Peter on his first day, or his second. But finally, after giving everyone plenty of notice, he had shown up on the family doorstep. Not the home he had left behind, a newer one, out in a northwest suburb. A nice brick house with a clean white front walk and no toys cluttering the yard. It made Greerdon uncomfortable.

Peter had answered the door. He stood there just looking at his father. "Petey," Greerdon said, and opened his arms.

The last time he had held his son the boy had been eight years old, a cute, skinny boy, and Greerdon had been on his way to prison for ninety-nine years. He had held his son so tightly he wanted to absorb him, take the boy with him, both of them running away together. He had known the hug had to last a long time. It had to be there to reassure his son that his father loved him, in the middle of a scary night, on his first day in a new school, when a bully picked on him.

Greerdon had seen Peter a few times after that in the prison visiting room, at increasingly longer intervals. But you couldn't maintain a relationship that way. It had been four years since the last time Peter's mother had brought him to see his father. Greerdon didn't blame her. It had been time to get on with life. The visits were so unsatisfactory anyway. He hadn't known the last one would be the last one, but didn't know what he would have said if he had.

The boy had been twelve by the time of that last visit, still skinny, still cute. Now he was a tall, bulky thing who looked almost like a man, who gave his father a half-hearted hug.

But standing there on that porch with Peter's hand on his back, Greerdon had thought he'd heard something almost spoken aloud: *Take me away.* Like a whisper from that long-gone boy.

But much more clearly he had felt from his son, *Leave me alone.* The two of them had missed a world of hugs, and walks, and games of catch. On the porch they had stood there awkwardly, with nothing on which to build a relationship.

Greerdon had seen over his son's shoulder Peter's mother, Greerdon's ex-wife. She didn't look as if eight years had passed. Dolores stood there with her arms folded, probably not realizing how defensive her posture looked, because her expression wasn't hostile. She watched her ex-husband with a little smile that he remembered, that asked ironically, *What are you going to do now?,* as if he had no good choice.

Dolores looked good, thin, fit, her face bearing few lines. She wore a white blouse and beige shorts, and her tan was even and smooth all the way down to the tops of her sandaled feet.

Then another man had come into view behind her, walking in from a back room. He stopped. When he realized Greerdon was watching him he said, "Hello, Steve."

Emerson obviously didn't like being there. He looked abashed, as if he had walked into someone else's house, instead of the other way around. There was no mistaking the situation, though. The living room held new-looking furniture in quiet tones of blue and white, the overall effect marred by the antique musket over the fireplace, which must have belonged to Emerson Blakely. Other signs of his long-term presence announced themselves around the room: pictures on the walls, a magazine stand holding issues of *Guns and Ammo* and hunting journals, a pipe in an ashtray, the wedding ring on Dolores's finger, a large diamond glinting off it. In all this house, the only thing remotely belonging to Greerdon was the boy.

He had taken his arms from his son and nodded politely to everyone.

Dr. Anne Greenwald usually interviewed patients in her office, which conventionally contained a desk, two chairs, a small table, and a couch. With wooden filing cabinets and framed diplomas, it looked very professional. The décor contrasted with the generally messy lives of her patients and reassured them that they were safe.

She also had another room in her suite of offices, which was furnished much less formally, with a couple of school desks, a table, slightly smaller chairs, cushions on the floor, and a small bookcase containing picture book favorites: *Goodnight, Moon; Miss Nelson Is Missing; Horton Hears a Who*. (Many of her patients identified with the hero of the last, who knew things he couldn't prove to anyone else.) This room represented a comfort zone for her youngest patients, and sometimes for Anne herself. For some reason she couldn't identify, she chose this room for her first meeting with Peter Greerdon. He certainly didn't look younger than his age, and his tests showed no sign of mental immaturity. Still, Anne led him into the kid room, sat at the table, and saw him look curiously at the bookcase. Peter chose to remain standing, and Anne didn't instruct him otherwise.

She set a legal pad and pen on the table, crossed her legs, and looked at him expectantly.

"I haven't done this before," he finally said.

"Yes, and Clarissa dragged you here against your will. There's no lock on the door, Peter. Any time you want to walk out, you can."

He made no move to do so. "Is she like your stepdaughter?" he asked.

Anne could have answered that question several ways. Mentally, she smiled at one of her answers. But to her patient she just said, "No. We're friends."

"Really?"

They weren't here to talk about her. "Peter, I'm surprised you haven't seen a counselor before this. I'd think before changing your school your parents would have had you see someone."

He shrugged. "I got into some trouble at my old school. They didn't like who I was hanging with."

"Have you made new friends at Berkshire?"

He just gave her a look: *Are you trying to be funny?* Anne shrugged apologetically. "So what's new?"

He seemed as if he wouldn't answer. Peter walked around the room looking at the pictures, put one finger atop a school desk and pushed down, almost tipping it over. He looked enormous in this room. After a full minute, turned sideways, he said, "My dad came back."

"That must be very strange for you. Were you glad to see him?"

He shrugged. Anne suspected she would see a lot of that. Peter answered very obliquely. "My mom got married again four years ago. So I've got a stepdad."

"And what's he like?"

Straightforwardly, he answered, "He's a cop too."

"I'm sorry, Peter, that doesn't explain it all to me."

The boy drew a little closer. Anne still hadn't moved to write a note. Peter said, "They don't leave it at the office, you know? They spend all day poking into people's lives, and when they ask questions they expect to get answers, and they deal with some rough people and they have to come off even tougher."

Now Anne's fingers twitched with eagerness to begin writing. That answer had conveyed so much, and given her so many possible directions to go. She sat watching the boy. He looked back at her earnestly, then began to look uncomfortable.

Silence is a psychological technique. Anne could use it well. But she doubted that any of her patients suspected how often her silence meant only that she didn't know what to ask next.

"What about your dad? When are you going to see him again?"

Peter laughed a strange, throaty chuckle. "I may not see him, but he'll be there."

Anne didn't know what that meant. "Is that how you've felt about him all along, while he's been in prison, that he was still with you somehow?"

He seemed as if he hadn't heard the question. Peter stood silently, unmoving. He had a talent for that, unusual for a teenager. After long seconds he shook his head, very sadly.

★

Chris said, "People are going to die tonight."

He didn't base that observation on statistics or police reports. It was just that kind of day. Chris and Jack Fine stood on the fourth floor balcony of the Justice Center in the middle of the afternoon, watching the dark half of the sky skid toward them, a few black clouds running ahead of the mass. It was only mid November, but a blue norther was blowing in. Within forty-five minutes it would lower the temperature ten degrees, and keep piling in. San Antonians who had been sleeping in air conditioning or with fans for months would drag heaters out of storage sheds and try to light pilot lights. Some of them wouldn't work right. The flames would blow out but the gas would keep pumping. A family sleeping five to a room would quietly begin inhaling the gas. Or some would use a kerosene heater that would spit fire and catch someone's blanket.

San Antonians could bear up under hundred-degree heat, but even a mild cold spell always caught them off guard. The incoming chill would make social changes, too. Men used to sitting on the porch drinking beer until they were ready for bed would be forced inside, into the midst of their families. The house would seem small. People would argue over the remote control.

"Yeah, they'll all be real easy to solve, too," Jack replied. Clearly his thoughts hadn't been running to broken heaters.

Chris moved to the railing of the balcony, still watching the sky rather than the ground. "Steve Greerdon says he's not interested in finding out who sent him to prison," he said quietly.

Jack kept his opinion of that to himself. "But everyone knows you are. I'm sure you're getting some great leads from the PD."

Chris nodded. Jack knew the course of the investigation better than he did. The police force appeared to be working very diligently to uncover the perpetrator of the crime for which their colleague had been set up. Many of those officers were probably sincere in their efforts, too.

"It doesn't matter what Greerdon says," Jack pointed out. "Whoever was behind this won't believe his lack of curiosity. They'll be watching him."

"According to him, there won't be anything to see, except him trying to develop a relationship with his son."

The first cool breeze reached them, slicing through the warm air like a wedge. After a long pause, Jack said, "You know they're watching you too, Chris. You're responsible for him now."

That was what the governor's spokesperson had as good as said, too. Chris pictured Steve Greerdon out there in the city somewhere, doing something or doing nothing, and whatever it was became Chris's responsibility.

They stood on the balcony feeling the cold front gather force. "Greerdon raised an interesting question," Chris said. "Maybe the cops running their protection racket and whatever other scheme didn't shut down the operation after he got sent to prison. Maybe they've never shut it down."

Jack, never restless, now became immobile. Chris could almost hear him thinking. "That might include manufacturing cases against other people, right?"

Chris nodded. This time Jack groaned audibly. "You know how many defendants tell me that all the time already?"

"Maybe some of them were telling the truth. We've got to look into it. While conducting our own investigation of who set up Steve Greerdon." Chris started to lean his arms on the balcony railing, glanced down at it and changed his mind. Pigeons liked this location. He looked down at the plaza where old people sat, passing the day. "Could they do that, Jack, feed us whatever they want and have us take it at face value? I'd like to think I'm smarter than I was eight years ago."

Jack didn't answer even obliquely, much more concerned with the practical aspect of what Chris had said. "What happens when police and I bump into each other, questioning the same witnesses and that kind of thing?"

"We're all cooperating," Chris said. "Why should they mind? Besides, you're an old colleague."

He clapped his investigator on the shoulder. Jack looked concerned. "You might want to assign someone with a lighter touch for this," he said. "And I'm not exactly the most beloved person over there."

"I'm sure you have more friends than you know," Chris said. "But you're right about needing someone else. Steve Greerdon's going to make things happen, whether he wants to or not. They'll be watching him. They may even try to get rid of him before he can do anything. We need to have someone who can keep an eye on him, see what develops. You have anyone who can do that?"

"Not really. All my guys are well known to the cops, they've worked together."

"Damn it, Jack, I count on you for this stuff. Can't you think of—"

"Well," Jack said slowly, looking thoughtful. "She might do."

"She who? Who're you—God! Damn it, don't do that!"

He had just turned and caught a glimpse over his shoulder of the girl who had come out onto the balcony behind them. Chris should have heard the door, but he hadn't. And the afternoon wasn't so late that the balcony held many shadows in which to hide. Nonetheless, the girl stood there, barely visible, not meeting Chris's eyes.

On second look, she wasn't a girl. She was thin and slight, but grown. In blue jeans and a tight blue top she could easily be taken for a teenager, but Chris remembered her. A new assistant investigator Jack had hired a few months ago. Chris hadn't heard anything about her work so far. The couple of times he'd asked how the new person was working out, Jack had just shrugged, which was his highest compliment.

Chris turned back to his chief investigator. "This could be dangerous," he said quietly.

"Really?" Jack raised his voice. "Hear that, Stephanie? The district attorney has a dangerous assignment for you."

No response came. Chris narrowed his eyes at Jack. "When I turn back around, is she going to be gone?"

"You just never know. That's the spooky thing about her."

After a moment Chris said, "I'll trust you with this aspect of the investigation," and turned and walked away. The young woman, Stephanie, remained on the balcony. She didn't meet Chris's eyes, as if shy.

After Chris left, Jack turned to her. "You heard?"

She nodded.

"Okay, just like we talked about. I'll give you backup, but they can't be very close. Any questions?"

She shook her head. Jack nodded, permission to depart, and she did so quickly. He stayed out on the balcony alone for a while, feeling the cold front wash over him.

Peter Greerdon unlocked the front door of his house and crept inside. Blue flickers from the living room told him he hadn't stayed out long enough. Peter began walking the other way, toward the kitchen and the hall to the bedrooms. But a growl came from behind his back.

"Where the hell've you been this late?"

Peter turned and stopped in the living room doorway. The only light came from the television, whose light washed over the sprawled figure of his stepfather, head back on the back of his black leather armchair, legs stretched across the matching ottoman. On the table beside him sat a drink, more brown than amber, and smoke hung in the air.

"Out with Dad," Peter said, blurting out the first thing that came to his mind.

It may have been the perfectly wrong thing to say. His stepfather's voice deepened. "He needs to learn the rules of this house. But you already know them."

Emerson Blakely stood suddenly. He was proud of this trick, springing from prone to tall in a moment. Peter had seen it a dozen times, but it still made him step back. "Where's Mom?" he asked.

"Out with the girls," Blakely said.

Uh oh. Peter thought about just going out the door again. If the next day he got into more trouble for staying out even later, it wouldn't be as bad as this, confronting his stepfather alone when Emerson hadn't drunk himself to sleep yet, and remained playful.

Instead Peter surprised them both by stepping down into the room. "Were you involved in the investigation of my father?" he asked quietly.

Emerson Blakely straightened up, didn't answer the question, but said, "Is that what he said?" His expression turned cagey, but still angry.

Peter shook his head. "Dad and I haven't talked about it. But it seems like we will one of these days, doesn't it?, and I'm going to feel pretty stupid if I have to say I never asked anybody about it, all those years while he was in prison. Don't you think I should have?"

"I would've."

"So?" Peter shrugged, as if he weren't curious, just performing a son's duty.

Emerson shook his head. "I wasn't in on it. And I wasn't friends with your dad. I knew him, but we'd never partnered or anything. I just followed it like in the newspaper. I remember it pissed me off. Investigation dragged on and on, then the trial. One dirty cop makes all the rest of us look bad, makes the job that much harder. That's all I thought about your father. I didn't meet your mother until years later. You know that."

He snapped out the last sentence more resolutely, as if he'd been accused. His eyes came back into focus.

Peter nodded thoughtfully, and brushed past Emerson, moving back toward his bedroom. He thought he'd pulled it off, but just before he stepped out of the zone of danger the big hand grabbed his arm, gripping hard. Peter turned back.

His stepfather had a strange look on his face. The perpetual anger predominated, but Peter also saw, to his shock, fear. That made Emerson glare and grip all the harder. "Don't forget curfew time again," he said tightly, "whether you're with him or not."

Peter stared at him. A bad move. He should have said something conciliatory. Instead he showed his stepfather something defiant in his gaze. Emerson's expression grew happier. "I'll help you remember," he said, and drew back his hand.

Peter, an acute observer of such things, saw that the hand remained open, for a slap. He hunched his shoulders involuntarily, but didn't try to jerk away.

Suddenly there was a knock at the door, a noisy *rap-rap-rap*. Both Emerson and Peter looked toward it. Emerson lowered his hand, expecting to see his wife. But Dolores wouldn't knock.

Nevertheless, the door came open, as if a family member had come home. Steve Greerdon stood there, not entering. "Sorry," he said to Emerson Blakely.

Blakely blinked at him, expecting trouble. But Greerdon spoke to his son again. "Peter, would you leave me and your stepfather alone for a minute?"

Peter was glad to get out. He walked away rubbing his shoulder, where his stepfather had gripped him. There would be four long bruises there in the morning, Peter knew, but he considered that a lucky escape. It could have been a lot worse. It had been before.

Steve Greerdon still didn't step inside the house. Emerson Blakely didn't invite him. Greerdon gave him a long, smoldering look, but spoke in a conciliatory way. "I'm sorry about getting Peter in this late. I don't know the rules of the house yet, but I'll learn them. Okay?"

This was a close enough approximation to what Blakely had said to make him wonder whether Greerdon had been listening. Greerdon didn't look confrontational, but he didn't leave, either. It was a delicate moment. Greerdon wanted to convey the threat he intended, but if he made Blakely mad he knew who would be the object of his anger.

Steve Greerdon had never been good at delicacy. But he made an effort. "And you know the rules of stepfatherhood, don't you, Emerson?"

Blakely didn't answer. Greerdon didn't press it. Finally he said, "Thanks for taking care of him while I've been away."

Blakely nodded and said gruffly, "Sure."

And Steve Greerdon turned and left, closing the door behind him. At least he'd gotten his son past the living room for this night. He couldn't be here very often, though. His being around too much would make matters worse.

Even in the most blended societies, ghettos persist. Some people liked to conduct their business in an environment where everybody is known, so an unfamiliar face stands out. There are other reasons as well. The comfort of familiarity. Lack of competition. Just let me sit here and not think about the outside world. But the world has grown more diverse even in the shadowed places. It's hard to keep even a ghetto pure. On the "heavily Hispanic west side" of San Antonio, where many of the billboards and store signs were in Spanish, brown skin may have predominated but wasn't exclusive. A restaurant or bar might even get a reputation for good food or authentic style that would draw people to it from outside the neighborhood. One such was Miguelito's, a Mexican restaurant but more of a cantina, where by eight P.M. or so the waiters almost stopped taking food orders with the drinks. A juke box would play quickly tripping Spanish, and the dance floor saw use.

Dance floors always meant trouble, Steve Greerdon thought. People dancing, maybe with someone else's partner, eyes communicating, blood moving faster, brief exchanges of words as dancers passed. It could turn competitive. Dancing made people hot, lustful, and thirsty. Drink had such different effects on people that bars such as this could be seen as ongoing experimental laboratories. *Let's add a drop of this. Now this. Now leave a knife in the pocket.*

Greerdon had no thought of getting involved, but he couldn't help being watchful. He sat near a doorway with his back to the wall and his eyes on the room. As far from the music as possible. The beer glass on his table hadn't been replenished in twenty minutes. When the waitress gave him a look from across the room he nodded, and a few minutes later she brought him a Tecate. In her wake came the bouncer. Greerdon didn't appear to notice him.

"Bouncer" was an inadequate description of Chip Riley's job. He wore a blue SAPD uniform and so provided not only security but a presence. Sometimes he stayed in the parking lot, sometimes he circulated among the tables. Regulars nodded to him and he stopped to chat with a few. Most nights between nine and two found him here. He even helped close up the place after closing time. Sometimes he and the manager, Luisa Gaines, stood behind the bar talking in low tones. Occasionally Chip Riley disappeared into her office. Sometimes he even filled in for her, like an assistant manager. On any given night he was one of the few Anglos in the building, but he was a fixture. He didn't go unnoticed, because part of his job was to be noticed, but he didn't disturb the patrons, either.

He stood leaning back against the bar, scanning the large room. Two couples danced, slowly. A few late diners finished their meals. It was a Wednesday night, it would probably be slow, but already some people would want to hurry the weekend. Chip yawned. He was a florid man, tall, lean except for the beginning of a pot belly. Five nights a week in a Mexican restaurant will do that to even the healthiest metabolism. Chip Riley was forty-eight years old, with more than enough years on the police force to retire, but still casting around for what came next. Anyway, he liked his life. He saw no reason to disturb it.

His eyes idly followed the waitress across the room and watched her set the can of Tecate on the small table with the single patron. The man looked like a solitary drinker of two or three beers, not a troublemaker. Chip Riley categorized him and moved on. Then his eyes snapped back to the table.

It was a tribute of sorts to Steve Greerdon that this was not his first evening in Miguelito's but it was the first time he'd drawn Chip Riley's attention. He kept his head down as Chip approached, but the meeting couldn't be avoided.

"Steve?" Chip asked, standing over him.

Greerdon looked up, letting the taller man see his face. After a pause he said, "Chip. How's business?"

Chip Riley stared at him. "I heard you got out, Steve. And you came here?" He looked around the room, searching for Greerdon's prey, his nervous hands betraying the thought that it might be him.

"I'm not looking for anyone," Greerdon said quietly. "Just having a beer. This is my neighborhood bar."

"Here?" Riley looked surprised. He considered the west side stretching around them, outside the bar. "Kind of a rough area."

Greerdon laughed quietly. "You should see my old neighborhood."

Chip Riley pulled a chair out from the table and sat, pushing it back against the wall too, so that he and Steve Greerdon sat more side by side than face to face. Chip made a small hand gesture and the same waitress brought him a Bud Lite in a bottle. No one in the room seemed to find this odd, even though Riley was in uniform. Riley turned and looked at his companion, obviously searching Greerdon's face for a sign of something, obviously not finding it. He raised his beer bottle and drank from it.

"Here's to you. Don't know how you pulled it off, man, but congrats. Lot of people thought you were buried in there."

"I was."

"Well—" Looking uneasy again, Chip Riley again made a small gesture, this time with two fingers. A minute later the waitress, a young woman beginning to smile, appeared with a tray and set two large shot glasses down in front of them. The liquid inside was golden.

Chip said, "Tequila, but the good stuff. What we keep for management. Here's to you."

Greerdon lifted the glass and pretended to sip. Chip shot his in one long drink, and set the glass down with a thump.

"So what's it now?" he said in a stronger voice. "The Count of Monte Crisco routine? Somebody else's turn in the grease?"

"I'm not looking for trouble," Greerdon said.

"Bullshit. How could you not be? Somebody put me in prison, I'd come out with a hate on bigger'n Dallas. Don't tell me. You're after them."

Greerdon shrugged. "You haven't been in. You don't know what it's like to be out. If I try to start any shit, they'll be better at it than I am, and more prepared. No, I'm just gonna sit quiet and be happy."

"Bullshit," Chip repeated, less emphatically.

Greerdon leaned his head toward him, and smiled into Chip's face. "And if that drives 'em crazier than anything else I could do, so be it."

Chip looked nervous again, then smiled back. "Why'd you come to me? You know I didn't have anything to do with what happened to you, Steve."

"I didn't come to you. I came to Miguelito's. What bar could I go to that wouldn't have some cop working off-duty security? Just my neighborhood place." He noticed again Riley's surprised look. "I like the west side," Greerdon continued. "Used to be my beat, remember? People mind their own business. Over there—"

He gestured vaguely northward and grimaced, as at bad memories.

Chip Riley watched Greerdon and came to an understanding. Hearing an Anglo say he was living on the west side of San Antonio surprised Chip because one expected people to congregate with their own kind. Even Anglos who owned west side businesses or worked over here went home to the right side of town at night. But that social compact had been broken irreparably for Steve Greerdon. After his years in prison the west side wouldn't hold any fears for him, and he had no reason to feel comforted among his own people. So it made sense to find him here. Chip settled back into his chair and looked around the room.

"Not a bad place," he said with a proprietary sound, and Greerdon nodded. "A few troublemakers, the usual," Chip continued. "You might even know some of 'em. Doesn't that worry you, hanging around over here? Someone recognizing you?"

Greerdon shook his head. "I've been gone eight years. That's like two generations on the street. Anybody I arrested is gone."

"You must've run into a few of them inside."

Steve Greerdon didn't answer for a while. The large room seemed to have grown smaller and darker. The music heated up. More people danced. Chip Riley watched them benignly.

"Sure I did," Greerdon said at last. "Some of them remembered me, and had friends. The first six months were bad."

Chip sat silent as if Greerdon had made a much longer statement, then asked, "How bad?"

"Whatever you're imagining. Yeah. But then they got tired, I broke a couple of noses, made a couple of friends of my own, blah blah. Sometimes shit happened to somebody who didn't like me." Greerdon shrugged. "Then we were all just neighbors. You get along."

Chip Riley watched him as if listening to a long narrative with plot twists and surprises. He knew that prison deaths got little publicity but happened regularly. He didn't ask his question.

Greerdon saw him thinking it. His face had grown darker as he talked, though his voice hadn't risen. He let his listener think what he wanted.

After a pause, when Chip realized Greerdon had finished talking about prison, Chip asked, "What're you going to do now?"

Greerdon laughed. "I'm a cop. Yeah, they reinstated me. Kind of on a long-term leave of absence, I guess. Think I should go into headquarters and get assigned?" He laughed again.

"Why not?" Chip shrugged. "Might be fun."

It might be lethal, too, Steve Greerdon going on calls with other cops, when he still didn't know who hated and feared him so much as to have put him in prison. "Anyway, I've got my own agenda. Try to get to know my son before it's too late. That kind of thing."

"You've got a lot of lost time to make up for," Chip said agreeably.

Greerdon shook his head and said, "You can't make up for lost time. It's gone. You can only make new time. In fact, you don't have any choice."

His voice had a shade of earnestness, as if someone had taught him this formula, or he had come up with it himself after long internal debate. Chip Riley, not given to philosophical musings, shrugged. They sat there for a while, quietly, like old friends. When the manager emerged from a back room, Chip pushed himself up from his chair. Greerdon threw a glance at the manager and a slight smile at Chip, who shrugged, looking surprisingly embarrassed. He crossed the room toward Luisa Gaines a little stiff-legged, and touched her arm.

Looking at her, Greerdon figured she had picked up her last name from a marriage, not at birth. She had light brown arms, thick black hair, and Cherokee-influenced features. Full lips barely parted over beautiful teeth as she spoke quietly. Luisa Gaines looked younger than Chip Riley, but that could just mean she had taken better care of herself. Her stare around the room appeared very experienced, including when it passed over Steve Greerdon. She said something in an undertone. Chip Riley answered the same way. They were obviously talking about the newcomer, but it was impossible to judge Luisa's opinion of his presence.

Steve Greerdon finished his beer, left the rest of his tequila untouched, and walked out of Miguelito's before ten. He had parked across the street and down a block or so, in a lot where a kid had held up a cardboard sign saying "$3" when Greerdon had arrived. The night was dark, the streetlight on this corner broken. When he turned a corner the few lights in houses looked far away. Greerdon walked on a couple of steps and then flattened himself against the wall of a closed store. He breathed very slowly as his hand went behind his back, to his belt.

He stayed there for a long minute, hearing footsteps, but they seemed to be going the other direction. Finally he moved slowly back to the corner of the building and looked around it. The street lay dark and nearly empty, except for a couple of cars moving slowly and two men walking away from the bar, apparently in no hurry to get anywhere else. Greerdon didn't believe anything in the scene. Any of them could be waiting for him to turn away again, then they'd resume their true identities.

He found his gun in his hand without remembering reaching for it. He put it away, but couldn't stop the adrenaline surging through his body, desperate for release. Anyone who jumped him now would be in bad trouble. But he had lost the sense of threat, unfortunately. Taking a deep breath, then blowing it out, he hurried to his car and drove away.

Chris Sinclair, the District Attorney of Bexar County, had a reputation of which he remained unaware. The word on him, among other high-ranking local officials, was that he didn't care about turf. He tended not to appear at those public ceremonies designed to remind voters of one's name. When anyone, including Chris himself, proposed joint initiatives that would require the cooperation of several agencies, he didn't push to take control of such task forces. And he just didn't seem to get the jostling for rank that went on constantly in local politics.

For example, when he called the chief of police to ask for a meeting, he asked when would be a good time and said he'd be at the chief's office then. No suggestion that the meeting should take place in Chris's own office. This made the chief of police suspicious, as similar behavior had made other local leaders wary. Didn't this young district attorney understand the jostle for superior position—and that he was giving up some of his by agreeing to go to the other guy's castle? Chris's behavior sometimes made other leaders feel outdated, as if someone had issued new rules and only the district attorney had gotten a copy.

The truth was, Chris's behavior in this matter was governed by nothing more sinister than the fact that he felt restless spending all day inside the Justice Center, and he grabbed opportunities to go elsewhere. So on a bright Tuesday morning he walked three blocks to police headquarters, unescorted, and waited for a few minutes, on his feet, before being ushered into the chief's office.

Chief of Police Lloyd Garza had held that position for only a year and a half, but he had been a police officer for twenty-two years, including half a dozen in the top command. Becoming chief had been the culmination of a life's ambition, but also signaled the end of his police career. No one remained chief for very long, since holding the job meant maintaining the good will of a majority of the nine-member city council. When you reached the top there was nowhere else to go except into retirement, and that day would come sooner rather than later.

Even though police solved cases and the district attorney's office prosecuted them, the two offices had surprisingly little overlap. Police were city, DAs county. The San Antonio Chief of Police was appointed by city council. The district attorney answered only to voters. They had, supposedly, similar goals but different masters.

However, Lloyd Garza never let it be apparent, in his own building, that there was any other boss than him. When Chris came in Garza stood up from his desk and shook hands firmly. Garza had strong features, black hair unflecked by gray combed straight back, and the same weight, within three pounds, as when he'd graduated from the police academy. He maintained a very military posture, which made his average height seem taller. And his constant demeanor was so stern that when he broke into a rare smile it seemed to make any occasion Christmas. Not many of his people felt personal loyalty to him, but no one bucked him.

"Hello, Chief."

"'Lloyd' will be fine in here, Chris. Thanks for coming." He spoke as if the meeting had been his idea, as he waved Chris to a chair.

"Steve Greerdon," Chris said without introductory remarks. "We've got to get to the bottom of what happened to him right away. I want to bring a case against someone quickly, and I don't want your department to be damaged any more in the process. That's why I asked to see you."

"'My department' hasn't been damaged at all," Garza answered. "A robbery defendant went to prison eight years ago, based on good evidence. Good enough for the district attorney's office, as you should well remember, and good enough for twelve jurors."

"Yes, but that's now been proven wrong."

"Has it?"

Chris shifted gears mentally, as Chief Garza pressed on. "A witness has changed her mind, after the passing of years, a witness whose memory may not have been very good to begin with, and which hasn't improved with age. And you proved Detective Greerdon didn't spill any blood at the scene, at least not that particular blood. That doesn't exonerate him in my book. Lots of armed robbers manage to pull off the crime without bleeding all over the scene. Usually it's their victims who do."

Chris stared, trying to read the man's rigid face. "So you still think he's guilty?"

Garza loosened up a little. "I'm not saying that. I'm not entitled to an opinion. Wasn't my case, I didn't have anything to do with it. I'm just saying that looking at it objectively, you yourself proved him guilty beyond a reasonable doubt, and it doesn't look to me as if the defensive evidence has been held to that same standard."

"Then why—?"

"I think a governor in an election year made a feel-good decision that gave him a nice photo op." Garza shrugged, as if speaking man to man.

"In the process he may have handed you and me a pretty problem, but it's not his problem."

"Do you really think a police officer could have been convicted falsely with other police officers gathering the evidence? You think they wouldn't have tested that case a lot more thoroughly before presenting it to the DA's office, unless someone was actually manufacturing that evidence to make a case against Greerdon?"

"As I said, I don't know that the evidence was false. But think about your premise. You're suggesting another officer, or group of officers, had such a grudge against Detective Greerdon that they set him up to go to prison. I can hardly imagine anything worse you could do to a police officer. Why would anyone have had such a powerful grudge against Steve Greerdon? Has he given you any suspects?"

"Not lately," Chris said, his frustration showing. Chief Garza watched him flatly, seeing that frustration, possibly seeing more. The chief himself gave nothing away. His speeches sounded like a debating exercise.

"Greerdon hasn't told me anything," Chris continued. "He doesn't even want me investigating. I can't—"

"You said 'not lately.' What does that mean?"

"He used to write me letters," Chris said. "After he first went to prison, and again when I first got elected district attorney. First when he obviously fiercely wanted to do anything to overturn his conviction. He'd throw out a dozen theories in one letter. Then later after he seemed to feel it was hopeless, but was still gnawing at the problem. I've reread all those letters. He had some theories that make sense now. He said of course that there had been a police conspiracy, he just hadn't been part of it. But he'd been approached to join the group. When he'd refused, that's when they'd decided to set him up. He named the officer who approached him, but only had guesses about the other people involved."

"Who was that officer?"

Chris hesitated, then said, "John Steger. The one who killed himself last year."

The chief of police turned over a hand with an ironic expression. Chris nodded, acknowledging how bad an answer that had been. "But I understand that officer left a letter. Maybe it gave some hints—"

Garza was already shaking his head. Chris continued doggedly.

"—or at least we could trace his career backward, see who he was partnered with back then, find out who they associated with."

"We'll do that. What about the other officers who were convicted of taking bribes or planning crimes?"

"We're talking to the one who's still in federal prison, Edward Newton. Another one's dead, and the one who agreed to testify against the others to escape prosecution himself has disappeared. He may have gone into the witness relocation program. I can't get anyone to tell me. I think he just dropped out on his own, personally. Made a new life somewhere. Maybe you could help find him."

"Absolutely," Garza said firmly. He sounded as if he were putting an end to the conversation. "But have you considered another idea? That maybe Steve Greerdon found out where he was first?"

Chris did consider that for a moment, but then continued. "What about you? Who have you assigned to the investigation?"

"Internal Affairs, of course. They've been on it for some time. I've also assigned Detectives Wardlow and Brown. Both of them transferred into the department from other agencies since Steve Greerdon's time, so there's no question they could have been involved."

Chris knew the two officers named, one as a thorough but unimaginative investigator, the other as one who took as much time off as possible. The fact that they couldn't possibly have been connected to the decade-old police scandal also meant they didn't have contacts from that time period. Chris didn't think them the best choices for the job.

Chris had the answers he needed, or at least the only ones he was going to get. He put his hands on the arms of his chair, but remained seated for one more question. "And just for the record, Chief, where were you nine or ten years ago?"

Garza let slip that smile. It was dazzling. "I was a sergeant with the juvenile gangs task force. Remember when we had a gang problem?"

So Garza wouldn't have been assigned to Steve Greerdon's precinct or to his Major Crimes unit. On the other hand, the gang task force had operated citywide.

"No," Garza said more emphatically. "I didn't know the man back then. Except by reputation."

Chris let that go. He thought he knew what Steve Greerdon's reputation had been. He put his hands on the arms of his chair, but Chief Garza stopped him, his smile disappearing. "By the way, Chris, I've been hearing some rumors. About you. Strictly speaking I probably shouldn't even tell you, but you know how this town is. You'd hear soon anyway."

"What about me?"

"We got an anonymous letter, with some documents. Suggesting irregularities during your campaign."

"I was extremely regular during my campaign." Chris didn't go on to make a joke. This took him completely by surprise. Garza looked uncomfortable, as if he felt conflicting responsibilities. "Are you investigating me?"

"That's what we do here. Like I said, I shouldn't even let you know. But I want to be straight with you."

Garza gave him a look to match what he'd just said. Some of Steve Greerdon's wisdom came back to Chris, revised for this situation: *The lead guy will believe what he's saying.*

"Thank you, Lloyd. I appreciate it."

Garza stood up. "I'm sure nothing will come of it. We get this kind of stuff all the time."

But when the two men shook hands it seemed to Chris that the chief's hand gripped his for an extra second, as if holding it in place while a handcuff came down.

While the chiefs' meeting ended inconclusively, a much lower-level encounter for which Chris had higher hopes took place on the west side, at a neighborhood park near Woodlawn Lake. Bonnie Janaway, assistant district attorney, had walked the jogging paths until she'd found a young man sitting on a bench. His perch looked perfect for a drug dealer, with long views in three directions and the lake guarding his back. On the other hand, he could have been watching his child play with others at a small playground fifty yards in front of him.

Looking at the young man, Bonnie thought he would much rather be taken for a pusher than for a responsible parent. He wore a thin blue jean jacket and sat with his arms stretched wide on the bench, as if oblivious to the chilly wind from the lake. He had longish hair, blowing uncombed around his head, a wide, sneering mouth, fleshy nose, and a pierced eyebrow that looked painful. Bonnie tried to ignore it as she studied his face, looking for a trace of resemblance to an old lady.

"David Guerra," she asked. Bonnie gave his first name its English pronunciation, accent on the first syllable, and only burred the double r of the last name, didn't roll it elaborately.

He looked up at her caustically. Or maybe that was only the effect of the pierced eyebrow. He said something to her in rapid Spanish. Bonnie shrugged her shoulders, and he switched to English in mid-sentence: "—not here to ask me for a dime bag, 'cause I'll just say 'Whazzat?' How stupid do you cops think I am?"

Bonnie Janaway stood straight, crossing her arms. "I'm not a police officer, Mr. Guerra. Don't you remember me? Bonnie Janaway. I'm the assistant district attorney who prosecuted the case that happened in your grandmother's store."

He didn't glance at her. David seemed to be waiting for an appointment. "Sorry. All you coconut chicks look alike to me. Besides, a prosecutor's some kind of cop, aren't you?"

"You'd be just as stupid to try to sell a dime bag to me as to a cop, yeah. But that's not what I came to talk about. You work at your grandmother's store sometimes, don't you?"

"I hang there when there's nothing better to do."

"Were you there when the robbery happened, eight years ago? You would've been, what, twelve, fourteen?"

"That's right, and I split out the back as soon as I heard something going down at the cash register."

"Leaving your grandmother and parents to fend for themselves?" Bonnie stared down at him. He ignored her gaze for a while, then looked up at her unblinkingly.

"That's right. What would you've done, Batgirl? Swung in on your rope and kicked all their asses?"

"I might've dialed nine one one."

He laughed. "Turned out I didn't need to call for cops, did I? They were already there."

She sat beside him on the bench. He had burly shoulders, hunched now, looking away from her. He *was* watching a child over there, she felt sure, and scanning the landscape beyond. Maybe David Guerra was a self-appointed protector, or maybe a restraining order kept him this precise distance from the child's mother. Bonnie's working life shaped her guesses.

"Did you see the man who committed the robbery back then? The one your grandmother identified in court?"

"Which one are you asking me?" Guerra replied caustically.

Bonnie's spine tingled. "You mean they weren't the same man? She identified the wrong person?"

Guerra shrugged. "How would I know? I was running away. She was the one right next to him, with his gun in her face."

He sounded as if he were joking, but his eyes remained flat and black and angry. Not sullen: angry. Bonnie Janaway knew the difference.

"Listen to me, David. I've gone through every member of the family. But I want to hear it from you. You've got the youngest eyes, and I hope the best memory. Listen, the—"

"I already told you, I didn't get a good look at him."

"I don't mean the robber, I'm asking about the cops who came to investigate the robbery afterwards. The ones who talked to your grandmother, and maybe to you. Do you remember them?"

She spread photographs on the bench between them. She'd gotten the pictures from personnel files. It wasn't a nice photo spread as a police officer would have assembled, with only one suspect and several other men of the same description. These were mostly cops, with only a few ringers scattered in.

To Bonnie's surprise, David Guerra took his time and really studied the photos. He picked out one and held it up before his face. "This was one of them."

"Listen. Were there any who came to see all of you eight years ago and then came back recently, to ask again?"

Guerra nodded slowly. Still studying the picture in his hands, he pointed casually to one still lying on the bench.

"Him?" Bonnie swore silently. "Are you sure?"

"Yeah, Coco, I'm sure. The second time he came he was so twitchy I thought he was gonna knock shit off the shelves. Then he went outside and just sat in his car for a long time, with his head down on the steering wheel."

It must have been shortly after that day that Detective John Steger had driven to a hospital parking lot, put his pistol in his mouth, and pulled the trigger. Bonnie wanted a better suspect than a dead man.

"Anyone else?"

"I've seen this guy recently," Guerra said of the photo he still held. "Is anything going to happen to these cops? Hell, I'll say it was all of them."

He laughed. But Bonnie had found more cooperation here than she'd expected. She gathered up her photos and said, "I'd like to talk to you again soon."

"Sure," he drawled, spreading his arms on the bench and smiling up at her. In Spanish again he said, "Next time your place, eh, Bonita?"

"Maybe so," she said levelly. She turned away, then turned back again. "And the last time being called a coconut hurt my feelings was so long ago I don't remember if it was third grade or fourth. That's what people like you call anybody who doesn't want to spend their life acting stupider than they are."

He shrugged, conceding her the duel of wits. Giving him a last look, Bonnie thought David Guerra appeared to be in disguise; the blue jean jacket and eyebrow pin looked unnatural on him. She would have guessed that it hadn't been long since he'd been called coconut himself.

Sergeant Richard "Rico" Fairis, forty-five, balding, thirty pounds overweight, jowly, looked like an illustration for the phrase "desk jockey." But he still hit the gym five days a week, he could bench press his desk if necessary, and though he couldn't outrun a twenty-year-old suspect, he could put a bullet in his leg at fifty yards. He had become a sergeant almost by accident, and still prided himself on being a street cop. He averaged eight arrests a week. When he loomed over a prisoner in the interrogation room, it was his eyes that did most of the intimidating. When Fairis dropped the veils from his eyes they were amber, almost yellow, very deep, had seen everything and balked at nothing.

He sat behind a desk in a classroom of the police academy where he taught one day a week. "Techniques of Interrogation." Fairis taught the course by the book and never, ever told the recruits the real stuff. They'd have to pick that up on their own.

Rico Fairis felt safe in this randomly chosen classroom because it wasn't his own and no one had any reason to wire it. His fellow officer Albert Reyes paced in front of him, his blue shirt still open a couple of buttons. The men had opened their shirts and patted each other down before beginning the conversation. This was not a male-bonding ritual.

"What's he doing lurking around the west side?" Rico asked.

"Just living there. That's all I can get. He's not talking to anybody, except Chip Riley a couple of times at that bar where he works. Doesn't seem to be trying to hunt anything down."

"He's waiting for us to get tired."

"Well, I'm there, Rico! I'm not just going to watch him for the rest of my life. Looking over my shoulder all the time, waiting for an indictment—"

Reyes ran his hands through his red-tinged black hair. He had coarse skin that made him look older than he was. It seemed only a few years ago that he'd been the golden boy, literally shining in the sun. Rico remembered with satisfaction. Pretty boys never lasted. Only ugly old guys like him and Steve Greerdon endured.

"The longest statute of limitations on any of that old stuff is ten years," Rico said calmly. " 'nother year, year and a half, we'll be as innocent as newborns. They can't—"

"For the old stuff, yeah." Reyes paced quickly back and forth. "How do we know what he's going to uncover? Besides, if Greerdon finds out who set him up, getting indicted's going to be the last of our concerns."

"If he knew anything, we'd know it by now. You think he's suddenly remembered something? Think he's figured out how his prints got on the weapon from the robbery? Remembers you tossing him that gun?"

"It was a perfectly ordinary nine-millimeter. Nothing memorable about it. How many guns does a cop handle during the course of a week?

He doesn't remember." But Reyes chewed his lip. He hadn't convinced himself.

Rico Fairis sat calmly on the desk, not moving except to swing one leg. He grinned. "You know what he's doing, Al? He's throwing us crazy. He's just waiting us out, until we do something stupid. He's probably learned a lot about how to wait, the last eight years."

Albert Reyes considered that idea, then shook his head. "I don't think so. If I came out of that place, I'd be so mad I'd hurt somebody the first day, even if it was the wrong person. You're wrong, Rico. What if he's already made his move and we don't even know it? You know, there's some guys who aren't on the force anymore, he might've tracked down one of them—"

"Why don't you find them all, then, Al? Just make sure you keep looking over your shoulder while you do. You don't want to lead Steve to them."

Reyes studied Fairis. He'd called Steve Greerdon by his first name. Rico and Greerdon had been partners once, hadn't they?

Fairis smiled. "Or if he's driving you so crazy, why don't you go ahead and take him out? Do you want my permission?"

Reyes didn't answer. He continued to study the burly sergeant in front of him and then asked suddenly, "Why did you send him to prison, Richard? Why didn't you just kill him?"

"Sentimental reasons."

"I can't imagine what it would be like to be a cop in a place like that. It'd be worse than hell. What would keep you going except waiting for the chance to get back at the people who put you there?"

Rico Fairis didn't respond. He looked like a man who slept well and never asked himself unanswerable questions. Reyes suddenly wondered why he was even having this conversation. The more he kept his own counsel in this matter the better off he'd be. But he'd never been good at that kind of thing.

Fairis reached into his desk drawer, pulled out a small chew of tobacco, and put it into his cheek. Reyes made a disgusted face and turned away.

"I'm taking off," he said abruptly. "If you decide to do something—never mind, don't even tell me."

Reyes put on his hat, the one with the braid on it.

Rico grinned. "Yes sir, Lieutenant. Is that an order?"

Reyes didn't look at him. He suddenly didn't want to see that grin anymore. As he walked away he buttoned his shirt and pulled his tie tight.

Anne Greenwald kept promising herself she was going to take off at least one morning a week, to work at home or exercise or just sleep late. But if she ever did, it certainly wouldn't be on a Monday. She seemed to get to the office earlier and earlier on Monday mornings. Always it seemed she'd gotten at least one frantic call over the weekend. Why did she give her mobile phone number to people, or how did they find her unlisted home number? She'd given it out too many times, that was why. But most of her patients were children, many had abusive parents, a few might be suicidal. They didn't take weekends off, so neither could she.

So she always woke early on Mondays, worrying about something, which ruined staying in bed. This Monday morning in November she'd awakened at four-something. After lying fruitlessly in bed for a while she'd gotten up and run through the dark neighborhood, until her thoughts caught up with her. Then she'd given up, showered, dressed, and driven through the city before the sun rose. The security guard in the parking garage had looked sleepy. He was the only person Anne had seen so far. Her footsteps echoed in the long hallway.

She came through her own outer office doors. The waiting room looked sterile, the chrome-and-brown-fabric chairs too perfectly aligned. Anne took a moment to mess up their order a little. It looked as if one of her patients had been in here obsessively straightening. Anne tended more in the opposite direction.

The staff wouldn't be in for another hour. The phone might start ringing any minute, though. Anne hoped to sit at her desk for an uninterrupted time, studying two or three particular files, maybe beginning to dictate a report. But she knew if the phone rang she wouldn't be able to resist picking it up.

At the door of her own office she hesitated. She couldn't have said why. Anne hadn't turned on the light in the hallway; the place seemed adequately lighted after her night run and drive. But the door of her office stood ajar. Nothing unusual in that. She couldn't remember if she'd closed it Friday, and the cleaning people might have left it open. But Anne seemed to catch a hint from within. She put out her hand but stopped, suddenly having a vision of her office ransacked, papers carpeting the floor.

She shook off the thought and pushed the door open wide. The vision had not been prophetic. Three stacks of files still cluttered her desk, along with notes and legal pads and mail, but it was no messier than ever.

The room did hold a surprise for her, though. As Anne stepped inside she gasped. A man stood against the filing cabinet, his arm resting on it. The youngish-looking man, roughly her own age, wore black jeans and a maroon sports shirt. A gold chain gleamed on his neck. He was a little over average height and slender. His hands, which he brought together and laced, were large.

Anne met his eyes. She didn't know him. He stared at her as if he'd been waiting, but also as if her appearance were an intrusion. He studied her reflectively, obviously trying to decide what to do about her.

Then he moved toward her.

CHAPTER *four*

★ As the stranger came toward her, Anne backed up a step. She could scream, but the nearest help sat far away. Quickly she reviewed her options: running, swinging her purse at his head, trying to talk reasonably to him. In her imagination all those choices ended badly for her.

The man stopped five feet in front of her, spread his hands, and said, "I'm sorry. I didn't mean to startle you. I guess I got here earlier than you start working. Nobody was here, I came in looking for somebody, and I just kept opening doors until I guess I came to the end of the line. Is this your office? Hi. Name's Eric Schwinn."

He held out his hand. Anne took it, moving stiffly. The man smiled a broad, winning smile. Eric Schwinn had a dimple in his chin, strong white teeth, laughing blue eyes. His thick black hair was a little curly and a little long.

Anne took her hand back from his and walked past him to her desk. She dropped her purse behind it and stood with her hands on the desk, one of them close to the phone. That put Eric Schwinn between her and the door, but that was all right, they were being reasonable. They were just going to talk.

"Who are you?" Anne said. Her manner had become deliberately cold and professional.

"Your new patient, I hope. I've heard great things about you."

Anne was not immediately won over. "Then

you should have heard, Mr. Schwinn, that for the most part I only treat children."

"I used to be a child."

He watched her, open and with the possibility of vulnerability. Anne smiled. She would have smiled anyway, to reassure him, but in fact she found his answer funny. She liked his expression, too. Eric Schwinn was charming. As a psychiatrist, Anne distrusted charm. She understood its roots. But that didn't make her unsusceptible.

"All right," she said. "Fill out a new patient information form. It's on a clipboard in the outer office. You're so good at finding your way, I'm sure you won't have any trouble. Then we'll make an appointment."

"Don't you have some time this morning?"

"Yes, I do. I came in early so I would have free time. But I don't intend to use it on you."

He continued staring at her, then nodded as if to say, *Fair enough,* and went out her door. Anne didn't relax. She half expected him to reappear with a knife. But in moments she heard him rummaging in her receptionist's office. A few minutes of silence followed. Anne spent the time clearing a space on her desk, choosing three files she considered the most urgent, and listening.

Eric Schwinn walked in a deliberately clumpy way when he returned. He stood barely in her sight and tapped on her doorframe.

"I'm sorry, there's no one out here to announce me," he said deferentially.

Anne joined him in the doorway. He smelled good, too—clean and not overly scented. She felt him watching her as she glanced over his form. Anne doubted his need for psychiatric treatment. His information sheet told her little. For the line "Reason for Referral," he'd written nothing.

Curious, she asked, "Were you suggesting that whatever you want to discuss started in childhood?"

"Oh, no. My childhood was great. The problem is this difficult transition to adulthood."

Anne laughed. His information form said he was thirty-four years old.

Eric Schwinn smiled. He knew he was funny.

"I know what you mean. Can you come back tomorrow afternoon? Say four o'clock?"

He hesitated. Anne knew he liked the time for the appointment, and was thinking of suggesting they have a drink afterwards. But he sensibly said only, "Fine. I'll look forward to it."

So would she, actually. Anne said good-bye, and they shook hands again. She listened to his footsteps going out, then took the clipboard back to the receptionist's office, and left his form there with a note to make a new file. At the same time she made certain he'd left, and she locked the door.

Off and on for the rest of the day she wondered what Eric Schwinn wanted, and who had recommended her to him.

Chris met with his assistant Bonnie Janaway with his crowded desk between them. A stack of files sat to his left, another to his right, with an open one in between. Chris saw Ms. Janaway glance at them.

"You can ask what I'm doing. Reviewing files of convictions. Trying to find a pattern of police testimony. Also reviewing cases in which an officer named John Steger testified."

"The one who committed suicide," Bonnie said. She sat, barely. She kept so far forward on the chair she seemed in danger of falling off.

"Yes."

"You think he killed himself over something he said in court?"

Chris laughed, but Bonnie Janaway didn't crack a smile. She didn't seem aware she'd said anything funny.

"I don't know. Frankly I don't know anything. I'm casting around. That's why I hoped you'd learn something from talking to the Rivera family again. Did you?"

"There's a grandson of the *abuela* who claims to know something about the police officers who questioned the family. Not about the crime itself. He hit the back door without looking back. But he told me John Steger and one other had come back recently to ask more questions."

"Do you believe him?"

"No." Bonnie spoke uncritically. "I don't disbelieve him, either. He certainly doesn't know enough to build a case against a police officer for tampering with evidence or anything like that."

"I didn't expect so."

She obviously had a question, and again didn't ask it. Chris said, "This police conspiracy is so far buried we may not be able to get into it. But they had to use some civilians to accomplish what they did against Steve Greerdon. That's my only hope. Just get me enough information to question one officer. If I can convince one I have evidence against him, maybe he'll turn. That's how these things break open."

"I understand. I'll keep looking." Bonnie stood up. "But may I ask you a question?"

"Of course." Chris leaned back in his chair and looked at her frankly.

"Why did you ask me to do this? This is more of an investigator's assignment."

"Believe me, all the investigators are busy with this too. I figured you had already met with all or most of the Rivera family, maybe you had a rapport with them."

Bonnie nodded slowly, obviously unconvinced. Chris cocked his head and waited.

"'Rapport,'" Bonnie repeated, as if the word had implications. "This isn't—some kind of punishment for not learning the old lady could speak a little English, and about the connection to the old robbery?"

Chris shook his head. "I know what it's like to be a trial prosecutor, Bonnie. The cases come in constantly, you have time to do a little investigation, talk to your witnesses for five minutes in the hall before you put them on the witness stand. It's not like you've been hired to defend O.J. Simpson and given an unlimited budget. I understand. You won the case, didn't you?"

Chris spoke nothing but the truth, but he left some things unsaid, and hoped she heard them as well. Sometimes it does pay to take just a little more time. Visit the scene of the crime, speak to the family member whose name didn't appear in the police offense report, see what kids hang around on the street outside. Understand for yourself whether a line of fire had been possible or not.

The District Attorney's Office had a teaching function. For most of

Chris's assistants this was their first job after law school, as it had been his twelve years ago. They needed to be trained. They would learn, if they were just thrown into a trial court with older prosecutors, but they would learn the rapid, skimming study those older prosecutors had learned. Once in a while Chris wanted them to step back and look around. This was such a time. Sometimes he saw in one of his assistants the potential for rising above the average, perhaps even for being a great trial lawyer. But not if they never raised their eyes from the case file, or saw the outside of the Justice Center.

Ironically, the best ones generally didn't last in the office long. Then it turned out Chris and others had trained those lawyers to oppose them in court. But good lawyers benefitted the system better than bad ones, on either side.

If Bonnie Janaway thought she was being punished for slipshod work, and so approached her next trial differently, the whole office would have benefitted. But mainly he just wanted her to do the job he had handed her.

"All right," she said, with cautious cheerfulness. "I'll let you know."

"Thanks."

Bonnie left slightly reassured. David Guerra had been right about her. She was a coconut: brown on the outside, white on the inside. She had come to that position by choice. She had indeed been born Bonita Rodriguez, her current last name acquired by marriage. Bonnie had come of age in a time when being Hispanic and female were more beneficial to employment than they were obstacles. But she'd chosen not to use those. She didn't like anyone assuming she knew Spanish, and definitely didn't like being thrown into the west side, as if she blended in there through natural coloration.

But she left Chris's office convinced that he might not even be aware of her ethnicity, and certainly didn't intend for her to use it. She also left determined to get back into a courtroom, and soon, and when she did to know more about the case than anyone else in the room, including the victims.

The brisk November wind outside the Cadena-Reeves Justice Center only added to her own sense of hurry.

Personnel matters were among Chris's least favorite parts of his job. On the other hand, handling people was about all there was to the job. Done with Bonnie Janaway, and tired of going through the closed files, he made a call and changed into shorts and a T-shirt. Fifteen minutes later he reached Braun Lake, deep on the south side. Lacing on running shoes, he took only a minute to warm up, then sprinted up from the parking lot and around the lake. There really wasn't a running path, so there were very few runners. But Braun Lake wasn't vast—calling it a lake at all would have struck some people from actual lake areas as laughable arrogance—and he soon spotted his prey. A broad figure moving more slowly soon hove into view up ahead. Chris put on a touch more speed and soon caught up to Steve Greerdon.

The cop, red-faced and huffing, glanced at him but didn't otherwise acknowledge his presence. From his sweat stains and breathing, Greerdon might have been running for hours. Chris slowed down to pace him. The ground was muddy, uneven, and regularly threw up interesting obstacles such as roots and fish heads. Cigarette butts littered the ground, along with discarded plastic bread bags, milk cartons, and soft drink cans. Fishermen apparently considered the lake not only a natural attraction, but a giant family-size trash can.

Smells kept one's attention, too. They passed through dead fish zones, smoking areas, and wetland preserves, each with its own pungent aroma. Chris finally spoke. "It's not just the exercise that's so great for you here. It's the fresh air."

Greerdon's foot slipped on a small slope of mud, he stumbled over a branch, and instead of recovering he put his hands on his hips and walked on slowly, breathing hard. Without glancing aside, he said, "How'd you find me?"

"Oh, this is my usual running track. I'm here every day at this time."

Greerdon snorted a chuckle.

"You must have come back really homesick," Chris continued. "You're certainly doing the whole San Antonio tour. West side, south side, all around the town. Have you been to the Alamo yet?"

Greerdon regained his breathing, though his face remained chili red. "When I was inside, I tried to use the treadmill as often as I could, but it's not the same. You forget you can trip over things. The landscape underfoot changes."

Chris thought of a couple of comparisons, but didn't make them. He thought he sensed gratitude on Greerdon's part for his restraint.

"I just need to get out a little," he said. "Staying in my room all day is too much like—you know."

Chris nodded. "Is it still a surprise that you can just open the door and go out?"

"The scary part is how seldom I even think about going out." He turned to face Chris, still with his big hands balled on his hips. "You don't even realize how weird life is, do you, because you've lived through it gradually. I've discovered it's a lot easier to be crazy these days. You can just sit in your room and have all this information come to you, just constantly. You know about this Internet thing?"

Chris nodded, trying not to look ironic.

"It's like a schizophrenic's dream. Those wackos with their conspiracy theories, they must have invented this thing. Everything's connected. You can just sit there for hours and let stuff pour over you. It's like being omniscient and crazy at the same time."

Chris wondered if Greerdon had had this good a vocabulary before he'd spent eight years in prison. They walked past a small family group, a father and two daughters, the girls' ages in the single digits. Both men fell silent until they were past. Chris asked, "What have you learned?"

Greerdon didn't look at him. "I'm not investigating, Chris. I'm just trying to learn my way through the world. Back into it."

"No stirrings. You haven't come across anything, seen any old friends?"

Greerdon looked at him. "Why don't you tell me?"

"I haven't heard anything." Chris picked up the pace a little. Greerdon lumbered along. "You know you've ruined my job for me? I don't believe anything anybody tells me anymore."

Greerdon just grunted, aware of the irony in Chris's voice. Then Chris grabbed his arm. "There's another thing, too. The chief of police told me an anonymous someone has sent him evidence against me. That wouldn't be you, would it?"

Greerdon stared at him flatly. "Does it sound like me?"

Maybe. Chris had no idea what the man in front of him was really like: his possibilities, his motivation. But he continued to feel an urge to question him. "When you first learned that you were suspected of something, when you got the first hints that something was wrong, what do you wish you had done?"

Greerdon shook his head. "I didn't get any hints. I didn't know shit 'til they came in and demanded my badge and my gun and booked me. I was an idiot. What should I have done? I don't know. Demand to see the evidence, confront whoever was accusing me."

"What do you think was the worst thing you did wrong?"

Greerdon put his fists on his hips and stared at Chris critically, as if wondering whether he was worthy of this information. Finally he said, "Believing in the system. Believing my innocence would protect me."

"But what could you have done differently? If it were happening now, knowing what you know, what would you do to stop it?"

"Anything. Whatever it took."

Greerdon stopped, as if he'd given away too much. Besides, the district attorney wouldn't take this advice.

Greerdon lightened the conversation. "By the way, I'm glad you've got that tail on me. Tell 'im not to lose me. I'll need the alibi one of these days."

"I don't know what you're talking about."

"Because you know what they'll try next, don't you? They'll try to send me up again, frame me for some other crime."

"Cheer up," Chris said. "Maybe they'll just try to kill you."

Greerdon did look slightly relieved at that idea. A physical attack he could handle. He would relish it.

Unconsciously, they had angled their path upward, rising above the lake. From a slight distance, it began to look prettier. Without a farewell, Chris circled around and headed back for the parking lot, running faster. In the parking lot he stood beside his car blowing for a minute. He and the investigator from his office, lurking in his own car, didn't acknowledge each other before Chris drove away. He noticed a patrol car making a slow circuit of the lake, and wondered if that was usual.

Peter Greerdon had to wait for Clarissa after school. She'd promised to drive him to his appointment, but first she had volleyball practice. At first Peter waited in the library, but he began to imagine stares on the back of his neck, so he got up and walked out, pulling on his jacket. Peter wore a school jacket from his former high school, which branded him here at Berkshire as out of his depth. He wore it defiantly.

Outside in the cool fall air he trudged along, eyes down. Today Peter sported a bruise on his chin, which at home had made him look vulnerable but here he hoped made him appear dangerous, not to be messed with. He passed a group of boys who lounged with a languidness he would never possess. Hearing a muttered remark, Peter turned and stared at the tallest, oldest boy, a senior who would be at Princeton next year, a legatee. Peter looked at him for a long time, trying to keep his eyes disinterested. *I'd kill you if it was worth the effort.* Princeton first sneered back, then as Peter's stare persisted the older boy dropped his eyes.

Peter knew better than to make a big deal of the moment. He trudged away, backpack over his shoulder. He heard snickers behind him but didn't turn back. He'd made his point. Princeton would remember.

Peter walked out of the school grounds and down the street. Within a block the character of the neighborhood changed. There were some fine, huge old homes but some of them stood next to places that hadn't been painted in decades. This was a very mixed area that had a high burglary rate. The kids from the stately homes attended private schools, but the kids who were really part of the neighborhood went to San Antonio School District schools that were old and tough—but not in the academic sense.

But today Peter felt strangely unintimidated. He didn't sense his father's presence, but he might be around. More important, he had taught Peter a few things in his brief time back in his life. Things like the intimidating stare. The lessons came naturally to the boy, who had longed for so many years to learn how not to be a loser. No one had ever taught him anything he really needed to know, until recently.

He walked down three blocks to a little no-name convenience store. A couple of boys lounged outside, but he didn't bother to use the stare on them. Inside he got a grape drink and a Payday and went back outside, beginning to unwrap the candy bar.

Someone stood in his way. Not paying attention, Peter stepped aside, but the obstruction moved too. He looked up to find the boys outside had been joined by their big brother. A gangly white boy with scraggly black hair and a nose ring stood squarely in front of him. When he had Peter's attention, the guy covered Peter's candy bar with his hand. "Go in and buy yourself another one," he said in a voice happy with threat.

"You kiddin'? What is this, like third grade?" Peter didn't have to fake being incredulous, partly because the last time he'd ventured out of his neighborhood he'd been threatened by armed drug dealers. This confrontation, by contrast, seemed silly.

"You callin' me retarded or somethin'?" The guy's dark eyes glared. "Fuck you, rich boy."

Peter stepped back. "I'm not rich. My father's a—just got out of prison."

"Yeah, right," the other guy sneered. "For what, tax fraud?"

He laughed, echoed by his two homeys behind him. Peter gave him the smoldering stare. The guy looked back at him with eyes genuinely dead. Nothing lay behind them to understand intimidation.

Uh oh. Peter had made a mistake. This wasn't a comic moment. You could get killed over a candy bar. It probably happened every day in this part of town.

This would be a good time for Superdad to make another surprise appearance. But if that were going to happen it would have by now. Peter suddenly felt clammy and cold.

The other guy saw it. He reached out his hand with a sneering smile. Peter's hand trembled.

But he found he couldn't hand over the candy bar. How could he trudge back to the school candyless and face down Princeton and his friends again? But Peter's reaction was more fundamental than that. The coldness departed. His cheeks flushed. Years of fear and resentment released themselves in the coursing of blood through his shoulders and arms. He pulled his hand out of the other's grip and turned away. He took two steps, not running.

The hand fell on his shoulder. Peter let it pull him around, turning faster on his own. The momentum brought up his hand. Just as the bigger guy's face came into view again, Peter smashed his fist into it. The guy looked merely startled, until Peter punched him again, just below the breastbone. His attacker went pale in a gush of lost breath. Peter knocked him down. For a moment he was so gripped by rage he drew back his foot, but then stopped himself.

The other two boys were staring at him. Peter glared. "How 'bout you two, you want some candy?" He lifted his hand that still held the bottle.

They kept their places. Peter backed up. The other two still didn't move, even to help their friend. Peter turned, hoisting his backpack onto his shoulder, and walked quickly. He looked back only once. The boys still stared at him. He imagined he looked like some fierce beast in retreat.

He felt great.

Anne and Eric Schwinn had sat in silence for most of twenty minutes. Anne remained behind her desk, uncluttered for this session. Schwinn sat in front of the desk, or occasionally stood to pace around the room, look at her diplomas and pictures, and glance back as if re-evaluating her in the light of each object. Anne sat patiently, an untouched pen and legal pad in front of her. She had started the session by asking her newest patient why he felt he needed to see her. At his shrug, she had said, "Try to put that into words." Then this long, placid time passed. He smiled at her in an embarrassed way from time to time, and Anne gave him a Mona Lisa in return, trying to show neither affection nor disapproval.

After a while she glanced at the clock and said, "This has been the easiest fifty dollars I've ever earned. I think we should go to three times a week, because frankly I need the rest."

Eric laughed. He stood across the office, fingering some small object from the top of her filing cabinet. He waved toward the small window. "Do you ever go outside the office?"

"Almost every night. Sometimes at lunch, too."

"No, I mean to have a session. Do you ever go—I don't know, for a walk?"

"Do you think my office is bugged?"

He smiled at her brilliantly and didn't otherwise answer. He had a good smile, which he seemed to know. Today he wore faded jeans, a long-sleeved reddish-brown shirt open at the collar, and boots that looked more workmanlike than cowboy. Anne did find herself curious about him. What he did for a living, for example. He could be a laborer, he had the shoulders for it. On the other hand, his fingernails were not only clean but buffed, and he had the air of someone used to being in charge, an entrepreneur. Anne would have bet that was one thing that made him uncomfortable about talking to her. If his trouble getting started continued, she would ask him about his job. That opened up most men.

"This is hard for me," he said suddenly. "I'm used to either not talking about myself or making shit up. Sorry."

Anne ignored both the obscenity and the apology. "What's your worst fear about talking to me? What's the worst thing you think will happen?"

He shrugged.

"Okay, what's the third worst thing? Let's start lower on the list."

Eric studied his hands. When Anne thought she was going to have to prod him again he suddenly looked into her face and said, "Giving up the mystery, you know? I'm afraid if I start telling you about myself I'll seem ordinary." He shrugged again. "That's like, maybe fourth on my list."

Anne said seriously. "Nobody is ordinary. Least of all you. Mystery doesn't interest me. Okay? The more I know, the more fascinated I get."

He watched her intently as she spoke. Anne feared he'd take her remarks more personally than she'd intended.

He sat down decisively. He shifted, put his hand to his mouth, deliberately lowered it to his lap. "I miss my old life."

"You mean your childhood? You mentioned—"

"No." Having steeled himself to begin talking, Eric cut her off. He wanted to continue. "I mean my job. My friends. I used to be part of a pretty big organization. I left a few years ago, went into business for myself. Now I'm the boss, which is what I wanted, but I kind of miss being one of the peons, taking orders and griping about the bosses."

"What do you do now?"

He moved his wide shoulders. "Not much. Sorry, I'm not trying to be mysterious. I have an Internet company. Buy stuff, mostly overseas, sell it on a Web site. Also put up information, you know, so people think they're in the know. It pretty much runs itself. I don't even own it any more, I sold it a couple of years ago before the bubble pop and did okay. I'm still a consultant to it, but I can do that from home."

"So you came here because you want to meet people?"

He shook his head, not smiling. Hunched forward, he picked through his words carefully. "I couldn't go back to my old life even if I wanted to. I changed. I didn't even realize it at the time, you know, you move on with your life, just thinking it's time for something new, not even realizing that you've changed yourself. Then when you think about going back you realize you can't and the reason is that you're not the same person and you never will be again, and maybe you liked that old person better."

He stopped abruptly, breathing as if he'd just run up stairs.

"What's wrong with the person you are now?" Anne asked quietly.

Eric Schwinn kept his eyes down, perhaps thinking about her question, perhaps still stuck in his problem he'd tried to articulate. "Nobody depends on me," he finally said. "I'm not part of a team, I'm not watching anybody's back, and I don't think I should be."

He said the last part very slowly. Obviously it was a painful admission.

"Why not?" Anne asked.

"It turned out I wasn't very good at it."

"You mean being a team player, or watching someone's back?"

Schwinn shook his head, easing his neck. "Both, I guess."

"No, you don't. Don't guess. You know exactly what you're talking about."

"And I guess you do too."

He glared at Anne. Sooner or later nearly all counseling reached this point, where the patient challenged the therapist's abilities. Anne and the new patient had come to it awfully early. She sat watching him steadily, but not speaking, sensing it was best not to answer his challenge.

Schwinn spoke more calmly. "Yeah, I failed to back somebody up when I should have."

"Was he killed?"

He gave her a penetrating glance. "No."

"If it wasn't fatal, then it's fixable, isn't it?"

He snorted, but without humor. Anne had managed in a very short time to kill Eric Schwinn's gleam of irony, which she considered a good achievement. A lot of patients approached therapy as if they were just fooling around. To get anywhere, Anne had to change that attitude. She had done it quickly in Schwinn's case. He looked angry.

"You know better than that, don't you?" he said.

Anne had sat patiently in her chair for more than half an hour without shifting. Now she folded her arms. "Why don't you give me some idea exactly what we're talking about?"

He shook his head. "What difference does it make? Don't you just want to ask how I 'feel' about it?"

"I think I can see how you feel about it. I want to know what 'it' is."

"Maybe next time."

Anne said, "This was a coworker, right?"

After a long moment, he nodded. Anne didn't think he'd answer any more questions along that line, so she shifted. "So have you been this unreliable in all aspects of your life? Have you ever been married?"

"No. You?"

"Long-term relationship?"

"Yeah, several. Sometimes two or three at the same time."

"Ba-dump-bump," Anne said, simulating a drum rimshot. She fell back into silence, making small rearrangements of objects on her desk. Schwinn watched her hands. Hostility left his expression.

"This is what I meant about the difficult transition to adulthood," he finally said. His voice reached for its former jauntiness and failed.

Anne just nodded.

"Don't you know this is hard?" he burst out. "Talking about why I'm a failure?"

She leaned toward him. "The easy part isn't worth shit."

Eric Schwinn smiled. He appeared to regain his poise, but at a different level. Anne hoped they had reached a new level of trust. "So tell me," she said, "what were you in your former life? Your profession."

He hesitated for a long time. Then, "Next time," he said. He rubbed his hands down the thighs of his jeans.

Anne sat back. "I thought we'd made some progress."

He smiled at her. "We did. I was planning to lie to you instead."

They made another appointment. Anne walked with him down the hallway toward the waiting room. Their shoulders bumped. For a moment it felt like the end of a first date. Anne sensed that Eric Schwinn thought so too. She stopped walking, folded her arms, and said good-bye. He gave her a look obviously meant to imply a personal relationship, and went out.

The door into the waiting area remained open. Across the large waiting room Anne saw Peter Greerdon, waiting to see her. He glanced up from his magazine, but not at her. Peter's eyes caught on the departing patient and followed him across the room. From her vantage Anne couldn't tell whether Eric Schwinn looked back at the boy. She didn't think so, from Peter's openly observant expression. Anne stepped softly to the doorway, but only in time to see Schwinn's back as he went out the outer door.

Peter stared after him, looking thoughtful.

By the time Peter Greerdon finished his session with Anne, it was close to six o'clock. He rode down in the elevator alone and trudged across the large lobby, watching for any man who might be watching him. Still, he didn't see anyone, and was surprised again when he sensed a presence close by and realized someone had fallen into step with him.

"Some people think if you don't cry or scream or wet your pants it wasn't a good session," Clarissa said lightly. "But Anne said it doesn't take that. She says sometimes you don't even know you learned something in the session until weeks later."

"I cried and screamed and wet my pants," Peter said. "But just to make her feel good." Clarissa laughed, to his immense gratification.

They crossed the street to the parking lot, traffic heavy on the downtown streets, and Clarissa led the way to her car, a yellow Volkswagen beetle her father had bought her at the start of this school year. Peter dropped his backpack into the back seat. Clarissa pulled out, slowly but confidently.

"What did we talk about today?" Clarissa asked. She wasn't talking about his session with Anne, and Peter knew it.

"Saving the environment one yard at a time," he said.

It was funny. Coming to see a psychiatrist might have been the healthiest thing Peter did, but he had to lie to his mother and stepfather about it. He needed a regular excuse, just as when he had slipped away with his friends to cruise bad neighborhoods and smoke marijuana. Clarissa supplied the excuse just as she did transportation to and from Peter's meetings with Anne. Somewhere she had come across a school club, Delta Epsilon Psi. The club actually existed, in case Peter's parents called the school to check, but it had been inactive since the previous school year. So Clarissa had adopted it for her own and Peter's use. DEP was a "service" club, formed to serve the community in various ways. One reason the club had gone cold was that the members had quit coming up with ideas for service. Now that task fell to Clarissa and Peter. They had formed, literally, their own secret society. Clarissa was thinking of electing herself president. Look good on her school record.

They had a pretty long drive to Peter's house, through some of the worst rush hour traffic in the city. Clarissa took it easy, and Peter relaxed beside her. That is, her driving didn't make him nervous. But Clarissa herself did. He kept wanting to ask her why she had adopted him. Scheduling appointments for him, giving him rides. He studied her in his peripheral vision: an intimidatingly pretty girl, clear-skinned, bright-eyed, with an expressive face and an unself-conscious laugh that made a boy want to devote his life to writing jokes. What on earth was she doing with him?

"When are you supposed to see Anne again?" Clarissa asked lightly.

This presented an opening for Peter to talk about the session if he wanted. He didn't. "Next week." But Peter did want to keep the conversation going. "You ever talk to anybody from Holmes?" The high school they'd both attended before transferring to Berkshire.

Clarissa watched the traffic, as if she hadn't heard, or as if the question didn't make sense to her. Then she shook her head no, quickly but emphatically.

Peter sensed he'd made a mistake. He quickly found another topic. "Do you know anything about Dr. Greenwald's other patients?"

"I've talked to a couple of them in the waiting room. Mostly, though, everybody wants to—keep a low profile, you know?"

"Are some of them really crazy?"

"I don't know. She doesn't say."

"Yeah, but, like— Some of them must be. I mean, just the percentages. How many people *not* seeing a psychiatrist are probably nuts? And if you already have enough of a problem that you need help . . ."

Clarissa smiled. "Are you worried about yourself, Peter?"

"Oh. No. Not me. Why? Do you think—?"

Clarissa laughed. "Don't worry about it. You're only going there because I told you to."

Peter gave a moment's thought to her confusing responses, then struggled back to his own meaning. "No, I mean I saw a guy, and he seemed, like, off. You know?"

Clarissa exited the expressway. She turned onto Babcock, a busy street, and looked for openings to angle across to the left lane. Peter sensed that his question bothered her. Or maybe she'd just lost interest in listening to him, which would make sense.

A few blocks farther on Clarissa made a left turn, into his neighborhood. Before they reached Peter's street, though, she pulled to the curb. "What do you mean, 'off'?"

Now she sounded serious. She looked at him carefully. He struggled to be worth her attention. "He came out with Dr. Greenwald walking with him, and they looked all friendly and like that, you know, but just as he turned away, with his back to her and before he stepped into the waiting room, he had this expression . . ."

Peter stopped, trying to recapture the memory. The man's face, handsome and rugged under his curly hair, had turned somehow alien: so briefly it could have been imaginary or a scrim of shadows. But his mouth had been compressed hard, as if in rage or determination.

"Did he look back at Anne before he left?" Clarissa asked seriously.

"I don't remember. Why? Do you think . . .?"

Clarissa shrugged. "Who knows anything? I just wonder if—you know, some of her patients get violent."

She began driving again. "Listen, maybe next week he'll have an appointment close to yours again."

"What if he does?" Peter sounded anxious. Clarissa looked strangely intense, and he was afraid he'd started something he hadn't intended.

"We'll decide then," Clarissa said. "At least I'll get a look at him. Here we are."

She had pulled to a stop in front of his house. Peter looked at it but didn't move to get out of the car. His mother's car wasn't in the driveway. His stepfather's was.

Clarissa saw his face tighten. "Want me to come in with you, show them you're really with somebody from school?"

"No, that's okay." Peter scrambled out. He opened the back door of the car and fumbled in the back seat for a minute, separating his backpack from Clarissa's. "Okay back there?" she said. "Yeah, fine," he said hurriedly, and slammed the car door too hard.

He stood on the sidewalk awkwardly before giving her a little nod and trudging up to the house. Clarissa got out of her car and stood beside it, waving. Something made her want to be seen by anyone watching from the house.

Peter turned and waved and disappeared inside.

Clarissa couldn't have explained why she had adopted Peter Greerdon. He'd just seemed to need help, and she felt a faint nostalgic fondness for him because he'd been a hanger-on of her old crowd. That school, that life, seemed years ago. She hadn't made a plan at all for taking up Peter. Clarissa didn't plan. She did things on instinct.

Sometimes that got her into trouble.

Anne, Chris, and Clarissa sat around the glass-topped table in Chris's condo. Chris had made his best dinner, which came in a variety of shapes and flavor. He called it Pasta with Stuff in It. This time the stuff was pretty good: capers and sun-dried tomatoes, chunks of salmon, and a thin threading of cheese. He had made a passable Caesar salad, too. There was nothing wrong with the food. In fact, Anne and Clarissa had both exclaimed over it at first bite. But by now the three of them had fallen into silence as if awkwardly unable to find a common conversation. But that wasn't it.

Chris was thinking about his conversation with Steve Greerdon, and with the chief of police. Someone had fed the police evidence against Chris. The same thing that had happened to Greerdon years earlier. Greerdon had said knowing what he did now, he would "do anything" to stop a false prosecution against him. Chris of course wouldn't do anything, and he didn't think much was required. Claims that he had violated campaign laws were probably just the usual rumors that always circulated through the legal community in San Antonio, the kind of conversation that kept life lively while lawyers tried to send people to prison or win them millions of dollars in compensation. Just the usual empty talk.

But that's what Steve Greerdon must have thought too, just before the train hit him.

Anne sat remembering her newest patient. They had just gotten to the interesting part, where he was on the verge of opening up, giving her what she demanded, but he still held out that last resistance. Keeping her interested. Next session, almost undoubtedly, he would give it up to her. Anne couldn't guess the details, but she thought she knew already the outlines of the confession she would soon hear. The details, though, those made it interesting. This is what kept her coming back to work. If she weren't interested in people she would never have become a psychiatrist. What none of her patients seemed to realize as they haltingly told the most intimate details of their psyches, and Anne sat with a determinedly unimpressed expression, was how much she relished those details. She wanted to help them, yes, but first came the gossip-rush of listening.

And Eric Schwinn promised to be interesting. Anne had forgotten the alarm she'd felt when she'd first found him in her office. But that shimmer of fear remained in her dealings with him, just below the level of consciousness, like the whisper along the skin one gets just before realizing that the empty room isn't empty.

Clarissa sat twirling angel hair around and around her fork, picturing the inside of Peter Greerdon's house. Clearly he didn't like going home, especially those last few feet of daylight to the front door. He wanted to stay away as long as possible. That was the only reason he had agreed to Clarissa's forceful suggestion that he begin seeing Anne. Clarissa knew that. She knew, too, that the boy had a growing crush on her. She resolutely did nothing to feed that—didn't touch him, sit close to him, lean an inch toward him as they walked or in her car. But she knew.

Her mother must have enjoyed this power. Clarissa had seen her exercise it, apparently unconsciously. But Clarissa knew better. Mom had worked to maintain her power over men. A gift that had deserted her at the end.

Clarissa shook off that line of thought and returned to Peter. She really did want to help him. That was the only reason she had suggested they investigate this patient who had caught Peter's attention. Another distraction for Peter to take his mind off what he feared at home.

Clarissa wondered how she could save him.

None of this made for dinner conversation. So the three of them sat in a silence that had grown by minutes. It wasn't an oppressive silence, because they remained unaware of it. After a few minutes Chris took a bite, Anne heard his movement and smiled at him. She moved her foot toward his under the table but then remembered that the tabletop was glass. Clarissa, noticing the movement and its abrupt halt, smiled and said, "I gave Peter Greerdon a ride home after your session this afternoon, Anne, and he said the weirdest thing."

"Oh? What?"

Clarissa grinned at her. "Nothing. I just wanted to see your face go all blank and indecipherable like that. Like whatever weird thing I come up with you're not going to confirm it or deny it."

Anne's face broke out of the shell of which she'd been unaware but which Clarissa had described perfectly, and the two of them laughed.

Chris said, "His father—" but then stopped, and the laughter covered his abortive attempt to join the conversation.

Clarissa rose from the table, taking her plate to the kitchen. Returning, she brought the wine bottle from the kitchen counter, set it pointedly between Anne and Chris, gave them a look, and went away to her room. She didn't look back over her shoulder, except figuratively. Anne smiled, moved closer to Chris, and poured them both more wine. Raising her glass, she leaned toward him.

"The girl has good instincts," she said.

As they leaned close, the air in the condo changed. There had been a sound, slight but unexpected. A background noise that didn't fit. Chris looked up sharply, toward the far end of the room where the glass patio doors stood uncurtained.

But the sound had come from Clarissa's room. It had been a sharp intake of breath from Clarissa, short of a scream but more than a gasp. She appeared in the doorway, backing out of her room as if from an armed intruder. Chris jumped to his feet.

But Clarissa's alarm was more subdued. She turned toward them, her eyes wide. "Come here, please. Now."

The words were unnecessary, except that they invited Anne to join Chris, who was already halfway across the long room. They joined Clarissa in the doorway and looked into her well-lighted room. Chris couldn't see anything amiss. The closet door was closed, the bed made. Clarissa's desk was the usual organized mess, but he didn't see anything more frightening than clutter there. Her backpack lay unzipped on the foot of the bed, a couple of books pulled out and dropped. She had obviously been about to begin homework.

"Look in my backpack," Clarissa said quietly.

Chris approached it cautiously. Anne stayed back with Clarissa. Still nothing looked threatening. If there'd been a snake in the bag Clarissa would have warned him. Chris pulled the backpack wider open and immediately spotted what she'd meant. It had been a long time, but the object was very recognizable. Chris found he was still holding his napkin. He used it to lift the clear plastic bag from the backpack, and turned, holding the marijuana high enough for the others to see.

"Dad, I swear—"

"I know." Chris put the Baggie down on the desk. It was packed very full, maybe holding more than four ounces. He had gotten easy convictions for such amounts. A misdemeanor, but the kind that could ruin school careers and future job prospects.

Chris had grown very alert, expecting the sound of a heavy hand knocking on the door. If this was a setup, it wouldn't be complete without an arrest. Still using the napkin, he opened the plastic bag, walked between the women in the doorway, and quickly to the kitchen, where he turned on the water and the garbage disposal and emptied the contents of the bag down the sink. A faint herbal smell entered his nostrils. Chris refused to feel nostalgic.

He still held the bag. He would take it to the office and have it checked for fingerprints, but he didn't think there would be any.

Clarissa had come into the living room and stood with her arms folded, looking defensive, almost hostile, a way she hadn't appeared in a long time. "Listen," she said quickly, "I called you in to see it. If it was mine I would have kept it hidden. I wanted you both—"

"I know," Chris repeated. "Now listen to me. Both of you. We have to be very, very careful from now on. The next time it could be heroin, Clarissa. It could be a gun."

Clarissa stared at him. She looked intense but not dismayed. Like Chris, she had become instantly alert.

Anne stared at Chris too, looking much more confused, and even concerned for his mental state.

"What the hell is going on?" she asked.

CHAPTER

five

★ Clarissa's bedtime was drawing near, and her homework still sat untouched in her room. She, Chris, and Anne sat in the living room, one lamp casting a soft light so that they looked like poker players or conspirators.

"So that's what's happening," Chris concluded. "I'm investigating the cops, they know it, and some of them are the kind who take matters like that seriously. Some of them invented a case against one of their own fellow officers. They wouldn't hesitate to do it to me, too. I've heard about their one attempt, and it seemed pretty harmless. Election law violations." He made a dismissive sound. "I didn't think about . . ."

He didn't finish the sentence, but took Clarissa's hand. In many ways Chris was still not used to being a parent. He hadn't had years of Clarissa's childhood to feel the vulnerability of having this extension of himself in the world, free of his supervision and often of his protection. Now he'd been reminded forcefully. He could protect himself, but that didn't make him safe.

"I haven't seen any police today," Clarissa said. "There weren't any near me, any time." She had adjusted to this idea much more quickly than her father. For Clarissa this conversation, about how to avoid cops that were out to get them, was an exercise in nostalgia. She sat with her elbows on her knees, paying close attention, and had wasted no time on disbelief or outrage.

"You wouldn't see them," Chris said. "Did you leave your backpack in your car any time while you weren't there? Police can get into a car faster than car thieves. Or it could have happened at school. During PE. You can't have your eye on your bag all the time. One of them could have even come to the school administrators with a search warrant. No one would tell you. Schoolchildren have no privacy rights."

As Chris spoke, he thought of the many cases he'd prosecuted or heard about in which the defendant's story was that evidence had been planted on him by police. Chris had always discredited such stories, and a jury had never once believed one. Given a choice between a cop and a criminal, which would a jury believe? Now Chris wondered how many of those stories had been true. Cops who would do such a thing knew how to choose their targets: habitual criminals with arrest records that would destroy their credibility. Would they grow so bold—or so threatened—as to try the same thing against Chris or his innocent child?

There was Anne too. They would know about his relationship with her. Chris turned to her. "And you're treating Steve Greerdon's son."

"That was my idea," Clarissa said quickly.

"Well, it wasn't a good one." Chris continued to look at Anne. "They may think he knows something, and that he'll tell you during the course of treatment. Can you send him to another therapist, at least until I get to the bottom of this?"

Anne stared at him, still with her look of concern, but that changed as her face became professional. She slowly shook her head. As Chris had known she would.

He sighed. "So there we are. Like I said, everybody has to be real careful."

Clarissa had withdrawn her hand from his and hunched her shoulders. She had gone cold, a chill from the past, from being outside, separated from society. She had almost forgotten this feeling, but it was her heritage, her upbringing. The easy life of the last year had just been revealed as a sham. Clarissa found herself oddly comfortable with that revelation.

Watch out? Oh yes, she could watch out. And everybody else better look out too.

Chris watched her worriedly, sensing her reaction and fearing it. "Can you just do that, darling? Be very, very careful?"

"Sure," Clarissa said carelessly.

Anne cleared her throat. "Is it possible you're overreacting?" she said to Chris. "I don't mean about what happened, but what caused it? Everything's not necessarily connected, you know. This could have a completely different explanation."

Chris raised his eyebrow at her, waiting. Anne said carefully:

"Maybe it was a gift."

Steve Greerdon had managed to lose his tail without ever spotting it. It is very difficult to stay close to a man who knows he's being followed. And Greerdon knew a few tricks. Turn down a lonely stretch of road, where the pursuer would have to hang back to avoid being spotted, turn quickly on a side street, quickly again, perhaps into an alley, or someone's long driveway. Outwait the bastard, then drive away.

Greerdon had a better one than that, though. He parked his car at his usual parking lot near Miguelito's on the west side, walked up the street as if going to the restaurant, then cut down an alley. At the far end sat a rusted-out Pontiac, an old clunker he'd bought for cash for exactly this reason. Greerdon got into it and drove off quickly. His follower would have been afoot by then, or watching Greerdon's first car expecting he'd have to return to it sooner or later.

He would, but he had business first, at which he didn't want to be observed.

By the time he reached the northwest side of town he felt even more confident he hadn't been followed. He parked the old car a block from his destination and walked the wrong way, then circled back. He seemed to be the only person walking in the neighborhood, and no car drifted by, either. Finally Greerdon cut quickly across somebody's carefully tended side yard and over the wooden fence. The back yard was nice too, with a large storage unit painted to look like a house, and a cocker spaniel that thought she was a German shepherd. Greerdon stood still, reaching out his hand until the dog gave up barking in order to smell his fingers. She barked again, not immediately taking to his smell, but as he made no threatening moves the dog sniffed his feet and then lost interest.

Once Greerdon had become part of the dog's nasal landscape, he walked quickly across the yard and jumped over the back fence. That set the dog yapping again, but he no longer cared.

This yard had more character than the one he'd left behind. The metal doors of its storage shed yawned open, displaying cardboard boxes and yard equipment heaped together in disorderly fashion. Nothing bothered his progress across the yard. Some cops don't like dogs. They're a pain in the ass at a crime scene, and after you've spent a few times trying to lure one away and lock it up so you can get a look at its owner's body you decide you don't want to come home to one jumping all over you, too.

He moved through the shadow cast by the house itself. It was four o'clock in the afternoon. Greerdon knew Emerson Blakely's working shift, three to eleven. Peter might be home from school soon, but that would be okay. Greerdon almost wanted to see him.

He crossed the concrete patio and looked at the glass patio doors. An almost-concealed wire gave away the alarm system. Okay. That made it a little harder, not much. He walked around, checking the bedroom windows. The first three he checked were locked, and he didn't want to break, just enter. The next window he tried gave to his upward pressure. It stuck, but after he created a small opening he could get his fingers under it and the window went up easily. Greerdon heaved himself up onto the sill and stepped through into his son's room, as he had guessed. Peter might use this window himself, for just this purpose. In and out. Greerdon remembered being sixteen.

The room's door that would lead into the house stood closed. Greerdon hadn't ever been in this room. He took his time to look it over. The decor made him nervous. It was too neat. Two pennants on the wall, one for Peter's old high school, one for the Florida Marlins. He wondered how old they were, and who had bought them.

No rock posters, no nearly naked girls. No marijuana-themed posters. The bookshelves held books, and several trophies on the top shelf. Greerdon took one down, a small one with a white fake marble base and a golden statuette of a boy with a bat. He remembered this one, from the machine-pitch team Petey had played on when he was six. It was the only trophy on the shelf Greerdon recognized. He stood there staring at them for a long minute. His eyes grew moist.

Eventually he put the trophy back and surveyed the rest of the room. A few pictures, papers on the desk, a dresser drawer hanging open, spewing out shirts. On a closet shelf Greerdon found a soccer ball and stood holding it for a minute, feeling the smoothness of its skin interrupted by the stitching. He wasn't used to this texture, had never felt it.

He found a couple of magazines under his son's mattress, which reassured him. At least Peter did have some secret teenage life here, it wasn't all elsewhere. And apparently he was heterosexual.

The neatness of the room had scared Greerdon. It looked like a disguise. Where was the anger, the rebellion? He knew it must be somewhere, and he hated to think of it all packed down inside Peter's head. That held the danger of explosion.

But a computer sat on the desk, humming furtively. That metal monster could hold worlds of secrets. He didn't know how to retrieve them, though. Greerdon didn't even bother to turn on the screen.

After pausing for a long moment behind the bedroom door, he turned the knob and opened it quietly. The air of the house felt undisturbed. He walked out into the corner of a hall. The next bedroom, its door open, was a home office. Another computer, a filing cabinet, an old leather sofa. The sliding closet door, half open, revealed coats and a couple of long dresses. Steve Greerdon looked at the filing cabinet and the desk drawers for a long moment, but then moved on.

The dining room was as neat as an unused room, the breakfast nook in the kitchen more homey. An inch of very stale coffee still sat in the glass carafe in the coffee maker. A bowl and a banana peel lay on the counter beside the sink. He stood there for a long minute. His fists clenched with an urge to smash everything, pick up the coffee carafe and hurl it through the window. This house had replaced his life. If he could destroy it, maybe his life would return. That wasn't what he thought, but it was what his body felt. Greerdon's face flushed; his expression would have made a grown man flinch. He moved toward the kitchen table, with its lightweight metal-legged chairs.

The layout of the house was that the front door was in the middle of the house. When one entered that way it was into the living room. Off to the left, through the dining room, was the hall to the two bedrooms Greerdon had seen. The other two bedrooms were on the other side, behind and beside the living room, so Peter's room and his mother's and stepfather's were separated by the whole house. Everyone must have liked things that way.

The kitchen was at the back. As Greerdon moved through it, toward the doorway to the other bedrooms, the front door of the house burst open. A muttered complaint was followed by the sound of objects being dropped. On purpose, apparently, because no one cursed or stopped to retrieve them. The front door slammed again, a heavy sound that made the whole house reverberate. Or maybe that was Greerdon's heart. He stood perfectly still in the kitchen, hidden for the moment, but if the new person came this way he would be as obvious as an elephant in a cemetery. Greerdon moved very slowly back toward the dining room exit, but that could be a mistake. He stopped and instead of retreating prepared a face to meet the newcomer. If it was Emerson Blakely they'd both be sorry a few minutes later.

But the sounds passed him by. The person went on toward the master bedroom, passing within a couple of feet of the kitchen doorway but not glancing inside. And Greerdon caught the breeze of passage and a scent. The footsteps, sharp but not heavy, the amount of air disturbed, a variety of clues he couldn't have identified told him this wasn't Emerson or Peter.

Straining to hear, he remained in the kitchen. He could go quietly down the hallway and back out the way he had come. Maybe he could slip out that heavy front door. But he might have been caught in doing either of those things, and he didn't want to look furtive. He was an intruder, but not a thief. And not a coward.

As he approached the bedroom his footsteps remained soft and again he tried to prepare an expression. Should he cough, call hello? He didn't want to frighten her. Or maybe he did.

His ex-wife Dolores was a secretary in an elementary school, a job that had given her good hours when Petey was young and needed her, and had remained convenient. It didn't hold any of her life, or hadn't. She looked forward to coming home, to stopping smiling constantly, to going out. From the darkened hallway he looked into the sunnier bedroom. She had already taken off her dress and her pantyhose, and sat on the edge of the bed pulling on jeans. Greerdon started to pull back, but she looked up and saw him.

He hadn't gotten his face ready in time, and her changing clothes had caught him off guard. Dolores just sat looking at him for a moment. She didn't gasp or change her expression. She just stared, waiting. Then she stood up, pulling the jeans up and zipping them. A T-shirt still lay on the bed.

Neither of them said hello. She continued to watch him. A lot of time could have passed by the time she spoke.

"What are you going to do now, rape me? Because that's what it would be."

He had entertained the fantasy that they were still in a sense married, that he would return to find she had been longing for him, as well. Her flesh was a revelation to him. He'd imagined it so long he had forgotten the reality. The swell of her breast sliding into the barely concealing, translucent bra. The tiny white scar of her appendectomy.

For Steve Greerdon, his trial had been yesterday. But everyone else's lives had gone on. He could see that in his son. A few years mattered so much in the life of a child. Greerdon had harbored the illusion that that wasn't true in adult lives. Time hadn't passed in his life. But it had in hers.

"No, of course not," he said.

He turned away, gave her privacy to pull on her shirt. There are moments in which one's life changes course, all in a moment. One says words, throwaway lines, that suddenly become true. One illusion fell away from Steve Greerdon in that moment: the hope, never said, never even coherently thought, that he could reconstruct the life he'd had. He was an innocent man. Dolores knew that now. His life had been taken from him unjustly. Justice required that he be given it back.

But life didn't work that way. She'd made a life without him, and it didn't matter that he was free again. Nothing from his past could be recaptured.

"So what are you doing here?" Dolores said, not unkindly. She had pulled on a T-shirt of broad pastel yellow and blue stripes, and stood with her arms folded.

"I brought you this." Greerdon took the envelope from his pocket and set it on edge on her dresser. The envelope was thin enough to be empty, but it wasn't. "Back child support," he said.

She opened the envelope and looked at the check, which required her to step within a foot of him. Greerdon watched her face. The thin lines radiating from her eyes had deepened a little, the skin of her cheeks grown slightly coarser. Her nose was strong and straight, and when she looked up at him her eyebrows raised in a way he remembered, showing surprise and asking a question. The size of the check had obviously startled her.

"I got a settlement from the state," he explained. "And it's for Petey. Start a college fund or—well, whatever you want. It's your money. I'm sorry I wasn't here to help."

"Steve—" Dolores suddenly stepped close and put her arms around him. He felt the blinking of her eyelashes and knew she was on the brink of crying. The hug felt wonderful. But he sensed her holding back, too, which was confirmed a moment later when she stepped away quickly and folded her arms again. "I'm so sorry about what happened to you. If I could—But you know, even if you hadn't gone to prison, you and I would probably be divorced by now. And I'm sorry, but I'm happy now. I don't want you to think there's a chance . . ."

He nodded. "You know I told you you were right to divorce me. And I wanted you to get married again. But why him, Dolores? Emerson Blakely. He was a bastard. If you knew the things I've heard about him—"

She sniffed, laughed, and wiped her eye all at the same time. "My God, Steve, don't you know that's what men always say? 'I don't mind you being with somebody else, but not him.' Not that one. Not any particular one. As a general idea it's okay, but not as reality."

"But another cop?"

"Think of that as a tribute to you," Dolores said, her voice beginning to grow harsh.

Greerdon shook his head and backed up. "You're right, it's none of my business."

She hadn't said that, but he knew she was about to. He turned and walked out, into the living room. Long before he reached the front door he turned back, knowing she had followed him. "But Peter is," he said. "I've missed half his life, and I'm not going to miss any more. I'm going to be here a lot. And if that puts a strain on things between you and your husband, that's not what I'm trying to do, but I'm not going to stop it, either."

She didn't answer. At the front door he turned back and they gave each other a long look. Their mouths twitched in matching rueful twists. Both of them could have said a lot more, but no more conversation would have mattered. The two of them had always been unusually communicative in silence. Apparently they still had that, if nothing else.

Steve Greerdon went out, closing the door carefully. Standing on the other side, he felt that whole house solidify against him. He stared out at the unfamiliar street with no idea where to go.

He walked slowly back to the old car, which seemed to have grown more decrepit while he'd been inside Dolores's house The street appeared to resent it.

Greerdon climbed behind the wheel and started the motor, but then just sat there. He had the vague idea he might wait here until Peter got home from school. He reached up to adjust the rearview mirror, to see whether any schoolkids were coming along the street yet. Then he froze.

"Hello, Steve," Rico Fairis said.

He sat in the back seat, directly behind Greerdon. He must have been lying over on the seat when Greerdon had gotten into the car, but now he sat as if he hadn't moved in hours. Rico had that gift. In a situation where everyone else paced or twitched, he could remain motionless for an inhumanly long time. He appeared immovable. Even when he smiled, a smile appeared to be the expression he'd been wearing all along.

"It's a whole new world, Stevie. I don't know if you can ever catch up.

Don't you know how easy it is to be followed now without you ever seeing a human?"

Steve Greerdon sat waiting, He wouldn't ask Rico what he wanted, because the answer wouldn't be trustworthy. Rico would tell him soon enough, if he wanted him to know. Greerdon didn't examine his feelings, either. His old partner sat behind him. They had shared a lot. In prison, Greerdon had realized that Rico must have been instrumental in sending him there. If nothing else, he had acquiesced. Yes, Greerdon could have killed him. He wouldn't be surprised to feel a wire come around his own throat, either. Rico sat in advantageous position, behind him.

"You pick up burglary skills in the joint?" Rico asked. "Was Dolores glad to see you?"

"You could at least have watched out for my son while I was away, Rico. Didn't you owe me that?"

"I did, Steve. He's never been arrested, has he?"

As Greerdon had known, he didn't trust Rico's answer. Was it true? Was it an implied threat? Greerdon turned in the seat so he could look back. Rico wore a brown jacket, a size too large for him; it could accommodate equipment. His stomach bulged out over his legs. He looked in lousy shape, but Greerdon knew that was deceptive, too. His big hands rested on his knees.

"How're you doin', Steve?" Rico asked with concern that sounded genuine if not deep. "We haven't seen you much at the station. Some people think maybe you're pursuing your own investigations."

"I'm not after you, Rico. You've been watching me, you know that. I just want to get on with my life. I know if I try to pursue what happened, you'll ruin me."

Rico nodded judiciously. "That's what I think, too. But, you know, proof is better than thinking. It'd put some minds at ease if you'd do me a little favor."

Steve Greerdon stared hard at his former partner, making his face implacable. He felt the tug of Rico's will. "I don't want anything to do with your business, Rico. I told you that before."

"Yeah, I remember." Rico nodded affably, then looked at Greerdon with what appeared genuine curiosity. "How'd that work out for you?"

Chris had suffered such a moment too, without realizing it. A moment like Steve Greerdon's realization in his wife's bedroom, when his life changed because he'd just lost a large portion of his motivating drive. For Chris, he had been forced to discard a major foundation of his belief system. After years spent in the justice system, he had remained a bit naive. He believed police officers pursued justice and that the great majority of prosecutions were justified. Becoming district attorney himself had only reinforced this belief, because then he could ensure the righteousness of his own cases.

But since hearing Steve Greerdon's story, since seeing the marijuana in Clarissa's backpack, he had realized he couldn't trust anyone, even his own team. The District Attorney's Office didn't investigate its own cases. Those cases were brought to them by police agencies: some by the same police officers who had framed Steve Greerdon and tried to do the same to Chris's daughter. Certainly they wouldn't hesitate to violate the rules of justice in pursuing criminals.

It remained true that most cops were honest and most cases just. But he could no longer trust any particular case. When a defendant claimed evidence had been planted, Chris wondered: Had someone wanted this guy bad enough? If so, why? The simplest case now held the possibility of tangled conspiracy.

Chris had become a functional madman. He didn't trust anything he was shown. Even his own perceptions had become suspect. He didn't recognize this as madness, he didn't show it. But he had begun to act on it.

"How many more of these guys are we going to listen to?" Jack Fine asked wearily. A scrawny man in an orange jumpsuit was being led out of his office by another investigator.

"I don't know," Chris said casually, reviewing his notes. "How many we got in jail?"

"About three thousand, any given day. But don't forget the ones we've already shipped off to state prison."

"I haven't," Chris said mildly. "I've had some bench warrants issued."

Jack stared. "What judge did you get to do that?"

Chris smiled, still with his eyes on the legal pad in front of him. "Why should I need a judge? I'm the district attorney."

Jack watched Chris closely. Even after working with him for almost two years, Jack couldn't always be sure when Chris was joking. He moved on.

"I didn't hear anything persuasive there." He gestured toward the empty doorway through which the latest conspiracy-theorist had exited. "You?"

"Maybe. The part about a police officer offering him a deal."

"Chris, the guy's confession is on videotape."

Chris gave him a look, as if Jack were the naive one. No matter what the videotape showed, there could have been another, off-camera exchange between the suspect and the arresting officer. "Okay, okay," Jack conceded. "But at some point you have to give more weight to the word of a police officer than a criminal. Even if they did cut some corners, they were still the good guys, and the ones who got arrested are in jail because they committed a crime."

Chris swiveled the stool on which he sat so he could face Jack directly. He gestured toward him with the legal pad. "Here's the idea I found interesting: that a police officer might make a deal like that sometimes. Say, 'You go find me evidence of a bigger crime and I'll forget about this one.' Take the handcuffs off a prisoner and push him out the back door of the police station. A cop setting a criminal free. Do you think that happens? Do you think it's *ever* happened?"

Jack didn't answer, which was answer enough.

"So we've got alliances between the good guys and the bad guys, Jack. I'm sure it makes sense to the investigator sometimes. 'I've got somebody here on possession of a small amount of heroin, he's not hurting anybody, maybe he can lead me to bigger fish.' But maybe the guy the cop is releasing *is* the bigger fish. Just because he was arrested for something small-time doesn't mean he's never done anything big-time. But now he's out on the street with a motivation to find a bigger case. To uncover a crime. Or invent one. Then if the cop cuts a little corner in making the new case, to protect his accomplice's identity, he and the first guy he arrested have become partners." Chris held up two intertwined fingers. "They're dependent on each other. And they both know something bad about the other. How long could a partnership like that continue, Jack? If it worked, if it was successful?"

This time Chris waited for an answer. After a minute Jack cleared his throat and said, "I knew a cop who had a snitch. Kind of like what you're talking about. The informant gave the cop tips, the cop cut him some slack on the small stuff. Then the snitch married the cop's cousin. Became a member of the family. They'd see each other at weddings and christenings. Made it harder to bust him when the time came."

Chris smiled. "That's not what I was talking about, but good point. Trust you to know better examples than I do."

"Steve Greerdon set all this off?" Jack asked. "Because you know, I still don't find him all that trustworthy."

"That's kind of my point, isn't it?" Chris returned to studying notes. Jack watched his face change back, to one so neutral of expression it displayed suspicion of everything. He saw his boss disappear.

"Let's talk to the other one we've got here," Chris said. "What else have we got to do?"

Jack wondered that himself, where all this was leading. Over his shoulder he said, "Send in our next contestant, Don Pardo."

They sat waiting for the shuffle of slippered feet, preparing to meet the fevered eyes of someone with a great story. Chris sat up straight.

The restaurant Miguelito's wasn't very crowded at seven o'clock on a Wednesday night. Steve Greerdon, eating *enchiladas de mole* and drinking iced tea, was prominent in a variety of ways, including his choice of beverage and his ethnic origin. Chip Riley leaned against the bar and watched him for a long minute, then looked slowly around the room. He saw a family of eight celebrating, three couples in booths, and one man looking furtive because the woman with him was not his wife. Small crowd, and Chip knew all their faces. He sauntered across the room and took a seat at Greerdon's table.

"A couple of guys have asked me about you," he said.

Greerdon put his hands flat on the table, looked at Chip straight, and said, "You want me to take my business elsewhere?"

Chip shook his head dismissively, as if to say he didn't take orders from anyone. He looked around and waved over the waitress who brought the good tequila. Chip downed his with a wince and a slam, then took a long drink of the beer the waitress had also brought him. As with many alcoholics, the one drink changed him. His face tightened as his body relaxed. He grinned. It was clear Chip felt taller, wider-shouldered, and in control. After one casual look around the room he said out of the side of his mouth, "I've got something to tell you."

Steve Greerdon didn't say anything. His expression grew more skeptical. He knew how to feed the urge to confess. That training hadn't deserted him.

"I don't know much," Chip said. "Just a couple of names. But you might be able to follow up. Here's how I looked at it back then, Steve." He leaned on his forearms and became more confidential. "You and I were never partners or anything, but I worked with you enough to know you were a good cop. When you got busted I figured, well, there'd been a lot I didn't know. You must've been into some stuff I didn't know about. But you didn't make a deal, you didn't take anybody down with you. So I figured something else."

Greerdon knew what he'd figured: that Greerdon had to take his punishment, knowing he'd be rewarded by his partners in crime.

"But now I see you in here, you don't look like a rich guy, you haven't taken off to the Bahamas, and in spite of what you say I can see you're hungry, Steve. You look like I used to look at the end of a month of being this close to taking down a big case. Don't deny it. I remember the look, Steve."

Greerdon didn't deny anything. Chip studied him, Chip's own tequila-ruddied face showing pride in his powers of perception. "Plus that DA says you were framed, and he seems like a good guy. Too much of a Boy Scout, but in this case that makes him even more convincing.

"So I've been doing a little digging myself, starting with what I knew back then. Steve, I think I can get inside."

Greerdon sat immobile. He felt like a man trying to catch a rabbit with a hand-held snare. If he moved, the hunt would be over, the prey gone. Steve Greerdon did not believe in generosity. The last eight years had taught him only self-protection. Chip Riley's offer of help sounded sincere, but Greerdon peered behind the offer. Why would he do this? It seemed more likely that this was a trap set up by Rico Fairris. If Greerdon said yes, he wanted to know, Chip would scurry back to Rico and the others with that information. Then they'd know that Steve Greerdon was indeed on the hunt. So what he needed to do here was reiterate that he had no desire to find out who had framed him. He needed to send Chip Riley away.

And yet the offer seemed genuine. So Steve Greerdon sat without moving. The simplest gesture seemed too heavy with consequences to make.

Finally he said slowly, "Look, Chip, I already told you—"

"Yeah, I know what you said, Steve. What you had to say. Don't worry, I get it." He picked up the other shot glass of tequila, forgetting it had supposedly been Greerdon's, and downed it slowly, savoring. His taste buds must have been almost ruined, it took strong flavors to reach him. He set the glass down, looked around the room, and saw the door behind the bar open. Chip lowered his voice again. "Listen, let's start by me telling you what little bit I know already. Not now, though. Come back about eleven. Can you do that? I should be able to slip out then. Out back, okay? Wait for me if I'm late. Don't come inside."

Steve Greerdon wondered suddenly how stupid everyone thought he was. Come to a dark alley at a time when no one would be around.

"Okay," he said.

Chip gave him a conspirator's wink. "Thanks, Steve. And just—just one other thing. I'm sorry." He laid his hand on Steve's arm, looking suddenly solemn, then stood up, using the back of a chair to do so. He'd better get something to eat soon. Instead he approached the pretty young waitress again, and put his head close to hers. Steve Greerdon watched him, thinking how good Chip Riley must have looked at one time: tall, lanky, moving easily, with a devilish grin coming easily. He should have had a gun on his hip and a Texas Ranger's badge on his shirt pocket. Must have cut a hell of a figure when he'd first started working here. Now he stood balanced precariously, both literally and figuratively: just about to tip over into ridiculous middle age.

Greerdon mused on Chip's last words. "I'm sorry." He had meant something more than sympathy for what had happened to Steve Greerdon. It had been a personal apology.

At that moment Luisa Gaines emerged from the office behind the bar. Her eyes landed first on Steve Greerdon. She did not look happy to see him. Her eyes moved alertly. Clearly she had noticed the two empty shot glasses on Greerdon's table. Then she found her manager. Her face went dead flat. She walked slowly and quietly along behind the bar until she stood right behind Chip Riley and the waitress. The young woman noticed her first, startling. Gaines said a sharp sentence in Spanish and the waitress went about her business. Chip gave Gaines a slow smile that must have worked in the past; he didn't notice how little effect it had now. Gaines noticed his color and his leaning on the bar.

"Do you just come here to flirt with my waitress and drink up my profits?"

Chip didn't lose his good humor. "No, not *just* for that."

He leaned across the bar and breathed tequila fumes at her. Luisa Gaines grimaced. "What have you been talking about with your friend?" she said.

"What friend?"

She gestured with her chin across the room, but when she looked in that direction she saw at the table only a half-empty plate. The Anglo with the heavy stare was gone.

"Sober up and stop being disgusting," Gaines snapped. "We have things to talk about."

Stephanie Valadez, DA's Office investigator, wished she had brought a book. She'd had such an easy night of keeping tabs on Steve Greerdon that her only problem was boredom. She coped with that problem in her own manner, by trying to take in more and more information. When Greerdon went into his favorite restaurant Stephanie stayed outside, a block away, but with a view of the front door. She stood very still on a street corner, letting sensations flow over her. If she did this well she had the impression that her senses were extending farther and farther outward. At first the closed bakery across the street overwhelmed her smell, but gradually she began to pick out flavors of the restaurant down the street, oil in the road, the leavings of animals, a trace of a smoker somewhere. She began to hear beneath the street noises slighter sounds: something small scurrying back up this alley, a late bird, a slight sizzle of

Christmas lights hung across the street, the barely perceptible sound of two voices, a man's and woman's. This was a commercial block, but some of the buildings had apartments above. Stephanie began looking around, trying to find what she was hearing. At the same time, she made sure to keep the door of Miguelito's in sight. It wouldn't do to let Steve Greerdon slip away while she explored the mystical world of the senses.

She also wanted to know why she hadn't seen anyone else following Greerdon. That worried her. Her boss had told her to expect someone else watching him, and on two or three days Stephanie had seen someone. Tonight, though, she felt alone. She didn't trust the feeling.

After an hour or so Greerdon emerged from the restaurant. He glanced both ways as she drew back behind the corner of the building. When she looked out again he was walking down the street away from her, in the direction of the lot where he'd parked his car. Stephanie hurried up the street and into an alley to where her own navy blue Jetta sat parked, and was ready when Greerdon drove past her. She hung very far back because the street carried little traffic, and his destination seemed apparent. Sure enough, Greerdon parked a mile or so away at the small apartment complex where he'd rented a place. He parked in his spot and went in, possibly for the night, but Stephanie decided to wait a while. She passed the time doing her Daredevil routine, trying to sense all the life around her. Sometimes that was too easy, as when a fight broke out in one of the other apartments. She also began to roam silently around the apartment block, looking for other surveillance and finding none. Still, she stayed on a while longer, checking to make sure Steve Greerdon's car remained in its parking space.

Some time before eleven her patience was rewarded. Greerdon reemerged from his apartment. He wore dark jeans and a dark brown leather jacket. The December night had grown chilly, around forty degrees. Stephanie had staved off the cold by continuing to move, but she found herself a little stiff as she had to run to her car.

Greerdon remained easy to follow, though. He seemed to be recreating his early evening, heading back up the street toward Miguelito's. This time he parked well short of the restaurant, on a dark side street, and walked. Stephanie parked on the same side street, but a block farther away, and hurried to keep Greerdon in sight. She passed a small white frame house and felt her heart stabbed by its white Christmas lights framing its two front windows. The porch sagged. Stephanie hurried past.

Miguelito's presented a formidable destination, framed completely in red and green lights itself, clashing with the neon beer signs. She barely caught a glimpse of Steve Greerdon turning the near corner, before he reached the restaurant. He slowed down. Stephanie did too. It was late on a weeknight, but the street wasn't silent. Across from the front entrance of the restaurant a man sat on a bus stop bench, singing in Spanish loudly enough for her to recognize the tune. A heavy man stood behind him wearing a long coat, his face in the shadows. He leaned slightly to spit, as if commenting on the other man's singing. It was impossible to tell whether the two were together or just waiting for the same bus. Across the street from them, nearer to Stephanie, a small crowd of other men stood just outside the restaurant's entrance, having a quiet consultation, Two of them wore long overcoats. All wore cowboy hats.

Stephanie looked down the side street and saw Steve Greerdon walking on, past the restaurant, disappearing down the residential block. She expected that he planned to circle back, or was deliberately trying to see whether he was being followed. So she looked for a stopping place herself. She would have liked to circle around the restaurant in front, coming around to intercept Greerdon on the other side, but those men presented problems. If they accosted her she felt confident of her ability to put them off or handle them—if worse came to worst she had a gun strapped to her belt at the small of her back—but she didn't want to be seen at all. The night no longer seemed black to her, she didn't feel sufficiently concealed. She slipped into the shadow of an overhanging bush, and waited. In a moment she would decide whether to follow Greerdon or slip to the back of the restaurant.

Why hadn't he just gone in? Had he made plans to meet someone down the street? Stephanie had a good tracker's paranoia. She thought he was just trying to catch her. She would counter that move by just waiting. He had to return.

Then she remembered Greerdon's car. It sat two blocks behind her. He could have walked down this street, knowing she would expect him to meet someone in or near the restaurant, only in order to keep her here while he slipped back to his car and went somewhere else entirely.

Stephanie panicked briefly. She wanted to run back to the car, she wanted to fly down the street and find where Greerdon had gone. She wanted to rush into the restaurant and look for anyone he might be meeting.

An argument had started among the men in front of the restaurant. They distracted her attention for a moment. Then she noticed the singing man had disappeared from across the street, though she hadn't noticed a bus come by. She didn't see the heavier man, either. Stephanie stepped out of the bush's enclosure and started down the street after Greerdon. A heavy impact on her back almost threw her to the ground. "*Oomph,*" she said, as arms encircled her, pinning her own arms to her sides, keeping her hands from her gun. The man draped himself over her, overwhelming her.

"Hey, chickie, chickie," the man mumbled into her ear, in what he must have thought a seductive croon. Stephanie tried to throw him off, but he held her more tightly. She turned her head to try to see him, and he breathed into her ear. It was the singing drunk who had been across the street. He had a several-days' growth of beard and a stench to match. Stephanie wanted to scream, but she didn't want to draw attention, either. The man wore an overcoat that enveloped them both. She could feel him pressing against the gun in her waistband, pressing it against her back. Stephanie drove both elbows back, but somehow he had already turned to avoid them. He put his leg around hers and pushed, and she fell to the ground, a moment later with the man on top of her. She had barely had time to turn, so that now they were face to face. He grinned at her.

"Oh yes, this is better," he chuckled.

She struggled. This would not happen. Her mind had gone fiercely blank. She turned herself into a fury, fighting with knees and hands and trying to butt him with her head. All these moves failed to dislodge him, but stopped his laughing. And she managed to wrench one hand free. She made it into a claw and went for his face. He rolled off her. "Okay, okay," he muttered. "I don't like it so rough."

Stephanie wasn't finished. Her rage roared in her ears. She had never been so mad in her life. She scrambled to her knees and reached behind her back. When she came out with her handgun, she pointed it straight at the bastard, both arms extended, and snapped out an order.

But he had already gone rigidly still. He crouched on both knees and one hand, the other hand up in front of him, looking more than anything like a pointing spaniel. His head was cocked, listening, his face straining.

He baffled Stephanie. She lowered her gun slightly. And in the next second she heard it too: a gunshot. Both loud and muffled, blocked by distance and perhaps more.

She looked across the street, thinking the argument in front of the restaurant must have erupted. But the men had dispersed, already running, and she didn't see a gun in anyone's hand. No one seemed to be on the ground.

Her mind replayed the sound and Stephanie jumped to her feet. It had come from behind the building. She jumped to her feet, ignoring the vagrant, and raced across the street. Veering to her left, she rounded the corner of the restaurant and came to a courtyard in back, an open space that held a Dumpster and loading area for supplies. Two cars sat parked back there.

Overhead a strong light burned, illuminating the body on the ground.

Stephanie slowed abruptly. She still had her gun out, and she quickly swung it in a circle, taking in the back of the restaurant, the large open space across from her, the Dumpster. Nothing living moved. Stephanie crept slowly across the dirty pavement to the man on the ground. He lay on his chest, a pool of blood seeping out from under him. She reached down and touched his throat. His flesh remained hot, but nothing pulsed within it.

She knew who he was, though they had never been introduced. Chip Riley. The cop and manager/security guard for this restaurant. He lay sprawled, his light jacket twisted, his eyes open in amazement. Stephanie looked all around the body, searching for evidence. She didn't see a weapon or shell casings. Then she looked for how the killer must have escaped. He could have gone out the other way, into the side street on the other side of the building. That was how Stephanie had expected Steve Greerdon to approach the building. Had he had time to do so? She couldn't be sure. Her time sense was confused.

The body lay about six feet from the back wall of the restaurant. Now she noticed a smoldering cigarette on the ground a few feet from the body. There was a door into the restaurant not far away. Stephanie started toward it, thinking someone could have escaped that way.

Then she heard a sound behind her, whirled with the gun ready, and confronted the vagrant who'd attacked her earlier: He was running, but skidded to a halt, staring at the body. "Oh, my God," he said, in a completely sober tone of voice.

"Stop," Stephanie said authoritatively, still with the gun leveled. "I'm an investigator for the District Attorney's Office."

The man stared at her, calculating. He glanced down at the body, then returned his gaze to Stephanie. "I know," he said, still in a changed voice. He held out both hands, then slowly reached behind his back with his left hand. Stephanie's finger tightened on the trigger. But the man continued to move very slowly, bringing his hand back into view. It didn't hold a weapon, at least not in the conventional sense.

He held a slender black wallet at arm's length, and let it fall open. Stephanie saw the gleam of a silver badge.

"I'm a cop," the vagrant said.

CHAPTER *six*

★ Jack Fine had his hand on the telephone before it finished its first ring. He had it to his ear before he came fully awake. But he snapped into the phone as if he'd been sitting there waiting for the call. "Yeah?"

Moments later he sat up on the side of the bed. Behind him his wife turned in the darkness, away from him.

On the phone, Stephanie Valadez sounded a little frantic. "There's an evidence team here already, Mr. Fine. It seemed like they got here in seconds. They've shoved me out of the way, they won't let me near the body anymore. I don't know who these officers are. Should I stay here and keep an eye on them?"

Jack made a quick decision. "No. Go into the restaurant. Talk to people."

"But the murder happened out here."

"Maybe because of something that happened inside. Get in and talk to people before the witnesses disperse."

"Yes sir."

"Do you have a camera or tape recorder?"

"No sir. I'm doing surveillance. I didn't think—"

"That's okay. Stephanie. Before you go inside. Are you still outside where the body is? Good. Take a deep breath. Calm yourself. Look at the scene. Just look. Don't focus on the body. Look all around it. Make vivid pictures in your head. Do that for one minute, then go inside. All right?"

"Yes sir."

She sounded a little calmer. She clicked *off,* and Jack sat on the side of his bed with the phone in his hand. He should call somebody. He was too old for this running off in the middle of the night.

Marjorie moaned and rolled toward him. They had been married three years. She hadn't been there through the many, many nights when calls like this interrupted his sleep. They had gotten married soon after Jack had retired from the police department. Marjorie was a dispatcher there, and after Jack retired they discovered they missed seeing each other every day. So far the marriage was fine, a middle-aged comfort for both of them.

Jack walked around the bed, leaned close to her face, and said, "I've got to go out."

"I know." She sounded fully awake. "Drive careful, there's drunks out there."

Jack grinned. Marjorie didn't even pretend to offer to make him coffee or anything else. She sounded like a veteran of these nights. He kissed her, then got dressed quickly. Five minutes after the phone call, he was in his car.

Chris didn't get a call until about five. No one needed him, and Jack didn't want to wake him until he knew something, which he never really did, not that night. Chris was at his desk in the DA's office by seven. When Jack came in, Chris was just hanging up the phone from calling to make sure Clarissa was awake. He had a slight smile, which disappeared entirely as Jack approached the desk.

"Are they going to bring me Steve Greerdon?" Chris asked.

Jack shrugged. He handed Chris a manila folder. Chris opened it to reveal photos and more. He took a long look at the body, wondering odd things such as whether the victim had still been alive when he'd fallen. Had landing on the cement hurt? Was it cold against the skin of his cheek? The ground looked dirty, littered with cigarette butts and stained by oil.

Chris knew this dead man was Chip Riley. Chris had never met him, but knew who he had been: a police officer, veteran enough to have worked with Steve Greerdon, casual enough about rules to be a suspect in the long-ago conspiracy. And apparently unimportant enough to events that someone might have killed him just to make a point, or to set up someone else.

Death had been assured from the moment Chris had made a phone call to the lieutenant governor. Not necessarily Chip Riley's death, but someone's. As soon as Chris had started taking steps to get Steve Greerdon released from prison, he had condemned someone to die. It could as easily have been Greerdon himself. Chris's powers remained far short of godlike, since he hadn't known whom he was condemning, or even that he was doing so. He hadn't thought far enough ahead, or known enough. But if not for him, Chip Riley would still be alive: asleep right now, maybe working an early shift, yawning, feeling grouchy. But feeling something. Not lying on soiled cement. Chris hadn't realized he was condemning someone, and he didn't blame himself now, but he felt strange and unworldly as he looked at pictures of the dead man, as if Chris had stepped without preparation into a new world.

If he had known this would happen, would he have left Steve Greerdon in prison? That question led too deep into the undergrowth of the past and moral obligations.

"I don't know yet," Jack said in answer to Chris's question about Greerdon. "They hadn't arrested anybody yet when I left. Greerdon wasn't around."

"But we know it wasn't him, right? Stephanie was watching him."

The silence that followed spoke eloquently. Chris closed his eyes and sighed.

"Stephanie lost him for a minute there," Jack finally said. When the district attorney's mouth clenched angrily, Jack said, "You want me to fire her? She's already about to shoot herself. You know how hard it is to keep somebody in sight every second without being spotted? Especially a guy like Steve Greerdon, who knows you're there and knows what he's doing."

Chris looked up at him in surprise. Jack shut up abruptly, looked pained, and then said, "I should've had two guys on him. At least."

"We don't have that many people. And if you had, he would have just outwaited us."

"I should've done it myself."

"Come on, Jack. It's not your fault." Chris stared off into a corner of the room. "It's my fault."

After a moment Jack laughed a bitter, surprised little laugh. He got the joke. He and Chris were people who took responsibility. They tried to be in charge of everything, every minute. Inevitably, they couldn't be.

Chris stood up and walked around, leaving the folder of photos open on his desk. "So he lost Stephanie just at the crucial time, just when he needed to, to shoot this guy? He must've really hated him."

Jack nodded. "I know. It doesn't make sense. Knowing that even if he'd shaken Stephanie for a minute she was still right there. She could place him at the scene." Jack spoke more smoothly. He had given up recriminations.

"Anybody ever see the two of them talk? Know what they were talking about?"

"They had talked earlier that evening. Stephanie interviewed a couple of people who saw them. Nobody heard what they were saying, though."

"Raised voices? Anything?"

Jack shook his head.

They settled down and began trying to piece together events, knowing there would be large holes in their puzzle. They knew more than that, too. That this case would be unlike any other Chris had ever prosecuted. Police would bring him a suspect. They would produce evidence suitable for securing a conviction in trial. And Chris wouldn't be able to trust any of it. He would have to put together his own case, based on questionable evidence and unreliable testimony. Probably he would never be able to tell whether someone was trying to manipulate him, but no re-creation of events would be trustworthy.

He expected that shortly he would be brought a neatly wrapped case of murder against Steve Greerdon, one designed to send him back to prison and leave Chris wondering what had really happened and who was behind yet another crime.

He was wrong.

"Is what I tell you confidential?"

Anne Greenwald looked steadily across her desk. "You've asked me that before. Yes."

On the other side of the desk, Eric Schwinn sat in the patient's chair rubbing his hands together. He had lost his ironic detachment. His wavy hair hung neglected, and his bright blue eyes looked very big, and red-veined. He wore a dark blue shirt, crisp black slacks, and black loafers, and was clean-shaven. In other words, he had left home looking sharp and ready for the day, but soon after he had come into Anne's office it had become obvious that some pressure had begun to tell on him.

"But what does confidential mean?" he insisted. "If you get subpoenaed to go to court, can they force you to tell them things I've said to you?"

"I'm not a lawyer. Maybe you should check with one. In Texas there is no psychiatrist-patient privilege in criminal cases. But will I testify about things you've told me? No."

Anne's posture made the statement believable. Schwinn studied her. Then he abruptly rose from his chair and paced the room. He grew angry suddenly. "Why should I tell you anything? Who says I have to?" He glared at her.

"I don't know. Why should you?" Anne said calmly. She had seen many people reach this point. They wanted to talk, they were about to break through, then suddenly questioned the whole premise of therapy. Why can't I just keep this to myself like I've always done? Anne would never say the answer. Instead she asked, "Why did you come here?"

Eric Schwinn returned to the chair. He grew apparently calmer. His left hand moved slowly, touching his lip, his earlobe. "You know I don't live in San Antonio anymore. And I don't really have a circle of people anymore. I mean, I know people. I've made friends." To his credit and Anne's great relief, he did not make air quotation marks with his fingers, but she heard them in what he said. "Get together for drinks, see people around. Last week I went to a birthday party. And sometimes they steer women toward me. I look like a good catch."

He looked steadily at her. After a long moment they smiled a little. They both realized he didn't need to tell her that.

"I've even—you know," he continued. "Had dates. Some great dates.

But it's all bullshit. Nothing's ever going to happen, because I'm an imposter. I'm not who they think I am. They think I'm this normal guy, carefree, easy laugh. Nobody knows that that's all fake. That inside . . ."

Anne waited to give him time to articulate a finish to his sentence. When it became clear he wouldn't, she said, "Eric. Everyone feels like that. There is no such thing as normal. Everybody on this planet feels likes a fraud. We all think, 'If everybody knew the truth about me, they'd never have anything to do with me again.' Don't you know that?"

She leaned forward compassionately. But the posture was wasted on Schwinn. He looked at her coldly. "As a matter of fact, I do know that. But that doesn't make me wrong, does it?"

Anne leaned back. Schwinn continued to stare, until he seemed to feel he had put her in her place. Then he began to speak again, slowly and coldly at first. "As it happens, I am a complete imposter. My name isn't Eric Schwinn. That's good enough, my real name wouldn't mean anything to you or to any of my 'friends' in Austin. I have a new identity because years ago I was involved in something. I was a police officer here in San Antonio. There was a scandal. Some officers were arrested, one killed himself, one went to prison."

Anne had grown very still again. She saw him watching her face for clues. She tried not to give any. But of course he was talking about Steve Greerdon.

"Did you know something about what had happened?" she asked.

"I knew everything. I wasn't involved, but people trusted me. When Steve got arrested, I skipped town. Made up a new name, got a different job. I didn't come back for the trial."

Anne nodded, looking wise and otherwise keeping her face impassive. She wouldn't condemn her patient overtly, but she understood his guilt. How could he live with himself? Letting his friend go to prison, when he could have stopped it. No wonder he suffered.

"I understand. You feel guilty because you didn't help your friend. But maybe your testimony wouldn't even have made a difference. At any rate, he's out now—"

"You don't understand." Schwinn put her in her place again, but not with a glare. He looked tired, as if he'd been up all night and it had just caught up to him. "I left because I didn't want to testify against Steve.

I would have put the last nail in his coffin. He *was* involved in that robbery. That's why I had to get away. I knew he was guilty."

Anne sat silent for a long moment, mulling over what she'd just been told. Then she said something she'd never said before during a therapy session. "Wow."

"Tell me about it," Eric Schwinn said, sounding self-satisfied. He had finally managed to prove to her that he wasn't like her other crazy patients, with their little problems.

"So you came back . . ." Anne said slowly.

"Because I figure Steve will want to tie up loose ends. And I'm one of them."

Anne continued to watch his face, while her mind raced. Schwinn looked relaxed now. He had shifted his burden to her.

"So what are you going to do?" she asked. "If you tell me you're planning a crime, that's not something I can keep secret. Besides, of course—"

"I'm not planning anything, except to try to stay alive. I just wanted somebody to know, in case something happens."

"So that's why you came to me?"

He shrugged. "I have enjoyed talking to you."

His secret had been an excuse to talk to a psychiatrist. He did have issues, as everyone does. What kind of person is willing to abandon his life completely and start over? Now he talked as if he were ready to start over again, shedding his new life like snakeskin. Anne guessed he wanted to explore himself.

Also, she imagined he knew her connection to Chris. He didn't want just anyone to know that he knew something incriminating about Steve Greerdon. He wanted someone who could get the information to someone who could do something with it.

Which she could do right now.

"You promised," he said, reading her mind. "That everything I say here is confidential."

"But Eric, I can help. I can—"

"He's already been pardoned for this crime, Anne. He can't be prosecuted for it again. It doesn't matter what I know about it."

She sat thinking. He watched her. Before Anne could speak again he said, "You promised, Anne. Everything I say to you is in confidence. I'm the one who gets to decide whether you can pass it on. I don't release you, unless I'm dead."

"All right," she said finally. Anne was thinking that she was treating Steve Greerdon's son. Now she knew more about Peter's father than Peter did. She couldn't reveal it to him, either.

She realized that silence had fallen for a while. Eric Schwinn sat at ease in his chair, smiling at her. "How about earning your money?" he said.

She had, whether he realized it or not. Coming to see Anne had worked a remarkable transformation in "Eric Schwinn." He sat looking rested and confident. Anne held up her pad and pen, indicating her willingness to listen.

Schwinn leaned back in his chair, put his hands behind his head, and stared half-lidded at a corner of the ceiling.

"The other night I had this dream. I was walking through some woods. It seemed like the trees were very tall. Then I realized that I was a raccoon."

Anne laughed. Schwinn smiled. She'd never had a relationship with a patient quite like this one.

Thursday night, about twenty-four hours after the killing, police went to Miguelito's and arrested Luisa Gaines for the murder of Chip Riley. The district attorney had to hear about it on the radio news Friday morning.

"Who?" Chris asked, once he had people in his office on another early morning. The radio report had been very sketchy, and the newspaper had had nothing, as the arrest had been made after the paper had been put to bed. "The owner of the restaurant where Chip Riley worked?"

"There was a lot more to it than that," Jack Fine said, and nodded toward Stephanie Valadez. Jack sat on the arm of the sofa, looking relaxed with a coffee cup. His youngest investigator stood tensely near him. Stephanie wore her usual black, but now it looked less authentic. She knew how far she had fallen. When her boss gave her the floor, she began talking quickly, sounding eager and nervous.

"Detective Riley spent more time at Miguelito's than he did working his shifts. He had worked there six years. Ms. Gaines has been the owner all that time. No one knew exactly what their financial arrangements were, but Riley acted like a part owner of the place. He was certainly the manager, not just there for security. And everyone assumed that he and Luisa Gaines had a romantic relationship."

"What happened the night he was killed?" Chris asked.

"They had a fight. A big one, two people said. It started in the restaurant, then they took it into the office. When he went outside for a smoke, she must have followed him."

" 'Must have'? Did anybody see her?"

Stephanie hesitated, and Jack stepped in to the pause. "You know how it is, Chris. Everybody was in the bathroom. A murder happens in one of these places, and these little closet-sized bathrooms were as crowded as a ladies' room at halftime of a Spurs game."

"I know," Chris said quietly but with force. He hadn't been criticizing the young investigator. It had been obvious the day before that Stephanie was beating herself up more than anyone else possibly could over having lost sight of Steve Greerdon just before the murder. She watched Chris now out of eyes unnaturally bright.

"When's the last time you slept?" he asked.

"When I heard about the arrest last night I went over there to see what I could find out. Nobody would talk to me, but I hung around just in case."

Chris wondered how she had "heard about" the arrest. Jack answered his unasked question. "Stephanie has a police scanner in her bedroom." When Chris gave him a look, Jack added quickly, "I'm just guessing. I haven't been there."

"Go home and get some sleep," Chris said to her.

She shook her head quickly. "I'll see what I can find out."

Chris shook his head more authoritatively. "Sleep. I need you rested and alerted. You may be up tonight when Jack and I are asleep in our nice warm beds." He turned his attention to his chief investigator. "Right now Jack and I have work to do."

They encountered some resistance getting to Luisa Gaines, as Chris had expected. He and Jack walked the few blocks to the downtown police station, reached the homicide offices without difficulty, then began to bog down as if they'd walked into a molasses swamp, their feet slowed, the air thick with impediments. People even seemed to speak more slowly up here on the third floor. "Ed, where's that suspect in Chip Riley's murder?" a young detective called across the room to an older, burlier man. "You take her back down to the holdover?"

"Not me," Ed answered. "She's still in interrogation room three as far as I know."

"I'll go check, sir," the young detective said. He had an earnest, tanned, barely lined face, and a helpful manner that didn't at all disguise the hostility in his eyes.

"I'll come with you," Chris said.

Again, that slowness intervened. The young detective hesitated. He glanced at Jack, who stood with his hands in his pockets looking unobtrusive, but still had an air of familiarity with this room. Without an answer, the detective turned and left the room, walking down a white corridor with Chris and Jack following. They passed windows into small rooms, all of them empty and dim. The third window on the right looked into an equally uninhabited interview room.

"Hmm," the detective said. "I guess they finished with her."

He stood without offering any suggestion. Chris said, "I'd like to talk to her myself. She's still in the building, isn't she?"

"Probably down in holdover," the detective said, not moving.

"Would you check, please?"

"She's probably asleep. May not want to talk to you. And if she doesn't—"

"I know the rules, Detective. I'll go down and ask her myself."

Chris took a step, and the young officer blocked his way. "I'll check."

He still looked at Chris coldly, and stood right in front of him as if to provoke a fight. Chris stared back at him tightly and said, "Are you mad at me about something, Detective?"

Jack said neutrally, "He wonders what you're doing here poking your nose into a police investigation."

Chris continued talking to the young detective. "You think this woman killed your colleague, right? Do you want to see her punished? There's only one person who can do that. You can arrest her eighty-five times, but unless I decide to prosecute her, she's a free woman. I'm sorry about Chip Riley, but it's my case. I'm going to put it together myself."

The detective looked unimpressed, but he lost some of his languor. He walked down the hall to a wall phone, spoke a couple of sentences into it, and called back down the hall, "They're bringing her up."

He started to turn away, and Chris asked, "Who's interrogated her already?"

"That would have been the night detectives who arrested her, sir. They've gone off duty. Ed and I just came on."

"I want a log of everyone who spoke to her last night."

"We don't keep a sign-in sheet, sir," the young detective said, and turned and left.

"They've had an eight-hour head start on us," Chris said. Jack nodded.

One reason for arresting a suspect late at night, or even getting him out of bed, is that he's tired. She, in this case. Police had arrested Luisa Gaines at the end of a long day of working in her restaurant, when her alertness would be gone, she'd be ready for sleep. The night officers would have been fresh, and could relieve each other while talking to her. Sometimes a suspect confessed just out of anxiety to have it over with. The urge to confess seemed strongest in the dead of night—and when a suspect was alone with a police officer.

"Anybody with a badge could have gotten to her by now," Chris continued. "Promised her anything, threatened . . ."

"Threatened her with something worse than prison?" Jack asked.

Chris stared down the hall, waiting. Yes, there were worse things than prison. Or more immediate, at any rate. Chris waited impatiently.

★

A uniformed officer appeared at the end of the hall fifteen minutes later, leading a handcuffed woman by the arm. They had taken her clothes, she wore a white jumpsuit, but someone had let her keep her black high heels, which looked very incongruous under the cuffs of the jail uniform. Her dark hair was tangled, her lipstick almost gone, her eye makeup very tired.

"Luisa Gaines?" Chris asked.

She just looked at him. Chris asked the uniformed officer, "Do you know if she's already given a statement?"

"Yes," the woman said suddenly. "Three. So can I go to sleep now?"

Chris looked her over and said casually, "Sure, if that's what you want. I'm Chris Sinclair, the district attorney . . ."

"I know."

"These police officers have arrested you for the murder of Chip Riley. They must have evidence against you. Maybe you've even confessed—"

She shook her head, to Chris's secret relief. He could still bargain with her.

"—but I'm the one who decides whether you're going to be prosecuted, and for what. So I want to talk to you myself. This is your chance to convince me, without anybody between us. But if you'd rather go back to your cell, or talk to a lawyer first, that's your right."

Gaines looked at him for several seconds, more and more searchingly, appearing to wake up as she studied Chris. Then she said listlessly, "Okay."

Jack motioned to the officer, who led the woman into one of the interrogation rooms, turned up the lights, and said, "I'll be right outside." Then he left the three of them in the room.

From this side, the window was a mirror, now that the lights were on. The uniformed officer could be watching. He could have called someone else by this time.

"This isn't the best place to talk," Luisa Gaines said ironically. A microphone sat on the table near her, and at the other end of the room there was a slot through which a videocamera could record.

"I know," Chris said. "But I don't think they're recording. If they are, I won't use it." He sat at the table. Gaines was at the end, he was on her left side. "Can we get you anything? Water? Coffee?"

Gaines smiled tiredly. "Eggs Benedict are my favorite. Hash browns on the side. But only after a good night's sleep."

Chris smiled in appreciation. Jack remained standing. He walked over close to the mirrored window, his back to Luisa Gaines, possibly blocking the view of somebody outside. Gaines suddenly leaned forward, close to Chris. "I don't mean this isn't a good place to talk just because of the recording equipment. I mean the police station. Why don't you get me to your office?"

"I will, later. Just a couple of quick questions this morning. How many officers questioned you?"

She shook her head tiredly. "Five, six? Any one that even spoke to me? Could have been twice that many."

Jack turned and looked over his shoulder. He seemed to have heard Chris's internal sigh. That's what he'd feared.

Staring at the back of her head, Jack said, "They say you killed Chip Riley."

Gaines turned and looked at him with an expression of ironic study. She dismissed Jack and turned back to Chris. "So which of you is the good cop and which one is bad? Who's going to be my friend?"

Chris had a sudden urge to play the scene for comedy, but suppressed it. "Nobody," he said. "I'm here because I just heard about your arrest and I wanted to talk to you as soon as I could. This is the only time you and I will get to talk directly. The next time we see each other, you'll have a lawyer. We'll probably be in court. Before that happens, I have to decide whether I'm going to prosecute you. Let me tell you, I will. I'll have a case. That's guaranteed."

Luisa Gaines sat up, beginning to look nervous. "They're setting me up. I'm being framed."

Chris didn't answer, just stared at her impassively. Jack intervened again. "If that's true, they'll do a good job of it. They know what he needs to get a conviction—" Nodding toward Chris. "—and they'll give it to him. A weapon, motive, the right timing. Probably somebody who saw you do it."

"But they can't. I didn't."

"Convince me," Chris said. "That's what I'm saying, this is your one chance."

"What do you mean? How can I prove something didn't happen?"

"That's not what I mean. Convince me that the other thing you said is true. You say you're being framed. Why?"

Gaines's mouth opened, then closed. Her eyes had become very bright. Chris saw the calculations going on behind her eyes.

"Don't think about it. Just tell me. Why would they frame you? Why do they want to get rid of you, or who are they trying to protect?"

"I don't know."

"We're almost done. When I walk out of here, it'll be to go back to my office and wait for the police to finish putting together a nice, tight case against you. Here's my last question: If you don't know why, then who? What police officer threatened you or promised you something?"

This time she didn't answer at all. Her calculations continued.

"Try to think clearly," Chris said calmly. "You want me to believe you're being set up by police officers. Am I just supposed to take your word for it? Give me something to investigate. Tell me what Chip Riley was into. Why did they want to get rid of him and you, too?"

"I don't know," she answered. Stubbornness had crept into her voice. "I just know I didn't kill him."

Chris stood up. "You can't tell me you're being framed and give me nothing else. If you think that, then you must have a good idea why. Or you know who's doing it."

"I don't know," she said quickly. Her tongue came out to touch her upper lip.

Jack leaned toward her. "Was Chip into something you knew about? You think that's why somebody wants to get you out of the way?"

They both saw her urge to speak, but then saw her hold back.

"I understand," Chris said gently. "This is your only chip, and you don't want to play it too soon. But listen to me. This is the only chance you're going to have. I'm your only hope."

She grabbed his hand. "Listen." He leaned down close to her. Gaines whispered. "Get me out of here. I can pretend to make a deal with them. I can pass it on to you."

She was talking quickly, but stopped when Chris shook his head sympathetically. "You don't understand, do you? Nobody's going to talk to you now. You've already gotten as deep into their organization as you're going to get. There's somebody out there, yes, but you won't ever see his face. The only thing you can tell me is what you already know."

But then her account would be empty. She would have given Chris everything, and would have to trust him to follow through. Luisa Gaines couldn't make that decision at eight o'clock in the morning, after a night of no sleep. Her life had taught her to hold on to secrets. They were currency. You didn't give them up just because a boyish-faced stranger talked nicely to you.

Chris gave up his study of her and walked to the door. "Wait!" Gaines called, whirling around. "You wouldn't do it. You won't charge me with murder if you don't think I did it."

"I won't just charge you, I'll prosecute you personally. You won't be the first innocent person I've convicted. It's not nearly as tough as you think."

His voice was flat. He walked out the door. In the dim hallway outside, the officer who had escorted the prisoner up from holdover lounged against the far wall, looking indifferent. The sound from the recording equipment could be piped to another room. Other officers Chris hadn't seen could have been listening to his brief conversation with Luisa Gaines.

Jack emerged too. Chris thanked the police officer and they walked out, through the homicide offices and into the main corridor. Jack stopped and seemed to listen, breathing in the life of the police station. He looked alert, not nostalgic, but Chris knew he missed the place, and the life.

"In spite of everything," Jack said, "I still believe that most of the people in this building do their jobs. Work hard and try to do the right thing. Almost all of them."

"I do too," Chris said. "The problem is . . ."

"Yeah."

They walked down the old, hard, heel-scuffed stairs, feeling observed. They didn't speak again until they were a block away.

That afternoon Clarissa drove her yellow Volkswagen to the entrance of the condo complex, punched in the access code, and after the gate pulled back drove in and parked in her assigned space. She lifted her backpack out of the back seat and got out, locking the car behind her. It was December, but not cold. Clarissa wore red shorts and a light jacket. She'd had a workout after school and felt good. Her blond ponytail bounced as she walked, the backpack hanging from one shoulder.

She didn't see anyone as she crossed the courtyard below her father's second-floor condominium. Clarissa made an exercise unit of the stairs, almost dancing up them, back down a few steps backwards, then all the way to the top. She had no idea how young she was, because she was the oldest she'd ever been. Early in life Clarissa had broken through the barrier between children and adults. She'd had responsibilities and worries. So she hadn't suffered what most teens did, the constant irritation of being thought a child while feeling ready to break out. Her mother had taught her that it was all a game. Her father was showing her otherwise, but Clarissa retained some of her mother's attitude. She took some things very seriously, but not necessarily the things people told her were important.

And on days like this she just felt good.

The shortest day of the year was approaching, the sun was already behind the buildings, creating a false twilight in the courtyard. Here and there darts of sunlight reflected in, giving the lie to the illusion. Clarissa looked down at the pond, shadowed by leaves floating on its surface, and felt unsettled for a moment. Then she went inside the condo and was surprised to find her father sitting on the couch in the living room.

"Hello, baby," he said quietly.

His tone of voice disturbed Clarissa. He sounded very affectionate, but also nostalgic, as if a phase of life were ending. Clarissa had had a lot of changes in her life. She thought she was used to them. But suddenly anxiety began to creep up as a coldness in her chest. "What's the matter?"

Chris stood up from the couch and smiled. He didn't say, Nothing. He gave her that much credit. Clarissa walked to meet him. Chris put his arms around her. Again, this wasn't an everyday experience, and felt like farewell.

"Don't you wish we had a house?" he said suddenly, stepping away from her and looking around the long main room of the condominium.

"Wouldn't you like to come home to a house, with a back yard, and neighbors?"

"And a swing set, and a puppy?" Clarissa laughed. Chris sometimes suffered pangs of remorse for having missed her childhood. "I like it here."

He had no idea. When Chris had found her she'd been living in a house with her mother, attending a suburban high school. He must still believe that had been her normal life, even though he knew better. Clarissa had lived more than a dozen places in her first fifteen years. She couldn't remember them all. There had been several memorable nights in children's shelters, huddled with her sister. Many of her accommodations had included other people, some of whom never got introduced to her. Nights in the car, sometimes traveling in what felt like flight, sometimes parked on a dark street. Very seldom had her life featured a house and a yard and sidewalks. She felt no longing for that life. She liked the condominium complex, the feeling of being surrounded by layers of normality between her and the street.

"I like having the pool," she continued. "Being able to walk to the grocery store and the video store. I like going up and down stairs." She grinned, recovering some of her good mood.

She was a wonderful girl. Chris felt terribly proud of her. And frightened for her. Putting his hand on her shoulder, he said, "I want you to go away for a little while. Go stay with your grandparents. I know it's hard, in the middle of your senior year, but I'll bring you back as soon as I can."

Her mouth pursed into a tiny opening, and her eyes looked haunted. "What have I done wrong?"

"Nothing, darling. It's not you. It's the business we talked about. The police. They've arrested somebody now for that murder of a police officer. I don't know what's going on. Somebody I don't know is going to be trying to put pressure on me. The best way is through you. I don't want to take any chances."

Clarissa felt a gush of relief. Warmth replaced the coldness in her chest. She smiled at him. "I won't go away."

His voice became uncharacteristically stern. "This is what I've decided, Clarissa. I hope it won't be for long, but for right now—"

She shook her head, speaking very seriously but in an almost lighthearted tone. "If you put me on an airplane I'll get off at the other end and hitchhike back. Or I'll stay with them for a day or two then run away while they think I'm at school. I'll get a job or steal the money and take a bus back here. You can't make me stay somewhere else. You can send me to South America and I'll find my way back. You know I can do it."

"I want you to be safe."

"I wouldn't be safe anywhere else. Only here with you."

She wouldn't ask him, but her desire was apparent in her posture, in the urgency growing in her voice, in the wetness of her shining eyes. Chris held her shoulders. She was trembling, but not out of fear.

She laughed. "At least here, if they frame me for something, I'm pretty sure the district attorney won't prosecute me."

Chris hugged her. There were ways around what she had said, and false accusation was far from the worst thing that could happen. But Clarissa was right, he would feel easier in his mind if she were close to him in the coming ordeal. "All right, baby," he said. "We'll just have to be very careful."

Clarissa nodded against his shoulder. Besides, she thought, she had to be here. Somebody had to keep *him* safe.

CHAPTER

seven

★ But Chris had another exposed flank. Anne. She stayed in his thoughts a lot—not that she didn't often preoccupy him at normal times. Anne was involved in this. She was treating Steve Greerdon's son. People might think she knew something. People might also think Chris's greatest vulnerability was through her.

Of course, Anne wouldn't stop treating Peter just because he asked her to stop, or because there might be danger in it. She certainly wouldn't go away for a while. In fact, she undoubtedly wouldn't do anything he asked her to do to make herself safer, such as stop seeing him for a while.

Damn women. Chris had a staff of more than two hundred people, almost all of whom would do exactly what he told them, as fast as they could. Many of them even tried to anticipate his wishes. But he had zero control over the two people who were most important to him. Funny thing.

Also intervening between him and this most important trial was an international holiday. The year was almost over, halfway through its last month, and the courthouse would virtually shut down very soon. Its revival in January would be sluggish and half-hearted. Chris could work, but he couldn't push this case to trial as fast as he wanted.

One day at lunchtime he walked through Rivercenter Mall, a few blocks from the Justice

Center. He wore an overcoat and felt like a spy, slipping furtively through the crowds of shoppers, some of them from out of town, almost all of them happy. Chris felt out of place, disguised. Yes, he had gifts to buy too. But much darker business held his thoughts. He felt watched all the time, not necessarily by some skulking underworld figure, but by normal people, looking at him and thinking, What's *that* man up to?"

He walked on the "fashion level" of the mall, past smaller, boutique-type stores. He went into a couple, but nothing held his attention, for either Clarissa or Anne. Sweaters. Yeah. They'd get maybe two months' of use in San Antonio, then spend months on a shelf. Blouses. Would Anne wear this? Would she wear it just on days when she'd see him, like a brooch her child had made in preschool?

Giving up and heading toward a jewelry store, he walked past the windows of a national chain store of women's intimate wear. He glanced at the photos of models, of course. Chris passed the store, blinked, and turned around and went back. Why not? Anne would look good in this. Or in that. It would be a gift on a whole new level, a subterranean one. No one else would ever know when she was wearing Chris's present. It wouldn't be displayed for anyone else's approval. And every time she wore it she would know he'd been thinking about her, thinking very specifically about her. It would be like touching her from a distance.

He walked in boldly. A pretty young woman smiled at him. Her name badge said "Caroline." Part of her job would be not to make him feel like a pervert. "Can I help you?"

"Not yet."

The rooms were small and light and airy, befitting the clothes. Nightgowns, bras, panties, more complicated undergarments that defied easy categorizing. First he had to decide on a type of clothing. He glanced through a rack and display of nightgowns, so wispy that their main material was imagination, but decided no, he wanted something Anne would wear during the day. That decision didn't make matters much simpler, though. There were rooms of bras and panties and merry-widow-type combinations. Red lace caught his eye, but he could imagine Anne's reaction to that. On the other hand, maybe she'd like that he'd thought her bolder than she usually was.

Another woman stood at his elbow, less young and less pale than the first. "Are you looking for a gift?"

He looked at her and they both laughed. The saleslady took him in hand. "Are you looking for something to wear under formal clothes, or for daily use?"

"Somewhere in between," Chris said. "Like with a business suit."

The woman nodded at him as if he'd said something very wise. "Women like that. Looking professional but feeling feminine. Over this way."

She showed him a nice selection of more conservative but still frilly sets, in colors from gray or black to floral-patterned. This of course started Chris wondering what the women he knew were wearing under their suits, or even the woman next to him. From her perpetual slight smile, she seemed to know this. "What's her coloring like? Closer to mine, or Ms. Wallace's at the front desk?"

That offered a wide gamut, since the saleslady was African-American and the other one looked like Norwegian wood. "Green eyes," Chris said. "Brown hair. Light brown. Pale skin but not whitewashed. The skin around her eyes is very light, because she wears sunglasses when she jogs. But her cheeks are pinkish, but also tanned, so they almost look orange at times. But in a good way. Her arms are brown but her shoulders are sort of taupe. And her chest has that sunset pink. But her natural color, like her stomach in March, before she's gone swimming at all, is—"

The saleslady, watching him studiously, held her breath. Chris cast around, through the colors of the store and in his mind, for the right phrase to describe what he pictured.

"—ivory. Not new ivory like you see in stores, and not like old piano keys, either. Not a hint of yellow. But as if you combined white and skipped right past yellow to the palest brown. Like a shade paler than beige, if beige weren't such a beige word. So I'd say she's . . ."

"Ivory," said the saleslady.

"Right, ivory. And when she blushes—which isn't very often—it goes all the way down to her chest."

The saleslady stared at him for a moment longer, imagining the hours of study that had allowed such a precise description, then recovered herself and said, "All right. Let's see what we have for a blotchy lady." But she said it in a kindly way, as if they both knew Anne well and wanted to please her. "What size?"

Chris was brought up short. He had no idea. "Let's try to estimate," the lady helping him said helpfully. "How tall is she?"

He described Anne some more, picturing her, which made him want to see her. His thoughts began to drift out of this fantasy store to Anne herself.

"Full-figured?" the saleslady asked. "Or more sleek?"

They had wonderful words for every body type. But Chris suddenly felt skittish. This was a delicate business. He didn't want to get something too small, and damned sure not too big. Even guessing Anne's dimensions exactly might seem insulting. He imagined Anne returning his gift to this store, holding something up to her chest, and sharing a laugh with the women salespeople. "Imagine what he thinks of me!"

Nevertheless, he boldly made a purchase. Ms. Wallace rang it up for him, her smile cooler, perhaps used to discouraging men from speculating about *her* secret life. Men who had brought themselves to make a purchase would feel such relieved expansiveness that they would be prone to that kind of thing. But Chris just gave her a smile as tight-lipped as her own, signed his credit card receipt, and carried his pink-and-white bag out into the mall, to find Steve Greerdon waiting for him.

Greerdon lounged back against a railing across the walkway. Behind him an atrium, a large open space, fell all the way to the river level, three stories below. A little push, a loss of balance, and Steve Greerdon could go hurtling down, no more problem to anyone. An engineer had anticipated this possibility, though, so that a wall of heavy clear plastic blocked the atrium, which made lounging back against the railing not such a daredevil act.

Chris walked straight across to him, making no pretense that this was a coincidental meeting at Christmastime in the mall. Greerdon looked bulky and protected in a heavy jacket. Big white tennis shoes encased his feet. He looked like a tourist, except for the focused expression on his face.

"Are you following me?" Chris asked without a greeting.

"Nah. I spend every day looking into the windows of this place, waiting for them to change the displays." He glanced down at Chris's pink and white bag with its thin twine handles, then back up into Chris's eyes, with a hint of amusement. Chris didn't take the bait, either to say something oblique about Anne or to return a comradely little half-smile-half-smirk. So Greerdon laid off. Instead he said, "You let me down."

"What the hell does that mean? I haven't done anything yet."

"You were supposed to keep me under constant surveillance. I wasn't supposed to have to worry that something would happen and I wouldn't have an alibi."

"You deliberately shook off my investigator."

"By walking down a street. I wasn't being real shifty. I expected her to follow me around the block."

"Somebody stopped her."

"Yeah. That's what concerns me. They wanted me alone when I walked in there."

Chris's eyes narrowed. "Walked in where?"

"To the loading area behind the restaurant. Where I was supposed to meet Chip Riley at eleven."

Chris stood without replying. This was news. His investigator hadn't known this. Police reports hadn't given it to Chris either. But some police officers might have known. Must have. Why had the undercover officer been there? And the evidence team arriving so quickly . . .

"Yeah," Steve Greerdon said again. "You want to go somewhere and talk?"

Ten minutes later they sat at a table on the Riverwalk. The wrought iron chairs were cold as a witch's touch, and the coffee had grown cool by the time the waiter got it to their table, but the place had the virtue of privacy. The few passersby hunched their shoulders and hurried by, frowning at having pursued the sun to San Antonio and found it missing. Chris's pink and white bag sat on the table between them, because the sidewalk at their feet was damp from the spray the wind threw off the river. Chris set the bag down boldly, as if he were such a tough guy he could have been wearing pink himself. On the walk from Rivercenter he had spotted Stephanie Valadez following them, and had waved her in closer. At first she shook off his signal like a big-league pitcher, but when he and Steve Greerdon took a table she sat at the one next to them, within earshot. Stephanie showed the cold, her face barely visible under a navy blue cap with earflaps pulled down. Native San Antonian, no doubt. She ignored Chris's shopping bag more assiduously than anyone else.

Steve Greerdon began abruptly. "I was in the place earlier and Chip talked to me for a minute, then asked me to come back at eleven and meet him out back. He had something he wanted to tell me."

"Did he say what?"

"No. Not a hint. Except he knew something about who'd set me up."

"That would be sure to bring you back. Do you think he was just making it up?"

"I don't know," Greerdon said honestly. "He certainly sounded like he meant it. He was a little drunk."

"His blood alcohol level when he died was point one five." Just about double the new level of legal intoxication in Texas.

Greerdon shrugged. "That was just a day at the office for Chip. His was probably point six when he woke up every morning."

"So he asked you to come back. Anybody else know about this meeting?"

Greerdon shrugged again. "Only if Chip told them. And I don't think he would. He acted awful sneaky about it."

"Unless he was making it all up," Chris said. "Maybe he was luring you in himself. Or thought he was. Maybe somebody had asked him to get you into that alley late at night."

Greerdon nodded. He had already considered this possibility. In fact, he must have thought of it early on. That's why he had circled the block to come at the meeting site from the opposite direction, and to look around for hidden watchers.

"Maybe that's why the undercover was there," Greerdon said. "Waiting for me."

"He says he was watching the four men Ms. Valadez saw coming out of the restaurant. He was on duty at the time, and that was his assignment. Three of the four men did have drug records."

"Anybody coming out of Miguelito's that time of night would be worth watching," Greerdon said.

"And he said he tackled me because he thought I was about to blow the surveillance," Stephanie said suddenly. She remained hunched and shivering. Chris wanted to tell her to dress more warmly.

"You believe him?" Greerdon asked. He waited watchfully for Stephanie's answer, according her the respect of a fellow professional. For a moment it occurred to Chris that Greerdon and Stephanie might have developed a bond over the last weeks, as hostages and kidnappers sometimes did.

"No," Stephanie said flatly. "But it could be true. I'll tell you one thing. He didn't seem to be expecting those shots. And when I found the body, he looked very surprised."

"Maybe just surprised it was Chip Riley," Chris said. "Maybe he was expecting to find our friend here face down back there."

"Killed by who?" Greerdon said. His shoulders moved, shrugging off the image of his death. "By Chip? Nobody would've given him an assignment like that, especially that late at night. Anybody who knew him knew he spent evenings drinking."

"Maybe that wasn't his job. His job was just to get you there."

"Then why was he still there?"

Chris said, "I'd say he screwed up. Just a guess."

Greerdon switched to the practical, to logistics. "Then who was there to do him? But then didn't go past Stephanie one way or me the other."

Stephanie spoke up for the first time in minutes. "Maybe it was just what it looked like. A domestic dispute. He and Luisa Gaines hadn't been getting along very well lately, I can tell you that from talking to people."

The two men considered her idea. Then Chris asked Steve Greerdon a question. "Did you see anything?"

It was odd that no one seemed to have asked him this question before. Greerdon was the secret witness, not interviewed by the police, unacknowledged. He shook his head slowly. "I must have just missed it. As I was getting close to the area I heard a shot. I ran up to the corner where I could see around the fence, and I saw Chip stagger and fall. It looked like he had just tripped. But I know a gunshot when I hear one. I think maybe I saw the back door of the restaurant closing, but I'm not positive of that. I didn't stay to look for clues, either. As soon as I saw what had happened, I thought it was a setup. Somebody was about to grab me and stick a gun in my hand. I ran. I turned around and ran back the way I'd come. Ran all the way to my car and went home. Spent the night waiting for a knock at the door."

"But they never came," Chris said.

Greerdon shook his head again. "Never did. Instead they've brought you Luisa Gaines."

Chris nodded. He looked over at Stephanie. She was sitting forward now, watching Steve Greerdon closely. She seemed less cold than she had been.

"I don't get it," Greerdon said simply. "Why her? What good does that do anybody?"

Chris sat back, against the cold wrought iron. "Maybe she's just guilty, like Stephanie said. Maybe they arrested the right person."

Greerdon laughed a small snort of sourness. Obviously he hadn't considered that possibility.

Chris sat watching him, and watching his investigator watch him. He would have liked Stephanie's opinion of Greerdon's trustworthiness, but didn't think she'd give it.

"I don't trust anything I'm told," Chris said. "Especially by police. And that's who's going to be making my case for me. I could use your help."

Greerdon sat staring at the moody green river. Then he glanced at Stephanie, as if asking her permission. He nodded abruptly. To Stephanie he said, "And you're going to stick close to me, right?"

She didn't answer, or need to. The determination in the stare she leveled at him answered his question clearly enough.

★

At four thirty Clarissa pulled the yellow Volkswagen to a stop beside the decorative boulder where Peter sat. He had his backpack packed and closed, having been watching her since she'd emerged from the gym. As he put his pack in the back seat, Peter noticed a couple of boys watching him. Trying to look enormously casual, he climbed into the front seat beside her, putting his hand on her seat an inch from her shoulder as he did.

Clarissa smiled at him. "Sorry I'm late."

She had showered and changed after volleyball practice, and smelled very fresh. Peter felt grungy. Nevertheless, he had his nerve up. After they had driven a few blocks and there was a lull in the conversation, he said, "Uh, listen, there's something I should have told you. Last week when you dropped me off, I left some grass in your backpack."

"You did," Clarissa said, with a slight accent on the first word. She turned to look at him, not smiling. Peter grinned big enough for both of them. The expression looked strange on his face.

"Maybe as long as we're just driving, you know, we could—share some." He pulled some rolling papers out of his shirt pocket and let her see them.

Clarissa barely glanced at the innocuous pink package. She kept her hands firmly on the steering wheel and stared straight ahead. Peter couldn't see her expression, which also was uncharacteristic on her normally lively face. She had gone perfectly flat. Clarissa had fled, into the past.

At her old school she had been one of the bad kids: the queen of them, in fact. Clarissa had the impulses and made the plans; the others trailed in her wake. She rode in the late night cars so cloudy you didn't have to smoke the passing joint; just breathe. At school Clarissa laughed when nothing funny had been said, taking the attention of any room she wanted in a way that couldn't draw a reprimand, just by tossing her hair and smiling to herself. Everyone would know mischief was afoot.

Peter had been one of the watchers who'd known her as queen. Her life must have seemed exotic and wild to him. It had been. Clarissa had forgotten. She didn't dwell on the past. But the sight of the cigarette papers brought it all back, in a rush of sensation that raised goosebumps on her forearms and made her feel soiled and sad and not to be trusted.

"No, thanks," she said.

Her voice was flat. Peter looked surprised, then confused. Looking down, Clarissa saw something besides the rolling papers. She saw Peter's hand close to her bare leg. Inwardly, she sighed. How stupid she'd been. You couldn't just pick up a boy and make friends with him. Even if you felt sorry for him, even if he knew that, eventually he'd think something else too. Clarissa had been the leader of the party crowd. Peter must have been remembering too.

She turned off McCullough and pulled the car to the curb of a residential street.

"You mean not with me," Peter said.

She glanced at his face and saw his confusion had turned to anger. In another minute she might have to push him out of the car. Clarissa slumped forward, forehead touching the steering wheel. "I quit all that," she said in a deadened voice.

Peter didn't answer. Clarissa continued. "I wanted a new start at Berkshire, Peter. I wanted to make myself over again. It was my choice. Not my father's, not anybody else's. I didn't want to be that girl anymore. When I saw you it reminded me of the good times, and I managed not to think about all the bad stuff. I'm sorry, I shouldn't have . . ."

Her voice trailed off, because any way she could express her regrets would probably sound insulting to him.

Now she would have to withdraw from him, let him know he'd read everything wrong. They would both feel bad every time they saw each other. Maybe one of them would have to transfer again. A few minutes ago she'd felt great, skin glowing, humming some tune. She had forgotten that in any given minute life could turn on you, make any day awkward and awful.

When she looked up, Peter's head had fallen back against the headrest. He no longer looked mad or like a seducer, clumsy or otherwise. He looked more slack-faced than Clarissa had a moment earlier. "That wasn't why I did it," he said, in such a mumble his lips barely moved.

"What?"

"That wasn't why I put the dope in your backpack."

She didn't say anything because she didn't know what to say, but Peter seemed to realize her attention remained fastened on him. His voice gaining some tone—a sad one with a memory of apprehension—he continued, "I saw my stepfather's car in the driveway. I didn't want to go inside with the dope in my bag. Sometimes he searches my backpack. I mean, like as soon as I get inside the door. Not every time, but I never know when it's going to happen. If he had found that—well, he's a cop, you know."

There was much more to it than that. Clarissa remembered the bruise on Peter's chin a couple of weeks ago. It had faded, but the bruised look in his eyes hadn't. She had also observed the tension in Peter every time they drew close to his house. Even if she'd managed to make him laugh earlier in the drive, he began to take on a defensive posture by the time he got home.

He glanced at her, embarrassed and afraid of her reaction. He drew in his legs, ready to grab the door handle and get out.

Clarissa looked at him sympathetically, but also with a similar embarrassment. "I'm sorry," they said simultaneously.

The sentence had a funny, echo-y resonance in the confines of the small car, as if they had burst into deliberate harmony. Then they both laughed.

They laughed longer than any witticism deserved. Peter bent his head and shook it and laughed a high-pitched giggle. Clarissa's shoulders shook. After a long minute they looked at each other and rolled their eyes and shrugged and laughed again.

Things could change that quickly. "I don't need my therapy session now," Peter said, and they both laughed again.

Somehow the papers had disappeared from his hand. Clarissa put the car in gear, thinking that she needed to tell her father something to ease his paranoia, but knowing that she wouldn't. It wasn't her secret to give away.

Peter's hands were back on his thighs, nowhere near hers. They started chatting again as Clarissa drove them downtown. Things seemed fairly easy again, with only their routine awkwardness, but Clarissa wasn't fooled. Their relationship had changed. Peter had revealed himself. She would have to be very careful. But she'd known that already. It didn't matter, though. She couldn't drop him now. Like an injured bird, once you'd picked it up you couldn't put it down again. It had become yours, until it could fly again.

Chris waited. Luisa Gaines didn't send him any messages. She hired a lawyer, a good one. The lawyer didn't call Chris, either. December waned. Chris managed to put the case out of his mind and finish his shopping. Clarissa was busy too, even after school ended. Chris watched her for signs of holiday sadness, but Clarissa seemed happy. Maybe Christmas hadn't been such a joyous time in her mother's households. Or maybe it had, and Clarissa refused to remember. The child had more mental discipline than anyone Chris had ever known.

One night Clarissa had a party and Chris had a date. Clarissa's party was at her friend Angelina's house and Clarissa was spending the night there afterward, so Chris could have a great date if things went well. It felt odd getting ready in the same condo with Clarissa, but less odd than it had felt six months earlier. She settled on a pair of jeans, then tried on sweater after sweater, in different combinations with blouses. Clarissa didn't overtly ask Chris's opinion, but she did step out of her bedroom with every try. He expressed enthusiasm over almost every outfit—not *every* one, that would have destroyed his credibility, and he tried to remain true to Clarissa's taste, not his own. After a few changes, Clarissa herself seemed to be changing along with her clothes. She came out in a holiday sweater smiling broadly, looking like one of Santa's helpers. For a subtler blue and gray number Clarissa looked pensive, her eyes bluer. In her next outfit, a severely-cut yellow, she looked older, ready to take her place in the professional world. Clarissa stared at him somberly, and Chris shook his head. She smiled in apparent agreement.

Chris had seen her mother Jean do this: try on moods, take a personality for a test drive. Her every persona had seemed perfectly sincere, but after seeing five of them in a minute how could Chris believe in any of them? How could he have trusted Jean at all? Yet he had.

He saw the same changeability in Clarissa, sometimes even more strongly—she was a teenager, after all—but in Clarissa Chris sensed more, a true center that she kept hidden most of the time and from almost everyone. Chris usually thought of this secret creature within his daughter as a child wanting protection, but it could have been something else entirely.

As the fashion parade continued Chris put on his tuxedo. The same tuxedo he had worn on his first date with Anne. The district attorney and Dr. Greenwald had yet another formal occasion. But he dressed with special care. Clarissa noticed, coming over to the living room mirror to give the final tug to his tie. Her head came above his shoulder. In the mirror they looked very much related. Clarissa smiled at him and seemed suddenly to have resolved the clothing dilemma. She looked like a schoolgirl: an especially pretty one, but not especially experienced or daring. Chris kissed her forehead and hugged her.

In the car he asked, "Is Peter Greerdon coming to this party?"

"I don't think so. He's just a sophomore, Dad, he hasn't worked his way up to this level yet."

"Do you have a date meeting you there?"

Clarissa shook her head, making her hair revolve. "It isn't a couples party."

She spoke offhandedly, but he didn't entirely believe her answer. At Clarissa's age most parties *would* be couples' parties, whether intentionally or not. He didn't press the inquiry, though. Clarissa seemed to have a problem with the idea of becoming a member of a couple. It was a problem Chris didn't mind.

Angelina's house burst with light. There didn't seem to be any guests yet, but Clarissa was the cohost, so earliness was appropriate. "Call me," Chris said, patting the pocket where he kept his cell phone, and Clarissa ran in happily. Chris watched her inside, looked around the street, didn't see any cars obviously keeping watch on the house, and so drove on to Anne's.

"Oh! You're early."

"I know," Chris said, standing on Anne's porch in tuxedoed splendor, holding a gift-wrapped box. "I came to help you get ready."

Anne was made up, but wore a white terry-cloth robe. Her hair was trapped more formally than usual, but not beaten into full submission. She smiled down at the box he carried. "Corsage?"

"Not this time."

She let him in and they kissed as they slipped past each other in the doorway. A light greeting kiss, the kind exchanged by people who've been intimate a long time. But Chris stood there a moment looking at her, until Anne laughed and pushed him into the living room.

This room was small and felt homelike to Chris, though not everyone would have thought so. The sofa and chairs had exposed blond-wood legs, giving them the somewhat transient look of a college room, as if they could walk away. But a wall of photos and keepsakes anchored the room, along with two tall bookcases filled to overflowing. Chris loved the room.

He took Anne's hand and they sat on the couch, she with a slyly curious look, as if she had some idea what he was up to, but didn't have all the details. "I brought you a present," Chris said, putting the box in her lap.

She made no move to open it. "Why?"

"This is the first night of Hannukah."

"Is it really?"

"Anne, I saw it on the calendar in your bathroom."

"You found my Jewish Day-by-Day calendar? Damn, now I have to kill you. Next you'll be learning our code words and secret rituals."

"Stop stalling and open the present."

She did it as greedily as a child, not making a slow-motion striptease out of the process. In a moment she had pulled the lid off the shirt-size white box and drawn back the tissue paper. Then she stopped, genuinely surprised. "Oh, my," she said after a moment, lifting out the present. "I think you got your boxes mixed up. You must have meant this for your other girlfriend."

Chris shook his head. "I know you're embarrassed, but try to act like an adult. Tell me what you really think."

The bra and panties had seemed demure in the wild profusion of the store, but in Anne's hands, here in her grown-up-hippie living room, the fabric seemed to have left some of its tameness in the box. The bra was a blue verging toward gray, almost translucent. The devilishness was in the details of its construction and the small touches such as the fabric flowers along its edge.

Anne found the tag, read it and looked up at him almost accusingly. "How did you guess my size?"

"How do you think? One day while you were in the shower I pawed through your underwear drawer. I'm a trial lawyer, I don't guess."

In fact, Chris had chickened out the first time he'd gone to the store, and bought Anne something a little less personal. But a week later, armed with exact knowledge of her size, he had returned and boldly made this purchase. Now his boldness began to ebb away, though, as Anne continued to sit there without squealing with delight. "Do you like them?"

She nodded slowly, and had grown sly again when she looked up at him. "Were you hoping I'd model them?"

"Not just now. But I would like you to wear them tonight. I hope they go with what you've got picked out."

"Well, since I didn't plan to—Never mind." She stood up abruptly and walked to her bedroom, closing the door. Chris examined her book titles again, finding changes. It was more than ten minutes before Anne emerged, fully dressed, in an evening dress he had seen before, a deep royal blue, almost a sheath, but with a relaxed skirt. There was no indication whether she also wore Chris's gift. Chris complimented her with a stare, which Anne acknowledged with a nod. She took his arm, still without speaking, and they started out. But on the porch, after she had locked the door, she pulled his head down close to hers and whispered, "They feel wonderful."

The Foundation to Save Worthy Causes, or something, had its annual dinner at the country club at La Sonterra, on the outer loop, where the large ballroom sat beside a large terrace with wonderful views of the golf course and the hills behind. The elegantly dressed guests, who had paid a minimum of a hundred dollars a plate, so that the evening with its silent auction and corporate contributions raised more than a hundred thousand dollars, mingled with each other in a self-congratulatory manner that was well deserved. Chris and Anne separated, rejoined, found each other across the room. Neither afterward remembered anything that had been said to them. After drinks and dinner and speeches they danced. Neither Anne nor Chris was much of a dancer, either in the sense of being particularly good at it or especially enjoying it. That didn't matter. It was just an excuse to hold each other.

It should have been one of those movie scenes where they rose alone to the star-filled skies, leaving the crowd behind. They did. For long minutes they remained unaware of anyone except each other. People might have stared. A speaker at the podium might have been calling for quiet, or announcing that the building was ablaze. Anne and Chris finished the dance, she retrieved her purse from the table, and they said good night to a few people, whose names they could not afterward have recalled. "Time for the modeling," Anne murmured in his ear as they left.

Chris drove very carefully, both hands on the steering wheel.

He woke with her head on his stomach and her hand on the waistband of his white briefs. Anne heard the change in his breathing and turned her head to look at him. "I should get you a present now," she said. "You look so dull compared to me. What color would you like?"

She still wore half her present, and a languid smile. When he reached for her she pulled away, walked across the room and into the bathroom. A minute after he heard the shower go on, he joined her. Her skin wet, Anne was hard to hold, and she seemed to enjoy being elusive. *Body type sleek,* Chris thought, *though tending toward full-figured.* What term would the nice saleslady have for Anne's type? Maybe he should get a photograph now, and take it into the store next time.

Later they sat at the table, dressed for the day and having coffee, unspokenly trying to decide whether to go out for breakfast or stall a little while longer and make it lunch. Anne gripped his hand for a moment as she took a section of newspaper from under it. A minute later she had regained some of her professionalism, and her worries. No particular article produced this effect; just reading about the world brought her back to that world, and to Chris's problem.

"Are you really going to prosecute this woman for murder?" she asked offhandedly.

"Quite definitely. The indictment should come down this week."

"Because you think she's guilty, or because you think she knows more?"

Chris glanced at Anne for a moment, and shrugged. "Both, I guess. She could convince me she didn't do it, if she comes up with someone who did. Or who had reason to."

"But how can you believe any evidence the cops bring you? Knowing what you know?"

Chris gave her a longer look. They had talked about this before. Why was Anne so curious now? "I've got my own people I trust," he said. "I can check out some of it."

"What about this what's-his-name, who you got out of prison? What's his position?"

"He's certainly not on the police team. He has more motive than anyone I can think of for wanting to help me."

Anne watched Chris, hoping the word "motive" would trigger a chain of thoughts in his head. But she saw she'd have to help. "Really? So you think you can trust him?"

"I don't know. I don't, exactly. But I think he wants what I want. And I know he didn't commit this murder. I think he has more reason for finding who did than for trying to frame someone for it."

"Really? Why are you so sure he didn't do it himself?"

Chris looked at her with a little frown. Anne knew the frown meant he was wondering at her curiosity. She usually stayed out of his business, except to offer the occasional advice. Some of her insights had been very helpful. But she didn't intrude. She returned her attention to the newspaper, but felt Chris's continuing stare.

"Because he was so angry that my investigator hadn't kept up with him. He wanted to be sure he had an alibi. And he had no reason for killing Chip Riley. Chip was supposed to give him some information."

"And you know that because—?" Anne asked lightly. But not lightly enough to fool Chris. He didn't answer until she looked back at him.

"Do you know something I don't?" he asked levelly.

Anne shrugged, and tried to make an ignorant expression. It didn't work well on her face.

"You're treating Peter Greerdon, aren't you?" Chris said, though he knew the answer. Anne just looked back at him placidly, as if waiting for a question. He knew how seriously she took her patients' confidentiality.

In one incident, before his tenure as district attorney, she had gone to jail rather than violate that confidence. She wouldn't abuse it for love, either.

Chris sat thinking. What could Steve Greerdon's son have told Anne that would make her distrust Greerdon? Steve wouldn't have confessed anything to his son, and the boy had been only eight when his father had gone to prison. He certainly couldn't have seen anything back then. Could he have overheard something, then or more recently?

No. He couldn't know anything. Steve Greerdon would have been more careful than that. Probably young Peter mistrusted his father. Even hated him, perhaps. After all, he was a teenager, with a dominating parent. And he would blame his father for missing most of his childhood, whether Steve Greerdon could have helped that or not.

Anne identified with her patients, always. Peter's attitude would have infected hers. After all, she hadn't even seen Steve Greerdon face to face. Chris thought some more, then put the problem aside. Just another case of him coming at the same problem from a different direction than Anne took. Not uncommon, that.

From the corner of her eye, Anne saw Chris think about what she'd suggested, then dismiss her concern. She'd been afraid of that. But she couldn't be any more explicit. She couldn't say that a patient had told her that Steve Greerdon had committed a crime. The most she could do was what she'd just done, give Chris a hint at what he should think. It didn't seem to have worked this morning, but she hoped he'd keep returning to the problem.

Then she had a new thought. What if she'd given Chris just enough of an idea so that he *did* begin to mistrust Steve Greerdon? But he didn't have anything concrete to think. He couldn't possibly learn what Anne had, from her secret source Eric Schwinn. So Chris's suspicion could never be more than that. But what if it began to show in his attitude, in the way he treated Steve Greerdon, what he told him and didn't tell him? Would Greerdon begin to get the idea that Chris knew something about him? Anne hadn't met Steve Greerdon, but from Peter and Eric she had a good idea of what he was like. And she could figure out for herself how a man like that would feel about going back to prison. If he thought the district attorney suspected him of something, what might such a man do?

Anne had just screwed up. If she couldn't give Chris more, she should have given him less.

She would have to keep an eye on this trial.

CHAPTER *eight*

★ When Chris Sinclair walked the halls of the District Attorney's Office, the atmosphere changed. He knew this because he had spent years as an assistant district attorney himself, and knew the normal air of the place: casual, interrupted by spots of intensity as someone prepared for trial, but with a prevailing lightheartedness. Most of his assistants were very young people. They performed well, but needed frequent release as well.

The appearance of the district attorney reminded them of the need to impress. He could feel people move, or freeze in place. Acknowledging greetings with nods and smiles, he kept moving through the government-white halls, so that people could resume their normal lives.

One fine morning in February, Chris appeared in Bonnie Janaway's doorway. "No trial this week?" he asked casually.

Bonnie had been leaning back in her chair, staring up at the ceiling. At her boss's appearance she sat up a little, but made no pretense of being hard at work. Bonnie's dark hair was pushed behind her ears, and she wore a charcoal gray suit. She looked very professional and well organized. But there were three stacks of files on her desk and two cardboard evidence boxes in the corner, on a wheeled carrier she would take to court. She said, "We started one, then the defendant changed his mind and pled."

"Really? How soon?"

"At the morning break, halfway through our first witness."

Chris didn't have to pretend to look impressed. "Must have been a hell of a witness."

Bonnie smiled. "Personally, I think it was my opening statement that did it."

"I don't think I've ever seen an opening statement accomplish that."

Bonnie's smile grew broader. Obviously she wanted an audience for this. "I aimed it right at the defendant. I said the State would be asking for the maximum penalty for this brutal, unprovoked assault."

"Aggravated assault?"

"We were calling it attempted murder. He beat this guy up badly enough that I thought we could make an assumption he wanted to kill him. That's what our first witness said, anyway. While Brian proved what a beating it was, and that the defendant and the victim hadn't even exchanged any words before it started, I watched the defendant squirm."

Chris took a seat in the slat-backed, uncushioned office chair. "What was your secret?"

Bonnie leaned forward. "The two guys were best friends. They liked the same girl. And every time the three of them were together, the victim would slip it to his friend. How dumb he was, how lousy he'd been with other girls. And it finally worked, the victim got the girl and the defendant got mad."

Bonnie's voice grew more animated. "But what I knew, see, was that the defendant would never get to tell his story, how he felt justified. Because he had a couple of priors we'd impeach him with if he took the stand, his lawyer knew it, and he would never have let his client testify. So the poor guy had to just sit there and take it, and never get to tell his story. Unless he changed his plea to guilty but with extenuating circumstances that he could explain to the nice judge."

"And you already knew this defendant wasn't very good at just sitting and taking it," Chris said admiringly.

Bonnie smiled again.

"What did he get?"

Bonnie said, "We reduced it to agg assault, which was really all we were hoping for anyway, and the judge gave him the maximum ten for that. And the defendant went off to prison happy."

She chuckled. Chris looked around her office. The day Bonnie had made felony this room had been a bare cubicle. It hadn't changed much in the two years since. The walls held two diplomas and a law license, but gave no hint as to whether Bonnie Janaway was married or had other family. The one photograph was of a landscape, unidentified. Chris, who felt uneasy in offices whose occupants used the wallspace to advertise their happy family lives and many achievements, respected his assistant's choices.

"I've come to ask you for a favor."

Bonnie looked wary. "Does it involve—? Never mind. I'm sorry. What? Sir."

"I'd like you to sit second with me when I prosecute Luisa Gaines for murder."

Bonnie looked no less wary. "Yes, sir."

"'Chris' is good enough. I have to say you don't look very honored." Immediately Bonnie pasted on the most insincere big smile he had ever seen. Chris laughed. He leaned toward her. "Are you maybe thinking that someone who sits second to the district attorney in a trial ends up doing all the work and not getting any of the fun stuff, or any credit?"

"I don't believe anyone's ever said that to me," Bonnie said carefully. An ambiguous answer.

"That's not what I want. I need a partner. Starting with investigation." He hesitated, not having planned whether he would tell her that the evidence might not all be trustworthy in this case. He'd get around to that. "All right?"

"Okay." This time Bonnie's voice held a trace of enthusiasm. Her eyes began to move around the office. He could see her thinking.

"Let me ask you something. Have you become friendly with any police officers?"

"Not really. You know, professional courtesy. Say hello in the halls. Why?"

"Just wondering." Chris stood up. "I'll have Jack brief you on what we've got so far. Then you and I will talk."

"All right." By comparison with her earlier attitude, Bonnie made these two words sound like a whoop of joy. Clearly she had begun to see the possibilities in such a high-profile prosecution.

"One more thing, Bonnie."

"Yes?" Instantly she looked wary again.

"I'll expect a hell of an opening statement."

She grinned, with a hint of slyness. Chris smiled back, and walked out.

Bonnie Janaway pressed four buttons on her office phone. "Hey, Brian, we've got some time off now. Want to go to lunch?"

Brian Janowicz looked uneasy when Bonnie Janaway parked her dusty blue Subaru in the gravel parking lot on West Commerce. "Are you sure about this?"

Brian had curly blond hair, a noble nose, and a very cautious attitude. Bonnie had seen him at someone's farewell party drink two beers, laugh raucously once, catch himself, then sip water for an hour and a half before he trusted himself to drive home. They had been trial partners for six months and he had never confided anything to her, but she suspected that he planned to be a senator some day.

"It's fine, Brian," she assured him, getting out of the car. "Cops eat here. Look, there's a patrol car."

February in San Antonio. The sky was crystal blue, untouched by white. The air was cool, but the sun had been bright all morning. Bonnie wore her suit jacket. Brian had come fully dressed too, in his navy blue trial suit. She watched him crunch across the caliche in the parking lot, could see him feeling the dust settle on his black shoes, and began to feel at home herself.

That was what had made her instantly suspicious of the district attorney's offer: the idea that he wanted her because this murder case happened on the west side, and Chris Sinclair thought Bonnie might have some insight into that culture. But he had no reason to think that, did he? She had successfully discarded her background years ago.

Miguelito's was a two-story building of old yellow stucco, adorned with tattered banners, posters for bygone fiestas, and beer signs. Sunlight splashed brightly on it, but as soon as Bonnie and Brian passed through the heavy wooden door the time of day became much more abstract. Inside, a dim interior felt compressed by an eight-foot ceiling. Three windows barred by elaborate burglar bars admitted filtered sunlight that made any spot it touched look dusty—even if that spot was on a human being. The restaurant's tables, covered by red or yellow cheesecloth, were also adorned by candles in glass bowls, wrapped in white plastic netting. Brian Janowicz seemed to stiffen beside her, but the former Bonita Rodriguez felt instantly at home. Smells in the air—of cilantro and baking cheese—drew her forward.

The main room held about twenty tables and a long bar. Bonnie looked for an exit on the far side of the room, didn't see one, but walked down that way. About half the tables were occupied, and the two assistant district attorneys in their suits drew some looks. Brian was the only Anglo in the place, and he clearly knew it. They sat at a table, and he folded his hands in his lap and smiled.

Two heavyset cops in uniform sat ten feet away. Bonnie didn't know them. The two appeared to have finished their meals, but felt no urgency to get back on patrol. They sat with a hand-radio on the table, working with toothpicks.

A card on the table, folded three ways to stand upright, offered five lunch specials. A young waitress put a bowl of chips and a dish of red salsa on the table, and said, "Something to drink?" When both the prosecutors ordered tea, she added, "You know what you want?" While Brian fumbled with the card—the first thing in the place he'd touched—Bonnie smiled and said, *"Gorditas."*

Brian obviously needed another minute. Bonnie decided to chat. "Is the owner here?"

The waitress shrugged. She could have exhausted all her English with her opening two sentences. Bonnie thought about switching to Spanish, but decided to hold that in reserve.

Brian ordered the regular plate, the waitress went away, and Brian said, "You come here often?"

Bonnie studied him for a moment before lying, "Only on special occasions."

In the daytime the restaurant seemed homey. At night it might grow heated—Chip Riley's had not been the first murder here—but the dangerous people were still asleep at this time of day. The lights were turned up brighter than they would be at night. The furnishings looked tired.

A few minutes after their food arrived, a woman emerged from a door behind the bar. As with the room itself, daylight didn't appear to be her natural element. It picked out glinting silver in her black hair, showed the lines around her eyes and the extra weight on her hips. But the woman moved very efficiently and her eyes snapped. The bartender, who had been leaning tiredly on the cash register, jerked to attention at her appearance. The woman strode to him with a fistful of cash register receipts, and started going over them with him in a low voice.

So this was Luisa Gaines. Murderess. Bonnie had been picturing her in jail whites, but here she was, obviously released on bond, which made sense. She was a solidly established member of the community. So she went about her business, even with a murder trial waiting in her near future. It seemed odd, as if the murder hadn't happened. But it gave Bonnie this chance to observe her, feeling like a spy. Gaines looked tired but energetic. Those two traits can go together: Her eyes drooped a little, but she drove herself.

And everyone else. When one of the police officers held up his empty iced tea glass, tinkling the cubes, Gaines spotted the gesture immediately. She walked quickly out from behind the bar and through the swinging door into the kitchen. Rapid-fire Spanish came from behind the door, and seemed to propel the young waitress through it, because she appeared a moment later, carrying the tea pitcher. As she poured his tea, the cop shrugged an apology for getting her in trouble.

"How're the *gorditas*?" Brian asked.

"Okay. Not as good as I expected, to tell you the truth. Bar food. I think they've been frozen."

The two police officers got up, pulling up their belts, heavy with equipment, and walked out slowly. Eyes followed them, including Brian Janowicz's. "Well, this has been special," he said, a line obviously intended to get them moving.

Bonnie would have liked to slip behind the bar and through that office doorway. She had no idea what she could hope to find. Not something to use at trial, just something to give her an insight into this woman. Did she have a picture of Chip Riley on her desk? Had she ever? What had they shared, outside this building?

She would also like to hear Luisa Gaines speak. Sometimes a whole trial could proceed from beginning to end without the prosecutor ever hearing the defendant's voice. His lawyer would announce, "Not guilty," and the accused would then sit there for two days, stripped of his power of speech. He might sometimes whisper to his lawyer, but no one else in the courtroom would hear him. Gradually as trial proceeded the defendant became an abstraction, an inanimate object. It was always a shock to hear his voice at the very end when the judge asked whether the defendant had any reason why sentence should not be pronounced.

Luisa Gaines was more real than that, moving through her life with a force of will that kept everything going. Bonnie was glad of this opportunity to have seen her, but didn't think she'd want to see her again until trial. She felt her sympathy beginning for this hard-working woman who appeared to have no one else to rely on.

It was a good thing she hadn't ducked behind the bar for a quick look into that office, because a moment later Luisa Gaines emerged from the office again. The woman moved like a snake, making unexpected appearances from all over. She must have kept her employees nervous. Bonnie even flinched a little herself.

"Ready?" Brian asked again, with more of an edge.

"Yeah," Bonnie said. "Let's go take a look around back before we leave."

He looked at her strangely, which made Bonnie smile as she led the way out of the restaurant.

On the Monday morning in March when jury selection was to begin, everything seemed like an omen. Clarissa dragged, making them run later than usual. In the car Chris spilled coffee on his pants. He had a spare navy blue pair in the office, but that meant he was no longer wearing a suit. The gray jacket and blue pants didn't clash, but they didn't match, either. He liked to look his best on opening day of a new prosecution, and now he looked as if he'd just thrown an outfit together.

When he and Bonnie Janaway got to the courtroom, its doors were locked.

It was nine o'clock on a Monday morning. People crowded the halls, especially the hall outside the 144th District Court. Lawyers struggled to get through the crush. Defendants with their families waited patiently to be admitted to the courtroom, most of them content to be kept waiting. Chris and Bonnie pushed their way to the front, to the heavy brown doors whose handles wouldn't budge. The doors didn't fit snug, Chris could peer through a small opening and in turn through the glass interior doors. He saw the court clerk at her desk, the bailiff at his, chatting and yawning. The court seemed to be going about its business, but with him excluded.

Bonnie could see his jaw muscles working. She said, "Shout through the door. Tell 'em who you are. Or do you want me just to break it down?"

"Good, hang onto your sense of humor. We'll fix that pretty soon."

Chris turned away from the door and shouldered his way back through the crowd, Bonnie following. They both carried heavy brown folders of jury lists and court documents, police and coroner's reports, all the dead minutiae that would soon become a murder conviction, they hoped. They passed through open doors at the end of the hall and around into a more private corridor that led past the court offices and the back doors to courtrooms. As they rounded a corner, Chris almost ran into Judge Helen Conners. He had to stop abruptly, meaning Bonnie bumped into his back. For a moment he felt very hemmed in, even more so by the fact that the judge carried a coffee cup and he had almost knocked it into her.

Standing aside, watching the near-smashup, stood a smiling man in a well-cut and pressed gray suit. He had a good tan even in this first week of March, smiling eyes, and a pleasant countenance. He carried only one slim file folder.

"Hello, Chris," he said pleasantly, but his voice carrying a residue of the chuckle he hadn't chuckled at sight of the prosecutor almost banging into the judge.

"Hello, John."

John Lincoln would never admit or deny his relationship to the revered president. He looked nothing like Honest Abe and came from Dallas, but he had a style of sometimes drawling in court and talking to jurors or witnesses as if they were all sitting on a porch, whittling. People who had never whittled a day in their lives felt the allure of his voice. Lincoln had probably adopted this style solely because of his name. In fact, he might have been born Jefferson Davis. He and Chris had been good friends in law school and still played tennis occasionally. They had tried a few cases against each other years earlier, but nothing of this magnitude.

"Good thing we ran into you," Judge Conners said. "John and I've just been talking, and thought it would be a good idea if the four of us got together for a few minutes to discuss the issues."

"The courtroom's locked," Chris said, and realized he sounded surly.

"Richard will take care of it," the judge said casually, referring to her bailiff. "I've got a visiting judge calling my regular docket this morning so we can devote all our time to this."

In other words, the judge was treating this as if it were a capital murder case. Probably because of its high-profile publicity. Another bad omen for this prosecution was having drawn Judge Helen Conners. A pleasant, cordial woman in her fifties, Judge Conners definitely fell into the "full-figured" category, though she always moved lightly, as if tiptoeing over dangerous terrain. She had almost no visible wrinkles, and her hair had grown blonder over the years. Outside the courthouse she sat on several charitable boards and always seemed to be doing something community-minded.

And she was married to a police officer. In fact, this morning's newspaper carried a picture of the judge's husband receiving an award for valor, with a beaming Helen Conners at his side.

The police connection should have put her solidly on the prosecution side, but that was not what Chris had observed over the four years of Conners's judgeship. She had been a defense lawyer for twenty years before her elevation to the bench, and what she seemed to have learned from her husband's work was how many of his colleagues had drinking or morality problems. Publicly she was the police department's staunchest supporter. Privately she had seen many of them screw up.

Judge Conners led the way to a small private conference room. John Lincoln sat immediately at her right hand, leaving Chris and Bonnie to take seats farther down the long table, on the left. Chris realized the other reason why he sounded surly is that John had been accompanying the judge down the hall. They had come from a cozy chat in her chambers.

The ex parte rule says that lawyers can't talk to a judge about a case without the other side present. This is probably the most violated rule in the books. In criminal cases, it certainly is. Prosecutors often spent all day with the judge of their assigned court, and as defense lawyers came and went the prosecutors remained, chatting with the judge, developing a relationship. Often their conversations were about the hearing that had just been held, or the one coming up.

Defense lawyers dropped by the judge's office to gossip, which the judges welcomed. You want to know what's going on in your building. Often these judges and lawyers had past relationships. They might even have been partners in the past. Once in a while, they married each other.

And in between the chatting and flirting and passing the time, these people talked about their work. About the cases at hand. It was inevitable, and no one really minded its illegality. It was presumed that judges put out of their minds these conversations when making a decision. Still, trial lawyers who always look for signs and foreshadowings also inevitably believe that the first lawyer to get his version of truth before the bench has an advantage. And John Lincoln had spent the first minutes of the morning with Judge Conners while Chris had peered through a narrow slot into a room from which he was excluded.

But it didn't matter. This case would be tried to a jury, not the judge.

After a few minutes of pleasantries, Judge Conners brought the lawyers to the case at hand with a vague question but a bright expression. "Anything I need to know about this trial?"

"I think you know it already," John Lincoln said immediately. "This case is more important to the police officers who investigated it than an ordinary case, because one of their own was murdered. They made significant mistakes in their eagerness to see someone punished for it. Oops, I just gave away my final argument." He shot a smile at his old friend Chris, but immediately looked sober again, leaning forward to press his index finger down on the table. "But I'm serious about this, Judge. Sometimes I'm the most casual lawyer you know, but in this case I'm really going to enforce the rules."

Judge Conners sat unmoved. "No, Mr. Lincoln, you're going to *ask* that the rules be enforced. *I'm* going to enforce them." But her stern look was followed immediately by a smile, as when one reprimands a favorite child.

Chris saw no reason to become involved in this discussion. He turned to Bonnie, who widened her eyes as if to say she didn't feel she had a place at this table.

"Mr. Sinclair?" the judge said, with a hint of impatience.

"It's just a murder case, your honor. Nothing unusual. I'll be happy to abide by the rules."

They all stood and began moving toward the door, except John Lincoln, who touched Chris's arm to stop him and said, "It's not an ordinary case, Chris. You know that."

Chris did know that. But he understood what the defense lawyer meant once jury selection began. Judge Conners, looking larger and more authoritative in her deep purple robe, made opening remarks to the jury panel for half an hour or more, explaining general aspects of the law and making everyone in the courtroom drowsy. Chris sat watching the sea of fifty people in front of him, restless in the spectator pews of the courtroom. It was hard to concentrate to pick out individual faces in such a crowd. Prospective jurors looked at him curiously, knowing who he was, then also studied the woman at the defense table, wondering what made her so dangerous as to require prosecuting by the district attorney himself.

Luisa Gaines had dressed in a vertically-striped dress that made her look more like a homemaker than a businesswoman. For the most part she sat with eyes downcast and her hands folded in her lap. Her lawyer, John Lincoln, seemed to follow the proceedings avidly, nodding along with the judge's remarks, looking through the audience as if to see whether they understood.

When Chris's turn came he had the urge to say something never before heard in a courtroom. He wanted to point at Luisa Gaines and say, *This woman has her fate in her own hands. If she would tell me what I need to know, she could walk free*. Of course, that had to remain his secret. But this trial felt fake to him in a way, a staged show to coerce a reaction from the defendant. The trial hadn't yet begun in earnest for Chris, though he was deadly serious. He kept his remarks to the jury panel brief.

John Lincoln, though, stood and walked around the courtroom like a game-show host. "This case will involve mainly testimony by police officers. Are there any of you who believe police officers are entitled to more belief than other witnesses?"

Several hands went up. Lincoln questioned one of them politely. The might-be juror said confidently, "They're trained to observe."

"Really?" John smiled. "Have you attended any of their training classes?"

The man shook his head. The defense lawyer let the subject go with a smile. "In this case," he said, "the victim was a police officer. Does that change anyone's opinion?"

The prospective jurors looked thoughtful, but no one raised a hand. The defense lawyer pointed at the witness chair. "You understand that when someone sits here, you judge not only the tone of their voice and their body language, but their reasons for saying what they do. When these people testify, can you forget that they're police officers and think of them as friends of the victim?"

Chris stood quickly and said, "Objection, your honor. The jurors will certainly not be required to forget the professions of the witnesses, or their training or experience." Chris felt his lethargy slipping off his shoulders. It felt good to stand up, to look at those faces from that perspective. He began to feel more solid. And he had said what he wanted the jurors to hear. Whether the judge sustained his objection or overruled it didn't matter.

"Granted," John Lincoln said. "But you must also remember that they're people, too. In fact, in the last few years we've had police officers who were indicted for crimes. Who've been kicked off the force, even gone to jail. Do you remember those cases, Mr.—" He consulted his jury list. "—Hernandez?"

The man called on nodded. "But those cases were about stealing or something."

"So you do believe that, properly motivated, a police officer might lie or steal or cheat just like any of the rest of us."

The prospective juror blinked and after a pause nodded. Others in that sea nodded as well.

The defense lawyer hammered home this theme with more individual questioning. Chris made objections sometimes, but didn't want to look as if he were trying to hide something from the jurors. When the morning ended he and Bonnie tried to strike the ten people they had thought most susceptible to the implications the defense lawyer had made.

And prepared to start their trial.

After lunch, everything was different, though they were the same people in the same courtroom. Twelve jurors were seated in the jury box, the rest dismissed. During jury selection the lawyers and prospective jurors had sat facing each other, questioning and answering, the lawyers trying to provoke a conversation. Now the twelve jurors sat separated in the jury box, and would be silent for the duration of the trial. The lawyers no longer faced them, or even looked at them openly.

The defendant turned once to look into the audience. Spectators had taken the places where prospective jurors had sat earlier. Among them were quite a few police officers, in uniform. The defense had objected to their presence, but Judge Conners had ruled that police had as much right to attend a public trial as other citizens.

Luisa Gaines's attention focused for a moment on one officer, a heavy man near the back of the room. Chris turned and looked, but he had never seen Rico Fairis before and so didn't recognize him. The defendant turned back to the front and never looked over her shoulder again. A few minutes later Fairis, having let his presence be known, rose and left the courtroom.

Bonnie Janaway made an opening statement that was brief and to the point. As she did she stood just in front of and between the defense and prosecution tables, facing the jury. She barely moved as she talked, though her hands were expressive. Her small gestures took in the defendant, as if inviting her to respond. "This is what we expect the evidence to show: The defendant sitting here is a successful businesswoman who owns a restaurant. A few years ago she hired someone to help her, Chip Riley. Eventually he became her partner, in every sense. He was her lover and her business partner, and he betrayed her in both realms. Or at least Luisa Gaines thought he did. And she couldn't get rid of him the ways a woman normally gets rid of a man. Not if Chip didn't want to go, and he didn't. He had a good deal. Ms. Gaines couldn't just kick him out. She couldn't divorce him. And she certainly couldn't call him a thief. Because Chip Riley was a police officer.

"One night he went too far, in Ms. Gaines's opinion. She found him in the loading area behind the restaurant and she shot him two times, with a gun she kept in her desk drawer.

"Her gun, her restaurant, her problem dealt with. This case is simple, as murder usually is. When it comes to you, we expect you will have no trouble finding Luisa Gaines guilty of murder."

Bonnie stood a moment longer, slender and morally upright in her pinstriped suit. Luisa Gaines looked down at the table, her lack of response making her look very suspicious. Bonnie sat to Chris's right, and he laid a hand briefly on her arm in congratulations. *Why couldn't they all do it like that?* he thought. *Simple and direct and immediately shifting the burden to the defense.*

"Mr. Lincoln?" Judge Conners said. "Would you like to make an opening statement now, or reserve it until your case begins?"

Immediately the defense lawyer had a dilemma. Lincoln was handsome in profile, and when he hesitated it was obvious he was really thinking. If he didn't make an opening statement now, he left Bonnie's unchallenged, the map the jurors could follow all through the prosecution's presentation of the case. On the other hand, if he made his own statement now, he would be giving away the defense's case, and locking himself into a certain theory of defense before he heard the State's evidence. Lincoln stood and said, "Your honor, I will rely on statements of the jurors that they will withhold judgment until the end of the evidence, and I will reserve my opening remarks until my turn comes to present evidence."

He sat again, not smiling but with good reason to be pleased with himself. He seemed to have had it both ways. Chris could have objected, but it was too late. The State called its first witness.

Jaime Guerrero was a slender young man with an inch-long scar across one cheek, a slashed mark that could have come from a knife or a broken bottle. The scar gave him a wary look, as if he were ducking behind it, but not fast enough. He slouched in the witness stand, dressed like a waiter in black slacks and a white *guyabera* shirt. Bonnie made him sit up straight by staring at him in silence before she asked a question. Quickly she established that Jaime had worked at Miguelito's for approximately three years before the murder.

"During that time, did you observe the relationship between Luisa Gaines and Chip Riley change from what it had been at first?"

"Yes," the young man said, leaning into the microphone. Bonnie had to prompt him to get a longer answer.

"He started off just being like security, somebody else who worked in the restaurant. Then later he started acting like the boss. If he told you to do something, you knew you'd better do it."

"Why?"

"Well, because either it came from Señora Gaines or she'd want the same thing."

"Can you give me a specific example?"

The young man appeared to think. "He told one guy, Jesse, not to take so many cigarette breaks, and when Jesse kept doing it, Señora Gaines fired him."

Bonnie nodded.

"You don't know the specific business relationship between Ms. Gaines and Mr. Riley, do you?"

The witness shook his head. When claiming ignorance, he looked very believable.

"Did you know that Mr. Riley had another job?"

"I don't see how," Guerrero said.

"What do you mean?"

"He always seemed to be at the restaurant. He was there more than I was."

John Lincoln stood laconically. "Objection, your honor. By its very terms, the witness couldn't possibly know that. What he just said is either speculation or based on hearsay."

"Sustained," Judge Conners nodded, and turned to the jurors. "I'll instruct the jury to disregard that last remark of the witness's."

"Just want the State to prove its case, not take it for granted," Lincoln drawled as he sat down. Chris gave him a sidelong look, and the judge looked at him directly, but the sidebar remark wasn't worth an objection. Not yet.

"What about the personal relationship between Luisa Gaines and Chip Riley, what was it like?"

"Same thing. At first it was just like he worked there, but he started—right away he was always like flirting with Señora Gaines, whispering to her, laughing. He was a big, good-looking man, Mr. Riley, and people thought he was fun to be around. The señora isn't like that, but it seemed like that made him all the more determined to get to her. One night he made her laugh, on a Friday night, and everybody in the place cheered."

"Did their relationship ever appear to change from just employer and employee?"

"Yeah," Guerrero said, leaning into the microphone again. "I mean, I wasn't there when it happened." This might have been dry wit or only simple observation. "But after a while, yeah, it was pretty obvious they were like boyfriend and girlfriend. Sometimes they left the bar together, sometimes they were the last two to close up. Some of those late nights . . ." He shrugged expressively.

Bonnie began another question, but John Lincoln rose quickly to his feet. "Your honor, I object to the witness leaving his sentence unfinished. It leaves a large implication hanging in the air, which I would like the record to show he made clear with his face and his body language."

"I can't rule on that, Mr. Lincoln," Judge Conners said drily, "because I wasn't looking at the witness. But I will instruct him to finish his answer. Go ahead, Mr. Guerrero."

The witness looked confused. "I just meant, it looked like the two of them—"

Lincoln, who had remained on his feet, immediately said, "Now, your honor, I object to speculation and hearsay."

"What?" the judge and the witness said together. Guerrero looked to the judge for instruction, and she stared at the defense lawyer. "But I thought you wanted him to finish the sentence."

"I want to make it clear, your honor, that he doesn't know what he's talking about. In fact you don't know, do you, sir, what the personal relationship was between Luisa and Chip Riley?"

Bonnie said, "I object to Mr. Lincoln interrupting my examination with questions of his own."

During the resulting confusion, Chris sat quietly and thought, *So we're going to be on a first-name basis with the defendant*. He had wondered how John would handle that. Would he make her the remote Ms. Gaines, too cold and removed from human events to have committed a crime of passion, or Luisa, who might evoke sympathy for her plight? For now, at least, there was an answer. The defense lawyer wanted to warm up his client's image—while keeping her reputation pristine, based on his handling of this witness.

"All right," Judge Conners said exasperatedly. "Mr. Lincoln, I suppose your last objection is sustained. Let's move on."

Bonnie sat for a moment, having lost the thread of her questioning. When her next question came, it was very tentative. "Did— You said it appeared obvious— Why do you say they seemed like boyfriend and girlfriend?"

After she finished her question, Bonnie wrote on a legal pad in large letters, *What was that all about?* Chris wrote back, *He wants to ruin your concentration. Don't let him.* He thought he felt Bonnie settle down again.

The defense lawyer obviously sat poised to stand and object again. The witness looked at him as he said cautiously, "You know, the things you notice about people. The whispering, like I said. And he would touch her sometimes. Even the way they argued sometimes. I don't know . . ." He shrugged.

"You say they argued? What about?"

"Sometimes Señora Gaines would say something to him about money. Where did some money go, or why there wasn't more money in the cash register. She got mad at him about how much he drank, too. She said something once like, 'We would have made a profit this week if you hadn't been here in the bar every night.'"

"Was that the only kind of thing she got mad at Chip Riley about, money and business?"

"Objection to any implication that this witness knew what Luisa was thinking or feeling," John said lazily, not standing. The judge just nodded.

Bonnie said, "Did you ever *see* the defendant appear to be angry at the victim over anything besides money?"

The witness stared at her, obviously intimidated by the exchanges between the lawyers. "You mean Teresita?" he asked. Someone in the audience snickered.

"Say whatever *you* mean to say, Mr. Guerrero," Bonnie snapped. "I'm not here to give the answers."

But it looked as if she were. Bonnie sat back in her chair as if to withdraw as far as possible, while Jaime Guerrero picked his way through an answer. "There was this waitress, Teresita, who just started a few months before. *Flaquita,* you know? She was . . ."

"No, Mr. Guerrero, we don't know. What does that mean?"

"Skinny. Skinny little girl, but with big—" He lifted his hands, then moved them to his face. "—eyes. Pretty little girl, you know. Very shy. She didn't have much English, she had just come from Mexico, I think. Anyway, Mr. Chip liked her too. Whispered to her and tried to make her laugh, too."

Surprising that a guy who had worked so hard to amuse so many people had ended up murdered, Chris thought ironically. He didn't like the way this witness had begun to portray their victim, but that was okay. Obviously Chip Riley *had* provoked someone beyond reason.

"Did you ever see how the defendant reacted to Officer Riley's attempts to amuse this young waitress?" Bonnie asked.

"She stared at them like fire, man. I was watching a couple of times when they didn't see Luisa looking and I thought they should both have felt her looking at them, her eyes were so hot. Then once she gabbed Mr. Chip by his arm and dragged him into the office and I heard yelling."

"Did you hear what she said?"

"Not exactly. It was a thick door to that office. I didn't want to hear, really. I got busy somewhere else."

Bonnie Janaway leaned forward, her face growing tighter, obviously willing her witness to concentrate. "Mr. Guerrero, were you working in Miguelito's the night Chip Riley was murdered?"

"Yes, ma'am."

"Describe the scene that night, please."

"A Wednesday night, but busier than usual. Mr. Riley was there, walking around, talking to people."

"Drinking?"

"Yes, ma'am. More than usual, I think. He seemed kind of tipsy pretty early on."

"Who was bringing him drinks?"

"Mainly this little Teresa I told you about. Mr. Riley would be at a table and he'd make a signal for Teresa to bring him a drink, then he'd hold her arm and ask her to sit with him."

A man screwing up his courage to make a confession to Steve Greerdon at eleven o'clock that night, Chris thought. *Or maybe enjoying the last of the good life if he thought that confession was going to get him into trouble.* But he hadn't expected to die. Someone must have already known about the planned meeting. That was the information Chris wanted from Luisa Gaines. She must have known. But in the months between the murder and trial, she had refused to save herself. She must have been more worried about the people she was protecting than she was about being prosecuted for murder. Chris and Bonnie had to make the threat of conviction and prison more real to her.

Bonnie asked, "Did Luisa Gaines see the flirtation going on?"

"I know she did once. She came out of the office once and glared at them. Later she even pulled him into that office, but he came out right away. I think he—"

"Objection," John Lincoln said simply, and the judge sustained him with equal simplicity.

"How did Officer Riley look when he came out of the office?" Bonnie asked precisely. "Frightened? Worried?"

"No, ma'am. He had a little smile on his face. He looked like a man who was happy with himself. And he had another shot of tequila right away."

"Do you remember about what time that was?"

"It was kind of late for a weeknight. After ten. But like I said, we were more crowded than usual. Some people were staying and drinking and playing the jukebox."

"Did anything else happen between the defendant and Luisa Gaines?"

Jaime Guerrero nodded. "Later he was sitting at a table, having a beer. Joking with people, you know. Teresita walked by and he grabbed her arm and pulled her down onto his lap. He was kissing her neck and whispering something."

"Did she struggle to get away?"

"No, ma'am. It seemed like— She kissed him back. Until she heard the door open. Then she jumped up."

"What do you mean, 'heard the door open'?

"The office door, ma'am. Señora Gaines's door. It was the only door inside the place, and its hinges squeaked. Believe me, we all knew the sound of that door opening. People jumped when she was coming out."

A ripple of whispers and chuckles ran through the spectators. John Lincoln's objection being sustained had no effect at all.

Bonnie said, "What happened?"

Guerrero began to appear animated by his narrative, like someone passing on good gossip. "Señora Gaines ran over there, and Mr. Riley just smiled up at her. She didn't yell, she kept her voice down, but I was close enough to hear. She said, 'Why don't you get out? Haven't you had enough fun for tonight?' "

"Did she say that in a friendly way, like giving him good advice, or—"

"No," the witness said ironically. "Even though I think it would have been good advice. If she'd said it to me the way she said it to him, I would've got out fast, believe me. But he just sat there smiling. He said something I couldn't hear that seemed to make her even madder. Then she started back behind the bar and he got up and followed her. It looked like he was going to go after her, but then he walked past her and went to the cash register. He opened the cash drawer—it had a loud bell, and she turned and looked at him—and he took some bills out of the drawer and stuck them in his pocket. Then he smiled at her again. She stared fire at him again, then she went into her office and slammed the door. And Mr. Riley came out from behind the bar and went out the other direction, sticking a cigarette in his mouth."

"Did you see either of them again that night?"

"A couple minutes later I heard gunshots. That wasn't all that strange in that neighborhood, but then somebody came running saying Mr. Riley was dead, and some of us decided to go home."

"One more subject, Mr. Guerrero. Had you been inside Luisa Gaines's office before?"

"A couple of times," the witness said, sounding as if these had been memorable but not happy occasions.

"Do you know whether she kept a gun in that office?" The legs of the defense lawyer's chair scraped the floor, and Bonnie added more precisely, "Have you ever seen such a gun?"

She had held John Lincoln at bay for the moment. "Yes," Guerrero said.

"Have you ever seen the defendant come out of that office with a gun in her hand?"

"Yes," the witness said again, once again too loudly into the microphone. "I think two times since I worked there. I heard about other—"

John Lincoln almost reached his feet, and Bonnie quickly interjected, "Only tell us about what you've seen personally, Mr. Guerrero. So you've actually seen Ms. Gaines holding a gun inside the restaurant."

"Yes. Pretty much everybody who owns a bar has a gun somewhere around. For fights and maybe robberies." He shrugged, as if to say that every business holds inherent dangers.

"Did you ever see Ms. Gaines use the gun?"

Guerrero nodded. "One night some men were fighting, and one pulled a knife. Mr. Riley went to break it up, and the man slashed at him, too. I saw Señora Gaines go into the office and she came out with the gun in her hand. She fired it into the ceiling. Things got very excited for a minute, then they calmed down. Mr. Riley had his gun out, too. He called police and they came and arrested one of the men. Nobody told them about the señora's gun."

Bonnie leaned forward again. "Listen carefully, Mr. Guerrero. This jury wants to know exactly what you saw. When Luisa Gaines went into the office on the night you're talking about, did she have the gun?"

"No. She wasn't carrying a purse or anything, and she didn't have it in her hand."

"But when she came back out of the office she was carrying the gun?"

"Yes, ma'am."

Chris felt Bonnie's hesitation. She asked the next question slowly, obviously expecting to be interrupted. "So the defendant kept this gun in her office?"

But no interruption came. John Lincoln sat at the defense table looking relaxed. "Yes, ma'am," Guerrero said.

Bonnie asked to approach the witness and did so, carrying a heavy item already tagged as State's Exhibit One. She put it on the witness stand in front of Jaime Guerrero.

"Mr. Guerrero, does this look like Luisa Gaines's gun?"

The witness examined it closely but without touching it. He seemed reluctant to pick it up. "Yes, ma'am," he finally said.

"Can you identify it positively as her gun?" Bonnie pressed.

Guerrero shook his head. "I never touched the gun, ma'am, or got very close to it. It looked like this one, but I can't say this is the exact same one."

Bonnie nodded as if satisfied, though Chris knew otherwise. She picked up the gun, which was a heavy old revolver with a long barrel. It would deliver a lot of bang for the buck. A good bar-owner's gun, because it looked intimidating and would be noisy when fired. If someone wanted to settle a dispute, this weapon would do it quickly. Bonnie opened the cylinder to show the gun was empty, then carried it, holding it up head-high, across the front of the courtroom to the defense table. She set it down between John Lincoln and his client.

"The State offers this Exhibit One for demonstrative purposes, your honor. I've tendered it to defense counsel for possible objections."

It would have been nice if Luisa Gaines had picked up the gun, but she wasn't remotely that stupid. Her hands remained under the table, in her lap. Lincoln didn't touch it either, in fact barely glanced at it before he stood and said, "Any objections I might have would go to whether this exhibit proves anything or not, your honor, not to its admissibility for demonstrative purposes. I would ask that the court explain to the jury what that means."

Bonnie carried the gun back to the judge's bench and set it on the shelf there as Judge Conners turned to the jurors and said, "This exhibit is being admitted for demonstration only. That means no one has identified this weapon positively as being involved in this case, but that it looks similar enough to the one you've heard testimony about that we can admit it just so you can see what that one looked like. On that basis, State's Exhibit One is admitted."

Bonnie was again seated at the prosecution table by the time the judge finished this explanation. Bonnie glanced at Chris, who shook his head in a tiny movement. "Pass the witness," she said.

John Lincoln took his time uncrossing his legs and pulling his chair closer to the defense table. "You say Luisa went into her office? Is that right, Mr. Guerrero?"

"That's right."

"And Chip Riley went the other direction, presumably toward the outside door?"

"He went that way. I guess so."

"Did Luisa come out of that office again before you heard the gunshots?"

"I didn't see her come out."

Lincoln sounded surprised. "You never saw Luisa come out of that office again before you heard the gunshots?"

"No, sir."

Chris looked at Bonnie, but she sat watching calmly, apparently unperturbed. He started to write a note to her, but Bonnie made a small hand gesture as if to tell him not to worry. So he sat back and listened.

John Lincoln said, "You don't work at Miguelito's anymore, do you, Mr. Guerrero?"

The witness shook his head, but the defense lawyer made him say it out loud: "No, I don't."

"Luisa Gaines fired you, didn't she?"

Guerrero's dark eyes looked at the defendant, but he kept his voice flat. "Yes, sir, after my name came out on the state's witness list."

Lincoln stood, holding a manila folder. "Well, in fact, your personnel file contains several reprimands, and in fact once you were suspended for a week by Mr. Riley himself, isn't that true?"

Guerrero leaned into the microphone again. "The señora wrote up everybody. She made sure if she ever fired anybody, she'd look like she had good reason."

"But she did have good reason to fire you, didn't she?"

"Yeah, she knew I was going to testify, about what happened."

"You're mad at her about that, aren't you?"

"No, sir," Guerrero said in that same flat voice. But his expression said something quite different He glared at Luisa Gaines, who kept her eyes demurely on the table, not dueling with him. "I've got a better job already." He almost sneered.

"So you don't mind burning this bridge, do you?" Lincoln asked.

"What do you mean, sir?"

"You're not going to need anything from Luisa Gaines again, so now you're free to get back at her from the witness stand. Isn't that right?"

The witness stared at the lawyer for a moment, clearly finding no good way to answer this question. Finally he said, "I'm free to tell the truth. Now she can't hurt me if I do."

"And in fact she'd be even less of a threat to you if she went to prison, wouldn't she?"

While Guerrero again tried to think of a comeback, the defense lawyer moved on. "Let me ask you about this gun that you said belonged to Luisa." Lincoln stood and strolled across the front of the courtroom as if he would pick up the revolver that had been admitted, but he just put his hand near it and faced the witness. "Do you remember a time, two or three weeks before the night of the murder, when Luisa's gun was missing?"

The witness paused, thinking, then nodded.

"Answer out loud, please, Mr. Guerrero."

"Yes. The señora was asking people what had happened to her gun and if one of us took it."

"So it was gone from her office?"

"I guess so."

"Do you know whether she ever found the gun again?"

"I guess she must have," Guerrero said.

"What makes you think she got it back?"

"Because she had it to shoot Mr. Riley with."

The witness sat back in his chair, looking quietly pleased with himself. But John Lincoln didn't object, or even look annoyed. He watched Jaime Guerrero, with a little smile. Finally he said, "You don't know for a fact whether the gun was still missing from Luisa Gaines's office on the night of the murder, do you?"

"No, sir."

Lincoln nodded in satisfaction, and started back to his seat before the judge ordered him to do so. With his back to the witness, he said, "Quite a few people knew about that gun, didn't they?"

"I don't know," Guerrero said, again too closely into the microphone, so his voice came out harsh and distorted.

"Well, you knew about it, and you weren't exactly Luisa's confidante, were you?"

"What do you mean?"

Back in his chair, the defense lawyer said patiently, "You knew about the gun because Luisa had had to bring it out before. So other people knew too, didn't they? Employees of the restaurant and even long-time customers."

"Yes sir, I suppose."

"And those people could have mentioned it to other people, couldn't they?"

Bonnie stood quickly and said, "I'll object to asking the witness to speculate, your honor."

"Sustained."

"At any rate," Lincoln said with a small, mischievous smile, "quite a few people knew about that gun, didn't they?"

"Yes, I guess."

"Did Luisa keep her office locked?"

"Sometimes, not all the time."

"Not most of the time, isn't that right?"

"I don't know," Guerrero said. "I didn't go try getting into the office all the time."

Chris sat and reflected that this witness must have listened to his instructions better than most did. Bonnie had told him to say 'I don't know' if he didn't know the answer to a question, and Guerrero had used the phrase several times already. However, he only claimed ignorance when answering defense questions, which made him look a little shifty, in Chris's opinion, as if he really were trying to get back at his former employer.

Lincoln continued, "In fact, her office was used as a sort of storeroom, wasn't it?"

"She kept some things there, yes."

"So sometimes employees went into the office to get a new roll of paper for the cash register or new credit card slips, things like that?"

"Yes sir, sometimes."

"You've been in that office, haven't you?"

"Like I said, a couple of times."

"And you knew about the gun kept in the desk drawer."

With a slight note of satisfaction, Guerrero said, "I didn't know it was in the desk, sir."

"But you knew it was in the office."

"Yes."

"And that gun went missing before Chip Riley was shot?"

"Objection," Bonnie said. "That's been asked and answered." The judge sustained her, but the defense lawyer's remark hadn't really been a question anyway.

"One last thing," Lincoln said. "Officer Riley carried a gun too, didn't he?"

"Oh, yes sir."

"Where did he keep it?"

"In a holster like on the back side of his belt."

"Did *he* ever pull his gun out inside the bar?"

"I only remember that one time I testified about."

"So you know he had one."

The witness shrugged. Lincoln let that answer suffice. "No more questions, your honor."

Bonnie leaned forward quickly. "Mr. Guerrero, you said after she had this argument with Chip Riley, Luisa Gaines went into her office and you didn't see her come out again before you heard the gunshots. Is that right?"

"Yes, ma'am."

"Did you know that there's another door out of her office, one that goes into the kitchen?"

Guerrero sat and thought, elaborately, turning his eyes up toward the ceiling. "No, ma'am, I didn't know that. Like I said, I wasn't in there very often."

"Well, hadn't you ever noticed that the defendant would go into her office and then a few minutes later come out of the kitchen?"

He nodded. "Now that you say it, yes. But I didn't know there was a door. I thought she could just pop up anywhere, like the devil."

No one laughed.

"On the night of the murder," Bonnie said intently, "you said people inside the restaurant heard gunshots, and some of them started leaving. Right?"

"Yes."

"There was quite a commotion?"

"Yes, ma'am. People talking and running around and some people trying to decide whether it was safe to go out the front door."

"During all this noise of gunfire and people shouting, did you see Luisa Gaines come running out of her office?"

"No, ma'am," Guerrero said. Chris wished he hadn't nodded and looked smug when he said it, but Bonnie had done a good job. After a few more perfunctory questions, both sides let the witness go. He walked past the defense table, almost swaggering, and sneered down at the defendant. She didn't look up at him.

Judge Conners took a short recess after this first witness. Chris turned to his trial partner. "How did you know there was another door out of Luisa's office?"

With barely a trace of a smile, Bonnie said, "Someone very wise once told me I should always go to the scene where the crime happened. I was there for lunch one day and saw Luisa go into the office, then come charging out of the kitchen a few minutes later."

Chris nodded, smiling at her. "It's a rare person who can learn from someone else's experience."

Bonnie didn't acknowledge the compliment. "Now we need to get a witness who can—"

"Yeah, I'll put Jack on it."

Chris hurried up the courtroom's aisle. At the back of the room he found a curious sight. Anne stood on one side, watching him. She didn't smile a greeting. She looked like a formal observer, perhaps sent from Geneva or the United Nations.

On the other side of the aisle, Steve Greerdon also stood at the back of the room, arms folded, leaning back against the wall. Chris spoke to him first. "What are you doing here?"

"I'm watching your back," Greerdon said, which in this instance was literally true.

"If you listen to testimony, you can't be called as a witness."

Greerdon looked at him flatly and ironically. "I'm aware of that rule, counselor. But I don't know anything about what happened that night. I thought something might come up I could help you with."

"All right. Thanks." Chris didn't offer to shake hands, a small, manly ritual he and Greerdon still had never performed. He stepped across the aisle and said, "Hi. What on earth are you doing here?"

Anne laid a hand on his shoulder. "I just came to see how things were going. How are they?"

"Fine so far. I haven't had to do anything." Chris looked at her quizzically. Her concerned expression remained centered on him, which made him feel very warm.

Anne inclined her head slightly toward Steve Greerdon across the aisle. "So is he on your trial team?"

Chris glanced that direction. "I guess so. I'm expecting him to help somehow. Why?"

Anne shook her head, a completely unconvincing claim of ignorance. "Just asking," she added.

Anne never "just asked." She always had reasons. "Going to stay for a while?"

"I can't. I probably have a full waiting room right now, and of course they're all disturbed. Carnage might ensue."

In fact, Chris found it very odd that she had dropped in like this for as long as she had. Anne very seldom had free time during the day.

Chris grinned at her. "So can I come watch you work sometime?"

Anne smiled. She put her hand on the back of his neck and pulled his head down close, but not to kiss him. She whispered, "Be careful."

"About what?" he said, but she turned and hurried out of the courtroom.

Looking after her, Chris found himself staring at Steve Greerdon. Greerdon's raised eyebrow asked a question. Chris shrugged his shoulders as if to say, *Women,* but continued to watch Greerdon. The cop looked relaxed and watchful at the back of the courtroom, just an idle spectator. Chris tried to think how he could use Greerdon to best advantage in this trial.

So his thoughts turned from Anne back to the trial. He stopped trying to make the connection she'd been hinting at.

Chris had let Bonnie Janaway question the first witness to settle her down. Just sitting and watching from a counsel table is perhaps the most difficult trial job there is. So Chris had done his assistant the favor of letting her loosen up first. Consequently, he felt a little stiff himself as he began to question the next witness, a small man wearing a white shirt, plaid sport coat, and very dull tie. The man had a high forehead and watery eyes that looked quizzical at even the simplest question.

"Please state your name."

"Ed Loudermilk." The man looked along the jurors' faces as if wondering whether they believed him.

"Mr. Loudermilk, do you know the woman seated to my left?"

"Yes. Luisa Gaines. She's a client of mine." The witness gave the defendant a very weak smile. She stared back at him levelly.

"What's your occupation, Mr. Loudermilk?"

"Oh, I'm sorry. I'm an accountant."

"No need to be sorry. I hadn't asked you anything yet." The witness's obvious nervousness began to calm Chris down. He felt in charge. "What accounting services do you provide for Luisa Gaines?"

"I keep her books from the restaurant, and do her income tax returns, and also help her with things like employee withholding and estimated taxes."

"So you're very familiar with her business affairs, is that right?"

"Well, I've only been in the restaurant two or three times. I do know its financial condition. That is, as much as anyone can tell from the recorded figures."

"What do you mean by that?" Chris asked, sounding genuinely curious.

Ed Loudermilk was twisting his hands together, probably unconsciously. They made a dry, whispery sound, like autumn leaves brushing against a windowpane.

"In any business that runs largely on cash, but especially like a restaurant or a bar, the books don't necessarily reflect the real cash flow. In fact, they probably don't."

"Are you accusing Ms. Gaines of anything?"

"Oh, no. No no no no no." He sounded appalled at the suggestion. "But one of the things I did for her was to try to reconcile payments received with the meal checks. But an employee could keep some of the money from a night's business simply by not writing the customer a check, and pocketing the cash. This is especially true of bartenders. If someone hands one of them a bill and says to keep the change, the transaction doesn't have to go through the register at all."

Chris asked carefully, "Are you speaking generally, or was this particularly a problem at the restaurant Miguelito's?"

Sure enough, this drew an objection from the defendant's lawyer, who rose quickly to say, "Only if he knows personally, your honor. I object to any hearsay."

"We haven't heard the answer yet," the judge ruled laconically. Chris nodded to the witness, who said, "Yes, it was a problem at Miguelito's."

"Let me take you back to last November, Mr. Loudermilk. Are you aware that Chip Riley was murdered at Miguelito's on the night of the seventeenth of that month?"

"Yes, I heard about it," the witness said drily.

"In the few weeks or couple of months before that night, had Luisa Gaines consulted you about as often as usual, or more or less often?"

"More often than usual," Loudermilk said. He had grown calmer on the witness stand, and stopped rubbing his hands. He looked directly at Chris the whole time, not at the jury or at his client.

"Why was that?" Chris heard the legs of Lincoln's chair scrape as he asked the question, and saw the defense lawyer poised to rise.

Loudermilk began, "There had been more discrepancies than usual between—"

Lincoln quickly said, "Objection, your honor. Again, I'd like the witness to say whether his testimony is based on hearsay."

Judge Conners looked down on the witness and said, "Sir, you may only testify to things you know personally, not to anything you may have heard from someone else."

Loudermilk answered, "I understand, your honor." He turned back to Chris. "There had been more discrepancies than usual—" Again the defense lawyer began to rise. The accountant looked directly at him and said, "I keep the books. I know this from the figures." Lincoln sat back down, with obvious reluctance. The witness continued, "There had been more discrepancies than usual between the tickets and the actual money received. Ms. Gaines was becoming increasingly upset about this."

Chris asked hurriedly, "You know that because she told you she was upset?"

"No, she never said that directly, but you can tell when someone is upset. She raised her voice. She got angry. She even asked me to do a study matching the food and liquor being consumed at the restaurant with the money that came in, so we could see whether someone was pocketing the money for meals and drinks served."

"Did you make such a study?"

"I found it impossible, sir. There are too many variables. Different bartenders put different amounts of tequila in margaritas, or the same one does it differently on different nights, depending on his mood. The same way with the food. Ms. Gaines tried to standardize this, but . . ." He shrugged.

Again Chris spoke carefully: "Do you know whether she suspected any particular person of stealing from her?"

Luisa Gaines's lawyer was on his feet before Chris finished the question. "Your honor, I object to hearsay. That's clearly the source of this answer. He couldn't have known this from her tone of voice or her facial expressions."

Chris stood as well. "Your honor, this is going to be an admission by a party opponent."

Judge Conners hesitated, then beckoned with one finger. "Approach, please."

As Chris walked to the bench, he reflected that John Lincoln hadn't been kidding when he'd said he was going to enforce the rules in this trial. Hearsay—what a witness had heard another person say—was not admissible in court. But there are many exceptions. One is where the person making the statement is the defendant—a "party opponent"—and the statement had been an admission of guilt or otherwise against the defendant's interest. A witness who had heard a defendant say, "I'm going to rob that bank," could testify to that fact.

In criminal trials, this rule was usually stretched loosely enough to allow testimony about anything a defendant had said. But in this trial, obviously, the prosecution's evidence was going to be held to a higher standard.

This was a subtle issue, and the judge knew it. At the bench she leaned close to the lawyers, covering her microphone with her palm, and said, "What's the answer going to be, Chris? Did she think the victim was stealing from her?"

In an equally low tone, Chris said, "In a roundabout way, your honor."

"Roundabout?" the judge said, frowning.

"She thought it was either Chip Riley or the waitress you've heard about, this Teresa."

Lincoln chimed in, "That's not an admission, your honor. She didn't do anything to Teresa, whoever she is."

"She's missing," Chris said. Lincoln rolled his eyes.

Judge Conners said, "But you're not accusing Ms. Gaines of having killed her, are you? At least not in this trial." She hesitated again, looking abstractedly across the courtroom. Then she ruled, "I'm going to sustain the objection, at least for now. We may revisit this if necessary."

"Thank you, your honor," Lincoln said, and walked quickly away.

Chris returned to his seat more slowly, thinking. He knew what the judge's ruling had meant. If after more evidence it appeared that the State's case was weak, Judge Conners might let this evidence in. Judges nearly always favor the prosecution, and Judge Conners was no exception. But she didn't like to be reversed on appeal, either.

Chris sat down, and glanced at the legal pad to see if his assistant had written anything there, but Bonnie had only drawn a question mark. Chris looked at his witness for a moment and said, "Mr. Loudermilk. After Ms. Gaines had aired her concerns to you, did you give her any advice?"

From the corner of his eye, Chris saw Lincoln frown, but the question wasn't objectionable. He was asking the witness what he himself had said.

"Yes, I did," the accountant said firmly.

"What was that?"

"I told her if she didn't trust her partner, she should get rid of him."

On that nice phrase, Chris passed the witness.

The defense attorney said quickly, "Mr. Loudermilk, how long have you known Luisa?"

"Oh, quite a while. We've been working together—" He looked to the defendant, as if she might supply the answer. "—seven years, I believe?"

"Does she strike you as a stupid woman?"

"No, not at all. She's a very capable business person."

"But if you told her she should get rid of her partner, and she immediately ran back to the restaurant and shot him to death, that wouldn't be the act of a smart person, would it?"

"It wouldn't be very smart, no."

Lincoln went on, his tone growing more sarcastic, "In fact, if she were going to get away with this crime of the century, ideally she should have killed you first, shouldn't she?"

The accountant widened his eyes at the defense lawyer. He had no answer.

Lincoln didn't need one. "In fact, it wasn't only Chip Riley who might have been stealing from Luisa, was it?"

"No, I don't think so."

"There were lots of suspects, true?"

Loudermilk said slowly, "Yes. As I said, in the restaurant or bar business it's almost a given that some employees are skimming cash."

"And yet there wasn't a wholesale bloodbath at Miguelito's, was there? Luisa didn't go into the restaurant and shoot everyone who worked for her, did she?"

"Not that I know of," the accountant said. He had grown comfortable enough to attempt humor. "I think I would have heard about that."

"When you said she should get rid of her partner if she didn't trust him, you didn't mean she should kill him, did you?"

"Of course not."

"I don't think the prosecution is suggesting that you're an accomplice to this murder, are they?"

Loudermilk frowned at the defense lawyer, not following his logic. "Certainly not," he said.

"Ms. Gaines is, as you said, a very capable business person, just as I assume you are. Wouldn't you expect her to take your advice in the same spirit you intended it?"

"That is what I expected. That she would confront him, perhaps tell him his services were no longer needed."

"So there's no reason to think she did anything else, is there?"

The accountant said, "Well, except that he's dead."

One question too many. But Chris didn't smile, and John Lincoln didn't pause as if injured. Immediately he said, "Mr. Loudermilk, do you know Chip Riley's other occupation, other than restaurant security?"

"Yes. He was a police officer."

"Are you familiar with the mortality rate of that profession?"

"No. Not really."

"But it's higher than working in the restaurant business, wouldn't you think?"

Chris felt Bonnie's elbow nudge him, but he didn't bother to rise to object that the defense lawyer was asking the witness to speculate. That was obvious. Besides, this witness was a cautious man. As Chris expected, Loudermilk shrugged and said, "I have no idea."

"Pass this witness," Lincoln said abruptly.

Chris paused, and looked at the list of questions in front of him. He had asked every one, and the defense hadn't raised any new issues that he thought needed response. Bonnie quickly wrote on the legal pad, "Luisa's temper?" but Chris thought another witness could answer that better than this one. He had an aversion to wasting time. He half rose and said, "No more questions, your honor."

The defendant's accountant climbed down from the witness stand and made his way slowly away from the front of the courtroom, nodding to his client. The prosecutor sat thinking. In two witnesses they had established that Luisa Gaines didn't trust her partner in either their personal or professional lives. They had given her motive, and they had more or less put the murder weapon in her hand. Now they only had to kill the victim.

Chris said, "The State calls Dr. Evelyn Reese."

A bailiff went out into the hall, and in a moment Dr. Reese came striding up the aisle. She was a tall woman made taller by high heels. She had flat cheeks, a thin nose, but a full mouth. Her light brown hair was arranged so as not to get in her way. Dr. Reese wore a light beige jacket that vaguely gave the impression of a lab coat, but in fact it was a suit jacket. She looked almost formal, not like the assistant medical examiners Chris was used to.

"Please state your name," Chris asked after the witness had been sworn in.

"Evelyn Reese."

Good. Chris didn't like doctors who used their titles as if they were part of their names. "What's your profession?"

"Medical doctor. Specifically I'm a pathologist."

"Are you in private practice?"

"I have a private practice, yes. I also teach at the medical school."

"Dr. Reese, have you testified in a criminal trial before?"

"No."

John Lincoln shot Chris a look. Both of them were used to the medical examiner or his first assistant Hal Parmenter, who both routinely testified that they had testified many, many times. The defense lawyer began to pay more attention.

"Please tell the jury your qualifications to perform autopsies."

She had those, in spades. Evelyn Reese rattled off degrees, postgraduate work, professional papers published. When the jurors' eyes began to glaze, Chris broke in to ask, "Have you performed few or many autopsies, Dr. Reese?"

"Many. Several dozen."

The defense lawyer remained alert. He was used to the medical examiner claiming autopsies in the thousands. It was a day at the office: get up, have coffee, cut up a body. Instead, for this witness, an autopsy was an uncommon event.

"Are you an employee of the Medical Examiner's Office?" Chris asked.

"No." Evelyn Reese smiled as if the suggestion were odd. "I'm sort of an auxiliary. They call me in as needed, which isn't very often. The autopsy in this case was performed during a week when the regular staff were at a conference. I filled in."

"Thank you. Dr. Reese, did you perform an autopsy on someone identified to you as Charles 'Chip' Riley?"

Formally she answered, "I performed an autopsy on the body of a man who had, according to our records, been known by that name in life. Yes."

The odd phrasing broke Chris's stride for a moment. Did the dead lose their names? For a moment the courtroom was haunted by his vision of groping ghosts, returning to try to recover those names by which they had been known in life.

"How did your examination begin?"

"With a visual examination of the exterior of the body. The body was measured and weighed: seventy-four inches long, two hundred forty-two pounds: overweight, as most Americans are these days, otherwise apparently healthy, a mature adult male with some gray in his hair, more so on the chest than the head."

Another detail Chris didn't ordinarily hear from his normal pathologist witness. He frowned. "Was there any obvious injury to the body, Doctor?"

"Yes. But I save that for last. As I tell my students, the obvious often makes us overlook the smaller details. Where someone has been bludgeoned, we might not do a toxic screening and discover he had in fact been poisoned."

Reese actually raised one finger while making this point. Chris grew more irritable. Sherlock Holmes would find no fault in this woman, but he did. He wanted to get on with the business of the gunshot wounds that had killed Chip Riley.

"So did you discover anything significant in your examination of the body, other than the obvious gunshot wounds?"

"Significant?" She shrugged. "That's not for me to say. I'm not a detective. I just try to note all the details. Among those: There was some lividity in the face. The blood had collected and come to rest in the front of the body."

"Meaning the body had been lying face down for a while after death?" Chris asked quickly.

"Yes. That is what that indicates. No trauma to the face or head. No signs that the subject had been in a fight shortly before his death. However, all four fingers of the right hand had been scraped."

"Scraped?"

"Yes. As if he had dragged his hand along a rough surface, or something similar. It happened very shortly before death, because the scrapes were fresh."

Chris had no idea what this detail indicated. He nodded wisely. "And now the gunshot wounds, Dr. Reese?"

"Yes. There were two, both in the front of the body. One entered through the abdomen and traveled upward through the rib cage, passing through a lung as well. That bullet made a larger exit wound under the right armpit."

"Was that a fatal wound, Doctor?"

"It would have been, yes, if not treated quickly. It collapsed the lung, started internal bleeding, and finally nicked an artery near its exit. That cut meant blood would flow freely, the subject would collapse in a matter of a minute or two and die shortly thereafter unless, as I said, medical attention had been provided promptly."

"What about the other wound, Doctor?"

"That was a shot through the heart." She raised her chin, looking at the jury directly. Surprisingly, for an academic, she didn't elaborate, but left the statement simple. That was one of Chris's pretrial instructions that had apparently taken.

"Did that bullet also travel at an upward angle in relation to the body?"

"No. It traveled downward."

"Could you please show us on the chart, Dr. Reese?"

A diagram of a human body had already been placed on an easel near her. The witness stood and, using a pointer, indicated a path through the body, directly into the outline's heart at a significant downward angle.

Chris noticed that John Lincoln watched attentively. So did his client. Luisa Gaines frowned, and her eyes glittered. Did she picture that outline as her dead lover? Did the bare, unadorned drawing recall the moment when she had shot him? In her face Chris thought he saw regret, and also anger. Anger at herself, at Chip Riley, at fate? Did this simple, clinical description recall to her the sound of a gunshot, a man gasping, a last exchange of looks? Most murders were committed in moments of fury. Chris believed that many killers would like to have that moment back, to reverse time. But remorse didn't appear to be the defendant's dominant emotion. Her mouth tightened angrily, and she looked down, away from the chart.

"How could the bullet come from that angle, Doctor?" Chris asked.

"Well, he would have to have been shot by a much taller person, or by someone standing above him, like on a staircase. Or the subject could have been lying down, face down, but lifting up on his hands."

"As if pleading for his life?"

The defense lawyer said angrily, "Object to asking for speculation as to what the victim was doing."

"Only if the witness can tell from her examination," Judge Conners ruled.

"In that posture, yes," the doctor said.

"Would that account for the scrapes to the hand you mentioned?"

"Possibly. Except they were only on one hand, and not on the palm, only the fingers. Still . . ." She trailed off with a shrug.

"Which wound came first, Doctor?"

"They came in the order I described them. The first produced what might be called a slower fatality. The wound to the heart would have killed the subject almost instantly."

"Killed instantly" was a phrase often heard in murder trials, but Chris didn't believe it. The human mind could move at such incredible speed, far faster than any known object, that Chris imagined every victim knew his death before it happened. Had long, long moments to see eternity coming, until one of those moments *became* eternity. Chris paused long enough to allow the jury to imagine such a moment themselves.

"Did you recover the bullets, Dr. Reese?"

"As I said, the bullet that produced the first wound passed all the way through the body. It was no longer present in the body. I did recover the bullet that pierced the heart. Well, the technician did. I saw its location."

"What did you do with that bullet?"

"There was a police officer standing by. An officer—" For the first time, Dr. Reese consulted her notes. "—Officer L. Hernandez. Badge number 42325."

"Did you see what he did with it?"

"He marked it in some way and put it in a Baggie. I believe the other officer may have examined it, then they—"

"Other officer?" Chris interrupted.

"There were several officers standing by, waiting for the results of the autopsy. I understand the deceased was a fellow officer, so naturally they were interested. I didn't know any of them. Only Officer Hernandez was the one—I don't know the terminology—the one assigned to take the evidence from me."

Chris stood and carried a plastic bag to the witness. Inside was a bullet, marked by being fired, but not squashed. "Doctor, this has been labeled State's Exhibit Twelve. Is this the bullet you removed from the body?"

She removed the bit of metal from the bag. In her long, elegant fingers it looked like a fashion accessory. "It appears the same. I don't know anything about guns. The officer would know."

The defense lawyer was making rapid notes on a legal pad. His client leaned over to speak quietly to him, and he nodded. "Thank you, Doctor," Chris said, trying to disguise his irritation. His normal medical examiner witness would have placed his own initials on the recovered bullet. Dr. Reese, the substitute, hadn't known the procedure, and no one had bothered to tell her, even with all those police officers jostling her elbow. "Just a couple of more questions. Can you tell whether a bullet was fired into a person at close range?"

"Yes. There are several indications. A burned area around the wound, stippling where gunpowder from the muzzle blast has blown into the skin . . ."

"Did you find any such indications here?"

"No, I didn't."

"From how far away would you say the shots were fired?"

"Three to five feet, I'd estimate."

"Officer Riley didn't shoot himself, did he?"

"No. Not possible." Again she looked at the jury for emphasis.

"Dr. Reese, from your examination, what was the cause of death?" As Chris asked the question, he returned to his seat and sat down, leaving the witness alone on stage.

"Gunshot wound," Dr. Reese said without hesitation. But that was all she said. Again Chris felt a little annoyed. His usual witness for this process would have added, "Homicide." In his last questions he had eliminated the possibility of suicide, so only murder remained. But Dr. Reese was too careful to say the legal word.

"Thank you, Doctor. I pass the witness."

His opposing counsel continued to write, raising his left hand as if asking permission to hold up the proceedings. Then he put down his pen, folded his hands on his abdomen, looked directly at the witness, and smiled. "Dr. Reese, we haven't met, except by phone. My name is John Lincoln. I represent the defendant in this case, Luisa Gaines." He gestured at his client, who did not smile in greeting. "Do you know her?"

"No." Dr. Reese shook her head politely.

"Did you know the deceased in this case, Chip Riley, before his death?"

"No, I didn't."

"Did you know any of the police officers involved, any of the ones who accompanied the body to your autopsy room?"

She shook her head again. "No."

Lincoln emphasized. "So you had no personal involvement in this case, only your professional duties, is that right?"

"Yes, that's right."

"Good. You may be unique in that."

"Objection to the sidebar remark," Chris said, just because it annoyed him. His objection, even after the judge sustained it, would have no effect except to call attention to what the defense lawyer had said. Lincoln smiled slightly.

"May I approach the witness, your honor?" As he did, he picked up the plastic bag from the judge's bench. "This bullet, State's Exhibit Twelve, you said it looked like the one you removed from the body, but you also said you don't know anything about guns. Are you sure this is the bullet you removed from the body?"

"No, I'm really not." The witness shrugged. "I believe I said that."

"Yes, you did." Lincoln took the bit of metal from the bag and held it up between them. "Do you know what caliber bullet this is, Dr. Reese?"

She glanced at it. "No idea."

"Whether it came from a rifle or a handgun?"

"Not really. It's pretty small, but . . ."

"It's still more or less held its shape, hasn't it?"

"Yes."

"You can see what it is. It isn't flattened like a bullet that's gone into a brick wall, for example."

"No."

"Can you tell us why *this* bullet didn't go all the way through the body, Doctor?"

"No. I don't understand your question, to tell the truth."

With his hand, Lincoln indicated a line through the diagram of the body, through the abdomen. "You described the other bullet as traveling a greater distance through the body, but it went all the way through and exited. Why did this one, after a much shorter passage, stop and not exit?"

"I can't explain that. Some bullets pass through bodies, some get trapped. I don't know whether some have less speed to begin with, if maybe sometimes a bullet gets manufactured with less gunpowder charge . . ."

"Because you don't know anything about guns, as you said. But you know about bodies. Did this bullet hit an obstruction? Bone, for example?"

"No. It went straight into the heart, and stayed there."

"Hmm," John Lincoln said, staring at the bullet. Again he held it up close to the witness's face. "Dr. Reese, you don't know for a fact that this is the bullet you took out of Chip Riley's body, do you?"

"Objection," Chris said. "That question has been asked and answered."

"Sustained," the judge said, but the defense lawyer continued speaking. "Yes, it has been. You said you can't identify the bullet by sight, didn't you? So for that we're going to have to rely on Officer Hernandez's testimony, right, Doctor?"

"Yes."

"Can you even be certain that was the officer's name?"

The doctor frowned in slight puzzlement. "He wore a name tag. And he gave me his badge number."

"Yes, he told you. You don't actually know anything except what he told you, do you?"

"I didn't know him personally, no."

"Did he put the bullet straight into a plastic bag, while he was standing there in front of you?"

"Yes."

"And then he went over to this group of other officers. And you didn't know any of them personally either, did you? How many were there? Three, a dozen?"

"Five or six, I'd say."

That shouldn't have happened. There should have only been one officer in the autopsy room, the one there to collect evidence. Chris turned and looked to the back of the courtroom. Steve Greerdon still stood there, arms folded, looking grim. He returned Chris's glance for only a moment, then nodded as if having been given instructions. He turned quickly and went out. Chris returned his attention to the defense lawyer's questioning of Chris's witness.

"Did Officer Hernandez pass the bag to one of these other officers?"

"I don't think so. I didn't see him do that," Dr. Reese answered carefully.

"But you're not sure? Isn't it part of your job to follow what happens to the bullet once you remove it from the body?"

"No. That's the police job."

"Yes," Lincoln said, with a triumphant emphasis. He put the bullet back down and returned to his seat. "One last thing, Dr. Reese. Which of these gunshot wounds killed the deceased?"

She continued to appear off balance. "Well, in a sense both. As I already testified, both were fatal wounds."

"But he was still alive when he was shot the second time, wasn't he?"

"Yes. That's clear from the—"

"So it wasn't the first shot that killed him. It was the second, wasn't it, Dr. Reese?"

"Well, technically speaking, yes. I suppose."

"Not just technically, but actually." Lincoln sounded suddenly passionate. "Chip Riley was killed by the second shot. Right, Doctor?"

"Yes. Although the first would have—"

"Thank you, Doctor. I pass the witness."

Chris didn't ask any more questions. Dr. Reese had begun with great confidence, then had appeared shaken by the defense attorney's questions, even though he hadn't seemed to prove or disprove anything. Lincoln and Chris knew, better than the jurors did, that the autopsy had been unusual: because of the doctor performing it, because normal routine had been breached a time or two, and because of that grim audience standing there awaiting the results of the autopsy. Cops. This early in the trial, the defense strategy began to show itself to Chris. Lincoln was going to put those cops on trial.

Even more troubling, Chris didn't believe all of them himself. And now, apparently, he had his own man on the case. He wondered where exactly Steve Greerdon had gone.

CHAPTER *nine*

★ Late that afternoon, Anne said, "I'd like your permission to tell Chris Sinclair, the district attorney, what you told me about Steve Greerdon. That he really did commit the crime he was convicted of."

She sat behind her desk. Her patient Eric Schwinn sat across from her. His elbows were on his knees, his hands in front of his mouth, his body hunched inward. He had been telling her how much he wanted to return to San Antonio and resume his old life, but that he knew he never could. The biggest drawback was that his old friend and partner was out of prison.

Schwinn didn't move for several seconds after Anne spoke. She sat waiting. Then their eyes met. His were troubled. Anne tried to reassure him by the steadiness of her gaze. Eric Schwinn stood up from his chair and came around her desk. He leaned over her, bringing his face close to hers. This was a serious breakdown in the doctor-patient relationship. An invisible wall was supposed to keep the patients away from this side of the desk. The desk represented Anne's authority. Sometimes she came out from behind it herself to hug a child or reassure one, but no patient was supposed to initiate such contact. Eric Schwinn had never been a usual patient, though. Anne didn't say anything.

He sounded very doubtful when he spoke. "If Steve hears that Sinclair knows that, he'll have a very good idea where the information came from."

"I won't give Chris your name, of course. Or any facts about you at all that might identify you."

"You wouldn't have to," Schwinn said softly. His hand was on the edge of the desk next to Anne's, touching her hand.

"It's your secret," Anne said. "I wouldn't reveal it without your permission. Even if you say I can, I won't tell him unless I really think it's necessary."

Schwinn watched her closely, as if trying to determine whether he could trust her. After another long minute he spoke very quietly. "All right, Doctor. Whatever you think."

"Thank you," Anne said. He hovered over her, very close. Much closer than a patient should ever get.

When Eric Schwinn left Anne's office it was nearly six o'clock. The building was almost empty of people. It would have been hard for Clarissa and Peter to hide in the lobby. But they knew Schwinn's routine by this time. They knew his car and which parking lot he used when he came for his appointments. In her yellow Volkswagen Clarissa waited down the block from that lot, and saw Schwinn when he came out of the building.

"There he is," Peter Greerdon said. Clarissa nodded.

She no longer knew exactly why she was doing this. Peter had been afraid of this man, and he intrigued Clarissa partly because he was one of Anne's few adult patients. Clarissa suspected he had come to her for something other than treatment. She hungered for mystery. It was a game. But she was getting bored with it. This would probably be her last surveillance.

Peter knew exactly why he was continuing to watch Eric Schwinn. Because it was something Clarissa wanted to do with him. "He's making the usual turn," he said alertly.

"Mmm huh," Clarissa said. Twice when they had followed Eric Schwinn he had just gotten on the highway to Austin. After following him past the city limits, they had turned back. That's why Clarissa was getting bored. The guy just came to town to see Anne, then he went back. His life was in another city.

Maybe this time she'd follow him all the way. It would mean she wouldn't get back home until late, she and Peter would get in trouble, and probably nothing would come of it except that she would learn where exactly this man lived. But Clarissa's foot felt light on the gas pedal. She had a sense of being able to reach beyond her boundaries. She laughed. Peter glanced at her. Clarissa couldn't have explained. She drove on, staying well back, hidden in traffic.

Luckily she didn't stay too far back, because this time Eric Schwinn took a different turn than usual. He turned onto the ramp that led to Interstate 10, the highway that went into northwest San Antonio. Anne almost missed him. She had to swerve sharply, so she and Peter were thrown together. He grabbed the door handle. Clarissa straightened up quickly, and they both stared straight ahead out the windshield.

"Maybe he's just lost," she said.

"At least we're heading toward home," Peter said.

They drove toward sunset. By the time they exited, dusk had begun to eat up vision. Clarissa edged closer to their quarry's white Buick. But once he made his way into a neighborhood she had to drop far back. "Where's he going?"

"Maybe he has a girlfriend," Peter said. They glanced at each other, the phrase sounding loud between them.

At least they weren't in Anne's neighborhood. Clarissa had half expected the man to be stalking his psychiatrist, or even meeting her with her approval. That idea had been in the back of her mind. Maybe she'd been spying for her father. But Eric Schwinn had something else going on. His car pulled to a curb. Half a block back, Clarissa did the same, behind a car already parked in front of someone's house. She and Peter watched, holding their breaths, as the man with the dark, wavy hair got out and looked around. That wasn't their imagination. Schwinn was afraid of being observed. But that could be for noncriminal reasons. Maybe he was meeting someone whose husband might be home. It was almost seven, time when people came home from work. But some workers worked unusual shifts. Police officers, for example.

Clarissa said, "I've got to go up there."

Peter nodded silently. His heart had sped up. He had started this business, by recognizing this man in Dr. Greenwald's waiting room, but Clarissa had pursued it much more earnestly than he. Now, though, Peter felt strangely frightened. He slid down in the seat, his eyes barely high enough to see out the side window.

"Get the address when I go by," Clarissa said, and Peter scrambled to find pencil and paper.

"Here we are. He's at the door. Okay, if I time this just right . . ." Clarissa slowed down. She might have been born for surveillance work. More importantly, she was lucky. As she cruised slowly by, the front door of the house Schwinn had approached had just opened. A man stood in the doorway, but Schwinn was blocking him. Clarissa slowed to a crawl, which would have been really stupid except that her quarry's attention was focused on the man who'd opened the door. The man reached out and put his hand on Schwinn's arm, then turned to usher him inside. Eric Schwinn went past, and for a moment the homeowner stood in his open doorway. He still wore a white shirt and suit pants, tie pulled loose. A tall man, of athletic good looks. Clarissa got a good look at his face.

"You know that guy?" she asked. Peter shook his head.

Clarissa didn't know him either. Her father had just spent the day with him, but Clarissa had been in school, not at the trial.

"Get the address?" she asked. Peter nodded, writing it down.

"There's a Web site where you can put in the address and get the name of the person who lives there. It doesn't work for everybody, but I'll try tonight."

"Okay, call me if you find out," Peter said. He sounded eager, but his eagerness only extended to the idea of Clarissa calling him. He didn't believe they had just solved some big mystery, or even deepened one. The guy they'd been following went to see some other guy. Big deal.

Clarissa might or might not get around to her self-assigned chore. If she did, she would discover that the homeowner Eric Schwinn had gone to see was named John Lincoln. But that wouldn't mean anything to Clarissa either. She had some investigative skills, but she was a teenager; she didn't read the newspaper. She didn't know the name of Luisa Gaines's defense lawyer.

Rico Fairis, in a beat-up Buick he'd informally confiscated from a drug suspect, hung back half a block, smiling at the scene before him. The pretty boy going to the defense lawyer's house hadn't spotted either of his tails. Rico shook his head. Very sloppy. But now the yellow Volkswagen with the amateur sleuths in it took his attention. The DA's daughter and Steve Greerdon's kid. An interesting combination that opened so many possibilities. Fairis chuckled. People had so many vulnerabilities, they couldn't even count them all.

He watched Peter Greerdon climb out of the Volkswagen, start up his sidewalk, then turn and watch wistfully as the car drove away, a slender hand raised from the driver's side in farewell. Fairis looked in his rearview mirror and saw Steve's car coming down the street. Crowded neighborhood tonight. Fairis had seen enough, anyway, and drove on past Peter without a glance. Fairis thought he knew what went on inside that house. Instead he followed the girl for a ways, wondering about these kids' relationship, and whether their fathers knew there was one.

Fairis rolled down his window and spat. He had a growing smile as he drove. Life was so entertaining. Why did anybody need to go to movies?

After leaving the courthouse, Steve Greerdon was busy for the rest of the afternoon and early evening. But his travels took him near his ex-wife's house, and he was surprised to see his son in a car with a girl.

Why the sight startled him, Greerdon couldn't have explained. Peter was sixteen, and likely to spend increasing amounts of time in cars with girls. But Greerdon hadn't given any thought to this aspect of his son's life. In fact, subconsciously he still thought of Peter as no more than twelve years old. It wasn't just a surprise to see him with a girl. It was a continuing surprise to see him more than five and a half feet tall with hairs on his upper lip and his chin.

The car was a yellow Volkswagen, driving slowly. It came to a stop at the four-way-stop intersection where Greerdon sat, and then the car just sat there, because the girl driving was so animated. She talked to Peter, gesturing with her hands, her face alight with odd pleasure. Peter just nodded along as the girl talked. Greerdon thought he understood exactly how the boy felt.

He sat unmoving too, watching them, feeling time's currents all around him. He could remember himself in just such a place and occasion as he now saw his son. The memories were both sweet and painful, but mainly long past. He would never be there again. Thank God. From the great height of his adult perspective it looked silly, but Greerdon also remembered the deeply serious possibilities of such encounters. He wished he had some good advice to offer his son, but he didn't. Adult perspective didn't mean insight. Sixteen was just something you had to live through.

Finally the girl looked up and saw him watching her. Greerdon waved, waggling his fingers. Uncertainly, the girl waved back. Greerdon saw his son's lips move, explaining. The girl looked at him again. Peter moved his hand in a much smaller greeting. Greerdon drove on. They were only a block or two from Peter's house. Greerdon circled the block, giving the kids time to talk and say good-bye, whatever. When he drove up to the front of the house where his former wife lived with Emerson Blakely, Peter was standing on the sidewalk and the yellow Volkswagen was at the far end of the block. Greerdon parked at the curb and got out. He walked up to stand beside his son, who slouched there with his backpack over one shoulder, staring at the departing car.

"Pretty girl," Greerdon said. Peter nodded.

"Isn't she the district attorney's daughter?"

"Her name's Clarissa," Peter said. Not dreamily, but giving the syllables emphasis, as if he usually didn't dare say her name aloud.

"That's right. What is she, like seventeen?"

Peter nodded. "She's a senior." He looked even younger as he said it. Greerdon noticed the puffiness of his cheeks, the cowlick at the back of his hair.

"I understand, son. She looks like a beautiful girl. But you know—"

"Dad, you don't have to tell me. I know she's so far out of my league I'm not even on the field. I'm just sitting in the stands watching her. But God, isn't that good enough?"

The most significant word of this speech was the first one. Peter had called him "Dad" before, but not often, and only in a grudging, awkward way. This time he'd said it easily, giving Greerdon the name unthinkingly. And he'd opened up in a way Greerdon didn't ever remember doing with his own father when he'd been a teenager.

He put his arm around his son's shoulder. "Peter, I'll tell you the only thing I've ever learned about women. There's no explaining them."

"Is that it?" Peter laughed.

"No, there's this little bit more. Sometimes the best girls—beautiful, smart—hook up with guys that it makes no sense at all. I think it's like a project they take on. Like buying an old house and fixing it up."

"Is that me?" Peter turned to look at him curiously.

"I don't know. But if it is, you need to listen to what she's saying. Is she trying to change you? You need to respond a little to her fix-up ideas. I mean, don't get perfect all of a sudden, or her work will be done and she'll move on. But you need to do a little bit of what she's trying to do with you, or she'll get bored. Get better gradually enough that she'll think you're still worth working on."

Peter looked as if he were really absorbing this. "Really?" he asked.

"Nah, it's all crap. Go back to the first thing I said. I don't have a clue."

Peter laughed. God, Greerdon's arm felt good around his shoulders. The boy started talking, explaining how this girl had just taken him up, maybe really like a project. Peter sounded confused and happy and eager to talk. Greerdon hadn't seen him in such a mood in years, since he'd been a small boy.

As Greerdon walked Peter up to the porch, he thought for the first time since he'd been released from prison that he could save a relationship with his son. He could know him as a person. Peter had become interested. And he needed his father.

"Isn't it kind of late to be getting home?" Greerdon asked. "Don't worry, we'll tell 'em you were with me."

Peter tried the door, but it was locked. Greerdon rang the bell. "Don't you have a key?" he asked, but then they heard movement inside.

The door jerked open abruptly. "About damned—" said a loud male voice. Emerson Blakely was already reaching through the open doorway when he saw Greerdon. His hand fell to his side.

"Hi, Emerson. Sorry for keeping Peter out. I picked him up from school and I had some errands to run. Okay?"

"Sure," Blakely mumbled. His face was flushed, and his breath smelled of alcohol. He remained in the doorway. Greerdon noticed the way Peter hung his head, both in subservience and as if he didn't want to notice anything inside this house. Greerdon felt a sudden burden.

"Mind if I come in for a second?" he said, gently moving Blakely aside. But rather than let himself be touched, Blakely suddenly turned and walked away, back toward the living room.

"Well," Greerdon said, "I'll call you later, Pete. What time—?"

Then he saw Dolores. She was standing in the living room, holding a hand up to her face. Greerdon stared at her. Peter wasn't moving. He didn't look at his mother.

"Hi, Steve," Dolores said. She dropped her hand and turned away, but not before Greerdon saw a bright spot on her cheek. It might have been high color, or it could have been blood. But Dolores's hot eyes looked like those of a woman who had been hit.

Steve walked into the room. His legs felt shaky. His heart suddenly beating faster made his hands tremble. He looked at Emerson Blakely, but Blakely dropped into his easy chair with his back turned to him. "Dolores . . ." Greerdon said slowly.

"Thanks for bringing Peter home," she said firmly, meaning she didn't want conversation with him. But Greerdon wanted something. She looked straight at him, the bright spot on her cheek beginning to darken. It would be a bruise by morning. He wondered what she would tell people at work, and if she'd ever had to make up such excuses before.

He looked at her and said, "Once it starts, it doesn't stop, you know."

Blakely must have heard him, but he didn't turn. Dolores didn't answer, even by nodding.

Peter was still standing there, still holding his backpack. His downcast face told Greerdon that this scene wasn't new to him.

Peter was what mattered. He was in danger here. Greerdon walked around so that he stood in front of Blakely, who looked up at him. Greerdon's fists were clenched. Deliberately, he opened them. He wanted so badly to beat up this bastard. He wanted to take him to jail. But Greerdon didn't have a place here. He could only make the situation worse.

Looking at Blakely, he said firmly, "Peter, why don't you come home with me tonight?"

Peter hesitated. But then he said, "Thanks, Dad, but I'd better stay here. I've got homework."

Greerdon looked at his son, wondering at his response. Peter looked scared, but also resolved. Greerdon said, "It'll be all right. He won't stop you."

"I know," Peter said.

Greerdon felt frozen. He stared at Blakely, trying to convey a message. Blakely dropped his eyes. *Don't humiliate him*. Greerdon thought. That would only make things worse. He'd been taught that years ago in the academy. So had Emerson Blakely.

Steve Greerdon took the hardest steps of his life slowly, stopping to put a hand on his son's shoulder. He turned at the doorway to give everyone one last chance, then went out, closing the door behind him. On the porch alone, he let out a deep breath and waited for his hands to stop shaking.

Peter had seen his father's fists clench. He knew Emerson had seen it too. His stepfather was afraid of his father. Before Emerson could turn and see the knowledge on Peter's face, Peter took his mother's arm and went with her to the kitchen to help with dinner.

But Peter remembered the lesson. You could be as nice and as reasonable as you could, but if the bully didn't fear you nothing else was worth anything.

Greerdon made one more stop that night, at the home of another police officer. Greerdon had spent the afternoon reading every police report involving Chip Riley's death. There were quite a few—many officers had taken a hand in the investigation of a fellow officer's death—so it had taken him time to fit things together. And not everyone who'd made the scene had written a report, not by a long shot. People wanted to help, but they didn't want to end up testifying. Greerdon understood. He hadn't written a report himself.

But Larry Hernandez had. He'd been the evidence technician assigned to retrieve any evidence recovered from the autopsy. Greerdon had read his report, and it had been very straightforward: Hernandez took the bullet from Dr. Reese, marked it for identification, then carried it straight to the evidence room and turned it in. But Greerdon knew that was just how reports were written. Life was messy. Written offense reports simplified events that in fact might have gotten a little tangled and open to interpretation. Officers learned that details could get you in trouble. So many offense reports read so similarly that they might have come from a form book. Greerdon wanted elaboration.

Hernandez came out onto his front porch, under a yellow light, and didn't invite Greerdon in, though he acted friendly enough. He stood there barefoot, in gray sweatpants and a white T-shirt, a big man with prominent cheeks and eyes that exaggerated his expressions. After a moment Hernandez led Greerdon out of the direct glare of the light to a porch swing. Hernandez gestured at it, and when Greerdon didn't accept the invitation Hernandez did. He lay his beefy arm along the back of the swing and sipped at a beer.

"Hell, yeah, there were other officers there," he said. "You know how it is, Steve. You get an 'officer down' call and everybody's interested. A couple of 'em followed me from the scene to the medical examiner's office. Two or three others met me there. Nothing to see, you know, but people want to get whatever info they can."

"Did Rico tell you anything?" Steve asked casually.

Hernandez looked at him steadily, not falling for it, his eyes shadowed. "Who?"

Greerdon had become convinced that Rico Fairis had been involved in this somehow. But the sergeant's name didn't appear in anyone's report. Nevertheless, while reading them Greerdon had sensed a lurking presence—or rather absence.

"Rico Fairis. I heard he was there, thought he must've had some input. He always does."

Hernandez merely looked puzzled. "Who told you that?"

Greerdon shrugged. Larry Hernandez stood up. He was as tall as Greerdon, with a gut and puffy cheeks, but younger than Greerdon and probably in good shape under the extra pounds. "He must've come after I left, then. I don't know what you've got against Rico, Steve, but I can't help you."

"Nah, nothing, man. I just heard . . ."

Hernandez concluded. "The highest-ranking officer at the ME's office was Lieutenant Reyes. But he didn't give any orders. He just came to see everything was done right."

"Why?"

"I told you. He was in the area, it was a cop-killing . . . People get aggravated. They want to do something. In fact, at first the lieutenant said he'd take the bullet right to the firearms examiner. They're in the same building, you know. But nobody there had the murder weapon. We didn't have a test-fired bullet for comparison. At first we said we'd all wait, but then the lieutenant said no, just take the bullet to the evidence room, somebody else would retrieve it in the morning. That's why the defendant wasn't arrested 'til the next night. There were a lot of forensics—"

But another part of the story had caught Steve Greerdon's attention. "So the lieutenant took the bullet from you?"

Hernandez looked at him stolidly, face to face. "No. He looked at it—"

"Larry, damn it."

"Steve, this isn't like with you. I know what happened to you, and I'm damned sorry. I was just a baby officer then. I barely knew you, but if I could have done anything . . . But this wasn't like that. Nobody's trying to pin anything on anybody, they just wanted to catch a cop-killer. The lieutenant might've gotten a little carried away. That happens. I don't want to get him in trouble."

"You haven't done that," Greerdon said.

Hernandez had nothing else, or at least would give him nothing else. Greerdon hadn't learned anything all day that implicated anyone other than Luisa Gaines in the murder of Chip Riley. On the other hand, he hadn't added to the case against her, either. He walked back to his car thoughtfully, jangling keys in his hand. Automatically he took in his surroundings, including a dark car parked down the block on the other side of the street. He waved. She wouldn't acknowledge him. Greerdon started walking toward the car. The driver's door opened, giving off no light—she must have unscrewed the bulb—and a slender form emerged from the car, no more than a silhouette. Literally his shadow. Greerdon felt tempted to raise his hands high and see if the shadow would emulate him.

"Just wanted to tell you I'm going home now," he called. "You can go off duty."

No answer came. Greerdon returned to his car, grinning, and when he started up and drove away the other car followed. She didn't trust him.

That same evening, late, Anne's voice came over Chris's phone line in a low murmur, slow, as if he had awakened her. In fact, Anne had called him. Chris hadn't been asleep, of course. He'd been making notes for his final argument and trying to anticipate the defense's case. Anne would know that. Her voice sounded intimate, but she spoke about work: "How's the trial going?"

"Fine. Good enough, I guess."

"What's the matter?"

Chris walked across his living room, wearing jeans and a blue T-shirt, looking like a law student pulling an all-nighter. A stuffed file folder and three legal pads lay scattered on the coffee table. Each pad had notes, different aspects of the trial, as his mind leaped around the problems.

He answered, "Oh, we've proved she was mad at her partner, she had reason to think he was stealing from her—or somebody was. And we've put the gun in her hand on another occasion. We're going to show she *could* have done it. But we don't have the big finish, the eyewitness or a confession."

"You can wring it out of her in cross-examination."

"Thanks. I'm glad I can count on me. To tell you the truth, I'm not convinced myself she did it. I've been wanting her to come to me and tell me she knows something else, Chip Riley was involved in something dirty, implicate other officers. But the way things are going, she probably doesn't even believe she's going to get convicted. So she has more incentive to keep quiet than to deal with me."

Anne hesitated, so her next question sounded important. "If she didn't do it, who did?"

"Good question. Maybe some mugger who just happened to be passing through the alley when Chip Riley went out for a smoke."

"For a what?"

"He went outside to have a cigarette, after fighting with the defendant."

"Why? He worked in a bar. Why did he have to go outside to smoke?"

Chris stopped and stood still, holding the phone against his ear, staring across the long room, but not seeing it. He remembered testimony. Chip Riley had been drinking more heavily than usual—and smoking. "He may have been meeting someone outside," he said slowly.

"Chris." Anne sounded very sure of herself. Unlike bullets and fingerprints, this was a subject on which she was entitled to an opinion. "Why does a woman kill a man? I don't think I've ever heard of one who did it over money."

Chris stood lost in thought for a few moments longer. Then energy returned to him. He began to pace again. "Damn, I wish I could find that waitress. Teresa, the one Chip Riley was flirting with. Maybe more. But nobody saw her with him outside."

"Well, if you can't prove where she *was* . . ."

"Yes," he said. "Yes." She heard the restlessness in his voice. He wanted to start writing on his legal pads. He wanted to think. He wanted to skip right over this night and get back into trial. His voice made Anne's sound drowsy. "Thank you, Anne."

"You would've thought of it yourself by tomorrow."

"Yeah, you're right. Okay. Hey! Are you going to come see me close up this case?"

"I've got work of my own, remember? How about if I just think about you longingly?"

"Don't talk like that, I can't get distracted now."

She laughed. "Good night, darling. And Chris? Be careful."

When he hung up the phone he wondered briefly what she meant by that, but then he was off and running on the new tack she had given him.

A few miles away, Anne hung up her phone and looked at it thoughtfully. Maybe she should have said more. Was it time yet? She couldn't tell, from this distance. She thought about Steve Greerdon hovering at Chris's shoulder, and what she knew about him. He had committed a crime. At least one. And he had a huge store of anger. Maybe it would be best if Chris *didn't* know any more about him. She didn't like keeping things from Chris, but that was part of her job. She held secrets. Because they weren't hers to release.

She yawned, truly, and went to bed.

Clarissa said the same thing to him the next morning at breakfast, in the same words. "How's the trial going?"

"Good." Chris hadn't slept much, he had been up and showered already when she'd staggered out of bed, but he looked eager for the day to start. "Today will be even better, I think."

"When you get in trial like this, do you miss seeing Anne?"

"She called last night, after you were asleep."

"Oh. Good." Clarissa still thought of the man she'd followed from Anne's office as a romantic rival for Anne's affections rather than any other kind of threat. That was probably the reason she'd pursued him. She wouldn't say she'd been protecting her father, even to herself. It had just been a silly project for Peter and her. But she was glad to hear that Anne had called.

"And how's school?" Chris asked distractedly. "Got a test or anything today?" But he didn't wait for the answer. "Sorry, honey, I've got to run."

He did, literally. Clarissa sat alone for a minute, then went to brush her teeth, thinking her job was done.

Steve Greerdon was waiting for Chris outside the main entrance to the DA's offices. A few feet from him, Stephanie Valadez leaned against a wall, looking sleepy. The receptionist wasn't on duty yet, it was still early, not yet eight o'clock. Chris let himself in with a key, and let the two others follow. "I've only got a minute, I've got to line up some witnesses . . ."

"Yeah, listen, you've got a hole in your chain of custody you don't know about."

Chris stopped and turned to give the man his full attention. They both knew well what "chain of custody" meant: In trial, when the prosecution wanted to use a piece of evidence that couldn't be identified just by appearance, Chris had to prove where that item had gone each step of the way from its original location to trial. Crime scene to police officer to lab technician, back to police officer, and finally into the courtroom. If any link in the chain was broken, the item wouldn't be admitted in evidence. "Custody of what?" Chris asked, knowing the answer.

"The bullet. The one that was taken out of Chip's body. Your evidence technician wasn't the only one who touched it in the ME's office."

Chris stared at Steve Greerdon, frowning. "What I really need this morning is a new problem."

"I know, I'm sorry. I thought you should know."

Over Greerdon's shoulder, Chris said, "Stephanie, go get Jack. No, never mind, I'll go to him. Come on."

He hurried through the maze of hallways, the other two not keeping up, and into the investigation section, which was a large nondescript room, with white posterboard walls and half a dozen metal desks. Occasionally a decorative item, a photographic or scenic calendar, got affixed to one of those bare walls, but never seemed to last. Jack Fine, looking at home in this institutional environment, was pouring himself a cup of coffee. When he turned at the noise of Chris's entrance he winced and made a sound like an arthritic man trying to climb out of a deep sofa. "You're in trial, man," he said harshly. "Leave everything else alone."

"This is for the trial," Chris said. "We start back at nine thirty, and I need you to do four or five things for me before then."

"How many of them are impossible?"

"Only one," Chris said thoughtfully. "At most two or three."

Jack rolled his eyes. "But you've brought me help." He gave Stephanie a small smile as she entered, then his eyes turned absolutely neutral as Steve Greerdon followed.

"First," Chris said, ticking off assignments on his fingers, "I really, really need that waitress, Teresa."

"I hope that's the one you think is impossible," Jack replied. "Because it is. She was an illegal, Chris. When someone is murdered and one of the witnesses is an illegal, *phhht!*" He made a sound of rapid escape and snapped his fingers like a magician. "The dead guy's a cop, it's double *phhht*. She's back in Mexico by now. I've got everything but wanted posters out, but I won't find her."

Jack's pessimism on this subject was one reason Chris had gone to trial early, figuring he had nothing to lose. But as trial had progressed the missing waitress had begun to seem more important. He shrugged, giving up on that one. "Okay, I need you to get a police officer over here. Lieutenant Reyes. First name, Steve?"

"Albert," Steve and Jack said together. "Sure," Jack added, "I'll give him a call and he'll run right over."

"Tell him we know everything about what he did in the medical examiner's office. Tell him he's looking at an indictment for tampering with evidence."

Jack's eyes widened. He went straight to his phone. Chris turned to his other investigator. "Stephanie, I think I'm going to call you as a witness this morning. I need to ask you about that door between Luisa Gaines's office and the kitchen. You did see it, right?"

"Yes, sir." She stood up straight and looked much more alert than she had a few minutes earlier.

"Another thing," Chris added. "You started outside, looking at the body, then you ran back through the restaurant collecting witnesses. Yes?"

She nodded.

"Did you see this waitress? Do you know the one I mean, Teresa?"

"Yes. No, I didn't see her."

Chris nodded. "Good."

Stephanie looked puzzled. "We need to round up some of those witnesses who were in the restaurant," Chris told her. "And one more thing. I need you to find whether something was collected at the scene. It was—no, damn it, it doesn't matter, it would have been different by the time the evidence technicians came along."

"Something I might have seen?" Stephanie asked quietly. Wearing her usual black, her long dark hair blending into her blouse, she looked, as always, like a schoolgirl.

"Well, yes, probably," Chris answered. "I wish you'd had a video camera."

"Ask her," Jack said from his desk, where he'd apparently been put on hold.

"It wouldn't be something—"

"Ask her," Jack repeated more forcefully. "When Stephanie called me from the scene, when she was standing over the body, I told her to take a good look at everything. She always follows directions."

Chris looked at the young woman skeptically. Steve Greerdon crossed his arms and kept his eyes on Jack, like an unbelieving audience member trying to see the ventriloquist's lips move.

"Can you picture the scene," Chris asked, "as it was just after you got there?"

Stephanie closed her eyes. She didn't frown in concentration. In fact, her face went even more smooth. "Yes," she said.

Chris felt as if he were hypnotizing her. "Stephanie, do you have a photographic memory?"

She opened her eyes. "I'm not sure what that means. I've never been tested. But if I see something, and I was paying attention, I remember it."

Chris stepped close to her and asked a soft question. Greerdon looked annoyed, as if he knew the secret were being kept from him.

Stephanie did frown at the question, and closed her eyes again. "Think about it," Chris said. "Let me know before trial starts."

"Yes, sir," she said, and hurried away. Chris was left standing next to Steve Greerdon, who did not appear to be waiting for an assignment.

Chris asked, "Do you want to be in the room when Jack and I talk to Lieutenant Reyes?"

Greerdon shook his head. "Don't let him know your source of information. If he thinks it's me he'll think I'm just out to get him."

Chris looked at him curiously. "Why would he think that?"

Greerdon moved his hands to his hips. He looked around the bare workroom, as if suddenly sick of such unadorned spaces. "There's a cop named Rico Fairis," he said slowly. "A sergeant. He and I were partners at one time. Rico got involved in something I didn't even want to know about. I was quite clear about looking the other way. But that wasn't good enough for Rico. He wanted me involved. I said no." Greerdon shook his head with regret, then looked Chris in the eyes. "The next thing I know, some young hotshot prosecutor is convicting me of robbery."

Chris stared at him openmouthed, guilt rushing back over him like a pillowcase over his head, cutting off his oxygen. "I've never heard of this Rico Fairis. He wasn't part of the team that brought me evidence against you."

Greerdon gave one short, bitter chuckle. "No, he wouldn't have been."

"Why didn't you tell me this? When you first got out, when I asked you?"

Greerdon said with great emphasis on every word, as if speaking to the hearing-impaired, "Because I didn't want to do anything about it. I told you that. I told Rico that. But he doesn't believe me. He wants me. Either under his thumb or back in prison."

"What does this have to do with Chip Riley?"

"One day a couple of weeks before Chip was killed, Rico asked me for a favor. One little favor. He said he thought since I was out somebody would come to me and offer me proof that I'd been framed. He just wanted me to tell him when that happened. And who said it to me."

"So you told him when Chip Riley approached you?"

"No! I told Rico I'd do it, and hoped that would throw him off, but I never intended to give him any name. I hoped it would just die away. And I thought I was safe because your girl was following me. But . . ." He lost the certainty in his voice. "I don't know." He shook his head again.

Chris sounded outraged, though that was tempered by the guilt he still felt. "Why didn't you tell me this right away, as soon as Riley was killed?"

"Because I had no evidence. It would've just sounded like me trying to get back at Rico. It still does, doesn't it? Besides, your case looked good. Jealous woman. It happens every week. I never found anything to make me think different."

"But now?"

"I don't know. I spent half a day yesterday looking for some sign that Rico was involved, but nobody would admit it. But this Lieutenant Reyes . . . When I heard he was there at the autopsy . . ."

"Why?"

"Because eight years ago he was a patrol officer," Greerdon said with no trace of nostalgic reminiscence. "He was one of Rico's protégés."

He had been more than that. Steve Greerdon remembered eight years earlier, after the robbery at the grocery store, but while the investigation into it had still been going on, in fact had been intensifying. As a detective, Greerdon had made the scene of another crime, a murder. When he arrived, only young Albert Reyes had been bending over the body, at the end of an alley behind a row of warehouses on the deep west side. A place where daylight never penetrated. Where a body looked even deader than it would somewhere else. Reyes had explained briefly that he'd received a dispatch for shots fired, had found the body and called for backup. He hadn't secured the scene yet. In fact, he wasn't sure suspects weren't still in the area. The young officer had been wearing thin latex gloves, Greerdon remembered. He looked at them approvingly at the time. That was more than most young officers thought to do. Reyes had obviously been concerned with not contaminating the crime scene, even while the crime was still hot.

Then something had happened, a tiny vignette of the kind that makes up a police officer's days. The sort of adrenaline spill that made some men love this line of work. Reyes had heard a noise. Greerdon hadn't, exactly, though the alley continually rustled with the sound of leaves and insects and rats and perhaps more. Reyes, who already had his gun out, whirled around, looking alarmed. With his left hand he'd quickly reached toward his ankle and pulled another gun, which he stuck butt-first into

Greerdon's gut. Greerdon had automatically taken the weapon, panning the alley with it. The two officers had stood up and walked slowly down the alley. They heard nothing more, nothing that sounded like running footsteps or a door slamming. After long moments they'd lowered their weapons and Reyes had grinned as if apologizing for his brief panic. Gently he took the gun from Greerdon's hand and returned it to his own ankle holster. "A little backup I keep," he'd explained almost sheepishly.

A lot of cops did that. Some over the years had made bad use of such weapons, Greerdon knew: dropping a throw-down piece beside the hand of a suspect who'd been unarmed when the officer shot him. Reyes didn't seem remotely the type, though. A clean-cut young officer obviously on the way up. He'd looked very neat, eminently professional. The latex gloves seemed to suit him.

The gloves he'd still been wearing when he handed Steve Greerdon the gun, and when he'd taken it away from him and put it back away.

A gun very much like the one young Chris Sinclair had later introduced into evidence at Steve Greerdon's trial: the gun that had been used in the robbery of the grocery store, and that had Greerdon's fingerprint on it.

Now, in the investigation section of the DA's office, he said, "You don't want me here when you talk to the lieutenant," and he faded away.

Jack and Chris looked at each other. Jack still looked skeptical, but then he always did. "What else is on your list?" he asked.

Lieutenant Albert Reyes wore a crisp blue uniform and an ironed white shirt. He carried his white hat with the gold braid. He didn't appear to be armed, but on a police officer it was hard to tell. He would walk around the metal detectors at the doors of the Justice Center by displaying his badge.

He came to Chris and Jack in the investigative office. Chris had decided to meet the senior officer here because it looked more clinical. A meeting in Chris's office would seem more like a high-level meeting, a courtesy extended to a fellow professional. Chris wanted Reyes to feel more like a suspect.

Chris had spent the interval of waiting getting mad. People were interfering with his trial. Usually he had only the defense and the judge to contend with. In this case he had to keep looking over his shoulder, wondering what his own team was up to behind his back. The defendant had become the least of his worries: He didn't understand anyone's motives. Steve Greerdon might well be lying to him, in fact almost certainly was in some respects. But so were other people. Now he finally had someone on whom to focus his anger at being unable to trust his own evidence.

"Lieutenant, thank you for coming," Jack Fine said, shaking hands. "I hope I didn't wake you."

"Of course not." The officer's brown eyes snapped with alertness and with a bit of amusement that anyone might suggest he ever slept. He turned to the district attorney, his hand moving forward.

"What were you doing at Chip Riley's autopsy?" Chris said abruptly. He sat on the edge of a desk and didn't extend his hand.

"Good morning to you, Mr. Sinclair," Reyes said wryly.

"Judge Conners is going to be telling me to call my next witness in about twelve minutes, and I have to decide whether that's going to be you. Answer my question."

Reyes immediately went to a deeper level of intensity himself. "You cannot understand what the words 'officer down' mean to every other police officer. They are the words we dread most. We imagine our own families receiving such news. When a police officer is killed, we do not sit at home and shake our heads and say 'tsk tsk.' We go to do something. A lot of officers went to the scene. By the time I heard what had happened, that part of the investigation was over. Besides, I live closer to the medical examiner's office. I went there. I wanted to coordinate. If my authority would help speed up the investigation, that's what I would do. I would do whatever I could."

"Why did you inject yourself into my chain of custody? You know better than that."

Reyes glared back at Chris. "It was *our* chain of custody at the time. And I didn't."

"Yes, you did. I have evidence."

"Chris," Jack said, cautioning.

The lieutenant smiled, suddenly looking at ease. He looked from Jack to Chris as he said, "I see. You are the good cop and you are the bad cop. I didn't realize I was being interrogated."

"No, we're trying to decide whether *you're* the bad cop," Chris said harshly. "What did you do with the bullet that was taken from Chip Riley's heart?"

"Nothing. I didn't touch it. If any witness says I did, he is mistaken."

"I didn't say anything about witnesses."

The lieutenant frowned, looking less sure of himself for the first time. "But you—"

"This is evidence that can't be mistaken," Jack said gently. "Your fingerprint."

"No," Reyes said emphatically. His face grew very hard again. "You do not have my fingerprint on the bullet."

"Not the bullet." Jack shook his head. "On the Baggie. You do know that plastic bags can hold fingerprints, don't you, Lieutenant? Under the new microscopes? Oh, yes."

Reyes lost his confidence again. His eyes dropped from their faces, the sure sign of a man in distress, thinking fast. "Eight minutes," Chris said, not looking at his watch.

"Perhaps I did," Reyes said slowly. "Touch just the bag. Held the bullet up to my eyes so I could get a good look at it."

"Damn it!" Chris said. He looked at Jack. "I have to give him up, don't I? Shit!"

The lieutenant's concern turned to alarm. "To who? To a grand jury? I didn't do anything."

"He has to give your name to the defense," Jack said patiently. He looked disgusted. "If you had just stuck to your story that you never touched the evidence he wouldn't."

"But you had my—" Understanding dawned on the officer's face. "Oh, God."

"Fingerprint on a Baggie," Jack said disgustedly. "God, you're easy. Don't ever commit a crime, Lieutenant. They'd have a confession out of you in ten minutes." He turned to Chris. "You only have to tell the defense something if it tends to prove the defendant's innocence. This doesn't. It just kind of messes things up." But Jack knew this argument wouldn't carry any weight with his boss. Chris was straightening his tie and putting on his suit coat. He shot an angry look at Reyes.

"Be prepared," he said angrily. "And stick around. He's yours, Jack."

He strode out of the investigative office, leaving two unhappy people.

When Judge Conners did call the case to order that morning, Chris Sinclair sat alone at the prosecution table. Bonnie Janaway was interviewing and coordinating the rest of the day's witnesses. John Lincoln turned toward Chris curiously, with a slight smile, as if he expected to be entertained. His client still stared stoically ahead. As usual, Chris wished he could read her thoughts. He wished he could just talk to her. But that wasn't allowed. Luisa Gaines had a lawyer. Chris could only address her through him. And John Lincoln would never allow her to make a deal with him while he thought there was a chance of winning an acquittal without such a deal.

When the judge prompted him, Chris said, "The State calls Stephanie Valadez."

Well before trial, the prosecution is required to give a list of its witnesses to the defense. If the name isn't listed, the person can't testify. So when it had become apparent that they would need more testimony about the layout of the restaurant, Chris had gone through his witness list to see whom he could use for that purpose. That was the main, simple reason for calling Stephanie. But now he had another use for her as well.

"Stephanie Valadez. I'm an investigator for the District Attorney's Office," she answered his first question. Stephanie had changed into a white blouse and a beige blazer and looked more conventionally feminine and less like a secret agent. She sat very straight in the witness chair but didn't appear nervous. Chris didn't think she had ever testified before, but she didn't show it.

"Have you been to the restaurant called Miguelito's, Ms. Valadez?"

"Yes, sir."

Chris paused ever so slightly, which gave Stephanie time to remember that he didn't like to be called "sir," and that she shouldn't be testifying as Chris's employee. "Did you go there the night Chip Riley was murdered?"

"Yes. I was there at the scene almost immediately after Officer Riley was killed. I heard the shots."

"Did you see who shot him?"

"No. When I came running into the loading dock area, he was already dead. I didn't see anyone else."

"Let's talk about the layout of the restaurant. Did you go into the restaurant that night?"

"Yes. I went through the back door, which opened into a short hallway. A few feet inside that door was a door to the kitchen. I went in there and through there to the restaurant."

"What was the atmosphere like inside the restaurant?"

Stephanie shifted a little in the witness chair and looked at the jury, beginning to tell them the story. "People had heard the shots. Someone shouted that someone had been shot. People were on their feet, milling around. Some were trying to get out quickly, while a few wanted to go see the body. It was rather chaotic."

"Did you try to gather up witnesses?"

"Yes. I started collecting people, asking what they had seen, making notes."

"And we've presented some of those witnesses in this trial, haven't we?"

"Yes, sir," she said, forgetting.

"I want to ask you about two people. Were you familiar with a waitress at the restaurant named Teresa, sometimes called Teresita?"

"Yes." Stephanie nodded to the jury. "I had been in the restaurant before and had seen her. A thin young woman with almost no English."

"Did you look for her that night?"

"Yes. I mean, not exclusively, not even in particular, but I did look for employees of the restaurant in particular, because I thought they would know more about what had happened than customers would."

"Did you see Teresa?"

"No, I didn't."

"Did you go all through the restaurant?"

"Yes, all the way out the front door. Other police officers were there by then, stopping people who tried to leave."

Chris felt intensity building at the table to his left. In his peripheral vision he saw Luisa Gaines leaning forward, studying this witness more than she had any other. But her lawyer leaned back, looking relaxed, still with a slight look of amusement. No, not amusement, Chris decided: expectancy.

"What about the defendant, Luisa Gaines? Did you know her?"

"Yes," Stephanie answered. "I knew her to be the owner of the restaurant."

"Was she there in the midst of all this chaotic activity?"

"No. She wasn't there. I noticed because the employees were looking around for someone in charge. Of course Officer Riley wasn't available, and Ms. Gaines didn't take charge, either."

"Did you ever see her?"

"Yes. After a couple of minutes she came out of her office. She looked surprised at all the confusion, but in a matter of moments she started trying to restore order."

"How did she look?" Chris asked curiously. This would have been Luisa Gaines's first public appearance after murdering her lover, according to the prosecution theory. How would she appear? "Distraught? Flushed? Short of breath?"

Stephanie shrugged. "Not really. Just like a woman taking charge of a crisis in her restaurant."

"She didn't have a gun in her hand, did she?"

"No."

Over at the defense table, John Lincoln hid a small smile with his hand. How stupid did Chris think his client was?

Chris nodded. "Now about the layout of the restaurant. You said the defendant came out of her office. Where was the door to that office?"

"Behind the bar."

"Did you go into that office later?"

"Yes, I did."

"Is there another exit from the office other than the door behind the bar?"

"Yes, there is. I found a door that you could easily miss at first. It didn't look as if it had been a door at first. It just looked like a section of the wall paneling. I opened it and found that it led out into a hallway. It's the same hallway that goes past the kitchen door and out the back door of the restaurant. The same hallway I'd come into when I'd come in from the loading dock area."

"So a person could go from the office out to the loading dock, or from the loading dock to the office, without going through the restaurant or the kitchen?"

"Yes," Stephanie said.

Chris made notes on a legal pad, letting the jury soak up that information. Stephanie had been a very good witness in a short space of time. She didn't even know how much she had done for the State's case. But she had one more important task.

"Let me take you back outside to the scene when you first arrived," Chris said seriously, clearly asking his witness to concentrate. The jury's attention was fastened on her. "After you determined that Chip Riley was dead, did you take a good look at the scene outside?"

"Yes, I did," Stephanie said.

"Other than the body, did you notice any other signs of human life?"

Stephanie knew what Chris meant, because he had told her in the investigative offices, and she had answered the question for him outside in the hall just before trial had resumed. On the witness stand, she nodded her head emphatically. "I noticed a burning cigarette. It lay on the ground just at the foot of the steps."

"Still burning, you say?"

"Yes."

"Only one?"

"There was only one there close to the body. But I looked around and I noticed another one about ten feet away, in the opposite direction from the way I had come into the area. It lay on the pavement, and it still had a glowing tip, too."

"A glowing tip?"

"Yes. I mean it was burning."

"Ms. Valadez, are you sure of this?"

"Objection," John Lincoln said quickly, on his feet and not looking amused at all. "He's asking his witness to bolster her own testimony."

Judge Conners glanced at Chris, who said, "Let me put it this way. Why did you look around the scene the way you did, Ms. Valadez?"

"I had called my supervisor on my cell phone. He told me before I went inside to take a careful look around and remember every detail." Without a hint of pride, she said to the jurors, "He knows I'm good at that."

"Thank you, Ms. Valadez. I pass the witness."

John Lincoln stared at Stephanie for a long moment. It appeared obvious to Chris that her testimony had bothered the defense lawyer. What she'd said hadn't seemed particularly damaging, but Lincoln saw the uses Chris would make of it. The defense lawyer and Chris had debated in law school, then had tried cases against each other over the years. John Lincoln had lost nearly all these encounters, but he was a very good lawyer. He would not have come into this trial without a plan. Stephanie Valadez seemed to stand in his way.

"Ms. Valadez," he finally said, "have you taken a good look at the jury?"

Stephanie glanced along their row, then back at the defense lawyer. "Yes."

Lincoln rose quickly to his feet. He walked away from the jury, and Stephanie's eyes naturally followed him. "Ms. Valadez, keep your eyes on me, please. Turn so your back is to the jury. Thank you."

The defense lawyer held up his index fingers, commanding Stephanie's gaze, but also looking as if he were conducting a very small orchestra. Lincoln glanced at Chris. Chris tried to keep from smiling. But looking at his old friend's face, John Lincoln suddenly knew he was making a mistake. He said slowly, "Ms. Valadez, how many men and how many women are on the jury?"

"Seven women and five men," Stephanie said at once. "Starting on the back row, it's man, then two women, another man—"

"Thank you, but that's not my question," Lincoln said. "There is a man on the front row, third from the right, one of the closest jurors to you. Can you tell us the color or pattern of the tie he's wearing?"

Stephanie closed her eyes. Chris was glad the jurors couldn't see her face, because this part looked fakey. Again her expression smoothed. After a few seconds she said, "That's not a man, Mr. Lincoln. The man is fourth from the right. His tie has a dark blue background with a pattern of sunbursts. His tie tack is a small gold cross. It's a little hard to make out, because it's on the edge of one of the—"

"Thank you, Ms. Valadez. I meant fourth from the right. I'm sorry, I wasn't trying to trick you."

Yeah, right. Chris thought, and so, from their expressions, did several of the jurors. John Lincoln walked quickly back to his seat. He didn't look at all defeated. In fact, he wore his own version of the small, almost invisible smile Chris had had a few moments earlier. "Ms. Valadez, with your remarkable powers of observation, could you tell whether this second burning cigarette you saw had lipstick on it?"

"No, sir. It was dark, I couldn't see it that well. All I could see was the burning tip."

"Have you ever noticed a nervous man, perhaps a man waiting for someone, light a cigarette without realizing he already has one going?"

Stephanie blinked and thought. "I can't say that I've ever actually seen that."

Not that it mattered. The question had been a statement. John Lincoln folded his hands together, leaned forward on his elbows, and said, "Ms. Valadez, what were you doing at Miguelito's restaurant that night?"

"I was on an assignment."

"And could you please tell us what that assignment was?"

Chris almost rose to object that the answer would be irrelevant. But he didn't want the jury to think he was keeping something from them. It was a close call.

"I was following a man named Steve Greerdon."

"Why?"

"Because my boss had told me to."

"Who is this man Steve Greerdon?"

Chris did stand then. "Objection, your honor. This is irrelevant. It has nothing to do with this case."

Also on his feet, John Lincoln said, "Maybe someone other than the district attorney should be allowed to determine that."

Judge Conners looked back and forth between the lawyers. Getting no reply from Chris, she said, "I'll allow you to inquire into this a little further."

Lincoln immediately seated himself and said, "Who is Steve Greerdon?"

"He's a police officer," Stephanie said hesitantly. "He was recently released from prison. My boss assigned me—"

"By 'boss' you mean Mr. Sinclair here."

"Yes, sir. Mr. Sinclair assigned me to—to escort Officer Greerdon. I went wherever he went."

"And he went to Miguelito's that night?"

"Well, to that area."

How close was he?"

"Within a block."

"In the area of the loading dock?"

"Well, in that general vicinity," Stephanie said. "But he was going around the block."

"You followed him around the block?"

"No, sir. I lost track of him for a minute or two—"

"A minute or two! When he was 'in the vicinity' of the loading dock? Was this at about the time the murder happened?"

"Yes, sir, at about that time." Stephanie tried to sound composed, but looked nervous.

John Lincoln jumped to his feet. He picked up his copy of the indictment and held it up. "Your honor, I request a mistrial! This man Steve Greerdon is not on the state's witness list. I haven't been informed of his existence before this! Here's another suspect lurking in the vicinity at the exact time the murder took place. This is evidence that tends to exonerate the defendant, and the defense hasn't been informed of it. I object that the state has been hiding exculpatory evidence. This is—"

"And I object to the defense lawyer testifying," Chris said quickly. "This isn't evidence. It has nothing to do with what's before the jury. The defense is just trying—"

"Gentlemen," Judge Conners said sharply, again looking back and forth between the two lawyers. She appeared startled. "Bailiff, take the jury out, please. We need to have a hearing on this."

The jurors trailed out. Lincoln watched them. Chris stood rigid, staring at the judge. As soon as the side door of the courtroom had closed behind the jurors, Chris opened the thick file in front of him and slammed it down on the table in front of him.

"There's the State's file! It's open. As it's been open through months of pretrial preparations. Everything in there has been available to the defense, including this!" He took out three closely printed pages. "This is Stephanie Valadez's written report to me. It begins, 'On the night of December thirteenth I was close to Miguelito's restaurant on an unrelated investigation . . .' There it is. Any time the defense wanted to pursue that, they were welcome to do so. Instead they chose to leave it unexplored so that they could make these implications in front of the jury."

"These aren't implications, your honor," the defense lawyer cut in. "And having an open file policy isn't good enough, when you don't inform the defense of specific exculpatory evidence, which in this case is that there was another suspect at the scene of the murder."

"Exculpatory" is a word only used in legal contexts. It is the opposite of incriminating. If the prosecution has evidence which tends to prove a defendant's innocence, the prosecutor must turn that evidence over to the defense. Hiding such evidence is one of the worst ethical violations of which a prosecutor can be accused. Chris's anger wasn't feigned.

"Steve Greerdon is not a suspect. He had nothing to do with this murder. He had no motive and no opportunity."

"He was closer to the victim than you've put my client," John Lincoln said coolly. Chris turned to him, eyeing him so intently that he might have considered the defense lawyer a suspect himself. Lincoln stared back levelly.

"We both know that's not true," Chris said.

"Perhaps you gentlemen won't mind if I make a legal ruling now," Judge Conners said wryly. "Mr. Lincoln, evidence that someone besides your client was in the neighborhood isn't exculpatory unless you demonstrate that this other person might have committed the crime."

"Fine, your honor. I'd like the opportunity to do that."

"Mr. Sinclair?"

"Absolutely, your honor. Officer Greerdon is in my offices. He can be here in five minutes."

"Fine, then." The judge tapped her gavel. "We'll continue this hearing as soon as he arrives."

"No, your honor," Chris said. He had used a word judges aren't used to hearing. Quickly he made his tone conciliatory, though his expression made clear his firmness. "I'd like this to be done in front of the jury, your honor. Mr. Lincoln accused me of hiding evidence in front of the jury. I don't want us to have a closed hearing and then have the jurors hear no more about it. If he's going to try to offer proof of another suspect, the jury should hear it."

"Fine," Lincoln said, staring at Chris as if accepting a dare.

Judge Conners looked briefly annoyed. She was supposed to make the rules. But in fact if both sides agreed on something, she would be inviting reversible error by overruling them. She shrugged. "Fine. Richard, as soon as we have a witness, bring the jury back."

The bailiff nodded. The judge left the bench. Everyone stood up, including the reporters in the front row of the spectator section. Chris could imagine the headlines they had already written in their minds. D.A. HIDING EVIDENCE. But he was more concerned with winning the trial. He looked at the defendant, who had sat remarkably unmoved through all the uproar around her. But for just a moment she looked up at him. Her expression gave nothing away, but Chris thought that the two of them had much to say to each other if they could. He was afraid the two of them were part of a larger game going on outside the trial. Evidence being found—or created—by both sides. Someone had promised Luisa Gaines something in exchange for her silence. That promise probably included acquittal. Chris had to make sure she didn't go free, no matter what he believed.

A few minutes later Steve Greerdon entered the courtroom, escorted by Jack Fine. He trudged up the aisle like an experienced bull entering the ring, looking warily left and right, not taking anything at face value. He walked up to Chris and said, "What's up?"

"The defense wants to prove you killed Chip Riley."

Chris said it flatly, watching Greerdon for reaction. The veteran cop and former inmate showed none. "'Course they do," he said. "Me or anybody else except her."

Normally Chris would have prepared his witness to testify. He hadn't had time to do that because he hadn't expected Greerdon to be a witness. But Greerdon looked confident. In fact, Chris saw a determination in Greerdon's expression that worried him a little. He remembered what Greerdon had said he should have done to avoid conviction at trial: anything. Whatever it took.

Chris looked past Greerdon, to John Lincoln, and waved his hand, offering the witness. Lincoln nodded and sat and took another legal pad out of his briefcase. Chris walked over to him. Lincoln pulled a file folder across the new legal pad, but not before Chris had seen the writing on it. Chris said confidentially, but loudly enough to be heard by the one reporter who lingered nearby, "John, next time you want to look outraged and surprised, don't have your questions for the surprise witness already written out."

Lincoln glared, then tried to smile.

When the jurors returned, Steve Greerdon sat in the witness stand. He was quite a replacement for Stephanie Valadez. Chris liked the contrast. He remained on his feet to say, "Your honor, this witness has been in the courtroom for some of the testimony."

John Lincoln quickly waved his hand and said airily, "I'll waive that, your honor." Chris sat down, letting the defense lawyer begin the questioning.

After getting the witness's name, Lincoln began quickly, "Officer Greerdon, what were you convicted of?"

"Aggravated robbery. I was also pardoned."

"But not before you spent eight years in prison, correct?"

"That's right."

"That must have been a very painful experience."

Greerdon looked at the defense lawyer coldly for a moment, then answered blandly, "Yes, it was."

"How long have you been out?"

"Almost six months."

"You were pardoned for the robbery. I assume you'll say you were innocent of that charge?"

"I was."

"How did you get convicted then?"

Greerdon nodded slightly toward Chris. "The prosecutor had evidence against me. It wasn't true, but he had a case."

"Was that evidence manufactured?"

Greerdon looked at him coldly again, and spoke slowly. "Yes."

"You were framed."

"I was set up, yes."

"By whom?"

Greerdon shrugged. His voice remained bland and his face stiff, but his eyes smoldered. "I wish I knew," he said mildly.

"You say they brought evidence to the district attorney. Usually it's police officers who do that. So you were framed by fellow police officers?"

"I have to think some of them were involved, yes."

"Officer, if people did that to me, I'd come out of prison wanting to make them sorry they were ever born."

There was a silence while the two of them looked at each other and the jurors looked curiously at Steve Greerdon, who appeared so self-contained but must have been stiff with rage inside. He finally spoke. "Is that a question?"

"My question is, don't you feel like that?"

"No."

"You don't care about finding the men who sent you to prison?"

"I'd like to know who did it, sure. I'm just saying it's not my main preoccupation. Mostly I just want to get on with my life. After being in prison, waking up free every morning is so wonderful you can't imagine it. Even sitting here is a great moment. I'm still amazed every day. That's more important than throwing away this new life obsessing over who got me."

John Lincoln sat and stared at him for a moment, just contemplating him, obviously unbelieving. He hoped the jurors would find Greerdon's placid demeanor unconvincing, too.

"Chip Riley was a police officer, wasn't he?"

"Yes."

"Did you know him when you were on the force, before you went to prison?"

"Yes. We never partnered, but we knew each other."

"Was he one of the officers who framed you?"

Greerdon was shaking his head before the question ended. "I have no reason to think so."

"But he could have been?"

"Since I don't know who did, I guess he was a possibility."

"Is that why you went to see him that night behind Miguelito's?"

"He asked me to meet him out there about eleven. He didn't exactly say he had information for me, but that was the impression he gave me."

"Did he seem remorseful, like he might have felt guilty over what had happened to you?"

"I don't think I ever saw Chip act sorry about anything." Greerdon smiled, a small smile but so incongruous on his stony face that it gave an impression of great amusement.

That expression seemed to make the defense lawyer angry. His voice grew harsher. "Chip Riley might have been one of the officers responsible for sending you to prison, mightn't he?"

Greerdon grew completely serious again. "He wasn't involved in the case."

"He didn't investigate the robbery case, but he could have had a motive for framing you, couldn't he?"

"I don't know why."

"Well, what motive did anyone have?" Lincoln asked, on the verge of sarcasm. "It was because you knew things about them, wasn't it? You were a danger to these other officers, weren't you?"

"Either that or they really didn't like me very much."

"You think this is funny, Officer? A man is dead. A man you had reason—"

"I don't think it's funny at all. There's nothing I take more seriously than a murdered police officer."

"You said you never saw Chip Riley remorseful. He didn't have much of a conscience, did he?"

"I didn't really know him well enough to—"

"You knew his reputation, didn't you? Wasn't he the kind of cop to be on the take? A dirty cop, the kind who would have had a reason to set you up and send you to prison?"

Because Chris sat close to the defense table, he noticed a very small movement. Luisa Gaines had pulled a legal pad close to her and begun writing. Everyone else's attention in the courtroom was fastened on Steve Greerdon. No one noticed her small, precise hand motions. She wrote very quickly, then dropped her hand beneath the table. She must have pinched her lawyer or otherwise gotten his attention, because Lincoln turned toward her quickly, looking startled. While Steve Greerdon on the witness stand denied having any reason to think Chip Riley had been involved in setting him up, Lincoln quickly read what his client had written. He seemed to recover himself. For a few minutes he had been so caught up in dueling with the witness he had forgotten his case.

Luisa Gaines quickly covered what she'd written. Chris knew he would never get a chance to see that page, but he had an idea what it had said. *Lay off,* or words to that effect. Proving Chip Riley had been involved in something crooked wouldn't help her case, since she had been his partner.

Besides, Chris thought, this was part of the defendant's bargain. She needed to keep the idea of corrupt cops out of this trial. At least one of those cops had promised her freedom, if she kept quiet. That was Chris's theory, and this brief exchange between the defendant and her lawyer convinced him further.

John Lincoln sat still for a moment, then got himself back on track. "What did Chip Riley say to you that night?" he asked quietly.

"Nothing. I never got close to him. I circled the block to come at the loading dock area from the opposite side. Before I got anywhere near, I heard a gunshot. I paused, because I wasn't sure where the sound had come from, and I didn't want to go charging into something. Then I heard another shot. I went to the corner and looked around at the loading dock, but by the time I got there Chip was down. It looked obvious to me he was dead."

"Did you see anyone else?"

This was a dangerous question from the defense. Greerdon obviously understood that the defense lawyer was accusing him of the murder. Lincoln had just given him an opening to solidify the case against Lincoln's client. Greerdon gave Luisa Gaines a long look, as if contemplating placing her standing over the victim's body, a smoking gun in her hand.

But it wouldn't have been a smart thing to say, and it wouldn't have been believable. The prosecution had known about Greerdon. If he had told them he'd seen Luisa Gaines murder her lover, Greerdon would have been the state's star witness. But he hadn't even been on the witness list.

After the pause he said, "No. I didn't see anyone."

"Why didn't you rush to the aid of your fellow police officer?"

"I told you it was obvious he was dead. And frankly I didn't want to put myself there. It looked like exactly the sort of thing that had happened to me nine years ago. I was afraid. Then I heard running footsteps and I saw Ms. Valadez come running up. A few seconds later another guy appeared who I recognized as an undercover officer. I knew they'd take charge of the scene, and get Chip help if he needed it. I wasn't going to do anybody any good there, so I left. I went home."

"You went home," Lincoln said flatly, disbelief apparent on his face.

"Yes, sir."

"Officer, is there any other light you can shed on who might have killed Chip Riley?"

"Not that I know of. I wish I could."

That sounded sincere. John Lincoln began wrapping up, getting the best he could get for his client from this witness. "You didn't see Luisa Gaines out there at all, did you?"

"I already said. No, I didn't."

"You didn't see her holding a gun, did you?"

"Not that night."

The moment froze. The defense lawyer obviously wanted to take back his last question, the one he shouldn't have asked. He sat unmoving, but with his mind obviously racing. Undo this or not? Pursue it or drop it? But in the meantime too much time had passed. Lincoln knew Chris had caught the answer, and understood its importance. He recovered himself in a matter of a couple of seconds, and probably most people in the room hadn't even noticed his pause. Lincoln said, "Your honor, I have no more questions for this witness."

Chris sat frozen too, staring at Steve Greerdon. Greerdon sat there with his hands folded together, placidly waiting, not looking at anyone. Chris found him unreadable. But he knew he had to pursue the last answer. He rose slowly and said, "Your honor, I have a few questions."

The judge nodded, but John Lincoln interrupted. "Your honor, I called this witness for a specific purpose. He wasn't on the State's witness list, and shouldn't be available to the prosecutor as a general witness."

Judge Conners remained leaning back in her chair, watching the defense lawyer and being careful not to smile. She knew the look of a man who had stepped in it. "Mr. Lincoln, when you call a witness the State has the right to cross-examine. Besides, you opened the door to this subject."

So the judge had understood the importance of Steve Greerdon's last answer, too. When one side in a trial "opens the door" to a subject, the other side has the right to walk through that inviting opening. The judge nodded to Chris.

"Officer Greerdon, you said you didn't see the defendant with a gun that night. Had you seen her holding a gun on another occasion?"

"Miguelito's is close to where I was living. I went in there very regularly. So yes, I had seen Ms. Gaines with a gun. I mean, she's a bar owner. Everybody knew she had a gun."

"As a police officer, didn't that concern you?"

Greerdon shrugged. "The first time I saw her bring it out when there was trouble, I asked Chip later whether she had a license, and he said sure. So I let it go."

Chris hesitated. He felt Greerdon leading him onto dangerous ground. But he had to ask. "Officer, when was the last time before Chip Riley's murder that you saw Luisa Gaines holding a gun?"

Greerdon stared into space, apparently thinking. Tension at the counsel tables mounted. Chris felt John Lincoln glance at him, but he wouldn't look that way.

"It was sometime in that last week," Greerdon said. "It was kind of late, I had just dropped in for a beer on my way home. Chip wasn't around at first. A fight started, and Luisa went into the office. I knew what she went for. I went over and broke up the fight myself before it got worse. Then Chip arrived. Luisa came out of the office and saw things were under control. She looked at us for a minute, then went back into the office."

"And she had the gun?"

Greerdon's voice grew more compelling, as if he were finally talking about his own field of expertise, or something that interested him. He leaned toward the jury. "She wasn't waving it around. She didn't have to. There's a way a person looks who's holding a gun. You can see it in their face. You may be panicked, but when your hand touches that handle you get a little calmer. You feel in charge. This is what gets people killed sometimes. You've got a gun in your hand, you feel at least a little invincible. That's the way Luisa looked that night when she came out of her office."

He leaned back and added casually, "Besides, I saw a flash of silver as she turned away, as she stuck it back in her pocket."

Chris walked slowly to the bench and picked up the pistol that had been admitted earlier. He handed it to the witness. "Does this look like the gun you saw the defendant holding?"

Greerdon turned it over carefully in his hands. "Yes. It looks like the same one."

"And when exactly would you say that was?"

"My best estimate, the Sunday night before Chip was killed on a Wednesday."

"No more questions, your honor," Chris said, and walked back to his place rather stiffly.

Lincoln, though, started asking questions at once. "Officer, why weren't you on the State's witness list to give this testimony?"

Greerdon frowned in apparent puzzlement. "I hadn't mentioned it to anyone."

"You hadn't told the prosecutor you'd seen Luisa Gaines holding a gun only a few days before the victim was murdered?"

"I didn't know it was an issue," Greerdon said calmly. "Like I said, everybody knew she had a gun."

"You didn't know that that gun had gone missing about two weeks before the murder?"

Greerdon looked surprised. "No."

Lincoln's eyes narrowed. "Did you take it yourself, Officer?"

Greerdon shook his head, still looking casual, not as if he were being accused. "I never got anywhere near it. I don't even know where she kept it."

Lincoln just watched him for a long pause, looking angry. But he also understood the futility of dueling with this witness any longer. "No more questions, your honor," he said.

Chris shook his head. "Neither do I," he said simply.

"Thank you, Officer," Judge Conners said. "This looks like a good time for a lunch break. We'll resume at one thirty."

The jurors left slowly, in the bailiff's charge. When they were gone, Luisa Gaines put her head down in her hands, looking discouraged for the first time. Chris should have been cheered by the sight. But he felt oddly hollow, completely unsettled. "Your honor, may we approach the bench?" he asked before the judge got away. She shrugged and gestured them forward, just the lawyers. Chris said, "Your honor, there's something I want to put on the record. I just learned this morning that a high-ranking police officer, Lieutenant Albert Reyes, was in the autopsy room when the victim in this case was autopsied. Lieutenant Reyes may have handled the bullet that was removed from the victim. At least he examined it closely. If called as a witness, I believe he would say he never touched the bullet, but I still wanted the defense to know about this."

"Very honorable of you," John Lincoln said dryly. "I'll give Lieutenant Reyes a call over lunch."

Judge Connors declared an official recess. She looked wryly at the two lawyers, like a teacher about to reprimand two of her favorite students. Then she merely rolled her eyes and left the bench.

Lincoln turned to Chris and said, "Another trap you're laying for me? You want me to call Reyes as a witness for you?"

Chris shook his head. "I didn't lay any trap for you, John." He decided not to say any more on that subject. He pulled the defense lawyer further aside, to where they couldn't be overheard. Chris paused, which made sure the other lawyer was watching him closely. "John, this is just between you and me. Do you think your client is innocent?"

"Of course I do," Lincoln said instantly and automatically. He didn't look receptive to a confidential conversation with Chris Sinclair, no matter what past they shared.

Chris said slowly, "What if I could convince you otherwise?"

Lincoln stared at him, first starting to get mad, then his expression turning more speculative. "What difference would it make? I'm not on the jury."

"She wrote you a note while you were questioning Steve Greerdon. She told you to get off the subject of dirty cops."

"That was a confidential communication!" Lincoln burst out. "You have no right to be looking over my—"

"I didn't see what she wrote, John. I just know. I know the deal she's made. I'm trying to tell you that it's a bad one. She should deal with me instead."

Lincoln paused for a long time. His face was handsome, usually full of eagerness, but suddenly he looked tired. He glanced over at his client, who looked at him curiously. "What are you offering?" he said quietly.

"I honestly don't know," Chris said. "Better than she'll get from this jury, if she'll give me good information. Dismissal of the case if she convinces me of her innocence."

Lincoln looked at him critically. "How could she possibly do that?"

"I have no idea. By giving me evidence against someone else, I guess."

Chris didn't think she could do that. He was still convinced of Luisa Gaines's guilt. He just thought that guilt covered others as well.

He spoke more quickly. "My case just got a lot stronger with that last witness, John. You know that. Now I've got the gun in her hand. And you've got no other suspect to offer."

"You don't know what I've got," the defense lawyer said. But he didn't sound hostile. Again he looked at his client. She was obviously waiting for him. Steve Greerdon stood a few feet away from her, but she wouldn't look at him.

John Lincoln wouldn't look at Chris again, either. But just before he turned away he said, "I'll talk to her."

Chris thought those words very hopeful. He found himself standing alone, and realized there was more work to do. The lunch recess had to be used, too. Bonnie Janaway had come back into the courtroom, and so had Stephanie Valadez. Steve Greerdon remained standing near the witness stand. He looked at Chris questioningly, obviously wondering if he could be used further. Chris walked toward him, gave him a studious look, and turned away, saying, "Come with me. We have to talk."

CHAPTER

ten

★ In Chris's private office he stood close in front of Steve Greerdon, close enough to feel the bigger man's breath. Chris glared at him and said, "I swear to God, I will prosecute you for perjury if I can prove it."

"What are you talking about?"

"You seeing Luisa Gaines holding a gun. Bullshit. When did that occur to you?"

"It happened," Greerdon said innocently. "Why would I make it up?"

Chris didn't know. But he thought Greerdon wanted to see the woman convicted even more strongly than Chris did. For one thing, that would remove any suspicion from Greerdon himself. But there was more to it than that. This trial had become a duel between Greerdon and his former partners, with both the defendant and Chris in the middle.

But right now he couldn't prove anything. As he turned away he snapped, "Don't do anything else. I don't need your help."

"Look," Greerdon said to Chris's back, and Chris turned around quickly, surprised. Because here was the anger, the rage that everyone had expected from Greerdon. His face was flushed with it, his shoulders hunched by the burden of it. His right fist was clenched, and he moved it as he spoke. "The last time I saw you in action, you screwed up big time, without my help."

"That was—"

"Different? Yeah, it's worse now. The stakes are higher and you still don't know who's on your team."

"If you're telling me there are cops out there messing with the evidence in this case, I know it. But I'm not going to respond the same way. If you—"

"Neither am I." Greerdon's voice became guttural as he said this, and his breath came harshly. "But you've got to counter everything they do. You've got to smoke them out."

"How am I supposed to do that, when you won't even tell me what you know?"

Greerdon began to grow calmer, but his eyes remained calculating. His shoulders lifted as his breathing slowed. He said, "Rico. Like I told you. He was there, I know it. He somehow had a hand in this. Listen. Recall me as a witness. I'll say that Chip dropped a couple of names to me that night when he asked me to come back at eleven."

Chris stared at him. "Is that true?"

Greerdon just looked back at him. After several seconds of this staring match, Chris turned on his heel again and headed toward the door.

Greerdon called, "You don't know what you're up against!"

That was damned true. Chris didn't even know who was in the room with him.

After Chris left, Steve Greerdon kicked the desk, hard enough to shove it across the floor a couple of feet. The effort only seemed to make him angrier. He picked up the desk chair, lifting it over his head.

Footsteps sounded outside. By the time Irma Garcia, Chris's secretary, opened the door, the chair was back in place behind the desk and Greerdon was walking rapidly toward her. Seeing his face, instead of reprimanding him, Irma stepped quickly aside. Greerdon stalked past her without a word.

Anne managed to catch Chris before he had to go back to trial. "How's it going?" she asked.

"Fine," Chris answered automatically. "Steve Greerdon saved my case for me this morning."

There was a pause from the other end of the phone line. Chris didn't notice. "Gotta go," he said. "I'll rehash everything for you tonight."

He turned off his cell phone, heading into the courtroom. He didn't have to stay connected to the outside world electronically. Chris was an important guy, if something big happened a person would come and get him.

Opening the courtroom doors, he didn't feel important at all. He felt like a pawn.

Several blocks away, at her desk, Anne heard the phone click off, and wished she had said something. But now wasn't the time. She would talk to Chris tonight. The subject couldn't be put off any longer.

She walked slowly through the short hallway outside her office door, to the office area. There were several message slips in her slot. She glanced through them. Eric Schwinn had called. So had Peter Greerdon. On both messages, the "urgent" box was checked. But it nearly always was on Anne's messages. The others were just from people losing confidence in their sanity. Anne put the messages back and looked out the window into the waiting room. Two children waited out there, one with his parents, the other with her grandmother. A boy of eight whose parents wanted drugs to fix his wandering attention, and what they called his "mood swings." In other words, sometimes he was less cheerful than other times. The ten-year-old girl across the room had genuine problems, including a half-hearted suicide attempt that might well have been a dress rehearsal.

Anne wanted to tell both these kids to ignore their families and not try to grow up too fast. Enjoy being children. Most children thought their problems would be solved by growing up. Anne hadn't observed that to be true.

She opened the door to the reception room and went back to work.

After lunch, there was a development.

When Chris came into the courtroom at 1:20, John Lincoln wasn't there, nor was his client. *Good,* Chris thought. That gave Bonnie and him a little more time to go over their few remaining witnesses. One thirty came and passed. Judge Conners, a rare judge who was usually more than punctual, assumed the bench. She raised eyebrows at Chris and he shrugged back at her. After another minute she asked, "Did you talk to opposing counsel since this morning?"

"Right after the morning's recess was declared I did, your honor. But I don't think I was so intimidating that I scared him away."

Judge Conners smiled. She also sent one bailiff into the hall to look for the missing trial participants and instructed a clerk to call Lincoln's office.

Chris remembered that John Lincoln had said he would talk to his client about making a deal with Chris. Had she said yes? Were they ironing out the details now, assuming a recess in the trial would be granted while the two sides bargained to a conclusion? Chris began subtly to relax, a lawyer beginning to believe he wasn't about to be back in trial.

At 1:40 John Lincoln rushed in through the back doors and up the aisle, putting away his cell phone as he came. He went straight up to the judge's bench without asking permission, motioning Chris to join him. At the bench, a little short of breath, he said, "Your honor, please excuse my lateness. My client isn't here. I've been waiting for her outside and calling her cell phone. But I can't reach her. I'm afraid something might have happened to her."

Judge Conners looked concerned. John Lincoln was a little flamboyant, but he didn't pull stunts, and he wasn't a liar. "Have you seen her since this morning, counselor?"

"We had lunch together, your honor, and discussed some serious matters." He gave Chris a significant look. "Then I had to run back to my office. Ms. Gaines wanted to make a phone call. We were supposed to meet back here. I'd like a brief recess in order to find her."

"Mr. Sinclair?" the judge asked.

Chris left the decision to her. "We're ready when you are, Judge. We expect to finish our case this afternoon. But we won't oppose a brief recess."

Judge Conners mulled it over. "I think we'll proceed. If Ms. Gaines appears she can join us. Otherwise I'm going to assume her absence is voluntary, and no reason to grant a continuance. Richard, bring the jury. Call your next witness, Mr. Sinclair."

Chris would rather have talked to his counterpart. But he walked back to his table while Bonnie Janaway, already there, stood and said, "Emilio Varga."

During the flurry of motion that followed, as the jurors were led in and the witness found in the hall, Chris watched the defense lawyer. Lincoln looked lost in thought, but the return of the jury brought him back. He felt Chris's attention and turned to him, giving Chris a very flat, almost hostile stare.

What was that about? Every time something went wrong, for anybody, they seemed to blame Chris. Was he really so all-powerful that he could ruin so many lives? He certainly didn't feel the part.

Bonnie questioned or requestioned two restaurant employees and one patron who had been in Miguelito's the night of the killing. She established two key facts through these witnesses: Luisa Gaines had not emerged from her office until the uproar in the restaurant was in more than full cry, and no one had seen the waitress Teresa in the crowd milling through the restaurant after the shooting. As far as anyone could remember, she had been gone from the restaurant area well before the patrons heard shots.

Privately, the prosecutors had questioned at least twice as many of their prospective witnesses. The witnesses they called were the three who remembered events as the prosecutors wanted them remembered. Others just hadn't noticed who was or wasn't in the restaurant after the gunfire. That wasn't cheating. It was how lawyers presented cases. The defense could call the other witnesses if they wanted. But they wouldn't, because Lincoln hadn't questioned them and didn't know what they would say. The prosecution always had more resources, including a police force full of investigators at their disposal. But as Chris sat and listened to his case being assembled satisfactorily, the whole enterprise began to seem fraudulent to him. No one could ever fully recreate what had happened. They could never know what detail had been missed, or its significance overlooked. That was true in a normal case. In this one, everything seemed suspect.

With one witness, Bonnie established something else. Several people in private interviews had told the prosecutors that Rosa Castillo was quite a party girl. On the witness stand she looked like a staid, middle-aged mom. She had been having a quiet meal in Miguelito's, she testified, at a table close to the kitchen. She had heard the first gunshot.

"Are you sure it was a gunshot?" Bonnie asked.

"Yes, ma'am. In my neighborhood you hear it often enough to recognize what it is." Mrs. Castillo sat with her purse in her lap and both hands holding it, as if she had found herself in a dangerous place surrounded by suspicious characters. Her broad face looked sober and reflective, intent on remembering.

"Did everyone else seem to notice the shot?" Bonnie asked.

"Not at first. People looked around like 'What was that,' you know. I knew. I was afraid it came from the kitchen. I stood up right away, and said to my friend who was with me, 'Let's go.' We started across the restaurant. Not running. We didn't want to get people stampeding. But I wanted out. I stopped at the cash register to leave money for my bill."

"Where is the cash register?"

"On the other side of the room, close to the front door."

"Were people jumping up and running out the door when you got to the cash register?"

"No, ma'am, not yet. But while I was saying I couldn't wait for the check, I had to leave, that's when we heard the second gunshot. Then everybody was for sure. That's when people started shouting and running around."

"So how much time do you think passed between the two gunshots?" Bonnie tilted her head and asked the question with a tone of curiosity, as if she'd never heard the answer.

"At least a minute," Rosa Castillo said. "Maybe two."

"Thank you, ma'am, I don't have any more questions."

Chris looked at the defense table again. There appeared to be a big blank spot there, where Luisa Gaines should have been sitting. Had Chris scared her so badly she had taken off? If so, what had scared her:

the prosecution's case against her, or the offer of clemency if she cooperated?

Jack Fine had been in the courtroom to note her disappearance, and of course he was spreading the word now. Police were already hunting Luisa Gaines. She was a fugitive from justice. Meanwhile, justice proceeded without her.

Her lawyer questioned Mrs. Castillo and the other State's witnesses only perfunctorily. However, with the last two prosecution witnesses, he came alive. When Stephanie stood and said, "Bill Renfro, your honor," Lincoln sat up and pulled another legal pad toward him.

Officer Renfro was an African-American man in his forties, with gray blurring his hair but still a youthful face. A tall man, he had a permanent slight stoop, a job hazard. He spent his life searching the ground.

"I was the evidence technician at the scene," he testified.

"What does the job of evidence technician entail?" Bonnie asked earnestly.

Officer Renfro spoke in a quiet, professorial manner, as if his job involved educating audiences, rather than blood and bullets and plucking discarded items from the trash. "I secure the scene, try to keep it uncontaminated. Then I collect whatever evidence I can find. Finally I take photographs and sometimes videotape the scene."

Bonnie led him through a recital of what he'd found at the scene of Chip Riley's murder. Renfro identified photos he'd taken of the body and the area around it. The victim lay face down, his face resting on its left cheek, eyes and mouth open. There was no sign of blood, at least in that photo. Chip Riley looked almost comic, like a drunk who had fallen down at a party. But the next photos showed the pool of blood underneath him, from another angle and after the body had been removed. Jurors looked at the photos soberly, a couple of the jurors barely glancing at them before passing them on.

Other photographs showed a dirty working area, asphalt pavement spread with the remains of food and cigarette butts.

"Officer Renfro," Bonnie asked, "did you find a bullet?"

"Yes, ma'am. I didn't find it personally, another officer did and called me over, about thirty yards away from the body. But I collected it."

Bonnie handed him a squashed piece of metal in a plastic bag. "Can you identify State's Exhibit Number Thirty-seven?"

"Yes, ma'am, this is a plastic bag holding the bullet that I collected from the scene."

"How can you be sure?"

"On the bullet I wrote my initials. Later that night I turned it in to the property room at police headquarters, and saw it tagged with this number that's on it now. This morning I picked it up from the property room and brought it here."

"Did you find any other bullets at the scene, Officer?"

Replacing the bullet in its bag, Renfro said, "No, ma'am."

"Did anyone else?"

"No. I was the evidence technician, they knew to call my attention to anything they found. There were no other bullets at the scene."

"Were there other officers besides you searching the area?"

Renfro smiled grimly. "The place was crawling with cops, ma'am. Everybody wanted to help. It was all I could do to clear them away and get them not to contaminate the scene. They know better than that, but people were a little excited."

Bonnie asked a few more questions about the location where the body was found. Asking dull questions would diminish the impact of those photos of the body lying on dirty pavement, and Bonnie realized that. She moved on.

"Did you collect a gun at the scene, Officer?"

"Yes, ma'am."

"Where was it?"

"Again, I wasn't the officer who initially found it, but they left it in place until I came to collect it. The pistol was in a desk drawer in the restaurant office. The middle drawer on the left hand side, if you were sitting at the desk. Toward the back."

Bonnie brought him the gun that had already been mentioned in testimony. "Officer, can you identify State's Exhibit Five?"

Renfro turned the silver pistol over in his long-fingered hands. "Yes, ma'am, this is the gun I found in the desk drawer. It has my initials on the barrel where I scratched them, and the tag number on it is the same one I saw put on it later that night."

Civilians were sometimes surprised at the seemingly casual way that police officers marked evidence they'd found, indelibly, by scratching their initials into the items. A juror had once protested to Chris after a trial, "But they're damaging private property." Chris had explained patiently that writing the officer's initials permanently was the only way to insure that the item could later be identified at trial. Yes, it marked forever that gun or bullet or other item. It might have slightly inconvenienced the owner. Compared to murder, though, such minor destruction was insignificant. Crime messes things up. The instruments and evidence of crime belong to the public after that.

Bonnie moved on. "Can you identify State's Exhibits Thirty-eight through Forty-three?"

"These are the bullets I found in the gun," Renfro said simply. He had a rare gift for getting to the point, not muddying the issue with jargon or roundabout explanations.

"Your Honor, I ask that State's Exhibits Five and Thirty-seven through Forty-three be admitted for all purposes," Bonnie said. She handed them over to the defense lawyer for examination.

Lincoln took his time. Stalling, Chris thought, hoping his client will reappear. But if John Lincoln was acting, he did a good job of it. He looked at the gun and the bullets carefully, and seemed to weigh the bullets in his hand before giving them back to the prosecutor. "No objection, your honor."

"They'll be admitted," Judge Conners ruled.

Bonnie asked, "Officer, when you found that gun, could you tell whether it had recently been fired?"

"Yes, it had been. There was a smell about it."

Bonnie Janaway sat down beside Chris again. She had very few more questions, and glanced at Chris for approval to finish. Chris quickly wrote a name on a legal pad while Bonnie asked another question of the witness. "Rico Fairis," Chris wrote.

Bonnie glanced down at the name and looked at her boss curiously. Chris quickly added, "Was he there?"

Without a pause, Bonnie asked the witness, "Officer, do you know another police officer named Rico Fairis?"

"Yes, ma'am."

Lincoln shot a look at Chris. But the question didn't seem to mean much to the witness.

"Was he there that night?" Bonnie asked.

"I don't know. I didn't notice."

"Would you have seen him if he had been there?"

"Not necessarily." For the first time, Renfro broke from appearing perfectly prepared. He sounded more conversational and even a little emotional as he added, "When a call goes out saying 'Officer down,' cops start showing up from all over. Even people who were off duty. I couldn't tell you the names of all the officers there. And I was concentrating on doing my job."

"Thank you, Officer. I pass the witness."

John Lincoln looked at Renfro speculatively. "Officer, I just noticed when I examined the evidence a few minutes ago. There were six bullets."

"Yes, sir." The police officer sounded a little puzzled, but still answered methodically.

"Those were in the gun when you found it—or rather when you had it called to your attention?"

"Yes, they were."

"Officer, how many bullets does that gun hold?"

"It's a standard thirty-eight caliber, sir. It holds six bullets."

"So it was fully loaded."

"Yes."

"Did you find any other bullets?"

"There was a box of bullets in another drawer of the desk."

"And did you collect those as well?"

"I did."

"Bring them to court today?"

"No, sir. I collected a lot of evidence. But I only brought to court today the things the prosecutors thought would be relevant."

"I understand. Let me ask you something else, Officer. Did you take fingerprints from the gun?"

"That's not my job, sir."

"I understand," Lincoln repeated. He did sound understanding, too, as if having a pleasant conversation. But he also continued to wear a puzzled expression that the jurors must have noticed.

"Officer, you didn't actually find either the bullet or the gun yourself, did you?"

"No. As I said."

"Who did?"

The bullet was located by a young patrolman named Matthew Sosa. I don't really remember who called my attention to the gun."

John Lincoln carefully wrote down the one name. Then he leaped to his feet and walked to the bench. He found the fired bullet and held it up before the officer again.

"Officer, has this bullet been fired?"

"Quite definitely, sir. It's compressed and scratched. Clearly it's been fired and hit something. Possibly more than one thing."

"Yes," Lincoln said. "But you can't tell when it was fired, can you?"

"I can't, no sir."

"For all we can tell, it could have been fired by someone who took Luisa Gaines's gun and shot it into the alley, maybe scaring away a cat."

"I don't know, sir."

Lincoln tossed the small, scarred bit of metal into the air, caught it, and set it back down on the bench in front of Judge Conners. He picked up the gun itself. "One more thing, Officer. You testified that you could tell this gun had been fired recently, when you found it that night. Could you tell how many times it had been fired?"

"No, sir," Renfro answered blandly. He was there to do his job, and wouldn't claim more than he knew.

"No more questions," Lincoln said, and returned to his table, still looking thoughtful, but now with a jaunty quality as well. The absence of his client didn't seem to be bothering him at all.

Bonnie had no more questions, either. Now that the gun was in evidence, it was time to wrap up. Chris went out into the hall to make sure the last two witnesses were there. They were. Both police officers, a fingerprint examiner and a firearms examiner. Chris sent the first one into the courtroom. Bonnie could handle him alone. He was there mainly to testify to what he hadn't found.

Chris turned on his cell phone and reached Jack Fine on his. "Where are you?"

"Right over your head. I'll be down."

Chris was at the bottom of the stairs when Jack came down. Jack wore a rumpled gray suit—did he *ever* send them to the cleaners?—a white shirt, and an oddly colorful tie, reddish in tone with a tangle of characters. It might have been a scene from a merry hell, and was obviously a gift. One Jack felt obligated to wear. Chris smiled at the thought of his investigator's secret life. But he said seriously, "Anything?"

Jack was already shaking his head as he descended the last couple of steps. "No sign of Luisa Gaines, if she's who you mean. Not at the restaurant, not at her house. Her car's parked over here in a lot a couple of blocks from here. If you've got her so worried she decided to run, she took a bus to do it."

"Or a cab to the airport."

Jack shook his head. "Pretty sure not. If she did she went in a very roundabout way. No cab downtown took a woman fitting her description to the airport, and none took anybody anywhere near her house."

Chris doubted the efficiency of cab records, but they could only work with the information they had. "Maybe she's just in a bar. Maybe she got bored with the testimony."

Jack shrugged, enduring his boss's sense of humor.

"Anything else?"

"Lieutenant Reyes left in a snit about one thirty," Jack said, as if it were a happy memory.

"I'd like to have Stephanie follow him instead of Steve Greerdon at this point," Chris mused.

"I already put her on it. But he'd have to be dumber than I think he is to lead her to anything. And Rico Fairis won't let him within fifty feet of him, I guarantee."

Chris nodded. "Where is Greerdon?"

Jack shrugged. *Out manufacturing more evidence*, Chris thought. "Okay, I'm going back in. We'll be resting this afternoon. Then we'll see what the defense has. Stay ready."

"Aye aye."

Jack often came up with such expressions, as if he spent his evenings watching TV stations no one else saw. Chris returned to the courtroom. Bonnie Janaway had already passed the fingerprint examiner to the defense. As Chris walked down the aisle, trying to be unobtrusive, John Lincoln was asking, "Is it your testimony that you didn't find *any* fingerprints on that gun?"

"Yes, sir," Officer Lopez said stolidly.

"And you didn't find any usable prints on the bullets, either?"

"No. As I said, I found partial prints on some of the bullets, but none that was clear enough to identify."

"I understand," Lincoln said. "On how many of the bullets did you find partial prints?"

Officer Lopez frowned at the odd question, and had to review his notes. "On five of them," he finally said. "But as I said—"

"Yes, they weren't identifiable," Lincoln said dismissively. "I remember. Thank you, Officer."

Bonnie Janaway looked at Lincoln curiously, then turned to Chris, who gave a tiny shrug. Bonnie stood to say, "The State calls Edward Simington."

The last witness they had planned, the firearms examiner, came rather heavily up the aisle of the courtroom. He was a police officer, but wasn't wearing a uniform. Today he wore a blue sports shirt and dark pants. Bonnie even asked him about this. "Officer Simington, do you normally wear a uniform when you're on duty?"

"Not normally, no, ma'am. Plus today's my day off."

"I'm sorry," Bonnie said. The witness, a heavyset man with a strong neck, sleepy brown eyes, and square jaw, just shrugged. He had to testify regularly, it came with the job.

Bonnie came to the point quickly. She handed Simington the gun and the two bullets, the one found at the scene and the other that had been removed from Chip Riley's body. "Officer, did you examine this gun and these bullets?"

"Yes, I did."

"Please explain to the jury what you do."

Simington turned toward them. "Under a microscope, I examine the bullets that have been submitted to me for comparison. There are certain identifying marks that a gun carves on bullets when it fires them.

'Lands and grooves,' we call them. Each gun barrel is unique, because of tiny flaws in its manufacture, so it leaves unique markings on bullets."

"Like fingerprints?" Bonnie asked.

"Yes."

"How can you identify whether those bullets were fired from that gun?"

Simington continued to explain patiently. "I fire bullets from the gun and recover them. At the forensic science center where I work, we have a water tank. I fire into that so the bullets can be recovered easily. Then I take one of those bullets that I know was fired from this weapon and do a side-by-side comparison, under the microscope, with it and one of the recovered bullets. I compare the marks on them."

"Did your comparison convince you these two bullets that are in evidence were fired from this gun?"

"Yes, ma'am. Their markings were identical."

Bonnie walked up to the witness stand and picked up the squashed, distorted bullet that had been recovered at the scene of the killing, behind Miguelito's. "Officer, this bullet is pretty messed up."

Simington nodded. "It certainly is. Going through a human body and hitting the ground or a fence will do that to a bullet."

"When it's this damaged, how can you be sure of your identification?"

"The damage doesn't obscure the markings," Simington said, taking the bullet from her and holding it up. His eyes narrowed as he appeared to see things no one else could. Several of the jurors also squinted at the bullet. "You can see them there now. In addition, we now have a computer program. I photograph the fired bullet and the software program kind of undoes the damage, showing me what the bullet would look like if it weren't so flattened. With that, it's easy to make the identification."

"Technology is making your job easier?" Bonnie asked with a small smile.

"In some ways," Simington said, with a more ambiguous expression.

"Pass the witness."

At the same time, Bonnie gave the bullet in question to the jury. They passed it from hand to hand, examining it closely, looking for the markings the officer had testified about. One woman in the front row just held the bullet in her palm, seeming to marvel at its lightness. Chris thought, *She gets it*. In trials he looked for this expression on the faces of jurors. Their recognition of the significance of some piece of dry evidence. This wasn't just State's Exhibit 37. It was also the shot that had passed through Chip Riley's body, taking his life with it. Holding the bullet clearly brought the reality of the murder home to the juror. Chris watched her repulsed fascination.

So did John Lincoln. He wouldn't begin his cross-examination while the jurors were distracted from what he had to ask. Lincoln was too experienced a trial lawyer for that. After a long minute's pause he stood and walked to the jury box and retrieved the bullet from the jury. "Excuse me, ma'am," he said politely, then turned to the witness. "Officer, you say you're certain this bullet was fired from that gun."

"Yes, sir," Simington said.

"Can you tell us when it was fired?"

"No. I can't tell that."

"It could have been the night before it was given to you, two weeks earlier, a year ago?"

Simington said, "Well, after a year I would think I'd notice the bullet's age, unless it had been stored very carefully. But within the last month or so, no, I don't think I could tell."

"Is the same true of this other bullet?" Lincoln picked up the less damaged bullet and held it out to the witness.

"Yes," Simington said, his puzzlement at the question obvious. "Up to a certain point, I have no idea when it was fired."

"Do you know where it came from?"

"This is the one that was taken from the body."

Lincoln held up a finger. "That's what you were *told,* Officer, but can you tell from your own examination that this bullet was fired into a body?"

Simington took the bullet and examined it with a curiosity he hadn't yet displayed. "No, not really," he finally said.

"In fact, it isn't significantly more damaged than the bullets you fired into a tank of water, is it?"

The witness looked at the bullet again, critically. "There are some markings on it, but no, it's not very damaged."

"So your testimony that a bullet fired from this gun killed Chip Riley is only based on things you were told about where the bullets were recovered, isn't that true?"

"That's not what I testified," Simington said a little defensively. "I only testified that these bullets were fired from this gun."

"Exactly," Lincoln said, though his air of triumph was lost on everyone in the courtroom. Even the judge was frowning at him curiously. "No more questions," Lincoln ended with a flourish, returning to his seat.

Chris had some idea what the defense lawyer was up to. But there was nothing to be done about it now. Bonnie looked at him and Chris nodded. She stood up and said, "Your honor, the State rests."

Scary words. At this moment Chris nearly always worried about what he'd forgotten or overlooked. And it never seemed he'd given the jury enough information to convict the defendant. This time, though, they had put her in the place where the murder was committed, explained why she'd want to kill the victim, shown he was killed with her gun, and, thanks to the unexpected testimony of Steve Greerdon, put the murder weapon in her hand—not the night of the murder, but not long before. She had handled the gun competently and familiarly, according to Greerdon.

Plus Luisa Gaines had fled during trial. The jurors had to be wondering about that.

Certainly that was on her lawyer's mind. John Lincoln looked a little surprised by Bonnie's announcement, though he must have expected it. Finally he rose to his feet and said, "Your honor, I'd like to make a motion outside the jury's presence."

Judge Conners turned to the jurors and said, "Why don't you take a short break? Joe, would you take them down to the cafeteria or wherever they want to go? Be back in fifteen minutes."

Everyone stood to watch the jurors exit. Chris noticed again how full the courtroom was. There were three reporters on the front row, two from television stations, one from the newspaper. Other people he didn't recognize almost filled the spectator pews. Chris wondered if any of them were plants, there to pass on to someone else how the trial was going, and whether any names had been mentioned. If so, Rico Fairis would hear shortly that his name had come up.

Steve Greerdon was no longer in attendance. Chris thought briefly that he might be looking for Luisa Gaines. Then again, he might be connected to her disappearance.

After the jury was gone, John Lincoln made a motion for directed verdict, asking the judge to find his client not guilty because the State had failed to prove its case. He said the words halfheartedly, partly because Judge Conners was shaking her head, patiently, all the time he talked. There was no chance she wouldn't let this case go to the jury.

"That will be denied," the judge said as soon as he finished talking. "Are you ready to proceed, counselor?"

"No."

The judge looked out at the spectator seats. "I believe people have said that word to me more times in this trial than in the rest of my judicial career put together. It's not a good precedent. Why aren't you ready, Mr. Lincoln?"

"Quite obviously, your honor, my client isn't here. I'd like time to try to find her. It wasn't much of a handicap not to have her here during the State's case, but I need her here for mine. It's after three o'clock already, Judge. I'm not asking for a very early recess."

Judge Conners mulled it over and looked at Chris, who said, "I have no objection, Judge."

"All right." She tapped her gavel. We'll give the jury some time off. Maybe they'll do some shopping and boost the downtown economy. But John, we're starting at nine thirty tomorrow morning whether your client is here or not."

"Understood, your honor."

The judge departed slowly, while everyone rose to their feet. Chris and Lincoln stood next to each other, and naturally turned toward each other. "Did you pass on my offer?" Chris asked.

Lincoln nodded slowly.

"So does that mean she's out gathering evidence for me right now?"

Lincoln stepped closer and lowered his voice, turning his back to the reporters in the front row. Very earnestly he said, "She's scared, Chris. You should be too."

Then he turned away and quickly packed up his briefcase.

"What do you mean by that?" Chris asked, but Lincoln didn't answer. As Lincoln turned away he said, "I'll have an answer for you in the morning. Assuming I can find her. Assuming she's alive to give me an answer."

He strode away. At the doors of the courtroom reporters caught up to him. John Lincoln stopped and flashed them his well-known smile. But then his eyes grew more haunted as he glanced around the courtroom. He made a brief remark and hurried out, past the television cameraman waiting just outside the door.

Chris turned to Bonnie, both with raised eyebrows. Lincoln avoiding the press? "Who was that?" Bonnie asked.

Chris shook his head. When his turn came to run the gauntlet, he had nothing to say either.

Changing back from a trial lawyer to a sort-of law enforcement officer, Chris conferred briefly with Jack in the investigative offices. There was no word at all on Luisa Gaines. Her home and business were being watched, as well as her car. Her employees, present and former, were glad to give police any leads they could think of. But she seemed to have had no friends, and her only relative in town, a sister, claimed not to have heard from her in weeks. "I talked to her myself," Jack said wryly. "The way she said Luisa's name made me think she's telling the truth."

"What if she just rented a car and headed straight for the border?" Chris asked. He had left his briefcase in his office but still wore his suit jacket and hadn't loosened his tie. He was still in trial mode, thinking quickly but not deeply, skipping from idea to idea.

Jack answered, "She'd have to show a driver's license to rent a car, and we've put out an alert on her."

"What if she borrowed a car, or got a friend to rent one and drive her?"

"She'd still have to show ID to cross the border, and they're a lot less casual down there than they used to be. I hope that's what she's doing. We'll have her by nightfall."

Just to throw Jack a curve, Chris said, "What if I meant the Oklahoma border?"

Jack's face turned craggier than usual as he worried about the possibility of their defendant running loose in America, but the idea also appeared to energize him. There was nothing Jack liked better than a puzzle to solve. Chris certainly thought they had enough of those on hand to keep Jack (relatively) happy for weeks.

"Any word from Stephanie?"

"Sergeant Rico Fairis is going about his duties in the manner of a quietly heroic, veteran police officer. In other words, like he thinks he's being followed by a documentary film crew."

"He's spotted Stephanie?"

Jack shrugged. "Doesn't matter. Rico's too smart to get caught at something now. He's going to be the cleanest officer on the force until this trial ends."

"What about Lieutenant Reyes?"

"Returned to police headquarters and hasn't emerged again. I thought about calling the chief and telling him we suspect Reyes of tampering with our evidence, so they'd keep an eye on him."

Chris thought for a moment, then shook his head. "Let him run free."

Jack nodded. "That's what I thought."

"You're way ahead of me, as usual," Chris said, and suddenly yawned. "I think I'll make an early day of it, go home and work on my closing argument. If Luisa Gaines doesn't turn up, it should be a quiet night."

He had seldom been more wrong.

First Chris called Anne as he was leaving the Justice Center, and she acted strangely flustered. "Why are you leaving so early?" she asked.

"Just because. I'm the boss, I can do what I want."

"But— Okay, but I wanted to come too. Listen, I'll— No, wait. Okay, I'll meet you at your place. Don't go anywhere else, okay?"

Chris smiled as he walked. "Anne, are you planning a surprise party for me? Am I messing up your plans?" He remembered a few months ago when she had sneaked into his condo and attacked him. But she would have pulled off a plan like that a lot more coolly than she was behaving now. He couldn't remember the last time he'd heard her stammer.

"Ha ha. Yes. Don't go anywhere or you'll destroy everything."

Chris drove home, found Clarissa not there, and went for a quick run around the neighborhood. In the shower afterward, his skin tingled, not just from blood rushing close to the surface but from anticipation. He kept thinking he heard noises of movement outside the bathroom.

Leaving her office as early as she could manage, Anne was surprised to find Clarissa in the waiting room. She sat placidly reading a magazine, looking more like a mother waiting for her child than like a troubled teenager needing counseling. "Clarissa?"

The girl looked up and smiled. "Oh, hi. Just thought I'd drop by. I had something else—so, hi. Leaving already? No late appointment today?" Clarissa looked over Anne's shoulder as if expecting to see someone following her out.

Anne shook her head. "I'm on my way to your house, as a matter of fact. Want a ride?"

Clarissa shook her head, looking, for some reason, relieved. "I've got my car. Besides, I've got to—do something else on the way home."

"Okay, I'll see you in a little while."

They walked out together and separated outside the lobby doors. Clarissa smiled at her in parting, a beautiful smile. She was *this close* to being grown, Anne thought. Clearly Clarissa was thinking something she wouldn't say, but she seemed to be harboring a woman's secret thoughts, not just being a sullen teenager refusing to speak. Anne felt more than fond of Clarissa, and lately that had become more of a sisterly feeling than a motherly one.

But today she was thinking more about Chris than about his daughter. She hurried to his home to set him straight—without, of course, letting him know that's what she was doing.

"What exactly did Steve Greerdon testify?" she asked half an hour later.

Chris grinned. "I've never known you to take this much interest in my work."

He was strangely relaxed for a man in the middle of a big trial. Chris sat on the couch wearing white jeans and a loose-fitting blue sport shirt. His feet were bare. He looked not much older than Clarissa. He gestured for her to come closer, but Anne stayed where she was, ten feet away, dressed very professionally. *She* had the intensity of a trial lawyer, not he.

Chris gave up on seduction and answered her question. "He testified he never got close to Chip Riley but did see him dead. He didn't see anyone else there. But he did give us some big help. He said he'd seen Luisa Gaines holding her gun just a few days before the murder. She had it back in her possession that soon before the killing. It had been missing for a while, you know. I was worried about how we were going to put the gun back in her possession, but Steve took care of that for us."

"'Steve'?" Anne asked. Chris shrugged. Yes, he and the cop he'd sent to prison were becoming more friendly. Their friendship usually worked best when they weren't in the same room, though.

Anne continued in her concerned voice. "Listen, there's something I need to tell you. I wish I had before this. But it wasn't my secret to tell. I've gotten permission, but I'm still afraid—"

"Too much build-up," Chris warned.

She nodded. He was right. Anne sat beside him on the couch, but not for affection, just to be able to look clearly into his eyes as she said, "Chris, you can't believe a word Steve Greerdon says to you. Not when he's under oath and not what he tells you in confidence. He's not what you think he is."

"I certainly don't trust him, if that's what you mean. He has more motive for murder than anyone I've ever heard of, let alone motive for lying. If somebody had sent me to prison on false evidence, they'd better leave town once I got out. I wouldn't rest—"

Anne put her hand on his knee to stop him talking. "That's just it, Chris. The evidence wasn't false. You didn't convict him wrongly eight years ago. He was guilty."

His face opened in surprise, then Anne saw relief. Chris wanted to believe. Believing Greerdon guilty of the crime for which he'd been convicted helped erase those images: eight years' worth of pictures of an innocent man in prison. She'd made him happy. But Anne kept her hand on Chris's leg as his mind and feelings raced to the next steps as well.

Realization struck him hard. If Greerdon had participated in the robbery of the grocery store nine years ago, then he had managed to manipulate Chris into winning his release from prison, in such a way that he could never be sent back.

And now he was on the prosecution team for this case.

"That's why I had to tell you," Anne said. "Especially after you told me about him coming forward with this important evidence. Everything he says is a lie. I don't know what he's up to, but you can't trust anything he tells you."

"I don't think so . . ." Chris said slowly.

"Doesn't this explain why he's not out there desperately hunting down the 'real criminals'? Like you said you'd do? Like anybody would do."

"I assumed he was lying to me about that," Chris said. "I figured he was, but on his own terms, and he didn't want any help."

"He didn't want to be watched, is more like it. Maybe what he's really trying to do is remove everybody who knew the truth. Maybe Steve Greerdon is your best suspect for Chip Riley's murder."

Chris thought about that. Anne saw his resistance to what she was telling him. She squeezed his hand. Chris's was jittering, his mind racing down avenues that did not include her.

He shook his head. "Greerdon thought he was being followed by Stephanie. He wouldn't have killed Chip Riley that night. He just—"

"Don't be so sure. He managed to shake her off, didn't he? And not get arrested even though he was right there?"

Chris kept thinking, turning what he knew of that night so that the pieces fell into a different pattern. "Riley was shot by Luisa Gaines's gun." But even as he said it, he himself saw the answer to that, and almost said it along with Anne, who quickly replied, "Which went missing two weeks earlier. And only one person says she got it back before the murder."

Chris stood up and walked slowly, thinking he'd have to ask for a continuance tomorrow, as he completely reconstructed his case, or a different case. Did this mean other people were different from what he'd been thinking? Lieutenant Albert Reyes was really the honorable, straight-arrow officer his record proclaimed him to be? Rico Fairis was just a hardworking, veteran street cop? Chris didn't know anything about these men himself, only what he'd been told. He didn't know anybody.

But then, neither did Anne. "How do you know this?"

She hesitated, but Anne had already gotten past the ethical question. "I learned it in confidence. But I decided you had to know, so I got permission to tell you."

"Meaning one of your patients told you. But how did *he* know, Anne? I assume you mean Peter Greerdon, Steve's son. But he couldn't possibly have known whether his father was guilty or not. He was eight years old at the time. Are you telling me Greerdon confessed to his son sometime? I can't believe that. He's not the type. It sounds more like a child's fantasy. Figure out a reason why your father got what he deserved. That would be better than thinking—"

Anne was shaking her head. "It wasn't Peter who told me this. And that's the last I'm going to say. I'm not going to let you eliminate my patients one by one. This is somebody you've never heard of, anyway. This patient came to me specifically because of unresolved feelings over what happened to Greerdon years ago. And was in a position to know the truth, believe me."

"So how did he know? Did he participate? Anne, how could someone possibly know 'the truth'? Did Greerdon confess to him? You know that's crap. He's not the confessing kind. If this person was 'in a position to know,' then he could have been part of the conspiracy against Greerdon, too. You have to give me more than this. You have to give me solid evidence, something I can use. If I'm going to turn my whole case around and point it in a different direction, I've got to be able to prove things."

She frowned at him, feeling offended. "I'm sorry, I'm not an investigator. I thought you needed to know this. Now your own people can follow up. Do you realize I've just violated not just professional ethics but my own sense of—"

He stepped to her quickly and held her arms. "I do, Anne. Believe me, I do. But you know what I'm saying. Right now there's nothing *to* follow up. I appreciate your telling me this, I really do. Listen, could you just ask your patient if he'd be willing to talk to me? Anonymously, if that's the only way. Or give me something more through you. Some hard facts. An evidence trail I can follow. This must be important to him, or he wouldn't have come to you. Ask him to give me something I can check out. Please?"

Anne relented. She nodded tightly. Then she pulled Chris close. "I just don't want you to get hurt," she said quietly. "I don't want people using you."

Chris chuckled. "You don't want me to trust anybody but you."

"That's right." She pulled his face down to hers. They both laughed, their lips vibrating against each other's.

After a moment he drew back to say, "But seriously—"

She drew him back. "No, don't be seriously." She murmured, "I've missed you. You're never really here when you're in trial."

"I'm here now."

She slipped off her jacket, dropped it without looking toward a chair and didn't notice that she'd missed. Chris's thumbs began to draw open her blouse, where it disappeared down into her skirt. Anne chuckled again, in a different key.

The telephone rang.

Chris grimaced. He decided to let the machine get it, then noticed past Anne's shoulder that it was dark outside, and realized how late it was without Clarissa's being home. The telephone's second ring sounded like the sudden jumping of his nerves, as he reacted like any parent. "Maybe she's had car trouble," he said, pulling away from Anne and hurrying to the phone.

"Chris Sinclair. Yes. Sergeant? What's happened?"

Chris fell silent, blinking as he absorbed the call. Anne bent and picked up her jacket. A moment earlier she'd felt sexy. Now she felt frumpy, standing in her stocking feet with her blouse coming untucked. She couldn't remember having stepped out of her shoes. She stepped back into them as she watched Chris. He was obviously getting bad news. Where was Clarissa?

"Oh, my God," Chris said into the phone. "Yes. Have you made any arrests? What about—? Yes, she was. Someone from my office. All right. Thank you for calling. Yes."

Standing across the room, Anne waited anxiously to hear the news, but part of her didn't want the phone call to end. She was afraid of what she would hear when Chris hung up.

But before he did she heard the sound of footsteps along the sidewalk outside the front door. Anne was sure she recognized that light step. The door opened without a knock. At the same time, Chris turned away from the door, listening intently to the voice on the phone. He stared at Anne. Something on his face did frighten her. For a moment she saw him wondering how much he could say to her.

It was dusk, nearly six o'clock, when Steve Greerdon pulled up in front of his ex-wife's house. Since being on the witness stand that morning, he'd spent the day trying to improve the prosecution's case, one way or another. Over his police radio he heard about Luisa Gaines's having gone missing, but didn't join in the search.

But as the day ended, he found himself wanting to see his son. Sitting on the witness stand and looking at the accused had reminded him of being in that position himself. He felt his freedom hang more precariously than it had at any time since his release from prison. It seemed illusory, a long fever dream from which he'd wake up in the prison infirmary.

Greerdon had done his best after he was out to steer clear of everyone and everything that had gotten him sent up eight years ago. But of course it was impossible. By the time he had decided to strike back, it might have become too late.

And so he wanted to see Petey. Both to convince himself that he was really out, and maybe, horribly, as a farewell.

He stood on the front yard in front of the house and stretched his arms and shoulders. The girl didn't seem to be following him today, which bothered him. He'd gotten used to her—a shy, black-clad guardian angel. Not sensing her nearby gave him the same faintly puzzled unease a man might feel if he no longer cast a shadow.

The house looked as solidly middle class as ever, with its redbrick walls and cement porch. Dolores seemed to have armored herself in the most solid image of respectability she could manage, perhaps to ward off memories of her first marriage. But the safety had proven imaginary, too. That was another reason why Greerdon had come. After his last visit, when he'd seen Dolores's bruised cheek and the tension in the house had been palpable, he'd wanted to check back as often as possible.

He rang the doorbell and no one answered. Greerdon frowned. Around him the suburb was coming alive, as people came home from work, tables were being set for dinner, kids worked on homework. He didn't believe in the silence from within. He pictured Emerson Blakely giving everyone a threatening look, telling them with glaring eyes not to answer the door. Greerdon resolved not to leave. He knocked on the door, hard. It rattled under his hand. Greerdon turned the knob and the door opened.

He decided he'd just stick his head in. "Hello?" he called into the dark house. There was a light somewhere far in the back, probably from the master bedroom, barely trickling out this far. Greerdon stepped inside and called toward his son's bedroom, "Peter?"

No one answered. The house had the stillness of a place where no one moved. He could feel its emptiness. But he felt something else, too. A waft of fresh air. This was March, the day had been pretty warm. If the house had been left closed all day it would be warm too. For the most part the air did lie heavy and warm, except for this wisp of air. Greerdon had felt this many times before, and his senses recognized it even if he didn't. An outside breeze slicing through the dead air of what should have been a closed-up house. It was the feeling on the skin at a crime scene, where the back door had been left open or a window broken. Where violence had recently happened, even if it was only violence to glass.

Greerdon's skin prickled. He stepped forward just slightly, toward the living room. Past Emerson Blakely's recliner he saw a foot. A boot-clad foot, lying sideways on the floor. For a long moment Steve Greerdon stopped dead. His whole body shut down, and his mind as well. It wasn't that he couldn't force himself to move. He had no inclination to move; no volition of his own at all. Subconsciously he wanted to remain in this moment forever, not step forward and discover what lay in front of him.

But the moment passed, he recovered control of his limbs, and he walked forward quickly, not running, still listening, and being careful not to step on anything significant. He circled to his left around the recliner until he could see the whole body. It was a man, wearing a black T-shirt and jeans. At least the remains of a T-shirt, what was left after the bullet had ripped through it, and through the man's chest. Even from ten feet away, Greerdon could see the bullet hole.

The victim's face was undamaged. He could see that as well, and recognized it. It was Emerson Blakely. He lay on the floor of his living room in his own house, close to his favorite chair, surrounded by his hunting magazines and artifacts of the manly life. Steve Greerdon closed his eyes and breathed a long sigh of relief.

Then his eyes snapped open again. "Shit," he breathed. He turned and looked at the open front door, expecting to see cops pouring through it.

He'd been set up again. Any moment, someone would try to hand him a gun.

Greerdon moved fast. He wanted badly to check the bedrooms, to find out whether Peter had been home when this happened. Instead he made himself turn and get back out of the house by the most direct line. He closed the door behind him and ran to his car. He wanted to get in it and fly away, but he couldn't. Peter might still be inside, or nearby. Instead he got on his radio and called in a report of a murder, like any good citizen. Then he waited to be part of the evidence team.

Five minutes later Greerdon stood just outside the front door of the house, listening. Far in the distance, he heard a siren. Turning, he saw a bulky figure coming toward him from down the street. Greerdon's hand went toward the small of his back, the holster there, but then he stopped as he recognized Peter, always bigger than he remembered and appearing to loom larger because of the backpack he carried by a strap over one shoulder. "Hey, Dad," the boy called casually.

"Peter." Greerdon stepped down off the porch and intercepted him.

"What's up? Mom home? How come it's so dark?" The boy sounded only slightly curious. Greerdon wanted to hug him. Peter's life was about to change again, all in a terrible moment, and once again it would be his father who would hand him that moment, as soon as Greerdon told him what had happened.

He delayed that moment. "Did you just get home?" he asked.

"Yeah. A friend dropped me off down at the corner. We stayed after school to work on a project. I called Mom, but nobody answered. What's—?" Peter's face changed. His posture grew more rigid. He looked at the dark front porch of his house, registering fear for the first time. He seemed suddenly to realize the oddness of a dark house and his father standing in the yard. "What's wrong, Dad?" He started around Greerdon. "Is Mom inside?" His voice grew more boyish with panic.

Greerdon stepped in front of him. "No. She's not there." Greerdon couldn't be sure of that, didn't know for certain whether his ex-wife lay dead in the master bedroom. But he wanted to reassure Peter as much as possible. "Do you know her cell phone number? Here, call her."

Peter took the phone his father held out and quickly pressed buttons. A long, tense moment followed. Greerdon turned to see headlights at the end of the block, quickly followed by more. The patrol car had cut its siren by now, showing good sense. Not a good idea to alarm the whole neighborhood, not yet.

"Mom? . . . Hi. Nothing, I was just wondering where you are. I just got home."

Greerdon closed his eyes in a moment of relief that surprised him by its strength. Dolores was okay. Gently, he took the phone from his son. "Dolores? Are you on your way?" She started saying something about a meeting after school, but he cut her off patiently. "It's okay. I'm here with Peter. But you need to get home. We'll wait for you. Okay. 'Bye."

A patrol car and an unmarked car pulled to a stop at the curb. The patrol car pointed a spotlight at the house. Greerdon waved, hoping they recognized him. He didn't know what he'd do if Rico Fairis stepped out of that unmarked car. In the moment they had, he turned to his son. "Listen, Peter, I'm sorry. It's your stepfather. Somebody's shot him."

Peter's mouth opened, but his breathing stopped. His eyes shot to the door. "Oh, my God. Mom and I weren't here." His eyes returned to his father, and suddenly widened. "Dad, you didn't—"

"No, Petey, not me. I just got here. The door was open and I walked in. I found him and I called these guys."

By that time four officers had walked up, two of them in uniform. Greerdon didn't recognize them, but the two detectives were familiar. Jones and Salinas. Known as thorough, unassuming workers. He'd never heard anything dirty about them and never known them to have any connection to Rico Fairis. He nodded to them and expanded his explanation to include them. "I walked around to the back yard. There's a window broken there in one of the bedrooms. Looks like maybe somebody came in that way. I saw the window and backed away. I didn't go near the windowsill, and I only walked into the living room far enough to see the body."

The detectives nodded. After quick instructions to the uniforms, they went inside. They didn't turn on a house light, but the flicker of their flashlights became visible. Greerdon put his arm around his son's shoulder and walked him away. Ten minutes later they were standing down by the curb when Dolores's car, being driven frantically, pulled into the driveway and screeched to a stop. She lunged out, saw Peter, and said, "Oh, thank God! Is he all right? What's—?"

"I'm fine, Mom. I'm okay."

She looked toward the house. "Then is it—?"

Greerdon grabbed her arm as gently as possible. "They won't let you go in, Dolores. I'm sorry."

Her face grew fractured. He didn't say the words, but she screamed anyway.

Chris was about to hang up, when his caller obviously stopped him. "What?" He looked at Clarissa, who had just walked in, then put his hand over the receiver. Without a greeting he said to his daughter, "Did you give Peter Greerdon a ride home today?"

Clarissa hesitated just a moment, looking as if she thought she was in trouble, then nodded.

Into the phone, Chris said, "Yes, she did." He listened another moment, then said to Clarissa, "Did you take him all the way up to his front door?"

She shook her head. "He's kind of weird about not letting his parents see who he's with." She shrugged, as if to say, *These crazy teenagers, who can explain them?*

Chris nodded, accepting, then turned back to the phone. Anne watched Clarissa. Clarissa raised her eyebrows, asking what was happening, but Anne didn't know.

Chris hung up the phone and without preamble said, "Emerson Blakely was killed a little while ago. Steve Greerdon's ex-wife's husband. A police officer."

"Oh, my God," Clarissa burst out. "Peter's stepdad. Is he okay? Peter?"

"Apparently. He didn't find the body. His father did. He was the first on the scene."

He looked at Anne grimly. Here was Greerdon at the scene of another crime. "I need more," he said to her.

Anne nodded. Clarissa began to tremble. She'd known much more than her share of violent death in her short life. Inevitably, this would remind her of others. Chris went and held her, stroking her back as if she were a much younger child.

Behind his back, Anne continued to stare at Clarissa.

"My God, am I going to find a dead body in every room I walk into?" Steve Greerdon said. By this time he sounded angry, but also weary and more than a little anxious. He sat in a small office at police headquarters. It wasn't an interrogation room, they'd given him that much professional courtesy, but everyone in the room understood the situation: the two detectives, the chief of police, the district attorney, and the district attorney's chief investigator. Greerdon sat in a hard-backed chair behind a metal desk, its top empty. It could have been his own office, already emptied of his things. The other men stood, in various postures. No one had tried to play the good cop or the bad cop. Chief Lloyd Garza handled the latter role without acting. He had already demanded Greerdon's resignation twice, and had Greerdon's badge in his pocket. The others looked frustrated.

"You know what's happened here, don't you?" Greerdon said it to Chris, ignoring the cops in the room. "He's getting more desperate. They've got to set me up, they've got to get rid of me. They think I'm getting close to finding the evidence on them."

"Are you?" Chris answered.

"No! But it must be connected to this trial. They're afraid of what Luisa Gaines knows. They're afraid I'm going to force it out of her." He got out of his chair and walked close to Chris, saying for his ears alone, "That's why she's gone missing."

"Who knew you were going to your ex-wife's house?" Detective Sidney Jones asked. Jones was a tall, thin, forty-four-year-old man invariably dressed in a suit. He had a way of blending into backgrounds so that his voice came as a surprise, as if out of nowhere.

"I told you, several people. I called in to dispatch and checked out, said I was going to see my son. I mentioned it to a couple of other people too."

"So somebody rushed over there and took the opportunity to shoot Emerson Blakely so you'd walk into it?"

"Yes," Greerdon insisted. "Then they tried to make it look like a break-in, but they didn't even do a good job of it." To Chris and Jack he said, "The broken glass of the window was mostly outside in the yard. Meaning it was probably broken from the inside instead of the outside. And they grabbed up a couple of things closest to hand, a little TV and a CD player, but not the things a real burglar would take."

"And we found those things in a Dumpster three blocks away," Ed Salinas said. His moustache seemed to droop in disbelief, or weariness. "He's right, they didn't try to make a good show of it. Whoever it was."

"Because they wanted it pinned on me," Greerdon insisted. "The crime scene looks like they were laughing at me while they set it up. If I'd wanted to kill Emerson, I would've done a hell of a lot better job of it."

"Yeah, how would you have done it?" Jack asked curiously. "I've always wondered how a professional would handle this kind of thing."

Chris glanced at his assistant. Jack looked genuinely interested. Not so many years ago, he'd been a police detective himself. He had extracted many confessions, and still had the techniques.

But Chief Garza stepped in again. "Unless you were mad," he said to Greerdon. "Unless you and Blakely got into a fight. Maybe you didn't like the way you thought he treated your son. Yeah, we know about that."

"Did it look like a fight?" Greerdon asked. Nobody answered him. The two detectives looked at Chris uneasily.

Chris hadn't said a word so far. This was their business. He'd just wanted to be here to see Steve Greerdon. Maybe to back him up, but mostly to see how he reacted to this latest accusation. So far he found Greerdon absolutely convincing. But he had ever since he'd first gotten Greerdon out of prison, and he could have been completely wrong about that.

Greerdon sat back down and gave Chris an accusing look. "Why didn't you have your girl keep following me? She was supposed to be there to protect me from crap like this."

"She had another assignment," Chris said shortly.

The chief stuck his index finger into the top of the metal desk in front of Greerdon. It looked like it must hurt, but the chief didn't flinch. "Your ex-wife was in a meeting at the school. Your son was with the DA's daughter here. That leaves you, Greerdon. That may not be enough to arrest you—" He shot an angry look at his two detectives, who looked back at him impassively. "—but it's damned sure enough to put you on administrative leave. And you're not coming back from this one, either."

They all knew how the chief of police felt. Steve Greerdon was ancient history in the department. He shouldn't have been this chief's problem. Garza wanted to be rid of him.

A cell phone rang. They all checked their pockets or belt holsters, everyone except Steve Greerdon, who rolled his eyes as he watched the technology scramble. It turned out to be Salinas's phone. He said his name into it, then just said "Yeah" half a dozen times in half a minute. "Okay, thanks, Doc. You'll fax over your report when you have it done?"

He hung up and said to everyone in general, "Medical examiner just finished the autopsy. He said his estimate is that Blakely died an hour before Steve called it in."

"I was here an hour before that," Greerdon burst out. "Writing a report. I was sitting right out there. Remember?"

The two detectives shrugged. Jones said, "Me and Ed were out, but I'm sure somebody from day shift will remember."

"Also," Detective Salinas added deferentially, speaking to the chief, "Emerson wasn't bruised or scratched. He didn't look like he'd been in a fight. Just shot."

Greerdon stood up and slapped his hand down on the desk. He stared straight at Lloyd Garza. "That does it. I wouldn't have just walked in and shot him. I damned sure would've punched him before I popped him. And look at me. Do I look like I've been in a fight?"

All the men in the room looked at him more carefully than they had. Even in the dim light of the office, it was clear Greerdon's face was unmarked. He turned on the desk lamp so they could be sure. It threw his features into angry relief, and hurled his shadow, big and menacing, against the wall behind him, as if Greerdon suddenly had backup.

"Maybe a gunfight," Garza said. But he sounded sullen, no longer angry. He knew he had no evidence against his officer. Everyone else in the room, veteran law-enforcement personnel, knew it too. What he might have instead was a major lawsuit for false arrest against the city of San Antonio. The city council members wouldn't like that, and they were the ones who got to decide who served as chief of police.

Steve Greerdon held out his hand, palm up. Garza only hesitated for a moment before reaching into his shirt pocket and pulling out the badge he'd demanded half an hour earlier. He dropped it on the desk beside Greerdon's hand, then turned and walked quickly out of the room.

"This'll be a fun place to work for the next week," Ed Salinas said wryly, but he slapped Greerdon on the back in congratulations. Greerdon looked at Chris. "Do me a favor, will you? Put your girl back on me."

"Tomorrow," Jack Fine answered for Chris. "I'll stick with you tonight." He turned toward Chris, who stood watching Greerdon speculatively. All his reactions seemed genuine. But Chris no longer trusted his own perceptions. "What about you?" Jack asked him.

Chris stirred himself and yawned, realizing how late it was. "I've got a trial to run, remember?"

CHAPTER

eleven

★ Trials are often won or lost during the *other* side's case. One's own case seems solid until the other side starts picking it apart. A lawyer puts a witness on the stand to prove an essential point, but on cross-examination the witness looks like such a liar that he damages his own side's case instead of helping it. Twice in Chris Sinclair's brief life as a defense lawyer a few years earlier, he had done such damage to the State's case in cross-examining the State's own witnesses that when his turn came he decided to put on no evidence, and the juries quickly acquitted. Much more often he'd had the experience as a prosecutor of presenting a fairly weak case, but then having the good luck of seeing the defendant take the stand. Often a defendant's story was so ridiculous or inherently unbelievable that he proved the case against himself.

So lawyers often win or lose not through careful preparation, but through quick reactions. Spotting those inconsistencies as they passed fleetingly in testimony and exploiting them in cross-examination. After a prosecutor rests his case, that's when he has to be at his best—his most alert, his quickest.

Chris didn't feel that way the next morning, after his short night and the thought he'd devoted to Anne's revelation and the new murder. His thoughts swirled uselessly. His mind wouldn't settle down to the job at hand. He decided he'd let Bonnie do most of the work this morning.

"Feel ready?" he asked her.

"For what?" she asked innocently, then chuckled. Yes, she was ready. He could tell.

The State's case against Luisa Gaines had not been very strong. John Lincoln was a veteran defense lawyer, he knew that defendants often lose cases for themselves by putting on weak or obviously false evidence. That's why so often the defense rests without ever putting on any evidence.

But on the morning of the day when Luisa Gaines would turn up again, Lincoln came out blasting. He started the day by asking for a longer continuance, given his client's continued absence. But when Judge Conners denied his request he didn't appear to care, quickly asking to make his opening statement. A few minutes later he stood confidently before the jury, looking each juror in the eyes as he spoke.

"Now I believe you will hear what really happened on the day Chip Riley was murdered. Luisa Gaines never went out in back of the restaurant. She had no reason to go there; she was busy running Miguelito's, just like every night of her life. She never held the murder weapon in her hand. In fact, she didn't know where it was.

"And most importantly, she had no reason to kill Chip Riley. He still worked for her, yes, but their personal relationship had faded away, and that was fine with Luisa. Whatever he was doing out behind the restaurant didn't concern her. Chip Riley had enemies. He was a police officer, he had crossed dangerous men. And it wasn't a very safe neighborhood where he went out to take a cigarette break."

He turned and pointed at the empty chair beside his own at the defense table. "Obviously you've noticed that Luisa Gaines isn't here. There is a good reason for that."

The legs of Chris's chair scraped the floor. He stood up, his hands folded in front of him. The defense lawyer looked at him, understanding. If Lincoln started to give an explanation for his client's absence, Chris would object to the lawyer testifying. They stared silently at each other for a moment. Chris didn't look challenging, just prepared.

Lincoln continued to the jury. "I don't believe you'll be allowed to hear why Luisa isn't here. Something may have happened to her—"

"Objection."

"Sustained. Please disregard that remark, ladies and gentlemen of the jury."

Lincoln shrugged at the jurors, to show that he'd explain if he could, but he was prevented from doing so. "You will probably learn after the trial is over. But don't let it affect your decision."

"I object to that as well," Chris said, "as a misstatement of the law."

When a defendant flees, either the scene of a crime or his own trial, that flight can be evidence of his guilt. If Luisa Gaines remained missing, Chris hoped the judge would instruct the jury that they could use that fact against her.

"That's sustained," Judge Conners said, holding the jury's attention. "When all the evidence is in, *I* will instruct you on the law that applies to this case. Not the attorneys for either side. Understand?"

The jurors nodded. John Lincoln waited patiently, then smiled at the judge before continuing. "Just remember, please, that *I* am here for Luisa. And I hope to bring you her complete story. Remember also one very important point. I hope to present evidence that will guide you in your decision. But the defense has no obligation to prove anything. The State has the entire burden of proof. I don't have to hand you another murderer and prove a case against him. I just have to show you that the State hasn't proven its case. Thank you for your attention. Your honor, the defense calls Juan Treviño."

A man stood up from the spectator seats. A tall Hispanic man with a thin, lined face and no gray in his black hair, he could have been a weary thirty or well-preserved forty-eight. He wore a white *guyabera,* the traditional Mexican straight-bottomed shirt, and black pants. A waiter's outfit, Chris thought. He turned to Bonnie. She whispered, "Waiter at Miguelito's. Police questioned him. He claimed not to know anything."

She seemed to know the case more thoroughly than Chris did. "Take him," he said softly.

Bonnie turned away from him, pulling a legal pad toward her. Her posture changed only slightly, but Chris could feel her attention intensify, even as he himself relaxed slightly. This would be Bonnie's witness when the time came for cross-examination. She began writing questions even before Juan Treviño took the witness stand.

John Lincoln said smoothly, "Mr. Treviño, what is your occupation?"

"I am a waiter at Miguelito's." He spoke formally, sitting up straight in the chair.

"Were you hired by Luisa Gaines?"

"Yes, sir. I have worked there almost a year."

"Are you still employed at Miguelito's?"

"Yes, sir. I am sort of keeping the place going while the señora is busy here."

Bonnie looked up at him. Managing a bar/restaurant like Miguelito's, whose customers largely paid in cash, would offer great opportunities for skimming. Luisa Gaines had literally handed the keys to the cash register to this witness. Giving him such responsibility amounted to a cash bribe. It was doubtful, though, that Bonnie could get the witness to admit this.

"Were you working at Miguelito's on the evening when Chip Riley was killed there?"

"Yes, sir. Earlier I was. I got off at eight that night."

Bonnie frowned. This was not an eyewitness.

John Lincoln continued smoothly. "Did Luisa keep a gun in the restaurant?"

"Yes, sir. I had seen it once, one night when there was trouble."

"While you were in the restaurant that evening, did something come up about the gun?"

"Yes. Ms. Gaines sent me to her office and asked me to find the gun. She told me where it was kept, in the desk drawer."

"Did you go and look for it?"

"Yes, I did. But it wasn't there."

"Did you look carefully?"

"Oh, yes, sir. I looked in every drawer of the desk. When the señora told you to do something, you'd better do a good job of it. But I couldn't find the gun."

"Did you tell Luisa that?"

"Yes, sir. She got upset. She came into the office with me and looked herself. But we neither of us could find the gun."

"Did Luisa seem upset about this?"

Juan Treviño shrugged. "Somewhat. She was worried that someone in the restaurant had taken it."

"What did she tell you to do?"

"Nothing else. Just go back to work and keep my eyes open. I did, but I didn't see anything else unusual that night."

Lincoln looked briefly stern. "Mr. Treviño, why didn't you come forward and tell the police what you knew about the gun being missing?"

The witness shrugged again. "I didn't know it was important. I wasn't there when Mr. Riley was killed. Police asked me about it later, but I didn't know they said he'd been shot by the señora's gun."

"Didn't you know that from the publicity about the case?"

Treviño shook his head. "I don't read the newspaper. It wasn't until you talked to me that I knew the gun was important. I didn't know I knew anything special. I thought Señora Gaines must have questioned every employee about the gun. When I knew it was important, I did try calling the police officers, but they didn't seem to pay attention."

"Did you call either of these prosecutors, or anyone else in the district attorney's office?"

"No, sir. Señora Gaines said they were determined to prove her guilty no matter—"

"Object to hearsay," Bonnie said, irritated at herself for having let the witness go on as long as he had. She had wanted to hear his answer herself.

"Sustained," Judge Conners said.

John Lincoln appeared unperturbed. "Thank you, Juan. Pass the witness."

Treviño turned toward Chris. He had obviously been prepared as a witness. He looked a bit surprised when it was the young woman at the prosecution table who sat forward and began questioning him. "Mr. Treviño, people in the restaurant talked about Officer Riley being murdered and Luisa Gaines, your boss, being arrested for it, didn't they?"

"Yes, somewhat."

"'Somewhat'? This hasn't been the hottest topic of conversation in Miguelito's for months?"

Trevino sat up straighter and looked more formal. "I suppose. But I don't join in the gossip. I try to keep to myself."

"So much so that you didn't know that Riley had been shot with Luisa Gaines's gun?"

The witness looked a little uneasy. "I think I heard something about it. But by that time, time had gone by. I had forgotten about the señora asking me to look for the gun, until Mr. Lincoln talked to me and I started thinking hard about it."

Bonnie's face opened up innocently and curiously. "Oh, so was it Mr. Lincoln who suggested to you that your search for the gun had happened on the night of the murder?"

"Oh, no."

"Did Luisa Gaines remind you of that?"

"We talked about it," Treviño said slowly. "But I remembered on my own."

"Uh huh." Bonnie let her skepticism show plainly, but moved on. "Are you now the manager of Miguelito's?"

"Well, not officially, I think. But I'm in charge when the señora isn't there."

"That's an important job. Yet you say you've only worked at Miguelito's less than a year. Weren't there other employees with more seniority than you, who should have been promoted to the manager's job?"

"You would have to ask Señora Gaines that."

"I'd like to do that," Bonnie said pointedly, glancing at the empty defendant's chair. "But surely you know there were other employees there with more experience than you."

"No," he said quickly. "Who may have worked at Miguelito's longer, but not with more experience than me. I managed a restaurant in Laredo before I moved to San Antonio. The señora knew that. That was why she hired me."

"What was the name of the restaurant in Laredo?" Bonnie asked, pen poised.

"La Hacienda del Rio," Treviño said quickly and with some pride. "Unfortunately, it closed. That is why I moved here."

"Who were the owners?"

"Two brothers named Luís and Esteban Flores. They left Laredo after they closed the restaurant, though. I think they returned to Mexico. No one is sure."

Bonnie narrowed her eyes, watching him. The witness's answers came easily and sincerely, and were perfect. There would be no way to check on his story. Bonnie decided to push him as far as he would go.

She set down her pen and leaned back in her chair, lacing her fingers across her stomach, growing conversational. "So it was because of your experience that Luisa Gaines placed such trust in you?"

"I suppose. I also think she liked it that I *didn't* gossip with the others."

"So naturally when her gun went missing, she asked you to look for it."

Treviño shrugged. "As I said, I thought she asked others as well."

"It seems likely to me she would have asked Officer Riley about a gun. Do you know if she did?"

"I never saw her talk to him that evening."

"No?" Bonnie sounded surprised. "Did they have an argument?"

"Not that I know. As I said, I didn't see them talk at all."

"While you worked at Miguelito's, Chip Riley was sort of the manager himself, wasn't he?"

Treviño frowned as if puzzled. "No. He was just sort of a security guard."

"He was more than that, Mr. Treviño. You know that, don't you?"

"What do you mean?" The man looked genuinely puzzled.

"Chip Riley and Luisa Gaines had a very personal relationship as well as being partners in the restaurant."

Treviño shook his head. "I never saw any sign of that. I heard they had been together, yes, but during my time there I never saw any—signs of affection pass between them. They just both did their jobs."

"So they had broken up?"

"I guess that is how you would say it."

"Really," Bonnie pressed. "And did Luisa Gaines seem upset about that?"

Trevino shook his head with a slight smile. "No. Truly not."

"Why do you say that, Mr. Treviño? And why do you smile?"

The witness dropped the smile, and looked uneasy at saying anything more, though he still had a confident look. Slowly, choosing his words carefully, he said, "I know that Officer Riley and the señora didn't have a—romantic involvement anymore. Maybe they did once, but it was all gone."

"How do you know? Isn't it possible they met outside the restaurant, that they spent time together elsewhere? Even that they lived together?"

"I suppose. But I don't think so."

"Why not?"

Treviño said, not blurting it out but as if the truth were being forced out of him, "Because Señora Gaines had someone else."

Bonnie just sat and stared at him. So did the jurors, as well as Judge Conners.

"What makes you think that?" Bonnie asked, with genuine curiosity in her voice.

"I saw them. One night when I was the last one in the restaurant except for the señora, he came to pick her up. An attractive man, well dressed even late at night. The señora had obviously been waiting for him. They left together."

"And how do you know they had a romantic relationship? Did she tell you?"

Juan shook his head. "No. Señora Gaines is a private person. But it was obvious. Her face lit up when he arrived. His, too. If you had seen them together, you would be sure." The witness looked at Bonnie as if he and she were sophisticated people who understood these things. Bonnie frowned.

"When was this that you saw them together?"

"Of that I am not certain. October, I think. Maybe September. Some time before Officer Riley was killed."

Chris looked over at the defense lawyer. Lincoln sat expressionless, watching his witness. But he obviously felt Chris's attention. He turned and gave Chris a look, and they both understood. Yes, the defense lawyer knew he had to produce this boyfriend. He would.

Meanwhile, Bonnie tried to discredit the testimony. "Have you heard people say that they heard Luisa Gaines and Chip Riley have what sounded like lovers' quarrels?"

He shook his head emphatically. "They didn't. She was not pleased with his work. She said he had grown very sloppy, and acted as if he owned the place. She was upset about that, nothing more personal."

"Haven't you heard that the defendant acted jealous over Chip Riley's flirtation with a waitress named Teresa?"

Treviño smiled indulgently, as if that were a silly joke. "That is simply untrue. She didn't like the flirting, true, because it kept the waitress from her work. She was unhappy with both of them, but it wasn't jealousy. She had no reason to be jealous."

"Let's go back to the question of the gun, Mr. Treviño. It was the defendant who sent you to look for it in her office, yes?"

"Yes."

"Why?"

"I don't know. Something had come up about it, I think. But I don't know what."

"Had she ever asked you to look for her gun before?"

"No."

"Had you ever heard her ask anyone else to look for the gun?"

"Not that I remember. But I don't hear everything that goes on in the restaurant."

"You seem to hear plenty," Bonnie said, "especially for someone who doesn't gossip."

The defense lawyer made a move as if to object. Before he could, Bonnie said, "I pass the witness."

So when Lincoln did rise it was only to say, "No more questions, your honor. The defense calls Enrique Galvan."

Chris touched Bonnie's arm and rose too, turning quickly to leave the courtroom. As he exited a man was entering: a tall, distinguished-looking man with gray at the temples, a large, handsome head, and very dark skin. He and Chris exchanged glances as they passed. The witness didn't seem to find anything unusual in the fact that the district attorney was leaving.

Chris went out into the hall and hurriedly called Jack. The investigator answered on the first ring. Chris spoke quietly. "Jack, the defense is calling a witness named Enrique Galvan. He's going to testify that he's Luisa Gaines's boyfriend. He looks like he's in his early fifties. I don't know anything else about him. Get down here and listen to his testimony, see what he says about himself. Then find out everything you can."

Chris slipped back into the courtroom, heard the witness testify that he was a contractor who owned a company called Gal-Tex Construction, and returned to the hall to relay that information to his investigator. Chris looked up and down the hallway, half expecting to see Luisa Gaines hurrying toward him looking apologetic, like a woman unforgivably late for lunch. Instead, after a very few minutes, he saw Jack Fine walking quickly toward him. Chris gave him what information he already had, and while Jack called upstairs to get someone started checking the witness's background, Chris went back inside. He walked quietly up the aisle of the courtroom toward his seat.

The witness, who wore a dark suit and sat a little slumped in the chair, was growing a reminiscent smile as he said, "I was a regular customer at the restaurant. Luisa would stop to ask me how things were. I started talking to her so she would stay longer. She has a beautiful smile. If you can ever make her forget her responsibilities for a minute, if you can make her laugh—well, believe me, it was well worth the effort." He smiled himself, and looked very handsome.

Chris saw that Bonnie had written nothing on the legal pad in front of her. She stared at the witness hostilely, obviously not believing a word he said.

Lincoln asked, "Did your relationship go further than occasional smiles in the restaurant?"

"Eventually, yes," Enrique Galvan said. "I finally asked her whether she ever had dinner any place else. Luisa knew what I meant. She asked me to recommend some place. I said I would pick her up." He shrugged. "We began seeing each other regularly."

"Did anyone ever see you on these dates you had?"

"Well, of course people saw us. We weren't skulking around. But we didn't try to be noticed, either. We went to different places. Or just to my house, or hers."

"When did this relationship start?"

"Last summer."

"Did you know that she had a personal relationship with someone else?"

"Of course I knew about the police officer who worked in the bar, Chip Riley. He made sure everyone noticed him. I saw how he touched Luisa sometimes. But I also saw her frown when he did. I saw her leave the room when he got too loud. It was obvious she didn't feel anything for him, if she ever had."

"And when the two of you started becoming involved, did she confirm that?"

This time Bonnie was ready. "Object to hearsay, your honor."

Judge Conners nodded. "Sustained."

Lincoln asked to approach the witness, then did, carrying a photograph. Handing it to Galvan, he asked, "Can you identify this exhibit?"

Galvan looked at the picture more than perfunctorily. A reminiscent smile spread up his face. "This is a picture of Luisa and me. It was taken in a restaurant."

"How did you happen to have your picture taken?"

"One of those men came around with a camera, asking if we wanted our picture taken for three dollars. I felt a little sorry for him. Besides, we didn't have any pictures of ourselves."

"Is that the date the picture was taken, down in the corner of the frame?"

"Yes."

"Is that date accurate?"

"Yes, sir. Before all this happened."

"Your honor, I offer this photo as defense Exhibit Number One, tender it to opposing counsel, and pass the witness."

John Lincoln did all this with slightly exaggerated gestures, offering the picture to Chris and Bonnie, then taking his seat, with a smile at his witness.

Bonnie held the photograph. She and Chris bent over it. In the picture Enrique Galvan and Luisa Gaines sat at a small table for two with glasses of wine in front of them. Galvan had his arm around Luisa and smiled broadly at the camera. She smiled too, but less openly, in a more guarded or rueful way. With her right hand she held the fingers of his hand that circled her shoulders. They looked happy, and they made a very attractive couple.

The date in the lower corner of the photo said October 21. About a month before the murder of Chip Riley.

Chris looked up at the judge and started to speak, but Bonnie stopped him with her hand on his arm. "No objection, your honor," she said clearly.

She was also announcing that she would cross-examine this witness. Chris sat back. Bonnie walked across the front of the courtroom to hand the picture to the jurors. She stood at the jury box watching them as they studied it. Silence lengthened until the judge said, "Ms. Janaway, are you going to cross-examine?"

"Oh, yes, your honor." She retrieved the picture from a juror and handed it to the witness. "Mr. Galvan, where was this picture taken?"

"A restaurant on the south side called Picador's. Rather late at night."

"Can you bring in the photographer who took it?"

"I doubt it. Those people don't last very long. They move on. I've been back to the restaurant to ask, but they said they haven't seen him in a while."

"So you can't produce him. Can you bring in anyone who saw you dining in Miguelito's, on one of these occasions when you flirted with the defendant?"

Galvan shrugged. "Usually I ate there alone. I'm a contractor, I go from job site to job site during the day. My men stay on the job. So I end up having lunch by myself a lot of times. Maybe that's why I had more time to notice Luisa. But I'm sure you could ask employees of the restaurant. Many of them must have seen me there."

Galvan had just scored a point, subtly shifting the burden of proof back to the prosecutor. As a clincher, he added, "Besides, as I said, once our relationship developed, we spent more time in private than in public."

"Were you embarrassed by each other?"

He shifted in his seat. "Not embarrassed, no, not at all. But—there were complications."

Bonnie waved at the jury. Chris could hear the edge of anger in her voice, and wondered if others could hear it as well. It became more obvious as Bonnie said, "This is the time to share, Mr. Galvan. Don't hold back. Why was your bright new love for Luisa Gaines complicated?"

Chris glanced at John Lincoln, expecting an objection, but the defense lawyer sat looking expectant. He knew this answer, and had deliberately not brought it out, leaving that for the prosecution.

Enrique Galvan shifted uneasily in his seat, but then looked forthrightly at Bonnie as he said, "You see, I am a married man."

Bonnie didn't say anything. She stared at the man from a few feet away. He continued, "My wife and I have been separated for years, but she is a devout Catholic, and begged me not to seek a divorce. It didn't matter to me, so I never did. After Luisa and I became serious it did begin to matter, but Luisa said— Oh. I know I can't repeat what she said. But we decided that what we had didn't need a marriage ceremony." He shrugged. "That is why we didn't want to advertise our relationship. I have children, and I didn't want to hurt my wife. And Luisa is very private by nature anyway."

"Did Chip Riley know about your relationship?"

"I don't know," Galvan said simply. "He and I never spoke of it. I know Luisa began acting more coldly toward him."

Bonnie returned to the picture. "Mr. Galvan, you testified that the October date on this picture is accurate. But is there anything in the photo itself that shows it wasn't taken, for example, last week?"

He looked down at it. "I don't see anything. We didn't know we had to have our picture taken with a calendar."

"No, but you know it needed to be dated. Do you know how you put this date on the photograph?"

The witness shrugged again. "The camera does it automatically."

"Yes, automatically," Bonnie said, "after you take a pin or a paper clip and press the little buttons to tell the camera what date it is. It doesn't know all by itself."

Galvan looked at her flatly. Her hostility had become apparent to him, if to no one else. "The date is accurate," he said.

"But we have to take your word for that. We also have to take your word that the relationship existed at all."

"It's true," he said earnestly.

"Were you and Ms. Gaines intimate?"

"Intimate? We were very close. We still—"

"Is it a sexual relationship, Mr. Galvan?"

The witness looked uncomfortable, which struck Chris as almost funny. A trial is no place for squeamishness, or for gentlemanly conventions. Galvan looked up at Judge Conners, who just looked back at him, not helping him out. Finally he answered, "Yes."

Bonnie's expression had flattened, though her eyes still looked angry. She saw now how far the witness was willing to go. But she was prepared to push matters to the edge, too. "Can you prove that?"

The witness looked up at her with something like alarm. "Prove it? What would you have me do? We didn't take pictures."

"Tell us something that only Luisa Gaines's lover would know," Bonnie challenged him.

Galvan looked flustered. Obviously his mind raced. With memories of passionate lovemaking, what she cried out in a vibrant moment? Or was he only trying to think of what he should say? It was impossible to say. "She—I don't know what to say. There is nothing—"

"Does she have a tattoo on her butt?"

The courtroom erupted. Some jurors stared at the prosecutor, a couple snickered. In the audience, people laughed outright. Collective gasps provided a rich background to the noise. John Lincoln leaped to his feet, saying indignantly, "Your honor!"

But Judge Conners didn't need instruction from him. She leaned forward over her bench, eyes blazing and face red, and said sternly, "Young lady, you will not use language like that in my courtroom. If you do again I will hold you in contempt."

Bonnie didn't back down. She folded her arms and said, "I apologize, your honor. I am a simple girl from the barrio. Can you please tell me how I should phrase that question?"

The judge replied tightly, "You are a simple girl who has graduated from college and law school. Figure it out."

Bonnie walked back to the prosecution table and took her seat. Chris wanted to whisper something to her, but also didn't want to break her concentration. He sat tight as Bonnie gave the witness a hard look and said, "Can you tell us anything that would substantiate your claim, Mr. Galvan? A mole she has in a place people wouldn't see? A freckle? An anatomical irregularity?" Glancing at the judge, she added, "Or decorative artwork somewhere that wouldn't be seen by anyone except Luisa Gaines's lover?"

Judge Conners returned Bonnie's glance, then turned her attention to the witness, as did everyone else in the courtroom. Enrique Galvan still looked uncomfortable, but he had straightened up to sit tall in the witness box and look forthrightly at the prosecutor. He had come up with his answer.

"I will not speak of such things," he said staunchly. "It would be a betrayal."

"You've already told us about the relationship," Bonnie said. "How is proving that what you said true any more—"

Lincoln stood to say, "Objection, your honor. She's arguing with the witness."

Judge Conners looked as if she were sorry to see the exchange interrupted, but sustained the objection.

The witness stared at Bonnie. "You have my answer," he said flatly.

Bonnie moved on, sounding bored with this man. "Mr. Galvan, were you at Miguelito's the night Chip Riley was killed?"

"No."

"Then you can't tell us about that, either."

"Object to the sidebar," Lincoln said, sounding angry for the first time during this witness's testimony. The judge sustained him.

Bonnie nodded toward the empty chair at the defense table. "Do you know where your girlfriend is now, Mr. Galvan?"

He looked sorrowful. "No. I am very worried about her."

"I'm sure. I pass the witness."

John Lincoln drew himself together and looked down at his legal pad, but he had apparently written no notes there. Like everyone else in the courtroom, he'd watched the duel between Bonnie and the defense witness. He cleared his throat and said, "Mr. Galvan, to your knowledge did Luisa Gaines have any reason to murder Chip Riley?"

"Asked and answered," Bonnie said quickly, out of the side of her mouth. She had turned so that she had her back to the defense lawyer and her profile to his witness, as if she could no longer bear the sight of either of them.

"Sustained," said Judge Conners.

Lincoln looked down again, thought briefly, and said, "No more questions."

Bonnie simply shook her head. The judge excused the witness. He stepped down cautiously and walked out past the defense table without looking back. It would have been a good moment for him to bend and squeeze Luisa Gaines's shoulder in an affectionate, reassuring manner. She could look up at him with eyes shining with gratitude and affection. Jurors could see a connection between them.

But of course Luisa Gaines was absent. So Enrique Galvan just walked stiffly out of the courtroom.

"Mr. Lincoln?"

The defense lawyer stood and said, "Your honor, the defense calls Anna Gomez."

As people waited, Chris turned toward his assistant with a questioning glance, asking about her attitude with the last witness. Bonnie understood. She shrugged, but not apologetically. Her eyes were still hot. "I hate liars," she muttered, almost loud enough to be heard by other people. The judge glanced toward her warningly.

Chris admired Bonnie's confidence in her ability to read people. Chris was sometimes troubled by the opposite in his own attitudes. He usually believed people, even people who said contradictory things. He seemed able to put himself in everyone's place. Often it wasn't until after a trial that he could figure out why someone must have been lying. Bonnie, though, had made a quick judgment and believed in it passionately. Her hostility toward the defense witness hadn't been faked. She still looked personally offended by his testimony.

The jurors' reactions were much harder to read, though. Bonnie had done a good job of cross-examining the defense witnesses, but as John Lincoln had said, the defense didn't have to prove anything. With his first two witnesses he had taken away the murder weapon and the motive. That is, if those witnesses were believed. Even if they weren't, they had certainly muddied the facts of the case.

The next defense witness appeared at the back of the courtroom. She stopped there, looking nervous. John Lincoln waved her forward. Anna Gomez was young, perhaps under twenty, small with thin arms. She wore a plain blue dress that was too big for her, as if it might have been borrowed for this occasion. She was pretty with youth but not distinctive. Her straight hair fell limply to her shoulders. She walked slowly, looking at no one until she reached the witness stand. Judge Conners swore her in and told her, with kindly gestures, to take a seat.

"Please state your name."

"Anna Gomez."

"How old are you, Anna?"

"Twenty-two."

"You'll need to speak up, dear, so everyone can hear you. Tell us, Anna, where did you work on the night of November twenty-eighth of last year?"

"At a restaurant called Miguelito's."

Chris and Bonnie looked at each other. She shrugged and whispered, "I don't remember seeing a statement from her."

Chris made a small hand gesture meaning he would take this witness. He began making notes as the defense lawyer continued questioning.

"Anna, what did you do at the restaurant?"

"I cleared tables and helped in the kitchen. Trying to work my way up to waitress."

"Do you remember a man named Chip Riley?"

"Oh, yes. He was a police officer and worked sort of as a security guard."

"Do you remember him there that night?"

"Yes, he was there, circulating, talking, laughing with people." Anna Gomez smiled as if at a pleasant memory. When the smile went away again, her face looked much too careworn for her age.

"Did you also know a waitress named Teresa Vasquez?"

"Teresita, yes. She was very nice. Quiet, but she and I talked sometimes during slow times."

"Do you remember whether November twenty-eighth was a slow night?"

"It was for a while, but then it got busy. Some large parties came in, people who had relatives in town for Thanksgiving. Things were very hectic for a while."

"Did you ever get a break?"

"Yes," Gomez said quietly. The jurors were leaning forward to hear her soft voice. "About nine o'clock I went outside, in the back. That's where I liked to take my breaks, to get away from the noise and the smoke."

"Were you smoking?"

"Oh, no," the witness said quickly. Her hands moved down her arms. One hand went across her abdomen and into her lap. "I don't smoke."

"All right." John Lincoln smiled at her reassuringly. "Anna, while you were outside taking your break, did you see anything unusual?"

"Yes. I was about to go back inside when the back door burst open.

Teresita came flying out. Then Señora Gaines followed her. She yelled. She said, 'Get out and don't come back!' "

"Luisa said this to Teresa?"

"Yes."

"Did she sound angry?"

"Yes, very."

"Could you tell why?"

"She said, 'I'm tired of your laziness! Customers are waiting and you can't be found!' She told Teresa she was useless, or some word like that, and said she was fired, right then, and to leave and never come back."

"This was at nine o'clock?" Lincoln asked.

"Yes, sir."

"Did Teresa leave?"

"Yes. She was crying. She walked away around the back and out toward the street."

"Did you see her again that night?"

"No, sir. I worked until the shots and until police came."

"Did you tell anyone else what had happened?"

"No. I didn't say anything."

"Were people asking what had happened to Teresa?"

"Not that I heard. We were busy for a while and then the shooting happened and everyone had other things to think about."

"When the police were questioning witnesses, did you tell them what you had seen?"

"No. They asked me if I'd seen anything out back or anyone threatening Officer Riley. I didn't think what I had seen had anything to do with that, so I didn't say anything about it."

Abruptly, John Lincoln said, "I pass the witness."

Once again Chris was taken by surprise. He understood the importance of this witness's testimony. If Teresa Vasquez had been fired and left the restaurant two hours before Chip Riley was shot, then he hadn't been flirting with her right before he was shot. Luisa Gaines hadn't come upon them and killed her lover in a fit of jealous rage.

And Anna Gomez appeared believable, partly because she didn't seem to understand the importance of her testimony. Chris must be careful cross-examining her. She appeared so fragile that a sharp question would break her. Nevertheless, he had to question her motivation, including possible gratitude to her employer.

"Anna," he asked kindly, "you said you were trying to work your way up to waitress. Have you made it? Have you been promoted to waitress?"

She smiled proudly. "Yes, sir."

"Congratulations. Do you still work at Miguelito's?"

"No, at another restaurant."

Damn. There went gratitude to Luisa Gaines. Chris managed not to look hurt. "During the time you worked at Miguelito's, had you seen Chip Riley flirting with Teresa? Whispering to her, trying to make her laugh?"

Other witnesses who worked in the restaurant had seen many such occasions, so if this witness said they hadn't happened she would look like a liar, and biased in favor of the defense. But she said shyly, "Yes, sir, I saw that."

"Did you see Luisa Gaines get angry on those occasions?"

The witness pondered, then answered carefully, "Sometimes, but not at the flirting. She got mad because Teresa wasn't doing her job. She got mad at anyone who didn't do their jobs."

"Well, you can't know why she was really mad, can you, Anna? You would have to read her mind to know that."

She shrugged, conceding the point. "That was just the way it seemed to me."

"On this night when you saw Ms. Gaines fire Teresa, did you hear either of them mention Officer Riley's name?"

Anna Gomez raised her eyes, appearing to think carefully. "No, I don't remember hearing that."

"Is it possible Ms. Gaines was firing Teresa because she'd been with Chip Riley when she should have been working?"

Gomez shrugged apologetically. "I don't know. I only know what I saw."

Chris gave up. "No more questions."

John Lincoln smiled tightly and said the same thing. "No more questions, your honor."

The witness looked up at the judge, then stood up carefully. Her loose-fitting dress tightened as she bent at the waist and stepped down.

Bonnie, who was staring at her thoughtfully, suddenly grabbed Chris's arm. "Oh, my God," she said under her breath.

"What?" Chris whispered back.

But Bonnie was already on her feet. "Your honor, may we recall this witness? Just for one minute's worth of questions."

Judge Conners frowned at her. "Recall? But she just— Well, I—"

Lincoln, clearly having no more idea what was going on than anyone else, naturally opposed the request. "Your honor, the State can recall her during their own rebuttal. We're on my time now."

"But the witness is here right now," Bonnie said reasonably. "It's just a continuation of cross-examination."

Judge Conners thought for a moment, and good sense prevailed over strict procedure. "All right. Take your seat again, please, Ms. Gomez. Briefly," she added emphatically to Bonnie, and gave her a look indicating she hadn't forgotten her earlier impropriety.

"Yes, your honor," Bonnie said with utmost submissiveness. When Anna Gomez turned and sat again, Bonnie watched her closely. Then she asked kindly, "Anna, are you married?"

John Lincoln jumped to his feet again, looking outraged and baffled. "What? Your honor, I object to relevance. What could this possibly have to do with anything?"

The judge turned to Bonnie, with the same question obviously written on her face.

"Your honor, it's about the witness's motivation," Bonnie explained without explaining. "If you will allow me one more question, it will become clear."

Staring at Bonnie, the judge said to the witness, "Answer the question, please."

Shyly looking down at her hands, Anna Gomez said softly, "No."

Bonnie licked her lips. She stared at the witness. Suddenly she looked afraid. But she said resolutely, in a gentle voice that still demanded answers, "Anna, are you pregnant?"

The witness looked up with alarm. The judge gaped at the young prosecutor. John Lincoln leaped to his feet again. "Your honor!"

"This is not proper impeachment of a witness," Judge Conners said sternly.

Bonnie answered, "That's not my objective, your honor. I'm not trying to make a moral judgment. I want to demonstrate that this witness is in a position to need help from the defendant."

"Phrase your question that way, then," the judge said coldly.

"I have to establish the predicate," Bonnie insisted. Chris sat beside her watching the witness. Anna was blushing. Her hands actively covered her stomach now. The answer to Bonnie's question had become obvious, at least to him.

Judge Conners stared coldly at Bonnie, who shrugged and sat.

"Ms. Gomez, has Luisa Gaines offered to help you with your baby when it comes? Help you with day care, find you a place, maybe, or give you a higher-paying job?"

The witness hesitated. Then she said, "No. She hasn't said anything like that."

The answer was probably true. Luisa Gaines wouldn't have put the offer into words, in case just such a question as this was asked during trial. Gaines would be too smart to make the offer explicit. But the witness's slight hesitation had been fatal, as far as Chris was concerned. There was an understanding between the witness and the defendant.

"Are you going to make her godmother of your child?" Bonnie asked kindly.

The witness smiled. "I have too many sisters and aunts for that."

Bonnie returned her smile, and released her. Still on his feet, John Lincoln also hesitated, but excused Gomez with no more questions. This time she stood even more carefully and walked slowly out between the two lawyers' tables.

A sigh seemed to circle the courtroom, an exhalation of breaths people didn't know they'd been holding. Judge Conners seemed to feel the release of tension. She sounded ironic as she said, "Any more witnesses, Mr. Lincoln?"

He glanced down at the empty chair next to him. "I'd like to call the defendant, your honor."

"Well, that's going to be a problem, isn't it?"

"If I could be given a little time to make one more effort, your honor . . . Also, I have one other witness to call, a police officer. He should be close at hand."

The judge glanced at the clock at the back of the room, which said it was not yet eleven o'clock. "I suppose we can give you an early lunch to try to find her." She turned to the jurors. "I'm sorry, but once again I'm going to give you some extra time. You'll need to be back here at one-fifteen." The jurors did not look displeased. They started to talk among themselves as they stood. Judge Conners said, "I want to see the lawyers in chambers."

Chris turned to Bonnie and said, "I'm going to have to transfer you out of this court. I think your effectiveness with this judge is going to be impaired after this."

Bonnie shrugged. "Oh, darn," she said scornfully.

Chris and John Lincoln followed the judge out of the door behind her bench and into the sparsely-traveled corridor behind the courtrooms. "Who's your police witness?" Chris asked casually.

Lincoln kept walking as if he wouldn't answer, then said, "Someone to say Steve Greerdon is a suspect in Emerson Blakely's murder."

Chris made a dismissive sound. The figure of Helen Conners, rather wide in her black robe, strode ahead of them quickly. As soon as she entered the door of her offices she whirled around, and it became clear that her energy was fueled by anger. Looking directly at Chris, she said, "You're going to have to get that girl out of my court."

"If you're speaking of Bonnie Janaway, your honor, that's a personnel matter of the District Attorney's Office. I make those decisions."

The judge glared at him. Chris added smoothly, "If you ever believe her guilty of any unethical conduct, though, I certainly hope you'll inform me immediately, and I'll launch a full investigation."

Judge Conners's eyes narrowed. She tried to read past his bland expression. Judges have limited powers—theoretically. In real life, they expect their whims to be obeyed by the people who come to them for decisions.

After a few seconds, though, Helen Conners suddenly laughed, a short, derisive outburst. "Tattoo on her butt! That was the laugh of the week." She turned, beginning to doff her robe, and led the way toward her private office. Over her shoulder she said, "Does she have a tattoo, John?"

Lincoln sputtered briefly. "I have no way of knowing, Judge."

"Yeah, right." In her office, Conners turned to face them again. "Any idea where she is?"

Lincoln shook his head. "All I can do is keep trying."

Conners looked at Chris. "Can you help him, Chris?"

"I'm doing my best, Judge. Believe me, we'd like to have her in custody, too."

The judge nodded. "Okay. I'll see you back here about one. Think we can wrap this thing up this afternoon?"

The lawyers looked at each other. "That all depends . . ." Lincoln said slowly.

"Yeah. Okay, 'bye."

She waved them out. The lawyers left side by side. They turned toward each other in the hall, but found they had nothing to say.

Chris and Bonnie had lunch in his office, along with Jack. Speaking of the judge, Bonnie asked, "Does she want me spanked in public, or just fired?"

"Both. I think I will leave you assigned to that court after this trial is over. The two of you should have fun."

Bonnie didn't look intimidated. Jack tried to turn the conversation to a more immediate topic. "Why does Lincoln want to prove Greerdon's a suspect in Emerson Blakely's murder? Which he's not, by the way."

"He just wants to cast suspicion everywhere he can, I'm sure. If Greerdon was at the scene of this murder and he's suspected in another one, both of police officers, it makes it look like he's on a vendetta, right? Makes it more likely he's the one who killed Chip Riley."

"Well, if he calls anyone who's really in on the investigation, they'll have to say he's been cleared as a suspect and is back on duty."

"But the suspicion will still linger . . ." Bonnie said thoughtfully. The men turned to look at her. "*Is* there a good suspect in Blakely's murder?"

"Not really," Jack said. "The best theory right now is that it was somebody trying to frame Greerdon for it. Someone who wants him taken away."

"Or wants him to look like a multiple murderer," Bonnie said in the same thoughtful tone.

Chris said, "You're thinking . . ."

"Her," Bonnie said. "Luisa. She's out there on the loose. We don't know where she is. Maybe *she* killed Emerson Blakely. Or had it done. To make it look like the best other suspect in her case is on a rampage."

Chris looked skeptical. Then he grew more thoughtful as well. "Or maybe her police friends did it for her," he said slowly.

They both turned to look at Jack. "I don't think so," he said wearily. "But to tell you the truth, I can't think of anything more plausible."

They sat in silence for a minute until Chris broke it. "I'll see you back in the courtroom. I want to call Anne."

Anne had little to say to him, though. She seemed distracted. They all did lately. "Let's go away after this is over," Chris said to her, striving for an intimate tone. "Just for the weekend, at least."

"That sounds wonderful," Anne said, but in the same tone she used to reassure patients that they weren't any crazier than anyone else.

After they said good-bye, Chris sat at his desk remembering Bonnie's cross-examination of Luisa Gaines's supposed boyfriend, and the question that had made Judge Conners laugh very belatedly. He wondered how he could prove that he was intimate with Anne. He knew so much about her, but far from everything. He would never know everything. She always had surprises for him.

After Anne hung up with Chris, she switched to another line and called Eric Schwinn's cell phone number. She thought she was going to get his voice mail, but on the fourth ring he answered, in a low voice.

"Am I interrupting something?"

"No, it's okay. What is it, Anne?" She heard him cover the phone partially and speak in an aside to someone else. All she could hear were the words, ". . . my shrink." The phrase sounded oddly intimate, and Anne felt herself oddly flattered.

But she kept her tone strictly professional as she said, "I need to see you again. Today."

She heard the grin in his voice as he answered, "Yes, ma'am. I'll be there as soon as I can. Is five all right?"

Anne would have to rearrange some things. "Yes. I'll be here."

"I'll see you then," he said, with emphasis on the "see." Anne hung up slowly, feeling she had just made a date rather than an appointment.

CHAPTER *twelve*

★ About one o'clock Luisa Gaines returned to the courtroom, late from lunch, late for her life. And in handcuffs.

The jurors were still assembling in the jury room, and the hall doors remained locked from the lunch break, so the spectator seats were empty. The bailiff sat at her desk talking to the court clerk, when the bailiff's phone rang and she answered quietly. After a moment she stood up and walked quickly to the table where Chris sat looking through his notes. She bent and whispered to him. Chris leaped to his feet and Bonnie looked up at him in alarm.

"She's here," Chris said. "They've arrested Luisa Gaines."

The defense table sat empty. "Call John Lincoln's office," Chris said, and walked hurriedly out to tell the judge.

In a few minutes the team was assembled: the lawyers, the judge, two bailiffs, the court clerk and coordinator, and Jack Fine. Jack stood behind the railing with his cell phone constantly to his ear.

"The surveillance team that had been keeping an eye on her house spotted her," he said to Chris in a low voice. But not so low that the defense lawyer didn't hear.

"Bullshit," Lincoln snapped at them.

Judge Conners said, in a light, brittle voice, "Did you say something, Mr. Lincoln?"

"No, your honor. Excuse me."

"Bring her out," the judge said to the bailiff. "What are we waiting for?" The ceremoniousness of the occasion seemed to annoy her. They all stood looking toward the side door of the courtroom, as if waiting for the entrance of the star.

The bailiff rapped on the door with her knuckles, then used a key on her belt chain to unlock it. This door led to a small holding cell next to the courtroom. The small space also contained an elevator, so prisoners could be brought directly up from the street level or the miniature jail between the first and second floors of the Justice Center. Prisoners were no longer brought through the halls in handcuffs and leg chains, as if their punishment included being made a spectacle. No one in the courtroom had yet seen Luisa Gaines.

The door opened and another sheriff's deputy, a cautious man with black glasses and gray at the temples, poked his head out, looked around, then withdrew. A moment later Gaines emerged. Her hands were cuffed in front of her. She wore a white coverall and thin slippers, and already had the prisoner shuffle, as if she'd been incarcerated for years. She kept her head down.

John Lincoln asked anxiously, "Luisa, are you all right?"

She didn't respond. Her lawyer turned an angry glare on the sheriff's deputies, who now numbered four. "What have you done to her?"

The cautious man said, "Brought her upstairs. SAPD delivered her to us downstairs, just like you see."

Judge Conners said to him, "Henry, we're in trial. You know I'm not going to let the jury see her like that."

"I know, Judge. I fussed at the officers about it. We're having clothes brought in now."

"Ms. Gaines," the judge said brusquely. "Are you injured? Or on drugs? Can you continue the trial?"

Gaines finally raised her head. She looked pale, except for the dark skin under her eyes. She had aged about twenty years. Dressed in the baggy coverall, she looked like the decrepit mother of the stylish, forceful woman who had begun the trial. Her voice was weak, too. "Yes, ma'am, I'm here. I'm not on anything. I'm ready."

No one took her assertion at face value. Lincoln stepped close to her and began whispering in her ear. It was impossible to tell whether she heard him. He took a step away and said to the judge, "I'd like the opportunity to confer with my client, your honor. Since we have to wait for her clothes anyway . . ."

The judge nodded. "I'd like to talk to her too," Chris muttered.

"You can use the courtroom," Judge Conners said, and rose abruptly. "Henry, let me know as soon as the clothes get here."

Lincoln began talking to his client again immediately. Luisa Gaines's lips moved. Almost immediately her lawyer looked alarmed. His eyes blazed as he looked up at Chris. "Your people did this to her!"

"My people? What people?"

Gaines was already trying to shush her lawyer, clutching his arm, but he snapped, "Cops."

Chris stepped close to them, looking down at Luisa Gaines. "I need to talk to you," he said in a low voice. "Not about the trial. I need to know what happened to you. Who."

She looked up fearfully, stepping back as if he had threatened her. For the first time she appeared animated. "No!" she cried. "I won't talk to you! I won't."

Then she did an odd thing. Outside the glass doors of the courtroom a small crowd was pressed to look at the drama inside. One of them was a television cameraman, with his camera pointed into the courtroom. Luisa Gaines glanced in their direction, but then stayed in profile to them, to the camera. She shook her head vehemently. The gesture seemed exaggerated, like that of a stage actress. "No," she said again. "I'm not telling you anything."

She also said this loudly enough to be heard by the four sheriff's deputies. She still sounded fearful. But for just a moment she looked into Chris's eyes. Hers weren't afraid, at least not of him. They blazed with desire to communicate.

Her lawyer saw it too. He gazed wonderingly from his client to Chris. "Let me talk to her," he said quietly.

Chris stepped away. What did Gaines want to tell him, while insisting loudly she wouldn't talk to him at all? What stopped her?

He withdrew to where Jack still stood outside the railing. Bonnie joined them. "Who arrested her?" Chris asked quietly. "Who brought her in? How did it happen?"

"I'll find out," Jack said briskly. He came through the railing and walked out the way the judge had, through the door at the back. Chris and Bonnie looked at each other curiously and walked that direction themselves. "We'll be in the conference room," Chris said to Lincoln over his shoulder. The defense lawyer was deep in whispered consultation with his client, and gave no indication he had heard.

Trial resumed forty-five minutes later with a strange appearance of normality. The defendant sat beside her lawyer, head held high. She wore one of her own dresses, a green one with a muted flower print, and she was carefully made up. Her face had regained most of its natural color, as well. She looked like herself again.

And the trial carried on as if she had never been missing. Judge Conners had decided to say nothing to the jury about the defendant's reappearance, as she had given them no explanation when she'd gone missing.

The only thing different from the early part of the trial was that when trial had begun Chris had sat in the left-hand chair of the prosecution table, which was on the right side of the courtroom from the spectators' perspective. The defendant had sat in the right-hand seat of her table, separated from him by only a few feet. Now she and her lawyer had switched places, so that Lincoln sat between Chris and his client, as if protecting her from the prosecutor. This wasn't just random seat selection. Lawyers like to sit close to the jury, to keep an eye on them, to aim their questions toward the jury box. But Lincoln had given up the preferred seat.

It still looked as if Luisa Gaines was afraid of Chris. She wanted to be as far from him as possible. Chris turned to his assistant and raised his eyebrows. "What did I do?"

Bonnie shrugged. "Did she run away because she was afraid of you? You do get this look sometimes. I haven't seen it, but other people talk about it."

She could have been kidding. He couldn't tell.

The defense called Detective Sidney Jones, the tall, lean detective with a long, expressionless face. Settling into the witness chair, Jones looked as if he knew a great deal, as if he could clear up many mysteries. But he didn't look eager to share.

"Are you the investigating detective in the murder of Emerson Blakely?" Lincoln began quickly.

"Yes, I am. One of them."

"Emerson Blakely was a police officer, wasn't he?"

"Yes."

Chris and Lincoln had had a brief hearing in front of Judge Conners before the defense had been allowed to call this witness. Chris had objected that all this was irrelevant to the murder for which the defendant was on trial. But the judge, being cautious, had ruled that the defense could put on this evidence, briefly.

"Detective, do you have a leading suspect in the murder of Officer Blakely?"

"Not at this time."

"You did have an initial suspect, though, didn't you? Wasn't Steve Greerdon the first person you questioned about the murder?"

"Detective Greerdon found the body. He was questioned as a witness."

"Well, isn't it true that the person who 'finds' the body often ends up being the person who murdered the victim?"

Jones shrugged. "Yes."

"And in fact Steve Greerdon was relieved of his badge and his gun before his interrogation began, wasn't he?"

Jones sat up straighter and paid more attention to the defense lawyer. "I wouldn't call it an interrogation. It was in Steve's office. But yes, the chief took away his badge and gun for a few minutes."

"So he was a suspect, wasn't he?"

"You start with what you've got," Jones explained. "So I guess, yes, without having any other idea, some people were briefly suspicious of Detective Greerdon."

"Why was that?"

"Well, like you said, he found the body."

Lincoln smiled grimly. "There's more to it than that, isn't there, Detective? In fact, Emerson Blakely was married to Greerdon's ex-wife, wasn't he? The woman who divorced Greerdon while he was in prison?"

"Yes."

"And Greerdon knows it was police officers who set him up to go to prison, doesn't he?"

"I don't know what he knows. We haven't discussed it."

"In fact, Steve Greerdon has good reason to bear a grudge against several of his fellow officers, doesn't he?"

Jones obviously didn't want to look evasive. But he was a very experienced witness, and refused to testify to something he didn't know. "If you believe some people's theories," he said shortly.

"You haven't developed another suspect in Emerson Blakely's murder, have you?"

Jones looked at the defendant. Obviously someone had talked to him about Bonnie's theory that Luisa Gaines might have killed Blakely to cast suspicion on Greerdon. But after a pause the detective just said, "No."

"Pass the witness."

Chris's cross-examination was brief. He let his annoyance at this distraction be obvious. "Detective Jones, has Officer Greerdon been cleared as a suspect in the murder of Chip Riley?"

"Yes."

"Has he been cleared as a suspect in the murder of Emerson Blakely?"

"Yes, he has." Jones gave these answers more quickly and with more evident satisfaction.

"Is Officer Greerdon still on active duty?"

"Yes."

"Still carrying his badge and his gun?"

"Yes, sir."

Chris slowed down and took the time to formulate his next question more carefully. "Detective, do you find it surprising that police officers should associate with each other even in their private lives?"

"No. You hang out with the people you know, and most people you know from work."

"So are your suspicions aroused by the fact that Detective Greerdon knew both these police officers?"

"No, they're not. As a matter of fact, I knew both of them myself. A lot of us did."

"Thank you. No more questions."

John Lincoln hadn't lost his easy look. "But you didn't see both these victims shortly before or after they were murdered, did you, Detective?"

"No," Jones said shortly.

"No more questions, your honor."

Chris let the witness go. He sensed they were done with the preliminaries. He was right. John Lincoln stood and said, "The defense calls Luisa Gaines, your honor."

He helped his client to her feet as if she were aged or infirm. But she stood straight and walked to the witness stand without looking left or right. When the judge swore her in, Gaines answered, "I do" in a loud, clear voice. She took her seat and looked straight at her lawyer, no one else.

"Please state your name and occupation."

"Luisa Gaines. I own a restaurant called Miguelito's and a couple of other small businesses."

"Luisa, first of all, are you all right?"

"Yes," she said shortly.

"You've been missing from this trial for two days. Did you run away because you're guilty of the crime you're charged with?"

"No," she said staunchly. For the first time she looked at the jury, with a stern look as if daring them not to believe her.

"Did you stay away of your own free will?"

"No."

Lincoln asked as if curious, "What happened?"

"I've been held hostage. During our lunch break two days ago, two men told me to come with them. We got into a car where a third man waited. As we drove away from the downtown area one of the men put a blindfold over my eyes. They took me somewhere and kept me there. That's where I've been ever since."

"Luisa, were these men police officers?"

The defendant looked hard at her lawyer. Obviously she hadn't instructed him to ask this question. "I don't know," she said quietly.

"How did you get away?"

"I didn't get away. This morning they took me to a place and let me out. But police officers were right there, and they must have been told I'd be coming. They arrested me right away."

"Then you were returned to this courtroom in handcuffs, correct?"

"Yes. But this is where I wanted to be. I wanted to tell my story."

Lincoln said with great sympathy, "Luisa, why did these men kidnap you?"

Chris stood and said carefully, "Your honor, I object to speculation. Unless she actually knows the motives of these supposed kidnappers."

He watched Luisa Gaines as he spoke. She sat blinking slowly, thinking hard.

Judge Conners said, "That's sustained. Unless she knows."

John Lincoln gave his client a prompting nod. She said, "I think they wanted to make me look guilty. That's what I heard them saying. 'This will get her convicted,' one of them said."

"Did you recognize any of them?"

"No."

Lincoln continued to speak quietly and reassuringly, like a doctor treating a very injured patient. "Luisa, did they mistreat you?"

Chris stood again. "Your honor, could we move on to testimony about the actual crime that this trial is about?"

"Is that a legal objection, Mr. Sinclair?"

"Relevance, your honor." Chris let a little of his impatience show.

"Sustained." The judge had just been having a moment's fun with him. It can get boring up on the bench, unable to participate.

"All right," Lincoln said, all business now. "Luisa, let's talk about your relationship with Chip Riley, say the last few months before his death?"

"It was professional," she said flatly, and certainly her face looked unemotional enough to make the statement believable. "He was an employee, and not a very good one."

"At one time you two had had a closer, personal relationship?"

"Yes. We had been lovers. But that was over. For me it was over completely. Charles—Officer Riley—sometimes didn't want it to be, but I made it clear I was no longer interested."

"What do you mean by 'sometimes' he didn't want your personal relationship to be over?"

"When he'd been drinking. When I was the only woman available."

"But you've heard people describing what sounded like jealous quarrels the two of you had. Isn't that true?"

"We had, months before Charles was killed. When we were breaking up." She made a face as if she smelled something bad, and turned to the jurors. "I hate using this high school language for something so important, but I don't know how else to put it."

A couple of the jurors nodded understandingly. Luisa continued, "But the arguments we had in the last couple of months were about how little he was working, and money he was taking from the cash register."

"And about the young waitress, too, isn't that true?" Lincoln asked.

"Only because he was taking her away from her duties. I shouldn't have blamed Teresita. I should have known myself how hard it was to resist his advances. But it wasn't jealousy. I had someone else. I was no longer interested in Charles Riley romantically."

Her voice had a strange quality when she said the name of her dead lover. Everyone else had called him Chip. The two of them had created a lovers' code by not using the nickname between them. Chris had known other couples who did the same thing. But the way Luisa Gaines said the name with no emphasis also sounded odd: a blank spot in her sentences from which intimacy had been erased. Chip Riley was missing from the world and from her feelings. She made him sound more dead than the medical examiner had.

"Did you fire the waitress Teresita that night?"

"Yes, I did. I was angry. She was neglecting her customers. My customers. It was because of Charles, but that was no excuse. It had been going on too long. I saw people waiting for their food, waiting for drink refills, and I waited and waited. I finally found her with him, in my office."

"What were they doing?"

"Standing very close. They had probably been kissing. Teresa had jumped away when I came in. I didn't care what they were doing, except that I was paying her and she wasn't working. That's when I took her out the back door of the restaurant and told her she was fired and not to come back. I didn't know anyone was watching."

Chris wondered if this was how it had happened. It was a defense witness who had testified to this scene. Obviously Gaines's testimony was coordinated with that witness's. What kind of story might the defense have come up with if they'd had some other evidence? Chris didn't believe that John Lincoln was an unethical lawyer. But he would go along with what his client said. If she presented him with a tale that hung together, he would put it in evidence for her, very capably.

"Did Chip Riley get mad about that?"

"He and I didn't speak again that night. The next time I saw him he gave me a little grin. That smile he had, that must have been charming when he was a little boy. Frankly, I hoped he would follow Teresa away, but he didn't."

Lincoln asked, "What about the witnesses who testified that they heard you and Riley arguing that night?"

Gaines nodded. "I did raise my voice when I was angry at Teresa, I admit. And Charles was yelling at me as I was pushing her out of the office and down the back hallway toward the door. It may have sounded as if Charles and I were yelling at each other. In fact, I didn't talk to him at all."

A good story. Bonnie tapped Chris's arm and he realized he'd been nodding along with the defendant. That didn't mean he believed her. He just admired the way her story hung together, how one scene answered several questions.

"How long did this happen before Officer Riley was shot later that night?"

Luisa shrugged. "Two hours? Maybe a little longer."

"Did you spend that time brooding about how he had betrayed you?"

Gaines smiled. "No. I didn't think about it at all. I was busy."

She looked like the hard, cold businesswoman who had come across in earlier witnesses' testimony about her managerial style. That style served Luisa Gaines well now. She didn't look at all like a woman who would kill out of jealousy, or any other emotion. Chris put down his pen, stopped making notes, and watched her carefully.

Lincoln cleared his throat and looked down at his notes. "Luisa, I want to ask you about your gun. Much has been made of your having that gun. Did you have it that night?"

She shook her head, looking a little perplexed herself. "No. I don't know what was going on with the gun. It had been missing earlier that month, then it had turned up again, then the night of the murder it was gone again. I didn't know what had happened. Too many people had come to know about that gun. I should have put it in a safe. But it needed to be handy when I did need it. I looked for it earlier that evening, thinking I needed to move it, and found it gone. I asked a couple of the employees, but no one claimed to have seen it."

"Did you ever find it again that night?"

"No."

"So you never saw it or touched it that night?"

"No."

"Did anything you saw or heard that night give you an idea of who might have taken the gun?"

"There was a police officer who knew Charles, who had come in several times and talked to him. He was there that night. Steve Greerdon. Once I looked around for him and didn't see him. I thought he had walked on his check, or that Charles had told him he didn't need to pay. But then a few minutes later I saw him sitting at his table again. I thought he must have gone to the men's room, but he could have gone into my office, too."

"Any other ideas?"

Bonnie touched Chris's arm. He was letting the witness speculate before the jury. But Chris shook his head minutely. He knew what he was doing. He might be making a mistake, but it wasn't unintentional.

Luisa Gaines frowned, apparently trying to recreate that night in her mind. "Charles could have taken it too. I heard him say he was going to meet this Officer Greerdon later. I thought they were friends, but maybe not. Charles could have been afraid that Greerdon blamed him for what had happened to him."

Gaines became more animated as she worked her way into her story. "I've heard Charles talk about police officers having 'backup guns.' Hidden guns other people wouldn't know about until they needed them.

I think Charles may have taken my gun to use as a backup when he went to his meeting."

Her lawyer nodded along with her. Then he settled down to business. "Luisa, did you kill Chip Riley?"

"No. Absolutely not." Gaines turned toward the jury and looked at them one by one. She had been well-coached.

"Did you have any reason to want him dead?"

"No."

"I pass the witness, your honor."

At the prosecution table, Bonnie looked questioningly at Chris. On the legal pad in front of her she had written at least two pages of notes and questions. The page in front of Chris was only half-filled. He also sat as if he hadn't heard the witness passed, continuing to stare at Luisa Gaines. But just as Bonnie leaned over to whisper to him whether she should cross-examine, Chris leaned forward and said very evenly, "Ms. Gaines, your story fits together very neatly and seems to remove you as a suspect in Chip Riley's murder."

"That's how the truth is," she said self-righteously.

"Really, has that been your experience, that the truth always makes perfect sense?"

She frowned at him, trying to think how she should answer. "Never mind," Chris said. "Let's stick to the facts, or at least your version of them. These men who kidnapped you and held you hostage for two days, did they threaten you?"

"No." She spoke emphatically and without hesitation.

"You say you think they were trying to make you look guilty by taking you away from the trial, right?"

"Yes, that's what I think."

"Yet they released you just in time for you to testify. That was considerate. Did they say anything to you about how you should testify?"

She shook her head. "No, sir."

"They didn't give you any instructions at all?"

Again she shook her head.

"All right, let's move on to the events of the murder. You testified you thought Chip Riley himself might have taken your gun. Yes?"

"He had the chance, and it seems to make sense."

"Well, the jury will decide that, Ms. Gaines. But what sense *does* it make? It was Chip himself who told you that police officers often carry backup guns. Right?"

She nodded emphatically. "Yes, that's how I know about that practice."

"If Chip knew about it, then he would have already had his own backup gun, wouldn't he?"

Gaines hesitated. Chris added helpfully, "So he wouldn't have needed to take yours. Isn't that right?"

"Maybe he didn't carry his usual backup when he was off duty," she said slowly. "That's why he needed mine."

Chris hoped the jury saw her making it up as she went along, which was how she looked to Chris. "You heard Steve Greerdon's testimony. Were you here for that part of trial? He said that Chip Riley asked him to meet him later. Remember?"

"Yes."

"Since Chip arranged the meeting himself, would he have needed to go to it doubly armed?"

She shrugged. "I have no idea why they wanted to meet. Charles could have felt threatened even though he'd set the meeting himself. Maybe he'd wanted to get their confrontation over with, and he wanted to be prepared for it."

"Well, he wasn't very prepared, was he? He let someone get close enough to him to put two bullets into him. And there was no sign that he reached for his own gun. Does that sound like what would have happened if he'd been meeting with someone he felt so threatened by that he had to take two guns?"

"I don't know." Gaines lowered her eyes.

"Doesn't it sound more like the murderer was someone he trusted? Someone he was close to?"

Softly she said, "I don't know what happened."

Chris moved on briskly. "Earlier that evening you went to your office looking for your gun. Why? No one has testified there was any kind of disturbance in the restaurant that night."

"No, but I felt uneasy. That Officer Greerdon made me uncomfortable, the way he disappeared and then came back. And knowing he and

Chip were going to meet later. I was afraid something bad might happen. I wanted to be sure the gun was available."

"During your direct testimony you said when you didn't see Detective Greerdon at his table you just assumed he'd gone to the men's room. Now you say that made you uneasy. Why?"

"He made me uncomfortable every time he came into the restaurant. The way he looked around. The way he stared at Charles when Charles wasn't watching. I was afraid of him, to tell you the truth."

As she said this, she raised her head and ended up looking directly at Chris. She appeared very forthright.

"Did you know why he and Chip Riley were going to meet that night, what they were going to talk about?"

"No."

"Didn't you ask Chip?"

"No. I wanted to be left out of it."

"Didn't you think it might concern you?"

"No." She looked genuinely surprised. The idea hadn't crossed her mind. She knew the meeting wasn't about her. To Chris, that meant she had known the purpose of the meeting.

"Did Chip Riley have information about the police officers who had framed Steve Greerdon and sent him to prison?"

"I have no idea."

"No? Once Greerdon showed up and started becoming a regular at your restaurant, Chip didn't talk to you about what he knew about him?"

"No. He just said they'd known each other in the past."

Chris put on an expression as if he'd just remembered an important fact. "That's right, by that time you and Chip Riley no longer had a personal relationship, right? You no longer had intimate talks."

"That's right."

"By this time you were romantically involved with— What was his name?"

Her eyes turned contemptuous, over his thinking he might catch her with such a simple trick. "Ricky. Enrique Galvan."

"Oh, you called him Ricky?"

"Yes, when we were alone."

That wasn't her pattern. She used a more formal name with Chip Riley than his friends did. This was hardly damning evidence, though.

Chris felt Bonnie glancing sidelong at him. He had a strong desire to ask Luisa Gaines whether her lover had a secret tattoo. Bonnie knew it. But he restrained himself and asked carefully, "Can you tell us something private about Mr. Galvan you learned in your many private chats with him?"

"You mean like a tattoo somewhere on his anatomy?" She sneered, but only for a moment. Her lawyer would have told her not to look arrogant or sarcastic in front of the jury. More quietly she added, "I won't say that. I can tell you that he's a very kind man. He thinks a great deal about his children. One of his daughters was sick for a long time when she was very young. For six months he went to San Fernando Cathedral every morning to light a candle for her. Even after she got well, he kept going for a month, just to be sure. And to tell God thank you."

She looked solemn, her hands folded in her lap. Luisa sniffed, the only sound in the courtroom. Chris didn't sneer. It was a touching story. If he said anything about it, he could only damage himself.

"Can you tell me what his favorite drink is?"

She smiled. "Iced tea. I served him myself several times."

"Come, Ms. Gaines, you know what I mean. When you went out on dates, is that what he drank?"

"Sometimes he would have scotch. Dewar's. But only one. He doesn't drink much." From her expression, that was another way her current lover was preferable to her old one.

"So by the time of Chip Riley's death, you and he were nothing more than business partners."

"Not even that," Gaines said dismissively. "He worked for me. And not very well, either."

"Is that so? Why didn't you fire him, then?"

Gaines shrugged and looked away. "Sentimental reasons, I suppose."

Chris put out his hand, and Bonnie placed a piece of paper in it. Chris walked up to the court reporter and had her mark the paper as a State's exhibit. Luisa Gaines watched the paper carefully as Chris held it casually. "Approach the witness?" he asked, and when the judge nodded, he walked slowly toward the witness stand. "Actually, sentiment had nothing to do with why Chip Riley continued to work at Miguelito's, did it, Ms. Gaines?"

"I don't know what you mean." Her voice had a faraway sound.

"Can you identify this document that's been marked State's Exhibit Seventeen?" Chris said, handing it to her.

Luisa looked it over carefully, though it was only one piece of paper, with one paragraph written on it. She looked up at Chris, then at her own lawyer. Lincoln gave no sign that he knew what was going on. Her pause lengthened, bringing all the jurors' attention on her. Chris waited patiently.

Finally Luisa Gaines cleared her throat and said, "This is a paper with Charles's name and mine on it."

"Not just your names, your signatures, correct?"

"Yes."

"And it's been notarized, hasn't it?"

Again she looked as if she wanted to deny the question, but she couldn't. "Yes," she said quietly.

"What is this document called?"

Gaines only glanced at it. "Partnership Agreement," she said.

Chris walked toward her lawyer, and with a perfectly neutral expression handed him the paper. "I'll offer State's Exhibit Seventeen, your honor."

John Lincoln looked down at it, then back up at Chris. He looked angry and surprised, but he only let that show for a moment, and not to the jury. "No objection," he said quietly. There was little else he could say. His client had already identified the signatures.

"It will be admitted," Judge Conners said, and reached out her hand. Chris handed her the paper. The judge read it quickly, then handed it back to him without expression, but with her gaze at him grown brighter. Judge Conners loved a good surprise.

Chris handed the paper back to Luisa Gaines and said, "Please read this to the jury."

Barely glancing at it, she read in a clear voice. "'We, Charles Riley and Luisa Gaines, agree to be partners in the business known as Miguelito's restaurant and other business ventures, not including Charles Riley's occupation as a police officer. In all other enterprises we agree to share profits equally.' Then it's signed by the two of us."

"Is there a date on it?"

"Yes," Luisa said, and read off a date almost two years before her partner's death.

Passing the document to the jurors, Chris said, "So Chip Riley was more than just an employee, wasn't he?"

"No," Gaines said, shaking her head. "At one time, yes. But not by the time of last summer. I didn't even know that document still existed. I had thrown mine away, and I thought Charles had too. We never referred to it anymore. We didn't share profits."

"Then you were in violation of your agreement, weren't you?"

She shook her head again. "I told you, the agreement was over. It was never valid anyway. You can tell it wasn't written by a lawyer. It was something Charles and I did one day because—" She waved a hand, in place of a much longer story. The gesture indicated recklessness and passion and perhaps even love. Her expression became a strange combination of distaste and fond recollection. "I don't know. We just did. But he never held me to it. And before I threw it away I showed it to a lawyer who said it wasn't binding. Because I didn't give any—what do you call it?"

Chris didn't help her out with a word.

"I didn't get anything in exchange for giving him half my business. So it was no good."

Chris nodded neutrally. He took the paper back from one of the jurors and looked it over. "This refers to other businesses," he observed. "And at the beginning of your testimony you also mentioned other businesses you own. What are those?"

She shook her head as if this were a minor matter. "Very small things. A storage place near the restaurant. A catering service. Things connected to Miguelito's."

"And did you share the profits of those with Chip Riley, either?"

Staring flatly at Chris, she said, "No. He never asked."

Chris walked to his seat. As he did, he said over his shoulder, "While you were gone, we heard from a witness who said you called him into your office the evening before the murder and told him to look for your gun. Is that true?"

"Yes. As I said, I was worried—"

Sitting, Chris said, "Thank you, Ms. Gaines, but that's not my question. My question is, had you ever done that before? Had you ever asked an employee to look for your gun?"

She stared at him. Her expression became absolutely still. Not even her eyes moved. Chris sensed frantic thought, but Luisa Gaines gave no sign of it. Finally, slowly, she said, "I'm trying to think. I'm sure I did. Once I sent someone to get it, when there was a fight. I can't remember. There may have been other times."

Chris sat silent, giving her time to think. But Luisa Gaines didn't expand her answer. She had been well coached.

"I'll pass the witness," Chris said.

Immediately John Lincoln said, "Luisa, had your gun ever gone missing before, other than these couple of weeks before Chip Riley was murdered?"

"No."

"So there wouldn't have been any occasion for you to ask an employee to try to find it, would there?"

"No," she said firmly—and with a hint of gratitude, Chris thought. Her lawyer had come up with a better answer than she had.

"Luisa, let's talk about this State's Exhibit Seventeen. Was this a serious partnership agreement?"

"No. I said what it was. A sort of love offering. Something to make us feel close. It wasn't really a business matter."

"Did Chip Riley ever try to enforce this agreement?"

"No."

"Even immediately after the two of you had signed it?"

"No. He understood what it was. We made fun of it sometimes."

"After things cooled personally between the two of you, did he try to hold you to this?"

"No. I had forgotten about it by that time. I'm sure he had too." Gaines looked at Chris curiously. He was huddled with his trial partner, looking at Bonnie's list of questions. One of them made Chris blush. "Just kidding," Bonnie whispered, and scratched out an extremely personal question she had suggested asking Gaines about her supposed lover. "My mind was wandering," she added.

Chris tapped one question, "Why didn't you come out of your office when everyone else heard the gunshots?" and shook his head. But it gave him an idea.

Gaines's defense lawyer was asking, "Luisa, after you fired Teresa, did you see her again that night?"

"No, I didn't."

"Did you go back out to the loading dock area that night?"

"No. Not until the police officers asked me to come out and identify Charles's body."

"You say you had seen Chip Riley and Teresa flirting with each other, or whispering intimately, that kind of thing."

"Yes, on several occasions."

"Did you also ever see them appear angry at each other?"

Luisa Gaines's voice had grown emotionless. She stared at her lawyer. "I saw her acting coldly toward him, especially after the times I reprimanded her for not doing her job. She appeared angry at him for getting her in trouble."

"How would Officer Riley react?"

"I knew from personal experience how Charles would respond to that sort of thing. He would get—more aggressive. A woman's acting cool toward him seemed to excite him. I saw this behavior with Teresa, too. When she would glare at him, so any other man would have the sense to keep his distance, Charles would grin at her as if she'd just passed him a love note."

"Did you see him act that way toward her that night?"

"Not that I recall. But I tried not to pay attention."

Her voice had grown deadly cold.

And Chris understood that her attorney had just developed another suspect in Chip Riley's murder. He heard just a trace of satisfaction in Lincoln's voice as he passed the witness again.

All business, Chris asked, "Ms. Gaines, where were you when you heard the gunshots from the alley?"

She hesitated for a moment. "I didn't hear the shots. I heard the noise of my customers afterwards. I was in my office then."

Chris sat silent for a long moment, watching the witness, trying to communicate with her. "There were a lot of police officers there after the shooting, weren't there, Ms. Gaines?"

"Yes."

"And you weren't arrested then, no one took you away. How long did you stay?"

"Two hours, three. I don't know. Until everyone had gone." She watched Chris seriously, wondering where he was going.

"One question then," Chris said. "Did you see a police officer named Rico Fairis?"

"I don't know who that is," Luisa Gaines said quickly. Her response put the ball back in Chris's court; people turned to him for an explanation. Chris continued to watch the defendant, though. Looking him in the eyes, she shook her head ever so minutely. She wasn't answering the question, he was sure. She was telling him she wouldn't answer.

He had tried once more to give her a way out, but she refused. "Thank you," Chris said. "No more questions."

The defense lawyer, the judge, his partner, and at least a couple of the jurors looked at Chris curiously. The other jurors turned back to the defendant. She stood and walked slowly back to her seat at the defense table, walking close to the jury box, staying as far from Chris as possible.

"Your next witness, Mr. Lincoln?" Judge Conners said.

He paused, put his hand over his client's, then stood and said, "The defense rests, your honor."

The judge turned to Chris. "Mr. Sinclair?"

"Your honor, the State will have one very brief rebuttal witness, who is not available until tomorrow morning."

Judge Conners looked at the clock and found the time satisfactory. "We can have our charge conference." She turned to the jurors. "Ladies and gentlemen, the attorneys and I have work to do, and it's too late in the day to have arguments and submit the case to you, anyway. You might find yourselves sequestered in a hotel tonight if I did that. I'm sure you would prefer to sleep in your own beds. So you are dismissed. Come tomorrow morning prepared to begin your own work. I'm sure the case will be coming to you then."

The jurors gave nothing away. Raggedly, not in unison, they stood and left the courtroom with the bailiff. The lawyers didn't even try to catch their eyes.

Most of the spectators left too. When the courtroom had almost emptied out, Judge Conners looked at the lawyers ironically and said, "Ready?" Then she said to the remaining bailiff, "I don't think we'll need the defendant here for this."

Luisa Gaines did something odd. She looked around the courtroom. Then she pulled her lawyer's arm. He bent his head to hers and she whispered something quickly. Lincoln looked at her in surprise. Then Luisa whispered something else, her eyes indicating Chris. Lincoln walked over to Chris, who stood in front of his table. Quietly, the defense lawyer said, "She said to tell you that Rico Fairis was there that night, in the restaurant."

"She said to tell me?"

Lincoln nodded. Chris stared after the departing figure of the defendant. She never looked back.

Anne paced around her office. Eric Schwinn was keeping her waiting. At five o'clock she let her staff go. Her next to last appointment of the day had canceled. The building grew noisier then quiet as it emptied out. Anne waited. She wondered if she'd been clear about the time. She walked out to the waiting room and made sure the door to the hallway remained unlocked.

When she turned back he was there, in the doorway she'd just come from, the one that opened into the hall to her office. Anne gasped. She had a very disconcerting feeling, that she was the patient in the waiting room and Eric Schwinn the doctor just calling her to come in for her appointment. She had a fluttery moment of nervousness, as if she were about to reveal her secrets. "How did you get there?" she snapped, sounding angrier than she felt.

He seemed to know that, smiling at her. "Just came back looking for somebody. Nobody was here. I thought somebody besides you might be in this little back office. I guess you and I passed each other."

She brushed past him. Anne wore a thin green blouse, a shade lighter than her eyes, and navy slacks. Schwinn wore one of his elegantly casual outfits, tan sport shirt with snap pockets, and pressed blue jeans. As Anne walked by she smelled his good clean scent.

He followed her closely, and in her office she had another moment of dislocation, as it seemed he would walk past her and take his seat behind the desk. Anne walked more quickly and got there, turning to find that he stood behind the visitor's chair. He showed no inclination to sit down. This wasn't a session. "You wanted to see me?"

"Yes." She waved a hand toward the chair, but when he ignored the gesture she sat. "You told me you know Steve Greerdon committed the robbery he was sent to prison for."

"Yes." He watched her closely, the smile fading from his lips but not from his eyes. Anne or the situation seemed to amuse him.

"How do you know?"

"I just know, believe me."

"That's the thing, it can't just be a matter of trust. I need to have proof."

"Why?"

"Chris," she said quickly. "The district attorney. I told him about this, but he won't just take my word for it. Lawyer, you know. He wants evidence." When Schwinn didn't answer she said, "Eric, this is important. The murder trial is wrapping up. I think they're about to convict the wrong person. You have information that points to Steve Greerdon. I think you think he killed Chip Riley. That's why you came to see me, isn't it? You're right, I want to see this thing through. But now we need to come up with real evidence."

"You don't believe me, do you?" He sounded hurt, but something more. He leaned toward her, his knuckles on the desk. His eyes glittered, but no longer with amusement.

Anne tried not to shift nervously in her chair, tried not to lose her edge of authority. "I told you, I do believe you, but to see the right person convicted we need more than belief. I want to help you."

The last phrase sounded tinny as it left her lips, the kind of thing a cop said to a defendant to extract a confession, or a nervous psychiatrist said to a patient about to slip off into a violent state.

Schwinn said, "I know because they asked me to participate. I said no. That's why I had to leave town. Even after Steve got convicted, I knew there were others who hadn't been caught. Others I didn't even know about. They'd get me somehow if I stayed on the force. That's why I had to give up my life. Because of him and his friends."

"Eric, I'm sorry. Did you testify against him at his trial?"

He didn't answer for a long while, then shook his head slowly. "I said I would, but they ended up not needing me. They had that other officer who turned and testified. The prosecutors decided that was enough. I was available all through the trial, but they didn't call me. It didn't matter, though. Too many people knew I knew."

Anne said, "Eric, we have another problem. What you've just told me isn't enough. I understand Steve Greerdon can't be convicted again for that robbery. He's been pardoned for it. But is there something else you know? Something about either of these recent murders? Did he have some reason for killing Chip Riley?"

Schwinn stood considering. His eyes remained on Anne, but with a faraway look. Then they focused sharply on her again. Blue eyes that looked so sincere. "That's what I've been trying to find out. And I think I have. Chip was in on it too, back in the bad old days. He was one of the gang. He and Steve must have worked together. And Steve didn't like taking the fall by himself. He's settling accounts now. He wants to get even, and he doesn't want anyone left who could mess up his new story that he was an innocent man convicted."

Anne nodded. This was what she had believed all along. But Chris didn't, she knew. "How do you know all this?" she asked.

Schwinn's eyes narrowed. "There's that question again. I know." He tried a smile. "Don't you believe me?"

"Of course I do." But he had begun to make Anne very nervous. She couldn't let him see that. She stood up from her desk, tapping a finger on it as if her mind were racing. "I wonder if they can get a continuance in the trial. Maybe we should go to the defense as well as the prosecution. Listen—" She turned toward him and discovered he'd moved. He was at the corner of the desk, moving slowly around. Anne couldn't get around the other way, because her computer set-up blocked it. Still trying to project energy, she said, "Could you come talk to Chris yourself?"

Schwinn took another step before answering. "Why should he believe me? He doesn't even know who I am, does he?"

"Of course I haven't told him anything about you. I told you I wouldn't, until—" She stopped, then hurried on. Anne rose and stepped toward him, moving her chair out of the way. She went toward him, not running away. That was not only Anne's style, but she had found it to be more effective. She would brush past him and try to catch him up in her apparent eagerness. "But once he knows how you were involved, we can turn the investigation."

She moved past him and turned the corner of the desk. Her office door stood open only a few feet away. She couldn't outrun him, but as soon as they got out of this confined space her possibilities would begin to open up.

Anne thought she was wrong, anyway, about the sudden nervousness she felt. After all, she had seen this man through several sessions, seen him open up about his past, seen him cry. He wasn't after her. He had come to her for help.

But something seemed to have changed in his eyes when she'd said no one other than Anne knew who he was. A moment of calculation had passed over his face, and the amusement in his eyes had vanished. Just her imagination, probably. She was so used to watching for tiny changes in people's expressions. Sometimes, Anne knew, she invented those changes, or the reasons behind them. Kind of a professional hazard.

"Maybe we can catch him right now, at the Justice Center," she said hurriedly. Then she took another step and everything changed.

A sudden sharp pain in her wrist made her cry out. She looked down to see a hand gripping her, and for a moment it seemed disconnected from the man in her office. Because she looked back at him and Eric Schwinn appeared unmoved. He was smiling again. But his hand had shot out and grabbed her.

"What are you doing?" she said harshly.

But he didn't feel the need to answer. He didn't have to explain to her anymore. He just stood there, holding her fast. Anne glared at him, but he didn't even respond to that. His smile continued to grow. Nothing she said or did could make any difference to him.

Everything had changed.

Chris and Bonnie and Jack met in Chris's office. The location was significant. Usually at the end of the trial day they'd been meeting in Jack's investigation office, as they talked about what new evidence they might need. Jack could quickly dispatch one of his investigators. Today, though, they had already sent tomorrow's one witness off on her assignment. Chris needed more than new evidence. He needed to think, which he did best in his own surroundings.

His office held a big desk centrally located in the room, and over in the corner by the windows a small living area, with a love seat and two wing chairs. Chris walked back and forth between the two areas. He stopped to take off his jacket and hang it over the back of his desk chair. His white shirt looked remarkably unrumpled after the long day. Jack stood, hands in his pockets. Bonnie was the only one who had taken a seat, in one of the wing chairs, watching her boss closely but with lively eyes. She wanted to win. She wanted it at least as much as the district attorney did. Bonnie didn't intend to be picked for the DA's team and then help him lose.

"Can we get tax records?" Chris asked Jack. "Show whether Chip Riley had any income from the restaurant?"

"He would have taken it all under the table. That's the advantage of a restaurant, it's such a cash business."

"Her records, then. Luisa's. She would have taken anything she paid him as a business expense."

Bonnie interrupted, rising. "This isn't about taxes, or money. Don't you know that? A woman doesn't kill over money. This is about passion."

"Passion?" Chris said. "You mean you think she was still in love with him?"

Bonnie tossed her hair, looking like a teacher with a slow student. "See, every time you hear the word passion, people think 'lust.' That's not what it always means. There are other kinds of passion. All kinds. It means strong feelings. It could be anger, jealousy. Passion makes you hot. Other kinds of hot. Your brain turns red with blood, it doesn't think anymore. Passion drives out reason. It destroys logic. No: creates its own. Passionate people see rationales that don't make sense to others."

Her expression had grown fierce, her eyes hot.

"Okay, you're scaring me now," Chris said.

"That's what I mean. Passion is frightening."

Chris and Jack looked at each other blankly. Bonnie rolled her eyes. "White people. I hope there aren't too many of you on the jury. Because this murder was about passion. If you try to figure out how she carefully planned it out, it will never make sense to you."

"But it does to you?" Chris asked seriously. "You believe she murdered Chip Riley?"

Bonnie looked momentarily confused. "Of course."

There was a tap at the office door, and Chris walked that direction. Bonnie continued, "She was the only person who would have felt strongly enough about the victim to kill him."

"That passion thing?"

"By the way," Jack said, raising his voice because Chris was across the room, "where did you get that partnership agreement between Chip and Luisa? I didn't find you that. Was it cops?"

Over his shoulder, Chris said, "I don't know." He opened his office door. His secretary, Irma Garcia, handed him a thickly padded envelope.

"For you. Just appeared up at the reception area, just like the last one."

"Thanks, Irma." Chris looked at the envelope. "It's been opened."

"Had to have the bomb squad check it out." Irma smiled. Very little went on in or near Chris's office without her learning every detail.

Chris closed the door and walked back toward his teammates. "You don't know?" Jack said, still talking about the partnership agreement.

"That's right. But I suspect it came from the same source as this." He overturned the envelope at his desk. A purple cell phone slid out. Chris looked into the envelope and found nothing else. As he picked up the phone, Bonnie turned over the envelope. Someone had written "District Attorney Sinclair" on the outside with a black marker. No address or postage. It had been intended for private delivery.

Chris looked suspiciously at the cell phone. It was on, its battery nearly full, according to an indicator on the small screen. "Is somebody supposed to call me?"

Jack said, "Why go to that trouble? They could just call your office from a pay phone."

"Maybe they're going to give me directions to some place."

Bonnie took the phone from Chris, who continued his earlier explanation. "The partnership agreement was just delivered here to the office, yesterday, while the trial was going on. Nobody knows who sent it. But it was a useful piece of evidence."

"Obviously from somebody who wants Luisa Gaines convicted," Jack said. "The same people who kidnapped her?"

"You believe her story?" Bonnie asked.

Jack shrugged. "Why not? It doesn't make sense that she'd just leave and then come back on her own. Why would she do that? It makes her look guilty."

Chris interjected, "So you think that was the kidnappers' objective? To make her look guilty?"

Jack almost nodded, then asked another question. "But then why release her in time for her to testify?"

They had returned to the same question. Bonnie, who didn't appear interested in the speculation, had been examining the phone. "This phone has a message on it."

She held it out toward Chris, indicating a blinking light on the screen. Bonnie pressed a couple of buttons, held the phone to her ear, then handed it to Chris. He listened intently. The message lasted less than a minute. Chris stared across the room. Then he gave the phone back to Bonnie and circled the desk to pick up his own phone.

"Who was it from? What was it?"

"I don't know," Chris said. "But the message was for Luisa Gaines. That's her phone."

Into his, he said, "Irma, call John Lincoln's office. If he's not there, make them give you his mobile phone number. I have to see him right now. Him and his client both."

Bonnie had been listening to the message on the cell phone, with Jack watching her. Bonnie's face was more expressive as she listened. Her eyes widened, then narrowed. Her nostrils flared. She looked suspicious, then aghast. After a moment she looked at Chris. "Did you hear the date at the beginning of the message?"

"Yes," he said, "Three o'clock in the afternoon on the day Chip Riley was murdered."

His own phone rang.

Anne spoke in a very controlled, calming voice. She looked directly into Eric Schwinn's eyes. "Why are you angry about this? I thought you wanted the truth to come out about Steve Greerdon. Isn't that the only way you can get your life back?"

He appeared to listen to her, but his grip on her arm didn't loosen. Anne felt trapped, but didn't know whether she should. So far he had done nothing more threatening than hold her in place. She kept talking. Anne sounded compassionate, and she was genuinely curious. What did this man want? She thought she had known.

"Are you afraid of what he might do if he isn't convicted? Is that it? But that's why we have to give Chris as much evidence as possible. And you're the only person who could do it."

She ran out of things to say and saw his eyes beginning to rekindle. Anne tried to jerk her arm out of his grasp, but that was futile. In fact, it broke the momentary spell her voice had cast. Eric's eyes went cold and dead again as he looked at her.

Just as Anne was thinking of screaming and wondering if anyone was left on this floor of the building, she and her patient both clearly heard the sound of a door opening. It was the front door of her offices, the one that opened from the hallway. "Hello?" a voice called.

Anne grew more frightened. The voice belonged to Clarissa. She called again, and then her steps moved toward them.

In the interior hallway just outside Anne's door, the light went on. "Anne? I know you're still here, I saw your car downstairs. Are you on the phone?"

Eric Schwinn released Anne but raised one finger warningly. He stepped toward the open doorway just as Clarissa stepped into it from the other direction.

"Oh, sorry." Clarissa looked at both of them. "I didn't know you were in session. Sorry. I'll wait out here."

"It's okay," Schwinn said charmingly, his easy smile back in place. "We're just chatting. Come on in."

He took another step toward her.

"I know you," Clarissa said, staring at him intently. Her statement stopped Schwinn. "I saw you talking to the defense lawyer in that murder case."

"Who?" he said, smiling at her easily. He moved toward Clarissa, away from Anne, but Anne stood rigid, her eyes trying to warn Clarissa. But the girl kept watching the smiling man. Anne wondered whether he had a gun. If she screamed, would he jump back to her, allowing Clarissa time to escape?

"What defense lawyer are you talking about?" Schwinn asked, and walked toward Clarissa as if to confer with her. He was almost there.

Clarissa glanced at Anne. She saw her anxious eyes.

Schwinn was close to Clarissa by then. His hand reached toward her.

But Clarissa was still just outside the open doorway and Schwinn just inside. Clarissa stepped quickly aside and he could no longer reach her without taking another step. While he hesitated, Clarissa did something very smart. She turned and ran, back toward the waiting room. When Clarissa acted, she didn't hesitate. One moment she was standing awkwardly in the doorway, the next she was gone, like an optical illusion.

Eric Schwinn hesitated again. Anne saw his dilemma. She thought she saw on his face an urge to run after Clarissa. But if he left this office, Anne would call a security guard. She would lock him out of the office, too. That meant he would have to disable Anne before he ran out. Clarissa was fast, too. And she would remember him. She already knew his face. Unless he caught her, he couldn't do anything to Anne.

But he had hesitated too long. As he started out the door he heard the hallway door slam back against the wall. Damn, the girl had been even faster than he'd expected. He'd never catch her now.

He gave Anne a puzzled half-smile. "Is that girl nuts, or is it just me?"

Anne had her arms folded and looked calm. Once again Clarissa had surprised her with her ingenuity. Most potential victims froze as they tried to think what to do, or wasted precious time negotiating with the person about to assault or murder them. Clarissa had had a thought and acted on it instantly. She split Eric Schwinn's thinking, left *him* with the bad choices.

"I have some pretty troubled people come here, as you know," Anne said. "That one's pretty sharp, though. She's a friend of mine."

"Whatever." Schwinn obviously dismissed Clarissa, putting all his concentration on Anne. He walked back close to her, with a frowning, thoughtful expression, then stopped two feet in front of her. "All right. I'll talk to the district attorney. We'd better make it fast, though, right?"

"I'll set up a meeting. Maybe tonight. The trial will probably be over tomorrow."

"Well, they can always do a motion for new trial, if new evidence turns up. I'm the new evidence."

He smiled at her. They were discussing practicalities. He appeared to be putting his life in her hands. The situation had completely reversed itself. Schwinn looked perfectly believable. He gave her a small, nervous smile that made him look boyish. "Well, you've got my cell number," he said. "I'll stay in town for a while. Give me a call."

He reached out and gave Anne's arm a friendly squeeze, an intimate gesture rather than a threatening one. "Sorry I overreacted. People coming up behind me makes me nervous. I've been looking over my shoulder a long time."

"That's understandable," Anne reassured him. She smiled back. He turned and walked away.

Anne returned to her desk. When she looked up, Schwinn still stood in her doorway. He smiled at her and disappeared. Anne stared at the empty space, wondering if she had read far too much into the man's hesitating for a few moments. The world wasn't really so sinister. What her speculation showed was how little she still knew her patient.

She was relieved to hear her outer office door close as she picked up the phone. She dialed a number she knew by heart and after a minute said, "Chris? There's someone I want you to talk to. Tonight. It has to be tonight . . . The one I told you about . . . Okay. When will you be through with that? Maybe around eight, then? All right, give me a call . . . Yes, I've seen her. She was here just a minute ago . . . Yes. Me too."

Anne hung up the phone. She wondered how much she would tell Chris before his meeting with Eric Schwinn. That she had trusted the man completely, but then he'd grabbed her by the wrist, with angry harshness? That memory was fading quickly. He had seemed so earnest at the end, just before he'd left, that she was beginning to believe she'd imagined that he was going to hurt her moments earlier. All he had done was hold her wrist.

Anne no longer knew what she thought. She started out of her office for the last time that day. As she reached for the light switch, Clarissa stepped into the doorway.

Anne gasped, then rolled her eyes and put her hand over her heart.

"Is he gone?" Clarissa asked. "I let him hear the door slam open, then I hid in the office and called security. They should be here in a second."

In fact, there was a heavy knock on the outer door, and they heard it open. "Dr. Greenwald?" a man's deep voice called.

"Back here! It's okay! We thought we had an intruder, but he's gone."

Clarissa was watching her with grave concern. "I'm sorry about running out on you. I thought it was the only—"

Anne reached over, put a hand behind Clarissa's neck, and pulled her in for a hug. "Girl, you were perfect."

Chris met with Luisa Gaines and John Lincoln in an office at the jail, a few blocks west of the Justice Center. Usually attorneys met with their clients in small cubicles with thick plastic separating them, but for this meeting the sheriff had courteously provided an office. There were two deputies stationed just outside the door, though, and the defendant clearly felt their presence. At first she kept her head down and would only mumble responses, except once when she said loudly, "I won't tell you anything!"

She said that to Chris, but he thought it was aimed past him. He looked over his shoulder, at the closed office door. "All right," he said. "I know that's your official position. That's the line you have to take."

He took a slow walk around the room, hands in his pockets. He and John Lincoln still wore their dark suits, with ties loosened. Lincoln looked suspicious but also very curious. It was not uncommon for plea negotiations to resume just before a case would go to a jury, but this felt different, as if aimed toward a purpose other than just concluding this trial. There in the bowels of the jail the night felt like five minutes to midnight, like the last few minutes before a deadline.

"Here," Chris said, and put the purple cell phone on the desk in front of Gaines. She picked it up and looked at him with little surprise. "My phone. Where did you get it?"

"There's a message on it." Chris took the phone from her, pressed a couple of buttons, and set it on the desk. They all huddled around it. Bonnie had raised the volume setting back in Chris's office, so now they could all hear the message. The caller spoke urgently in a male voice roughened by smoke or anxiety.

"Luisa, it's me," the phone said. "Listen, you need to know. You think Chip's cheating you and cheating on you, but it's more than that. He and that little waitress, they don't just want to rob you, they're going to kill you. I heard them talking. I think it's going to be tonight."

The message ended. Gaines continued to stare at the phone. She had gone pale, and she had barely enough breath to say, "I never heard that message before in my life."

"Tell that to the jury tomorrow. I don't think they'll believe you."

"Where did you get that?" Lincoln asked.

"That's what I've been wondering. Maybe your client could tell me."

"What do you mean by that?"

"She knows," Chris said, nodding toward Gaines. Both men looked at her. She kept her head lowered. She turned the phone over and over in her hand, as if looking for a clue. Chris watched her.

Arms folded, Chris said, "I've been trying to figure out why a defendant would run away during a trial but then come back. Maybe she was just careless enough to let herself get arrested, but I don't think Ms. Gaines is careless.

"So I've been trying to make sense of her story. That somebody kidnapped her, but then released her just in time for her testimony. Why? Because they wanted to make it look like she ran away because she knew she was guilty? But then why let her go again? They should have waited until the trial was over, so she couldn't testify, and so the jury would go to their deliberations with the sight of her empty chair, and with me telling them that running away from trial is a sign of guilt.

"So why would anyone do those two things?"

He leaned on his hands on the desk, bringing his head close to hers. She still refused to look up.

Lincoln cleared his throat and said, "Luisa, you don't have to say anything. But if you think it would help for you to explain something . . ."

She gave no sign she had heard. After a pause Chris began talking again. "I finally came up with a theory. Based on a minor thing I'd been overlooking."

Lincoln looked at him curiously. Chris answered his unspoken question. "What happens if a defendant voluntarily absents herself during a trial? If she gets found, and brought back to court, the judge will revoke her bond. Sure as hell. She'll spend the rest of the trial in custody."

They both looked down at Luisa Gaines in her jail coverall.

"So?" Lincoln said. But he looked around his surroundings as if realizing for the first time that they were all confined.

"So she'll be right under the thumb of law enforcement officers. Somebody's telling her bluntly, We've got you and you're not getting away. It's more obvious even than a patrol car parked outside your house all night. Pretty much any police officer who says he's investigating a case can check out an inmate for questioning. So now you're like their personal pet. Right, Luisa? Did someone tell you you'd better behave during trial?"

She shook her head, but it was a jerky motion, like a physical reaction to being prodded.

"I wondered," Chris continued, "why your defense didn't try to imply that Chip Riley might have been murdered by one of the police officers with whom he'd supposedly been involved in the scheme that had sent Steve Greerdon to prison. You cast suspicion on every other possible suspect, so why not cops?"

He looked at John Lincoln, who shrugged and said, "I might still do that in final argument."

Chris leaned over Luisa Gaines again. "But she didn't say anything like it in her testimony. Because those are your orders, aren't they, Luisa? Don't give us up, or things will go bad for you. They were supposed to help you in your defense, weren't they? Those other cops. And they did, a little. They gave you some evidentiary help.

"But then you told your attorney the name Rico Fairis, and he let it drop to me. I guess Fairis is the main one threatening you, and you hoped I could get him arrested. But you need evidence for that, Ms. Gaines, and I don't have any yet."

She raised her face to him finally, and he saw utter hopelessness. Not the look of a person who's never had expectations, but of one in whom hope had recently bloomed and then been crushed. Gaines's face showed disappointment as deep as the loss of faith. Her eyes were black and sunken, her mouth closed in a thin, small line. Chris felt a quick twist of guilt, as if he should have known she was relying on him.

"But somehow they found out you gave me the name, and they punished you for it. First with that contract between you and Riley, which just turned up in my office, and now with this." He nodded toward the cell phone still in her hand.

Chris stood with his hands on hips and stared down at her grimly. He didn't sound triumphant as he said, "They're throwing you away, Luisa. That's the last piece of evidence I need to put you away. I guess they think once you're convicted, no one will believe anything you have to say anyway. And once you get to prison, you'll really be in their hands. I'm sure they have friends there, among guards and inmates. If you try to talk then, you'll never come out alive."

The defense lawyer finally took a more forceful role. "Okay, Chris, you've scared her to death. Is that what you came for? Or do you have an offer?"

"Yes. Twenty years. In exchange for her guilty plea *and* for truthful information that leads to the arrest of police officers for corruption and any other felonies."

"What if they weren't police officers?"

"She could convince me of that, but it would be real hard. Let's just say information that leads to the arrest of those persons responsible for the false conviction of Steve Greerdon."

"Not including you, right?" Lincoln grinned briefly. Chris didn't respond. Lincoln quickly said, "But twenty is too much. Make it better. Besides, what if she didn't kill Chip Riley? What if we could prove to you someone else did that?"

Luisa Gaines looked up at her lawyer sharply. He didn't notice, but Chris did.

"If you could prove that, you'd have done it in trial," Chris said.

"Maybe," Lincoln said slowly. "Unless there was evidence she wouldn't let me use." He looked down at his client. She looked back at him steadily in return, with an unreadable expression.

"That should be part of the package, then," Chris answered. "If you have other evidence of her innocence, I won't object to your bringing it up in a motion for new trial hearing. If it convinces the judge . . . In the meantime, though, twenty is my best offer. Because I still believe she murdered Chip Riley. I'm only willing to go that low because she knows things about people who are going to be a lot more dangerous than she is if they're allowed to continue to operate."

A small silence fell. Lincoln looked at his client for a sign, but she had transferred her gaze to Chris, as if trying to gauge his honesty. Her unusual involvement in the criminal justice system had given her a very jaded view of that establishment.

"Well?" Chris finally asked. "Do you want to talk to your client alone?"

Lincoln nodded, but Luisa Gaines suddenly stood up and said loudly, "No! I won't help you. I don't know anything like what you're saying. Here!"

She thrust the purple cell phone at him, and Chris took it. He looked disappointed but not upset by her outburst. "Still think they're going to save you, Luisa?"

She leaned toward him and said very softly, "There are worse things than prison."

Chris nodded sadly. "I was afraid that's what you'd think. We need help to change things."

She didn't respond. He turned away.

"What are you going to do now?" Lincoln asked Chris.

He turned back and said firmly, "Tomorrow I'm going to convict her of murder." He looked at the cell phone and then put it down on the desk near Gaines's hand. "But I'm going to do it without this."

Lincoln said, "You're not going to use the phone message? Why?"

Chris spoke with an edge of anger that wasn't directed at either of them. "Because I don't believe in it. I think it's manufactured evidence. So I'm not going to use it."

He turned and walked quickly out of the room. Outside, after he passed the deputies, Chris stopped and leaned against a wall. His hands were shaking. He found his breath shallow. The phone had felt hot in his hand. He had the feeling he hadn't had nine years ago, that he was being manipulated. Being in jail felt right. Was he about to convict another innocent person? He couldn't let that happen.

Outside, his cell phone rang and he found he had another meeting that night.

Downtown San Antonio doesn't fold up at night as do the business districts of most big American cities. The restaurants along the Riverwalk remain busy into the night, and pedestrians keep walking near the downtown hotels. But parts of the city empty out. The parts where people work in offices. The courthouse complex almost shuts down completely. Anyone left inside after sunset gets an eerie feeling that the world has suffered some catastrophe that hasn't quite overtaken him yet. Most of the restaurants that serve the area close at midafternoon.

So when Anne called, even though they were all downtown they drove a ways, to the Liberty Bar, a building from the 1880s that looked as if it should have been condemned decades ago. It leaned visibly. If you stayed there long enough, you didn't notice.

Inside, old-fashioned wooden tables were covered with white paper. Anne and a stranger sat at a table about halfway along the wall. They remained deep in conversation until Chris stood right over them, when Anne jumped up and touched him briefly in greeting. The stranger, an overly handsome guy with bright eyes and black, curly hair, extended his hand for a manly shake. They were having drinks. Chris ordered coffee, then thought of the hot liquid hitting his empty stomach and changed his mind and made it a scotch.

"I'm not trying to be rude," he said as soon as he sat down, "but it's been a long day and I have a closing argument to write and a child to take care of. So can we get to the point quickly?"

"How do you think the trial's going to come out?" Anne asked.

"I don't know. I don't even know what I hope." He looked her in the eyes and they continued the conversation silently. Chris knew that Anne had never trusted Steve Greerdon from the first day he'd been released. She saw that he feared, more than anything, convicting an innocent person. She hoped to save him from that. Anne put her hand over Chris's. His felt cold.

"My name's Bret Hendrix." He glanced apologetically at Anne. "I told you I didn't give you my real name. I haven't used it in almost ten years." Back to Chris, he said, "Steve tried to recruit me to join him in the robbery of the grocery store. We'd been partners once, he thought he could trust me. I didn't rat him out, but I didn't join, either. After he got arrested, I told my story to my lieutenant, who passed it on to the DA's office."

"How come I didn't hear about you back then?" Chris asked.

"Your boss decided to keep me out of it. I didn't really know any details. But my problem was, there were other people involved, and they knew who I was. A couple of them were afraid Steve might have told me their names, too. I had to quit the department and leave town. I've been looking over my shoulder ever since. But you've got him covering your back, man. Feeding you 'information.'" Bret Hendrix made air quotes with his fingers. "He's out to convict this woman to take the heat off him. I couldn't let that happen."

Chris looked unemotional, or just dead tired. "*Did* he tell you any names back then of other officers who were involved in the corruption?"

The man Anne knew as Eric Schwinn leaned forward, with his hands clasped on the table. "Needless to say, they don't let you know too much until you're in, until you've committed yourself so much you can't back out. Steve only told me one other name."

"Who was that?"

"Chip Riley."

Chris closed his eyes and blew a long breath. He looked at Anne, who nodded. His drink arrived and Chris downed half of it. "What about Emerson Blakely?"

"I don't think so," Hendrix said. "I think that one was personal. That's another reason I knew I had to tell you this. It looks like Steve's cleaning house. He'll work his way around to me sooner or later."

They talked for ten more minutes. Chris felt lightheaded, and not from the drink. Anne could see the effect on him. Under her hand, his trembled. Finally Chris said to Hendrix, "Do you mind if Anne and I talk for a minute?"

"Sure, sure." Hendrix stood up hastily. Quietly he said, "Thanks, Dr. Greenwald. Mr. Sinclair."

"Keep in touch," Chris told him. "I may call you later tonight or in the morning."

"Yes, sir," Hendrix said without irony. He walked hurriedly out of the restaurant.

Chris said, "He went all boyish there at the end."

She nodded. "He does that sometimes. So do you."

"Does it make me sound more sincere? Should I try it tomorrow with the jury?"

"Chris, I know you're not going forward with this trial with the uncertainty you have now."

"Really?" He sounded curious, as if she knew him better than he did himself. "Then what will I do next?"

Anne smiled. "Go home and not sleep. And when it gets late and very empty, call me."

Chris leaned forward and kissed her, very intimately. This room already felt empty of anyone else. He realized how much he had missed her during this trial.

"We need to go away."

She squeezed his hand. "We will."

"Eric Schwinn" had parked a block away, so he could walk to and from the restaurant, making sure he wasn't followed. But there are other ways. Just as he unlocked his BMW with the clicker on his keychain, the car rocked a little, as if he had set off a small explosive.

But the car rocked because a heavy man had just come out of the shadows and leaned against it. Steve Greerdon looked at ease sitting on the hood of the expensive car.

"Hello, Bret," he said. "We need to talk."

CHAPTER

thirteen

★ The next morning Jack Fine testified very briefly for the State. At first Chris planned to use Stephanie Valadez to provide this testimony, but then Bonnie pointed out that he had already proven that Stephanie had nearly supernatural powers, so maybe they should use someone more . . . Here words had failed Bonnie, as she looked at Jack.

"Some old fart whose ears are going bad?" Jack said.

"I'm sure I would have found a better way to put that if you'd given me another couple of seconds," Bonnie answered, blushing.

But it was a good point, so that morning Jack appeared as the last witness of the trial. He had been the subject of an experiment in which he sat in Luisa Gaines's office while a police officer out by the loading dock fired two gunshots into the air.

"I heard them clearly," Jack testified.

"Were all the doors between you and the loading dock area closed?"

"Yes, sir. I made sure of that."

"Pass the witness."

Jack's testimony had been so brief and matter-of-fact that it seemed to leave little room for cross-examination, but Lincoln thought of some.

"Mr. Fine, when you ran this experiment, was there any noise coming from the dining area?"

"It was a Thursday evening and the restaurant was open. There were people eating and drinking and talking. We had a police officer out there to calm them down after the shots were fired."

"I doubt the crowd was its usual lively self with a police officer sitting in their midst, wouldn't you?"

"Well, they always used to have Chip Riley there, and everybody knew he was a cop."

Lincoln smiled wryly. "You do a good job for your boss, Mr. Fine. No more questions."

And abruptly the evidence portion of trial was over. The jury suddenly appeared more prominent, as if their box had moved forward on invisible rails. The prosecution and defense both rested and closed. Their chance of putting on evidence was gone. This was always a scary moment for a lawyer, but that anxiety was increased in this case, because both sides knew very well they had evidence they hadn't brought forward. Bonnie glanced at Chris questioningly. She'd known his decision about the cell phone, but since announcing his intention not to use it he hadn't shown any doubt. Even if he lost this trial, he wouldn't use evidence he didn't believe in. This case continued to remind him of his prosecution of Steve Greerdon eight years earlier. He'd used false evidence then, unknowingly. He wouldn't ever again use evidence about which he had any doubt.

"Both sides ready for argument?" Judge Conners said. "State?"

Bonnie stood up quickly. She wore a severe suit this morning, and an expression to match. She stood right in front of the jury and in a serious tone of voice opened with a joke.

"'Hers was the not unusual case of not wanting him herself, but not wanting anyone else to have him, either.' Dorothy Parker. She had keen insight." Looking along the jurors, she asked, "Do you men know that's how women feel? A lot of men do, too. Yes, we'll break up with you, spit in your face, tell you to get out and never come back—but you'd damned well better not try to replace us. A certain kind of woman won't stand for that. You're supposed to spend the rest of your life broken-hearted over her, not find somebody else. And you'd sure better not rub her nose in it by flirting with that woman every night in front of her."

Over at the defense table, Enrique Galvan had come out of the audience to sit beside Luisa Gaines, holding her hand. She didn't look at him. Bonnie turned and invited the jury's attention to this tender scene.

"Luisa told you she didn't care about Chip Riley because she had a new man in her life. Personally I don't buy this relationship, but you're welcome to your own opinion. But it doesn't matter. Even if she did have someone new, that doesn't mean the old boyfriend can go scot free. He still has to be punished for breaking up with her. Especially since he continues to spend every night in *her* place, Luisa's restaurant, laughing and drinking and acting like he owned the place. Why was he there? He was just an employee who'd slipped into the boss's bed. He wasn't good for that anymore, and he didn't belong in the business anymore, either, drinking her tequila and taking her money and flirting with her waitress."

Bonnie's voice rode up and down the musical scale. She wasn't a cold reciter of the evidence. Her eyes were fierce and her face flushed. She lived the emotions she talked about. The jurors not only hung on her words, they watched her warily, as if she might do something crazy. Suddenly Bonnie pointed at the defendant. They looked like sisters.

"I don't believe there ever was a breakup. She told you what Chip Riley was like. If you tried to push him away, he just laughed and got closer. He wouldn't let himself be thrown out of her life. And Luisa Gaines isn't the type of woman to break up with a man and then continue to see him every night just as a business arrangement. No. If she broke up with a man she would tell him to get the hell out, now, this minute. She wouldn't want him in her face and her cash register anymore."

Bonnie walked toward the defendant. "No, it was still going on. The fighting in front of strangers, the kisses in the office, the pushing, pulling, scratching, making up, the hatred, the lovemaking, the passion. You can see it in her face."

Enrique Galvan looked a little alarmed as Bonnie approached. Gaines sat rigidly, her mouth tight and eyes downcast, looking like a stone Aztec mask. But blood was creeping up her chest and neck and into her face. If she raised her eyes, they would burn somebody.

"Luisa is a strong woman. Admirable in many ways. She built up a business by herself, in a tough part of town in a man's world. She would do what had to be done. Make the deals, keep the staff in line, pay a police officer to keep the place safe, have a gun on hand she was willing to use if necessary. Luisa Gaines took care of herself. She did this time too. Maybe she *wanted* to break up with Chip Riley. But she knew he wouldn't stand for that. He'd try to blackmail her with that partnership agreement if nothing else. She would never be rid of him.

"This was all in her mind, but what broke her was finding him kissing the waitress, Teresa Vasquez. Teresita. This child Luisa had taken in and given a job. Was Luisa going to let this girl take her place? She'd already yelled at her that night, maybe fired her. And when Chip Riley went missing, Luisa knew where he was.

"She had taken steps to protect herself. Luisa hadn't lost her mind in jealousy. She made plans. She brought in another employee to show him that her gun was missing. But it wasn't. Luisa had just hidden it somewhere else. She carried it outside that night. Where she found two people. How do we know that? Because Stephanie Valadez came on the scene right after the shots were fired. She found a dead man with a cigarette near his hand, and another burning cigarette several feet away. Chip had been out there, but not alone. He wasn't taking a cigarette break. He could have smoked in the restaurant. This isn't California. We've got smoky bars here. He wasn't out there just for a cigarette. He was sharing his cigarettes. He was sharing something else, too. You think if Chip Riley found himself alone out there with little Teresa he wouldn't try to take advantage of the situation? He did it right in front of other people. How much further would he go if he was alone in the dark with her?

"That's what Luisa came outside and saw. And that was the last straw. She wasn't going to let him do this to her. She raised the gun and shot him. Not the girl. Chip Riley. Him. Her lover. She didn't care enough about the girl to kill her. She knew she didn't have to worry about her as a witness, either. She knew little Teresa would run scared all the way back to Mexico. And she was right, because nobody's been able to find her.

"No, you don't shoot the stranger. She hasn't betrayed you. You shoot the one you loved."

One woman on the back row of the jury nodded, caught herself, and sat still, but with her attention caught on Bonnie.

Bonnie continued, "Luisa knew what she was doing. She wasn't overcome by rage. She shot Chip once, which would have killed him but didn't do it right away. The medical examiner told you that. Chip fell down on his hands and knees. We know that from the blood evidence and the stains on his clothes. He reached out to her. He talked to her. Probably asking her not to kill him. Telling her he loved her. But Luisa didn't want to hear that. Her next shot went straight through his heart. The heart that had been hers. It still was. She made sure of that."

Bonnie waved toward the male lawyers. John Lincoln watched her admiringly. Chris sat absolutely still, staring at his hands. "They may try to tell you other motives for murder. About money or revenge or other things. But that's not what causes murder. Passion does. It takes deep feeling to pull that trigger. Strangers don't shoot each other. Lovers do. You have to care about somebody an awful lot to kill him.

"There's only one person who had what it took to kill Chip Riley."

Bonnie stared at the jury with a look so strong it could have sent them running for the jury room right now. Then she turned and swept past Luisa Gaines, who maintained enough control not to look at her.

The defense lawyer had a little trouble getting started after that. But he sounded eminently reasonable. He rose to his feet, acknowledged the judge and his opposing counsel courteously, and as he walked toward the jury said, "Well, as we know, people get killed every day by people they never slept with. Sometimes it's not passion that leads to murder. It's cold calculation. Or determination fed by years of brooding about someone who did you wrong."

He stood in the place Bonnie had held, right at the jury rail, and said, "I cannot believe you think you've heard enough evidence in this case to say beyond a reasonable doubt that this woman murdered Chip Riley. Did anyone see her shoot him? No. Did anyone hear her say she was going to kill him? Did anyone see her heading outside the restaurant that night? Did anyone see her with the gun in her hand? No.

"You have been told that you have a terrible responsibility. To discover the truth and convict a murderer. That's what the prosecution wants you to think. But that is not your responsibility. It's the job of the police to solve this mystery and bring you the killer. You do not have to sift through all the clues, or go and investigate yourself, and decide who killed Chip Riley. Your only job is to say, have they proven this particular case against this particular suspect? The answer is no. And when you tell them the answer is no, then the police will go back, they'll re-examine their evidence, they'll look for more. Maybe this time they'll look hard enough for

Teresa Vasquez, who can tell them what happened. This time they'll do their job. Do you think they'll just let it go? No. This was one of their own who was murdered. They'll find out the truth, after you tell them there's no evidence that this woman murdered Chip Riley.

"Think about that. This was a police officer who was murdered. The murder scene swarmed with investigating officers afterwards. There were even police officers in the autopsy room, waiting for the results."

Chris stirred. He raised his eyes, which slowly swept the front of the courtroom, unseeing. No one noticed.

John Lincoln held out his hand. "There were police officers right on the scene, who stopped the witnesses and preserved the scene and scoured that neighborhood. Yet what you heard in this courtroom is all the evidence they found against Luisa Gaines. Doesn't that tell you something? They didn't bring you Teresa Vasquez. Maybe they didn't look very hard, because she would have been a witness against them. She would have testified that Luisa fired her earlier that evening and she left, so she wasn't out there in that alleyway kissing Chip Riley. She wasn't there to set off a jealous rage. That never happened."

He lowered his voice, and leaned closer to the jurors. "Or let me suggest something else. Maybe they *did* find Teresita."

Bonnie glanced sharply at Chris, but he didn't object. Maybe the defense lawyer was right.

Lincoln raised his voice again, having gotten away with his speculation. "The State has a lot more power to investigate than the defense does. Police officers, subpoenas, the power to arrest potential witnesses. Then in this courtroom they bring you the evidence they want."

This time Bonnie shot to her feet. "Objection, your honor. The prosecution has an obligation to reveal to the defense any evidence that tends to prove the defendant's innocence, as Mr. Lincoln very well knows."

"Sus—" Judge Conners began, but Lincoln interrupted her ruling. "I'm not accusing these prosecutors of anything," he said earnestly. "They are good, honorable public servants. But they have to depend on others to bring them evidence. And in this case in spite of all their power they brought you very thin evidence against this defendant. Why? Because she's the wrong suspect. She was from the beginning."

He turned and looked out into the courtroom. "You know, you can sit here and watch Luisa during the arguments. You can make your judgments about her character. But you know who you don't see? Steve Greerdon. Look around. Wouldn't you think he'd be here?"

Indeed there were a great many uniformed officers in the audience, most with arms folded, watching stonily for the outcome of this trial. But Greerdon was not among them. Lincoln turned back to the jury and lowered his voice again as if telling them a secret. "They don't want you to have another look at him. But you remember him, don't you? Steve Greerdon, who just 'happened' to appear on the scene immediately 'after' the murder."

Lincoln made air quotes with his fingers. Chris noticed the gesture.

"Steve Greerdon, who spent eight years in prison because of evidence submitted by his fellow police officers. Who was pardoned and came out again. And in the short time since then two police officers he knew are dead. Think of Steve Greerdon. Who had a better motive for murder than he does? Ms. Janaway talked to you about passion. Think of Steve Greerdon's passion. They took his life. And he had long years to do nothing but brood about what happened to him. If he thought, if he even suspected Chip Riley was one of those officers who put him there, do you think he'd hesitate to kill him?

"Officer Greerdon told you Chip Riley was supposed to give him information about who had set him up. Maybe he did. And maybe Riley's information showed that he himself had been involved. So after he told Greerdon everything he knew, he was no longer any use to Steve Greerdon. Who took his revenge there behind the loading dock. He had the opportunity to take Luisa's gun earlier in the day, so he'd have a murder weapon that wouldn't be traced to him.

"He had the opportunity to set up everything. This is a man expert in gathering evidence. That means he knows how to create evidence, too. How to arrange a crime scene. How to kill someone and make sure someone else gets blamed for it. Especially since he's still a police officer.

"Wouldn't that account for the lack of evidence against Luisa? Steve Greerdon covered up any evidence that pointed to him."

Lincoln turned to pace away from the jurors, and as he did he shot a glance at Chris, as if asking him to join in this theory. Then Lincoln turned back to his argument.

"I'll suggest another possibility. Maybe, as the prosecution says, Teresa Vasquez didn't leave immediately after Luisa fired her. Maybe she slipped back into the restaurant. She knew where Luisa's gun was. Everyone did. But she couldn't shoot her employer in the restaurant. She waited outside. Teresa had just lost everything. Losing her job meant she'd have to leave the country, probably. And who had lost her that job? Yes, Luisa Gaines fired her, but it was because of Chip Riley. When he came out to have a cigarette, Teresita shot him. Maybe she'd been waiting for Luisa instead, but Chip Riley was every bit as much to blame.

"Then she would have run, and she wouldn't let herself be found. There's another possibility."

Lincoln tapped one hand against another, counting slowly. "There are just too many possibilities. You cannot convict this woman with this many other possibilities remaining open. If there had been a solid case to put together, police would have. Why couldn't they?

"You know why. Because she's not guilty."

He held their gazes a moment longer, then returned quickly to his seat, putting his hand on his client's shoulder. Gaines raised her hand to his, her most human gesture of the trial.

Chris sat. Attention gathered in his direction. Finally he stood, and it looked for a moment as if he would turn away from the jury and walk toward the courtroom doors. But instead he walked slowly toward the jury box. At first he wouldn't look at them.

"It's not as easy as Mr. Lincoln says," he began quietly, "to put together an ironclad case against a careful, determined murderer. Especially one who's working on her own turf. Who has the power to fire or promote the witnesses, who can suggest things they should say. Who could set the scene up earlier in the day, or even much earlier. Who ever said Luisa Gaines's gun was missing? She did. Or someone she arranged to have say it. Could police have prevented that? Or broken down her story? No. She didn't give a statement to police. Smart woman, Luisa Gaines. She knows what to do."

Chris spoke slowly, as if pondering to himself. He paced along the jury rail. "Let's dispose of these defense theories. Teresa Vasquez? Please. 'Little Teresa,' everyone called her. She was afraid of her boss. Do you honestly think she would have crept back into that restaurant to try to steal her boss's gun after that boss had told her to get out and not come back? Please. What she might have done was linger in the alley. Waiting there because she had nowhere else to go. Mr. Lincoln is right about one thing. If Ms. Gaines did fire Teresa, it left Teresa in a terrible spot. She was in this country illegally. Without a job she stood a good chance of becoming homeless quickly. Do you think she had savings, on her salary?

"She only had one friend. Chip Riley. She might have waited until he came out, then she would approach him, share a cigarette, beg for his help. Riley, of course, would have showed her that help came at a price. That's what Luisa Gaines would have seen when she came outside.

"That's if she fired Teresa at all that evening, which I doubt. Again, her only witness to that is someone who owes her his livelihood.

"So let's turn then to Officer Steve Greerdon. Mr. Lincoln has told you how clever he is at manufacturing evidence, and getting rid of evidence that might point to him as the murderer. So he suggests that Steve Greerdon killed Chip Riley. On a night when other people knew he was supposed to meet Officer Riley out there behind the restaurant. At a time when Steve Greerdon was being followed everywhere he went by someone from my office, and *Officer Greerdon knew that*. He told you about it himself. So this is the time and place that he chose to murder Chip Riley? When he was right there, knowing he had a witness, and with no alibi?

"No." Chris shook his head decisively. "If Steve Greerdon had decided to murder this man, you would never have heard the name Steve Greerdon. He would have arranged things a lot better than this."

As if he had convinced himself, Chris began to come alive. His voice firmed up. He looked at the jurors directly, then he turned and looked at the defendant.

For a moment he hesitated over what to call her. John Lincoln had made a point throughout trial of calling her by her first name, humanizing her for the jury. The prosecution usually tried to do the opposite, of course. But Chris did feel as if he knew this woman. This trial felt more oddly intimate than any he'd ever prosecuted. Both sides were conspiring together to keep things from the jury. And Chris still wanted something from this defendant, and was willing to give her something in return.

"So let's return to the evidence against this woman. Her gun. Her lover. The man who was stealing from her. Who held her future hostage because she had signed a contract with him.

"We cannot re-create that moment of murder for you. Not completely. Luisa came out there with her gun. She knew Chip Riley was outside, either because she remembered he was meeting with Steve Greerdon, or because she'd looked around the restaurant and found him missing and knew where he'd be. Either way, she went outside to find him, and she was carrying a gun. This isn't an impulsive woman. She had a plan. It was probably the fact that she knew Chip was going to meet Steve Greerdon that made her think she could get away with this.

"So she went outside already armed. She saw her lover with another woman. Maybe if not for that she would have just threatened him and gone back inside. But that sight gave her the last nudge she needed. He turned toward her—probably smiling, starting an explanation, reaching for her. Chip Riley was wearing a gun on the back of his belt, but there was no sign he reached for it at all. And he wasn't carrying a backup as Ms. Gaines told you about. He wouldn't have let anyone else get that close to him and left himself so unprotected. No: He reached for Luisa, thinking he could talk his way back into her affections, as he had so often in the past.

"And she shot him, that quickly. She had to do it fast, before he saw the gun, perhaps before she could change her mind."

Chris looked across the courtroom at the defendant. She had her eyes down, but then she raised them. Her gaze held on Chris's face. Nothing else moved in her expression. Then with a visible effort she looked at the jurors. She shook her head slightly, then looked down again. Chris walked slowly toward her.

"That first shot was sort of impulsive. A quick reaction to what she'd seen. And the medical examiner told you that shot would have killed Chip Riley if he didn't get medical attention. But not right away. He was still alive, down on his hands and knees." Chris had an urge to go down on the ground himself. He had never done anything so dramatic in trial, didn't like lawyers who did, and didn't do it now. He did reach out a hand toward Luisa Gaines, as if begging for his life. "Chip reached for her. He was still trying to make up. Still thought he could save himself. A few seconds passed. Ms. Gaines heard his voice. She hesitated. Maybe she listened to what he was saying.

"And then she shot him again, straight through the heart." Chris dropped his hand to his side. He had walked up to the edge of the defense table, as close as he could get to the defendant. She looked into his eyes again. Luisa no longer appeared afraid of Chris. They held a long look, while Chris talked to the jury.

"That first shot was intentional. She'd brought the gun out there to use it. But it was still the work of a passionate moment, as Ms. Janaway told you. But then Luisa had an opportunity. She could save her lover's life. Call for an ambulance, get immediate help, keep him alive. So if you have a problem with that first shot, skip ahead. Don't convict her for that shot. Find her guilty of murder because of that coldly calculated second shot. The one that went right through his heart."

Luisa Gaines's eyes gave him no clue. Then she closed them, with a tiny sigh.

Chris turned back to the jury. "Do you know what's wrong with the defense's theories of who else shot Chip Riley?" He pointed at Luisa Gaines again. "Her gun. "The police officer gathering evidence found it back in her desk drawer. Carefully reloaded. Who could have put it there *after* the murder? Steve Greerdon? Little Teresa? Either of them would have turned and ran after the shooting—*away* from the restaurant. Neither of them was seen inside it after the shooting. Only one person would have carried that gun back to Luisa Gaines's office, her sanctuary, and put it away again. Only Luisa Gaines could have done that."

"No!" Her voice shrill, the defendant bolted to her feet. "I didn't!" she screamed. "I didn't, I didn't put it there!"

"Then who did?" Chris said directly to her.

Judge Conners was already banging her gavel. Now John Lincoln jumped to his feet too. "Objection! This isn't the evidence portion of trial. He can't cross-examine her!"

"No," the judge said sternly, glaring at the defendant. "Nor can your client testify any more. Both of you sit down. No more questions, Mr. Sinclair. And no outbursts," she added, pointing to the defense table. "You can all finish this trial in handcuffs."

"I apologize, your honor." But Chris wasn't the least bit sorry. He turned back to the jurors. "You've heard about the aftermath of the shooting. Police were nearby, my investigator. People inside heard the shots. People milled around immediately, some of them trying to get out, people shouting and calling. It was a chaotic moment. The kind of moment in which in the past Luisa Gaines had taken charge. This was her restaurant, she didn't allow disturbances. Everyone else reacted to the shots.

"But no one saw Luisa Gaines. She didn't emerge from the office where she told you she was. We know she could have heard the shots from there. But she didn't come out to take charge. Why? You know why. Because she wasn't there. She was coming back in from the loading dock area, hiding her gun, covering up the evidence, composing herself to face police questioning. If she had been sitting in her office as she testified, you know she would have come charging out into the restaurant. That's what she'd always done in the past. Because Luisa Gaines was always in control. She knew what she was doing.

"Just as she knew what she was doing that night. You know too, that she is guilty of murder."

He turned and walked quickly to his table. Judge Conners dismissed the jurors after final brief instructions. Chris turned speculatively to the defense table. The main part of his argument had been aimed at Luisa Gaines. But she wouldn't look at him again. She had nothing to lose now, but she still wouldn't speak.

"Good job," Bonnie said. "You want to wait here for a little while, or go up to the office?"

"Neither. I've got work to do," Chris said. "If you get a verdict, call me on my cell phone, okay?" Chris spoke quickly, and hurriedly rose from the table.

"Where are you going? The trial's over. New evidence isn't going to do us any good."

Chris didn't answer. He glanced at the courtroom doors, saw the congestion there, and walked quickly across the front of the room and out the door the judge had taken.

Bonnie and John Lincoln looked at each other blankly.

"I thought you knew everything now," Peter Greerdon said.

Watching traffic carefully, Clarissa didn't answer at first. She drove her yellow Volkswagen around a corner onto a calmer street, then turned to look at Peter in the passenger seat. "I do," she said.

He wouldn't look back at her. "Then why are we still following her?"

"We're not following her."

Peter gestured at Anne's car, half a block ahead. The green Volvo made another turn and Clarissa thought she recognized their destination, the Justice Center. "I mean, we're not following her to find out where she's going. I just want to make sure nobody *else* is following her. We're not spies, we're bodyguards," she concluded disingenuously.

Peter shrugged. He'd accept whatever explanation Clarissa gave him. He wore baggy cargo pants and a short-sleeved blue shirt with a collar. For him, this outfit was the equivalent of a suit and tie. Clarissa had invited him along on the spur of the moment, but she wondered if he'd been expecting the invitation, or hoping for one. Clarissa sighed mentally. At a stoplight she turned and studied the boy beside her. That's what he looked like: a boy. Cheeks stubbled patchily, baby fat still blurring his features. Peter clearly felt her attention but wouldn't look back at her until the light turned green, and Clarissa continued to sit. Then he looked at her in slight alarm and said, "What?"

She kept her eyes on him. Peter couldn't hold her stare. He looked momentarily angry, then dropped his eyes.

Putting the car in gear, Clarissa said casually, "How's your mom doing?"

"She's okay. Goes to work every day. I'm just a little worried about this summer, when it's just her and me in the house every day."

"Yeah," Clarissa said, investing the one syllable with as much significance as she could. Peter glanced aside at her.

Then Clarissa frowned at the traffic up ahead. "She's not parking. She's speeding up again. Why aren't we stopping?"

"I thought I saw her on her cell phone," Peter observed. "You think she was talking to him?"

He obviously didn't mean Clarissa's father. Clarissa's expression grew determined. She passed a car on the right, catching sight of the green Volvo as it turned a corner on Alamo Street, heading toward an expressway entrance. "I don't know."

Peter reached for his seat belt and pulled it across his chest. "Are we still just being bodyguards?" he asked.

CHAPTER

fourteen

★ Steve Greerdon drove his nondescript Pontiac along a near east side street within a couple of blocks of where he'd made his first arrest as a rookie policeman. The arrest had been for prostitution, the girl so drunk she didn't even notice him standing nearby when she propositioned some guy leaving a club. She had turned out to be seventeen. Greerdon wondered whether she was still alive.

He would have liked a more glorious start to his police career, but that first arrest had turned out to be close to typical. Bad guys were rare. The world was much more cluttered with pathetic people scrambling to get by. There might be truly mean, vile-intentioned people exploiting those people, but you wouldn't find them standing on a street corner waiting to be arrested.

Greerdon pulled up to a closed garage door next to an alley, got out of his car, and a man stepped out of the mouth of the alley. A man with chiseled features and tousled hair, but this late afternoon with a drawn expression as if the descending sun made him nervous. "Hello, Bret," Greerdon said, investing the two words with a load of sarcasm. "Stand still for it."

He gave the former police officer a pat-down that was quick, but thorough enough to uncover two guns, one in a back-belt holster and the other at his ankle. Hendrix—the former "Eric Schwinn"—shrugged when Greerdon took the first one, but glared at the second.

Greerdon examined the backup pistol. "This gun killed anybody, Bret? What if I have it traced? What would it tell me?"

"It's got no connection to me," Bret said sullenly. "Give it back." He reached for the gun.

Greerdon closed the space between them in an instant, slamming Hendrix back against the wall. Greerdon's face in his, the gun jammed between them. "Take it from me," Greerdon said fiercely.

His eyes looked crazed. Clearly he wanted to kill someone. Bret Hendrix turned his face away, then pushed as hard as he could, giving himself a few inches of breathing room. He jumped aside.

Greerdon still held the gun. His finger found the trigger and tightened. Then he recovered himself, by small increments, first moving his finger, then making his hand stop shaking. He threw the gun down the alley, smashing it against another wall.

"Let's go," he said shortly. "You drive."

In the car, after Greerdon settled into the passenger seat and Hendrix started driving, Greerdon laughed bitterly and said, "Eric Schwinn. Where'd you come up with that one? You been a bicycle messenger since you left the force?"

"You said you wanted to talk," Hendrix said nervously. "What do you want with me?"

"Nothing. I want this shit to stop. I don't want to be looking over my shoulder for the rest of my life. I'm giving you up."

"I didn't do anything!"

Greerdon gave him a sneering glance. "Please."

Hendrix turned a corner onto a run-down street that used to be commercial but was now mostly abandoned storefronts. "You're going to have me arrested?"

Greerdon laughed bitterly. "Let's say I'm giving you to the cops. Rico asked me to tell him if anybody came to me to make a deal. I'm going to give him you."

Hendrix looked in the rearview mirror. "Where's your tail? I thought you were followed all the time now."

"I got rid of her. Wanted to keep this private."

Hendrix turned two more corners quickly, as if testing this claim. No car followed them.

"Take a left up here," Greerdon said. "We're heading back to the west side."

"Sure," Hendix said, but instead he made a sharp turn into an alley on the right and zoomed down it. Greerdon was shouting at him to stop, but Hendrix aimed at the wall at the end of the alley. At the last minute he screeched to a stop, inches from the wall. Greerdon turned toward him with the gun. Hendrix reached for the door handle, but Greerdon grabbed his arm. Then he looked back behind them.

A black sedan filled the alley behind them. It came to a slow stop, blocking them in. Slowly, a bulky figure climbed out from behind the wheel. Rico Fairis stood, spat, and walked slowly up the alley, around his car to the passenger window of the one Hendrix was driving. Fairis made a finger gesture of rolling down the window. Instead Greerdon locked the door with his elbow. "I'll kill him!" he shouted.

A gun appeared in Rico's hand. He fired, cracking the window, then smashed it to pieces with the gun. Greerdon ducked from the rain of glass. A moment later the muzzle of the gun was against Greerdon's neck. But Greerdon still had the gun in his hand, pointed at Bret Hendrix. "I'll kill him," he said more quietly.

"So fucking what?" Rico Fairis said.

Furious thought filled Greerdon's features. "We can work our way out of this, Rico. Everything can go smoothly."

A shrill woman's voice called from a window above, "What's going on down there? I'm calling the cops."

Fairis started to look up, stopped, and looked speculative. "Maybe we can," he said. "Let's go to my place."

In Fairis's car, Hendrix driving, Fairis heavy in the back, and Greerdon, disarmed, in the passenger seat, they headed deeper east, which made sense. After a couple of miles they'd left cityscape behind and the land became much more sparsely populated. Most big cities extend suburbs for miles around them. In San Antonio, if you drive in the right direction you can see cows inside the city limits. Developers haven't gotten to all those areas yet, and the east side was considered not very desirable for such prospects. In a few minutes Bret Hendrix turned onto a graveled road and came to a tall fence. He got out and opened the gate, which was closed but not locked. A chain dangled from one side.

Rico Fairis opened his back door, but only to spit brown juice onto the gravel. Greerdon turned and looked down at the stain. "Couldn't you have developed a more disgusting habit, Rico?"

Fairis grinned. "Nasty, isn't it? I worked security at the rodeo one year and a cowboy offered me some. I thought I'd just try it, but what do you know, I got to like it."

Greerdon shrugged. Hendrix got back in the car and drove. This was to be the site of an industrial plant, but its construction had gotten bogged down in protests and city council turf wars and construction had stopped almost as soon as it had begun. Land had been cleared, though there were still clumps of trees scattered around. A few tall walls had been built, but they stood roofless, propped up by plywood. Hendrix drove to the approximate middle of this compound, and stopped. Fairis got out of the car and with his gun hand gestured Greerdon out as well. Fairis spread his arms. "I thought you'd feel comfortable here, Stevie. Nobody close by. Lots of space to talk. Or scream, for that matter."

Greerdon said, "I'm not as dumb as I used to be, Rico. Know what I've spent the last few weeks doing? Writing down everything I could remember and everything I've learned."

"A biography of me?" Fairis smiled.

"Not just you, Rico. Your friends. I knew a little. I've learned more. Like about Bret here."

"You've got nothing on me," Hendrix snapped. He had emerged from the car and come around it, standing about five feet from Greerdon, holding a gun. Fairis had put his away, somewhere behind his wide backside. With his finger he cleared the tobacco out of his mouth, which made both the other two look away.

Greerdon turned to Hendrix and said, "The money you used to start your Internet business was extorted from a drug dealer you arrested on Grayson Street, near Fort Sam. You didn't make an arrest report, but dispatch records show that's where you were that night. And amazingly enough, the dealer's still alive."

"My word against a drug dealer's," Hendrix said with a yawn. "You're terrifying me."

"His word and a tape from the apartment building's surveillance camera, showing the two of you having a conversation and then you walking away folding something and putting it in your pocket. He's saved the tape all these years, until he thought he might need it. Now I've got it."

"Bullshit."

Greerdon shrugged, turning back to Rico Fairis. "There's more. Some about you, some about your associates. Enough that one of them will cave and give you up, Rico. You want to rely on the likes of him to watch your back? It's all in a safe deposit box that gets opened in the event of my death."

"I don't believe it," Hendrix said angrily. "And if it does turn up I can convince the DA's girlfriend it's all fake. Trust me, I can."

Fairis didn't even glance at him. Clearly "trust" didn't cross his mind. "What do you want?" he said to his old partner.

"I want you where I was," Greerdon said. He tried to keep it quiet, but the words skittered out as his eyes grew hot. His hands tightened and clenched. Rico Fairis watched these reactions. He shook his head. "Not gonna happen."

"Why not?" Greerdon said. "I'm not worried about dying. That hasn't scared me for a long time. So what're you going to do, torture me?"

"Yeah. With two words. Ready? Your son."

Steve Greerdon didn't answer. His eyes stared into his former partner's. Greerdon's were dark, deep, brimming with old emotion. Fairis's remained all surface. He continued, "You want our colleagues to have evidence of his activities the last couple of years? Enough to put him inside, Steve, I promise you. And you know what that's like."

Greerdon stared. He didn't bother saying silly phrases like *You wouldn't*. Rico sat back on a workbench, and swung his leg casually. They both knew he would do whatever it took to survive. "So maybe you can tell us how to defuse this bomb threat of yours," he said quietly.

Bret Hendrix spoke up. "There's only one way he won't ever be a threat to us again."

Without looking at him, Fairis said, "Shut up, bicycle boy. We all know that. Do your job."

Hendrix glared for a moment, then put away his gun and went to Fairis's car. He pulled equipment out of the trunk and began setting it up. First he went over Steve Greerdon with a handheld wand.

"We're very high-tech now," Fairis explained. "This tells him you're not wearing a wire or a recorder. Really, Steve? You didn't try to record this meeting?" He frowned, pushed Hendrix out of the way, and ran his hands over Greerdon's chest and legs himself. He seemed satisfied. He pointed at the other equipment. "One of these things tells us there aren't any listening devices aimed at us, and the other is a white noise transmitter that'll ruin any reception if there is. We don't want to be overheard."

"You know that's not my style."

"It didn't used to be, Steve, but people change. Looks like you haven't, though. So we can talk a little." He sat on the hood of his car.

"He doesn't know anything we need to know," Hendrix said angrily.

"I think he does, and I think you should speak when you're spoken to." Fairis shrugged apologetically at his old partner. They had an unspoken communication. *It could have been you and me, Steve. Then I wouldn't have to use this lousy help I've got today.* "So who have you told about me?"

"Nobody," Greerdon said. "She did, though. Luisa."

"Yeah. But she's a liar and a murderer, so who'd believe her? I'm more concerned about you."

"You know I wanted to take care of things myself."

"That's certainly the way it looks."

"But I want to do it straight out, Rico. Not like you. Trying to frame me for Chip Riley. Don't you have any new tricks after all this time? I know you've been sending this punk to the defense lawyer to feed him stuff about me. But you couldn't interest the police in me. Even after you added Emerson Blakely."

Fairis shot him a look. He took the time to light a cigarette, then said, "This isn't one of those scenes where I break down and confess to all my sins because I think you're about to be dead. You already know what you know, and that's enough."

Steve pointed his thumb over his shoulder. "Tell me about him, then."

Fairis looked that direction and his expression became disgusted.

"What do you think? He helped set you up, but for the rest he was worthless. When it comes to wet work, his all happens in his pants."

"Shut up," Hendrix said fiercely.

"I can't hear you, son. Come over here a little closer and repeat that." Nothing happened. Again Fairis shrugged apologetically at Greerdon. "Well, come on, Steve. I would've preferred to send you back, but you know I can't have you running around, talking to people and turning over stuff. Tell me where this supposed safe deposit box is, and I'll leave your kid alone."

A long pause followed while Greerdon thought furiously. Fairis added, "Give me your stash and your son gets a free pass for as long as I can provide it. And I always keep my promises, Steve."

"I know that."

But still nothing happened. Rico gestured at Bret Hendrix to come closer. The ex-cop moved cautiously, wary of Greerdon. Greerdon didn't move. "Tell me one thing, Rico. Why did you set me up, all those years ago? Why didn't you just kill me then?"

Fairis shrugged. It appeared he wouldn't answer. Then he looked his old partner in the eye and said, "A dead cop isn't all that much of an attention-grabber, you know that. Happens every day. But a former cop in prison, now that's a picture. For most of us, that's the worst fear. You were my example, Stevie, of what happened to people who crossed me. You were my recruiting poster."

They stared at each other, both showing mixtures of emotion. Rico Fairis looked genuinely sentimental. His face held a trace of nostalgia, as if he and Greerdon were meeting over a beer and talking about how the new kids couldn't measure up to the old days. Greerdon showed a measure of relief. He nodded as if finally getting the full story.

Then Fairis nodded toward his new partner again. Greerdon moved suddenly away. Hendrix had been about to clip him in the side of the head with the gun. Now he shifted his grip to a shooting position.

Greerdon just stood there, looking at his former partner. "You're right, Rico. Dead isn't the worst thing. I haven't worried about that in a long time."

He stepped away, backwards, spreading his arms.

Fairis spoke quietly and reasonably. "Steve, come back. Just tell me a couple of little things and we'll make this—" Then he looked up, past the retreating Greerdon. Raising his view to the near horizon stopped Fairis's voice.

"What?" Bret Hendrix said. Then he too saw what Fairis had seen: a small group had stepped out from behind a wall fifty yards away.

"There's more over that way," Greerdon said helpfully. "And up there on that tower sort of thing behind you."

Fairis was shaking his head. "Nobody could have followed us."

Greerdon nodded. "Nobody did. You got to pick this spot, Rico, but I picked the part of town to meet Hendrix in. And I checked and found out you provide security for this place. We had a couple of other locations staked out, but this was my bet. I figured you out. No electronic surveillance, just educated guesses. What we used to call police work."

Bret Hendrix was looking around wildly, still with his gun drawn. "Let's go. We can get out—"

"Calm down, son. We're not going to be fugitives. We haven't done anything wrong except chat with an old friend. It'd look better if you could stop waving that gun around, though."

The group that had stepped out from behind the wall began walking down toward them.

Chris and Jack came down the slight incline, along with the two police detectives and the young woman. Jack stopped. "Go back up," he told her.

She gestured to him impatiently, but he was insistent. The woman backed up, raising her binoculars again and keeping them trained on the three men down by the cars.

"We should stay here, too," Jack said.

Chris nodded and kept walking.

Up above, from the other side of the wide cement block wall, Anne stepped into view. Behind her Clarissa and Peter looked out, like shy children not wanting to be introduced to strangers. A young man, also with binoculars, stood with them.

Bret Hendrix had lowered his gun, but still had a wild look. "You're right," he said. "We can talk our way out of this. Why don't you go ahead and arrest him, Rico? Say he was trying to blackmail you, whatever. He'll be that much less believable once he's back in jail."

Rico Fairis frowned up at the groups by the wall. "I see the DA, I see a couple of familiar faces. But who're the civilians?"

"Those would be lip-readers," Steve Greerdon said. "And those things around their necks would be binoculars." He turned to Hendrix. "Pretty low-tech, but it works. I'm sure they got the gist of our conversation."

Hendrix's eyes shot around. His lips moved as he tried to replay events of the last few minutes. "I didn't say anything!" He put his hand over his mouth. "I didn't admit to nothing."

"Your partner here did that for you. When he talked about you helping to create the evidence against me."

Hendrix's eyes grew wild again. He stared upward. Then his eyes lit on a familiar figure. "Doc," he whispered. His features smoothed. "She'll get me out of this." He holstered his gun and began climbing upward. He turned to say, "You're on your own, Rico. I've got a friend over there."

Greerdon followed Hendrix's gaze upward, where he saw his son. Greerdon instantly frowned. He waved, gesturing Peter away. But the boy continued to stand there, staring down. Greerdon turned back to Fairis, who had also been looking upward. Their eyes met for a moment.

Then the district attorney arrived. "Sergeant Fairis, you're under arrest."

"Why? Because of what this guy told you? Talk to him, he doesn't know anything. Just speculation. He doesn't have any proof against me. Ask him yourself. Isn't that right, Steve?"

"We don't need anything from Detective Greerdon." Jack stepped into the conversation. "Luisa Gaines told us you were at the restaurant the night Chip Riley was killed."

"She'd say anything—"

"We know you were, Sergeant. After we showed my investigator Stephanie Valadez your picture, she remembered seeing you out in front of Miguelito's before the shots were fired. She thought you were just waiting for a bus like the other guy, but the other guy turned out to be an undercover cop, so it makes sense you were with him. Other officers saw you later, and thought you had just come when the call went out. There were a ton of cops there. But you were the first. You were already inside. Mr. Sinclair here figured out the rest."

"Figured out what? There's nothing to figure out."

Chris said quietly, "From the fact that your partner, Lieutenant Reyes, was in the autopsy room, waiting for the bullets from Chip Riley's body. That was so unusual I kept coming back to it. Especially his taking the evidence bullet and looking at it. He's a veteran officer, he knows better than that. But he did what you ordered him to do, didn't he? Made a quick switch of the bullets. The one that passed through Chip's body and was found at the scene, and the one that was removed from Chip Riley's heart. Oh, they matched by the time I got them, by the time they became 'evidence.'" Chris did not make air quotation marks with his fingers. In fact he stood perfectly still, engaged in a stare-down with Rico Fairis, who watched him, trying to gauge his character as well as how much he knew. "But the second bullet that was fired into Officer Riley came from your gun, Sergeant.

"You were there on the scene. You knew about the meeting that was going to happen that night. Probably Riley told you. Maybe he even offered to set it up, so you could deal with Steve Greerdon. But Riley was a problem. You knew he couldn't be trusted never to talk. He'd already talked too much.

"Then you got really lucky. Events took a new course. Luisa Gaines shot her lover. She caught him out there and she'd finally had enough and in a moment of rage she shot him. Then she came running back in. You saw what had happened and stepped outside just to make sure. That was a mistake. Chip Riley saw you there, and he wasn't dead yet. He was down, but not dead. He could still talk. In his state of mind, he'd probably implicate everybody he could, in anything he could think of. Dying people tend to do that. And you knew Steve Greerdon was close by as well as undercover police officers. The gunshot would bring them there in seconds. With Chip Riley still conscious. So you ended it. The second shot was yours, Sergeant. The one that made him instantly dead. And you went back inside and waited for the crowd of police to arrive, so you could blend in."

Rico Fairis smiled. "Luisa Gaines tell you that? I'm surprised she didn't say it to the jury. She'd say—"

"No. She didn't tell me all that. That's not our source."

Jack Fine said, "We've got Reyes in custody, Rico. When we told him he faced either tampering with evidence or accomplice to murder, depending on what he said, he opened right up. He was easy."

Fairis's smile went far, far away. Suddenly he looked like any other criminal, sweating under lights, looking around at his interrogators, looking for an opening or a friendly face. He didn't find any. He lit on Steve Greerdon, who stared at him grimly but with a suggestion of pity.

"And then you threw Emerson Blakely into the mix," Greerdon said, "just to point more suspicion at me."

"No," Fairis said, then paused a long moment while he continued to stare at his old partner. Finally he added, "That one you'll never be able to prove."

He turned and ran toward his car. By this time there were half a dozen police officers on the scene, and more arriving. The two detectives who were closest drew their weapons. Steve Greerdon and Jack said simultaneously, "No!"

Rico Fairis turned at the car door, now with his gun in his hand. He didn't point it, he had it down to the side, but he was raising his hand.

There is an event known as suicide-by-cop. Desperate men who want to be dead but don't have the nerve to shoot themselves sometimes try it, creating a hostage situation or otherwise making themselves look dangerous so that police will gun them down. Steve Greerdon had never heard of a cop pulling this himself, but then he'd never seen a cop about to go to prison. Other than himself, and maybe he'd been making a stab at suicide-by-cop back in that courtroom eight years ago, when his guilty verdict was announced and he'd gone berserk.

There is no fate worse for a police officer than going to prison. It's a vision of hell. Greerdon saw that vision pass across Rico Fairis's face. Surely he would rather be dead than endure that. He raised the gun.

But the veteran officers waited. Their guns were aimed, but they intended to give Fairis his last opportunity.

And Rico Fairis's eyes lit again on his old partner. Greerdon, who stood unarmed, stared levelly back at him, without anger or sympathy. Fairis held on that expression, then his own eyes dropped. He didn't say another word. His fingers opened and his handgun clattered to the asphalt.

They stood in their tableau for a long moment before the two detectives remembered how to arrest a suspect, and went forward with their handcuffs.

Fifty yards above them, Bret Hendrix arrived panting at the other small group. A uniformed officer put out a cautioning hand, and Hendix took the pistol from his belt and handed it over. Then he stood directly in front of Anne, drawing a heavy breath. He ran his hand through his thick hair, smiled shyly, and became Eric Schwinn again. He looked abashed and boyish and appealing.

"Anne. Thank God you're here. You know what I was doing. Why I had to be here. I really thought Greerdon was setting me up. Turns out it was both of them setting up each other. But you know—"

He stopped suddenly and looked at the teenagers standing nearby. "You're the girl," he said to Clarissa. He turned to Peter and added, "And aren't you Steve's son? You two've been following me all along, haven't you? Why?"

Clarissa folded her arms, looked straight into his eyes, and lied. "Because we knew you were going to try something like this. I thought you were trying to send Peter's father back to prison."

"No, that's not it. Not exactly. If he's really innocent, if I've been wrong all this time, then I can help him more than anybody. Right, Doctor?"

Anne stared at him, not smiling. Schwinn—no, Hendrix—faltered, looking even more in need of her help. "You're the only one who knows everything, Anne. You'll tell them, won't you?"

God, he was good-looking. Anne said coldly, "All I can repeat is what you've told me. Which was all lies, wasn't it? That's why you came to see me in the first place."

"No, Anne, listen—" He had begun to sweat again.

"I'll recommend another therapist for you," Anne said, turning away. "You need more help than I can give you."

CHAPTER

fifteen

★ Later that evening Chris returned to the Justice Center for the verdict in Luisa Gaines's murder trial. He was surprised to find that only two hours had passed. All the other participants waited for him: Bonnie, Judge Conners, John Lincoln, the defendant. Everyone looked at him coming up the aisle except her. "Where've you been?" Lincoln asked curiously.

"Arresting Rico Fairis."

At that, Luisa Gaines looked up. She shook her head. "Yes," Chris said quietly. "He's in custody. I don't lie. Ask your defense lawyer."

Gaines didn't. Her eyes stayed on the district attorney's face. "What are you going to prosecute him for?"

Her curiosity seemed odd, with her own jury filtering back into the jury box. "That may be up to you," Chris said.

"Which of you is the presiding juror?" Judge Conners asked. "Mrs. Johnson? Do you have a verdict?"

"Yes, your honor." A petite lady with quiet poise stood up on the front row. A kindergarten teacher, as Chris remembered. The perfect person to run a jury. She didn't wait for the judge's instructions and she didn't read from the paper in her hand. She looked straight at the standing defendant and said, "We find the defendant guilty as charged in the indictment."

Luisa Gaines didn't make a sound. She continued to stare across the courtroom as if she hadn't heard. The next day's newspaper story would report that the defendant showed no emotion. But before she was taken away she did turn toward Chris and say quietly, "Rico Fairis was the one who kidnapped me."

"I thought so," Chris answered.

The room began to empty quickly. Chris turned to Bonnie. "Passion," he said. She grinned. He turned to find Anne and Clarissa in the courtroom. By then the judge had dismissed the jury and exited herself. Both Bonnie and the defense lawyer followed the jurors out to ask them questions. Chris's group was alone in the room. Clarissa came down the aisle and put her arms around him. "I'm still mad at you," Chris said. "You shouldn't have been there this afternoon. You could have gotten hurt."

"I was there to protect you," Clarissa answered.

There was nothing to do about her. Chris took Anne's hand and went outside, where the air, as it always does after a trial, tasted better and freer than any other day's air.

Lieutenant Reyes got a misdemeanor conviction. He had to leave the police force, of course, but he kept his pension and got only probation. In exchange he continued to give information, which upon investigation proved accurate, until charges of extortion and assault mounted against Rico Fairis, along with the kidnapping of Luisa Gaines.

But not murder. "I could make the case that he killed Chip Riley," Chris said stubbornly, sitting behind the desk in his office on another evening weeks later.

"You already proved that one," Jack said. "Can you convict two people of the same murder?"

"Yes," Chris said. "They both intended to kill him. In a sense they both did. It would be two intents."

"Yes, it would," Jack said, and Chris realized he'd misunderstood. The whole atmosphere around such a trial would be too intense for anyone's good. "Why don't you just be satisfied? Rico pled to everything and got thirty years. He'll never see the light of day again, anyway."

Chris looked across his desk at his chief investigator. "I just hate to see a crime go unpunished."

"Tell me about it," Jack said wearily. He made Chris smile.

So Rico Fairis went to prison uncharged with any murder. No one even made a serious effort to charge him with the murder of Emerson Blakely, but Fairis's denial of it had been so lame that investigators considered the case closed. And soon after Fairis's incarceration, the phone on Steve Greerdon's desk rang. He was back at work, working undercover in an informal way. This week the chief of police had given him an assignment for the first time. Progress of a sort. The detectives' room, with its old wooden desks and acoustic-tiled walls, felt both alien and familiar. Greerdon stopped typing a report on his old typewriter and answered the phone by saying his name.

"Still at the job," Rico Fairis said sarcastically. "I knew I'd find you there. How's the family?"

"How the hell'd you manage this?" Greerdon said.

"Thought you could help me out a little," Fairis went on easily. "Tell me a couple of names, point me in the right direction. I figure to own this place within a couple of months, but if you could give me a head start I'd appreciate it."

He was amazing. And Greerdon knew Rico wasn't just boasting. Getting a phone call was a rare privilege for an inmate, and here he was managing it after only two weeks inside.

But it was his gall that was truly awe-inspiring. Calling the man he'd put in prison to ask for help. Greerdon sat silent, too many replies running through his head.

"We both know you owe me a favor, partner," Fairis said quietly.

Greerdon didn't answer that. After a moment he said, "Try to get a job in the library. It's inside work, and all the smart people pass through there sooner or later. There's a guy there named Ernie Jackson, if he's still inside. For a Snickers bar he can get you anything."

He talked for another minute. By the time he stopped the line had gone dead. He didn't know whether Rico had hung up or run out of time. Greerdon stared at the phone for a few seconds, then got an outside line and called his son.

Anne opened the door into her waiting room. Only two people sat there in the late afternoon. One of them was Clarissa, who waved to her and went back to reading her magazine. Clarissa and Anne jointly held secrets now, and neither would ever mention them. Anne suspected Clarissa had become suspicious of the stranger, "Eric Schwinn," not because he posed a threat to Peter and his family, but because she'd seen an attraction between Eric and Anne. He'd been a threat to Clarissa's family. She was an insightful girl. She and Anne wouldn't ever talk about it.

Their other secret was much more significant. Anne knew that Clarissa had lied to her father. She'd said that she had been with Peter Greerdon at the time of Emerson Blakely's murder. In fact, she had been with Anne.

They would never talk of it. Anne had never told Chris, and never would. Chris's job was trying to punish crime, but Anne's business involved keeping secrets.

Peter shuffled toward her, displaying an odd mixture of emotions. He still showed the traces of happiness at being with Clarissa, but as he approached his therapist he seemed to take up the burden of his turmoil of feelings. In other words, he looked like a teenager.

Anne led him to the little-kid room. Peter stood, while she sat in one of the small chairs.

Stalling for time, he asked, "What happened to—you know, the guy who used to come here?"

"All they could charge him with was tampering with evidence and interfering with justice. He was planning much worse, I'm sure, but those were all they could get him for. He pled guilty and went to Judge Conners for punishment. I know he expected to get probation. He said all the right things at his hearing, about the community service he was doing and what he'd continue to do on probation. And he looked great, very contrite.

"Chris Sinclair only said one sentence to the judge. Did you hear what it was?"

Peter shook his head.

"He said, 'He lied a fellow police officer into prison and left him there for eight years, even knowing he had a wife and a young son who needed him.' And the judge sentenced him to the maximum ten years. Eric—I mean Bret Hendrix—went absolutely white. He'll be eligible for parole in three or four years, but I don't think he'll make it. Not like your father."

"My father's very strong."

"So are you, Peter. I mean Bret doesn't have your father's incentive. He was always thinking of you, Peter. Unfortunately, he was gone for a long time, and you got used to relying on yourself. Even when your father got out, you wouldn't turn to him for help."

Anne took a deep breath. Her hard work was about to begin. She spoke loudly enough that Peter wouldn't miss a word, and she looked right at him, while his eyes stayed mostly on the floor.

"Your stepfather was a hard man, wasn't he, Peter? I wish he would have sought treatment. I think I understand him. Your father coming back set him off. Emerson had taken your father's place. He probably felt guilty about it, and he wasn't secure in his position. All those guns and gun magazines— Even if your father didn't do anything, he threatened Emerson's authority just by being there. Your stepfather was a screamer already. You'd told me that. Now he became a hitter. You don't have to tell me, Peter, I know. There was a bruise on your mother's face one day. Once that starts, it doesn't stop. You came home to find Emerson mad. That had happened before, hadn't it? But this time he was drunk, too. The autopsy showed that. This time he was mad enough to really hurt somebody. Maybe he even had a gun out. With all those guns he had in the house—"

Peter didn't answer, just stared down at the floor.

"Let me tell you the rules," Anne said quietly. "If you tell me you're planning a crime, I have to report that. But if you tell me something you've already done, that will be just between you and me forever. Technically, what a patient tells a therapist isn't privileged in a criminal case, but I have my own standards. Anything you tell me won't leave this room. I've gone to jail for a patient before, and I'd do it again. And I think you need to talk."

Several seconds of silence passed. Long time. The boy mumbled, and Anne leaned in to hear. "I tried to stand up to him. I forgot what I learned from my dad. Sometimes you have to back it up. And besides, I couldn't just leave. My mother was coming home in a few minutes."

Peter had begun to cry very quietly. Anne closed her eyes, stood up, and put her arms around him.

"We have a lot of work to do," she said.

about the author

Jay Brandon is the author of more than a dozen novels. *Grudge Match* is his fourth novel featuring District Attorney Chris Sinclair and child psychologist Anne Greenwald. An Edgar Award finalist for *Fade the Heat*, Brandon has been called "perhaps the finest writer of legal thrillers in America." He's been a lawyer for nearly twenty years, and lives in San Antonio, Texas.

ink mark noted - no where else in book
ABD